The Raven and The Rose

Leanne Blakemore & Adra Mayfield

WARRINGTON
PUBLISHING

Danbury, Connecticut

The Raven & The Rose
Copyright © 2026 by Leanne Blakemore & Adra Mayfield

Published by Warrington Publishing
Danbury, CT
www.warringtonpublishing.com

Printed in the United States of America
First Edition
ISBN: 978-1-969359-13-2 (paperback)
         978-1-969359-12-5 (ebook)
         978-1-969359-14-9 (hardcover)

Cover designed by Melody Simmons (bookcoversbymelody.com)
Edited by Mike Waitz at Sticks and Stones

This book is a work of fiction. Names, characters, places, and incidents either are products of the author's imagination or are used fictitiously. Any resemblance to actual persons, living or dead, events, or locales is entirely coincidental.

To my beloved parents, who gifted me the magic of storytelling and the courage to write my own. Your love was an inspiration, always.

—Adra

To Mom and Pops – You imparted a love of the woods, the flowers, and all things green, instilled the importance of education, and ALWAYS encouraged me to be exactly who I am, no matter what the world expects. Love and Miss you always.

—Leanne

Englebright Manor

1840

Chapter One

Lady Rosalind Arabella Englebright was running for her life. The normal tumult of her thoughts had turned into a riotous cacophony as she ran full tilt through the dark woods. *Why, why did I let Papa get me into this mess?* she fretted to herself. *No…it is unfair to Papa.* She bore the responsibility. Her thoughts spun around her as she ran on. She should have been enjoying a nice visit in Newcastle or a talk with her friend, Nan.

Instead, here she was running through a dark forest in skirts not intended for this purpose, being chased by the one man she could not bear to catch her. What to do, what to do, she frantically sifted through options, almost losing her way. Her first impulse had been to run…just run and run…the second that man had uttered the word…die. Though she knew the forest like her own home, the thick canopy hid the light of the full moon, making it difficult to tell shrub from rock, tree from stalking man waiting to snatch her. *My fate is not yet sealed.* It was the only hope she held as she ran on, and branches whipped across her skin, stinging like tiny branding irons everywhere they touched.

Oh, Lord, she thought. *What if he does manage to catch me?* Startled, she screamed a curse as she came upon a young elm that moments before, she had sworn was a man lurking in the dark. *Bloody hell, I am no schoolgirl,* she thought, trying to slow her racing heart. She knew she had to quicken her pace and pay attention, or she would surely be found and never reach her destination, but her corset was making breathing more and more difficult.

Blast it all. Why did Nan have to make this gown so bulky? she thought as she desperately tugged the skirts from the shrub they had snagged on, nearly dragging her to the ground. She knew she would not be able to remove her stays alone, but at least she could free herself of the leg-shackling heaps of fabric swirling around her ankles.

"Why do women insist we dress like a decorative pudding?" she wondered, mumbling under her breath.

Thank goodness I wore sensible slippers this eve. She stopped behind a copse of trees and began pulling at the mass of silk and chiffon around her, and managed to rip the heavy stitching at her waist as her breathing slowed. She continued ripping; each tear like a shattering tumult in the quiet evening air. She cursed softly to herself as she continued heaving and tugging. Finally, the heavy skirts and crinoline fell to the ground in a rush of silken rustles. She looked at them in satisfaction, but they did look like a pudding, and she had not eaten nearly as much as she would have liked at dinner. Her shoulders slumped as a belly growl echoed through the night.

"Deuces and devils," she groaned, having no idea what the phrase she had learned from the twins meant, but it made her feel more in control, and there was no one to chastise her. Her belly grumbled again as if in protest to her poor choice of words.

Hidden in the dark, he grinned wickedly as he watched her skirts fall to the ground.

She knew she could run more freely in her bloomers, but the cool night air sent shivers up her bare legs as tendrils of fog crawled around her ankles, caressing her like fingers from a specter seeping from the ground. She was now naked to mid-thigh. The bit of light that made its way through the deep forest illuminated her pale skin. *Lord,* she thought to herself, *I am glowing like some ethereal faerie;* a stark contrast to the darkness. This was worse than the small gems from her skirts catching the little light. Anyone within a stone's throw would think the forest haunted by a pale pair of legs. Looking down at her white flesh, she shook her head. Perhaps she had been a bit hasty. Well, there was nothing for it now. Done was done. Looking about her one last time, she began to run anew as the fear began to build.

Standing silently in the dark, his blood quickened at the sight of her bared flesh.

Rosalind ran on and on. If only she could make it to her mother's cottage. It was so well-hidden, she would be safe…at least for a time. Maybe upon sunrise, she would head for the coast, gain a boat, and keep running to the States, she frantically thought. Surely, he would not follow her there.

She backtracked as she ran, weaving between trees, stitching a path as intricate as the laces on her corset. It was an attempt to obscure her trail so it would be difficult to follow. Her intricately woven braid ripped free painfully as it caught upon a low-hanging limb, eliciting yet another unladylike curse from her and leaving her auburn hair a tangled mass flowing into her face. Every new tree snag littered the forest floor with small, white daisies and crystal pins as they fell free from her styled locks.

"I'll be bald by the time I get there," she huffed aloud.

It took her much longer than anticipated to reach the cottage. She had not been thinking clearly and had lost her way in the darkness several times. She had never been so frightened in all her twenty years. *He had said 'die.' The end result is always death.* She shuddered at the thought. Finally, she spotted the thatched roof above the low-growing shrubbery.

I have made it, she nearly cried to the night sky, giving praise to her maker.

Slowing as she neared the neatly cobbled walkway leading to the door, she let out a long sigh of relief and inhaled the floral bouquet of the yellow roses lining the path, which helped calm her somewhat. Fearfully, she took one last look behind her into the dark wood as she turned the handle to the cheerful blue cottage door and slid inside. Gently closing the door behind her, she sagged against it and attempted to catch her ragged breath. The binding corset left her breasts heaving above her tight bodice. In truth, she was having a hard time gaining enough air.

Maybe I can find a blade and cut it free as soon as the lightness in my head settles, she thought.

Nan would kill her if she knew what she had done to her creation. As she melted against the door, slowly falling to a sitting position, legs splayed in front of her, she could not help letting free the whimper she had been holding back. Then she cursed aloud again.

"Blasted bollocks," she whispered. "Bloody, buggering bastard." *Oh, Michael would be proud of that one*, she thought. The horrid words helped bolster her nerves and stayed her whimpers of distress. She sighed. She had made it to safety at last. She could decide what to do on the morrow when she was thinking more clearly. She closed her eyes and tried to relax.

"Forget something, my Love?" asked a sultry, baritone voice from the middle of the pitch-black cottage. The cadence of a nearly absent accent swept across her like an ice-cold caress, causing goosebumps to flow down her flesh.

Rosalind gasped as she tried to stand, but lost her balance in shock and fell to a jumbled heap upon the soft rug that adorned the cottage floor. Her breath came in ragged flutters as she lay on her back looking up at him. She could barely make out his broad shoulders from the dim moonlight shining in the small window, but she *could* clearly see what he held in his hand. It glinted, flashing silver in the scant light as he slowly advanced upon her. She could not move or breathe as the fear took her. He stopped but a whisper away, slowly kneeling beside her. He reached under and around her waist with his free hand and pulled her to her feet as if she weighed no more than a child. She knew it was pointless to fight, and she was so lightheaded and tired, she couldn't quite muster the energy anyway.

His one arm held her firmly to him; there was but a sliver of moonlight visible between their bodies. She could feel the heat of his thighs spreading like warm honey over her cold legs, and though she fought against enjoying the sensation, her body was betraying her.

He slowly, ever so slowly, lowered his head so their mouths nearly touched. His breath whispered across her lips; the smell of mint and a bit of scotch tickled her senses.

"You are mine," he breathed over her chin as he brushed a kiss upon her tingling flesh.

A thousand tiny nerves were beginning to hum all along her body, as if his voice were just the right vibration to bring her to life. She was having difficulty remembering why she should not want this. Her mind was so muddled.

He traced her jaw with gentle nips, then captured her lips for a soft kiss, just brushing his mouth across hers for the briefest of moments, then returning to the other side of her neck. The kiss was like a butterfly dancing across her. Her belly fluttered with each press of his lips.

*The kiss of death; wasn't that what Nan had said? He would give a gentle caress before…before…*She could not catch the thought, but the fear was trying to work through the haze of her thoughts.

Her chest began to heave once again, but she knew not if it was from fear or this fever he was awakening within her. Sensation, near to overwhelming, danced upon her bare skin as her belly warmed, body responding though she willed it to stop. No…this was all wrong. Death…it all came back to death.

"Oh, God, oh, God, oh, God," she whispered over and over, not realizing the sound escaped.

She breathed in the masculine scent, a dangerously sensuous mixture of spearmint and sandalwood with a hint of salty heat that made her legs wobble like a newborn colt.

He whispered against the bare flesh of her neck, "So sweet."

The heat of his breath sent shivers to places they had no right to be.

"I would rather help you undress," he growled low in her ear as he nipped the lobe with his teeth.

She sucked in a breath as her head fell to the side, giving him better access. His kisses traced her skin like wisps of fire licking at her, beginning to consume her like overly dry wood.

"But if you prefer to do it for me, then please…continue." She felt his grin brush across her skin as another kiss scorched her shoulder.

He raised his head and looked down into her eyes, seeming to dare her to fight against him. She was frozen in panic, realizing he had her at his mercy. He then lifted his other hand in front of her, showing her again what he held, rotating his hand back and forth so she could better see the sparkling and shining in the moonlight.

He smiled, and she saw the raw hunger now in his eyes right before he leaned down to claim her open mouth nearly savagely. She felt him raise his hand above her as his lips sealed on hers. He was overwhelming her senses as his tongue licked across her bottom lip. *He said die,* was all she could think. Then she felt the rush of air as his hand fell, and he let go of the mass of silk and gems he had been holding.

She watched as her wedding skirts dropped to the floor. He must have found them in the woods. The crystal jewels lining the lace caught the moonlight, dancing like a thousand tiny stars glittering silver as the skirts fell and hit the rug.

Or were those stars in her eyes, she wondered. Surely not, she thought, mortified. She felt a true lightness settle in her head, a dizziness, really. His warm breath was now on her neck and made her both shiver and feel so hot, and just a bit…nauseated. Her vision began to blur around the edges as she began to get a grip on her traitorous body.

Dear Lord in heaven, am I going to swoon? She had never swooned in her life.

"Oh, damn, oh, damn," she continued murmuring. *What can he do to me if I am unconscious?*

She thought she would prefer to lose her supper on him than swoon. *Anything but that,* she begged God, not realizing she spoke aloud.

"Anything but what?" he questioned in that sultry, deep voice that sounded as rich as freshly polished mahogany. Not waiting for a reply, he dipped his head and again kissed her ear.

Ye gods, he can bring me to my knees just by speaking to me. She tried to bat the thought away as her hope of escape began to fade. *He is much too dangerous.* The words he had spoken spun in her head. *Die,* he had said it, but an hour ago, reminding her of all that was at risk. *I have to escape.*

He was placing gentle kisses along her jawline, as he ran one hand over her almost bare hip and trailed a gentle caress down her cheek with the other. *Going in for the kill.* She tried to snag the thought, but it was as if her mind had been filled with naught but vapor, and he was a hot breeze blowing her every thought into nothingness. The heat in her belly was spreading like warm butter, suffusing all the intimate places that had been only hers before he came along.

She thought she heard a smile in his voice as she trembled at his touch, and her breath quickened. He seemed inordinately pleased with her reaction to him and then kissed the dip between her collarbone and shoulder. That dip was a perfect fit for his tongue to flick across and taste her skin. She tried to stop the whimper as it escaped her lips.

"Surely, it is not as bad as all that." He murmured the hot words across her shoulder, writing her fate upon her like bare parchment waiting for a tale of seduction and desire. It ignited something within her that she was sorely trying to tamp down.

She suddenly could not breathe. "You said die," she gasped out. "I'll…I'll not have it!" Panic was setting in, making her heart gallop like one of her papa's stallions. She knew she was making no sense…and her vision…dear Lord, she now saw flashing lights in her periphery…more stars falling, she mused in confusion. She began to struggle in his arms, trying to push him away. She tried to raise her knee to incapacitate him in his private regions as her brothers had taught her, but he reached down and pulled her hips so close to his that she could not move. He was brazenly kissing her neck now, and she felt a firmness press into her belly.

Is that his…oh, my.

He wanted her. The knowledge sent unwanted bolts of lightning coursing through her, even as she struggled to catch a thought. She felt herself drawn into him, cradling that hardness to her. It held dark promises. She was panting now, her corset growing ever tighter, giving her no option but to give up the struggle and fall against his chest. Her breathing was too constricted to continue resisting; each intake sounded as a squeak in her ears. Somewhere there was rushing water, roaring through her mind.

How odd, the stream is not close, she thought.

She felt him wrap his arms around her and start pulling on her corset strings. She could not muster the strength to fight him off. She thought she heard him calling her a damned fool as he tugged at the garment.

How odd, she thought as her now overly heavy head began to lull to one side.

Damn it all, was all she could think. *The blackguard has caught me,* her mind tried to scream, but she was falling into darkness…

And damn it all, I am going to swoon!

Her last thought before darkness overtook her was that she hoped her new husband caught her before she hit the floor.

Chapter Two

One Week Prior

The tantalizing aroma of Mrs. Gowan's famous nutty buns wafted through the manor, luring Rosalind to their source. A nice, neat pyramid of buns was sitting next to the oven in the big kitchen. A river of caramel sauce erupted from the peak and dripped down, oozing onto the platter and gathering into a golden pool too irresistible to pass.

Rosalind peeked around the corner; the kitchen was presently unoccupied, likely due to Mrs. Mary going to fetch additional supplies for the remainder of the feast she was no doubt preparing for breakfast. Rosalind stole into the kitchen and then dipped a very slender finger into the warm sauce and popped it into her mouth. She closed her eyes and savored the sweet, buttery goodness, letting out a soft moan of contentment. *How very fortunate we are to have Mary Gowan to keep us all heartily fed.* Mrs. Mary had been in the employ of her father's household longer than Rosalind had been in existence. The woman's talent at creating culinary delights had no bounds. Because Rosalind adored eating, she thought Mrs. Mary might just be her favorite member of the household. Of course, she would never tell Mrs. Ingrid or Elsa…or any of their other precious staff.

'The absence of just one…maybe two buns will not be noticed, surely," Rosalind whispered to the tray before her, as she peeked behind her again.

This was her usual morning routine, and Mrs. Mary had not caught her yet. She grabbed a pristinely white cloth off the counter and then approached the platter as if it were a conquest. Rosalind took her eating very seriously. It always made the local ladies fuming with envy that she "ate nonstop and never had to let out her laces." Her father always said she was graced with her mother's vibrancy and thus had to eat more than other girls to maintain it. *Mother was ever so vibrant*, Rosalind thought sadly.

"No time for being maudlin on such a fine day…and not with nutty buns to pilfer," she laughed aloud…then quickly stifled the giggle and peeked around her again. She quickly placed one bun between her lips and held it in place with her teeth. She pulled another one from the middle of the tower, where the caramel sauce was most saturated. She tucked it into the napkin and then stuffed the bundle into the pocket of the breeches she had procured from one of the stable lads just that morning.

"I really don't know what all the fuss is about dresses. Throw some lace on these, and I am sure they would be just as fashionable," she muttered through a mouthful of her tasty treat. The young man had certainly been happy to give them up to her; why, he all but tripped over his own feet when she had asked for his pants. Of course, he had been a bit mistaken in exactly what she meant, but that was no nevermind. In the end, she made her request clear, and he ran to fetch a spare pair of the woolen breeches for her. She promised, of course, to replace them with some just as nice and comfortable.

Happily chewing, Rosalind headed toward the door and nearly missed the block of fresh white cheese and some sausages helplessly perched on the counter. "Just a few of these for Mrs. Willoughby, I think," she said as she stuffed the cheese and sausages into yet another pristine cloth. Mrs. Ingrid, the housekeeper and head of household as far as Rosalind was concerned, would have her hide if she knew what she was doing to her linens, Rosalind chuckled to herself.

Mrs. Ingrid was a stickler for cleanliness, propriety, and minding one's own business. Rosalind loved her dearly. If she had a sixpence for each time the dear soul had told the staff to "nose out of M'lady's business," then Rosalind would be wealthier than the queen of England herself.

Looking out the open door to the sky, Rosalind noted the brilliant reds and oranges streaked across the horizon as if someone had set them ablaze with the stroke of a paintbrush. She could see the green just beginning to glow from the tops of the large trees in the forest across the lawn. The dew sparkled like jewels in the growing light. The sun was breaking dawn in grand splendor, which meant it was time she was off.

She quickly poked the remainder of the sticky bun into her mouth and began licking the caramel from her fingers as she headed out the door. With a spring in her steps, she bounded down the back steps that led from the kitchens. She paused and inhaled the perfumed smell of the late spring roses lining the kitchen walls. She never turned back to see Mrs. Mary peering out the window with a knowing smirk on her face and a shake of her head, eyeing the bulging of Rosalind's pockets.

Rosalind had just finished a quick stretch and was breaking into a full run across the gardens when she heard what sounded like it could have been a very loud and disapproving gasp from behind her. The sound of wind blowing through her curtain of auburn locks made it impossible to tell, but it sounded as though Elsa, her lady's maid, was greatly put out with her for some reason or another.

What in the world could she have done this time, she thought as her pace quickened, knowing full well it was her breeches that were the source of offense. She laughed as she breathed in the crisp morning air. No time for worries today. She had villagers to visit, her new building project to look in on, and adventures to embark upon.

Rosalind loved her early morning runs; the wind whipping through her hair, the smell of the brooks, and the verdant aroma of the leaves crushed underfoot enveloped her like a perfume crafted from God's own creation. She headed for one of her less-used running paths through the thick woods, thinking it was shorter and would allow her to get to the village a bit faster. She was on a mission today and was anxious to see it complete. Excitement at her new endeavor had her giddy as she ran along. The sun shone warmly on her face. She laughed aloud as she heard Elsa in her mind, "A lady's visage should be as porcelain, not port wine."

Rosalind was so caught up in the joy of the day that she almost tumbled headlong into a large hole in her path. She jumped mid-stride just in time to save herself, but managed to catch the edge with her booted toe and tumbled to the ground, ripping the knee of her new breeches and tangling her hair in a broken branch lying at the edge of the path. Rosalind, who normally prided herself on being nothing like those other "delicate" ladies, let out a rather ladylike scream as she fell. Sprawled out upon the dew-dampened ground, she flung her mussed hair out of her face and looked over her shoulder at the damaged earth.

I must look a sight, she thought, as she tried to rub the dirt from her palms. Regaining her feet with some rather inelegant comments, she moved to examine the hole more closely. It was nearly a meter deep and as much around. The edges were perfectly smooth as if chiseled precisely by a Renaissance sculptor. *How odd.* She would surely have broken her leg if she had fallen in. She looked all around for the pile of earth that must have been removed, but saw nothing. Twigs and leaves rained down from her tangled tresses as she turned in a circle in disbelief. What manner of creature could have dug this? she thought. It seemed an odd place for a den.

"Oh, hang it all," Rosalind sighed in frustration. Putting the thoughts aside, she turned to head on to Nan's cottage, not quite certain of what she wished to do. She could not go into the village proper looking as though she had been pillaged. She warred with her thoughts as she turned and looked back toward home. She could return home to clean up a bit, but then risked Elsa physically dragging her out of her breeches and stuffing her into a dress like a sausage into a casing. Now in a rather sour disposition, she decided to change her plans and just head on to Nan's. There she could clean up, have a good pout, and her friend would listen dutifully.

Nan was her best friend for nearly thirteen years. Although they were only a year apart, Nan had already lived a lifetime of sorrow. Her dear husband suddenly died from an unexplained illness slightly more than two years ago. They had been married for only two years when it happened. It was swift. He woke with a fever and rash that quickly turned into labored breathing and difficulty swallowing. Even the help from Old Maude could not save poor Erwin. Nan had already lost her dear mother as well. Having lost her father to a war before she was old enough to even remember the man, Nan was left all alone in the world. It broke Rosalind's heart to see the suffering of someone she loved so deeply. Although they were not blood sisters, they were sisters at heart.

Her meandering thoughts caused her to nearly fall into an identical hole not fifty meters from the first. "This is simply unacceptable! How is a girl supposed to run without breaking her neck?" she shouted to the trees. They remained resolutely silent at her rantings.

Rosalind walked more carefully the rest of the way, getting surlier with each additional hole she found in *her* running path…and there were many. She had found fifteen neatly manicured holes in all by the time she reached the edge of the woods that led into the small village.

She had planned to visit with some of the younger mothers of the village and see if they needed any help with their little ones this fine morning before heading to her new project and then on to Nan's. Rosalind loved the village and the people, but none more than the children. She thought it was extremely important for them to learn reading and mathematics, though it was not a popular thought amongst the *Ton* of larger cities. Many "highborns," as they were called, believed that the country folk and commoners should remain uneducated, or they would forget their station in life. She thought that was stuff and nonsense.

She had begun to teach the little ones in the village their letters and reading, as well as songs and a bit of French, as time allowed. She had already obtained support from an important member of parliament to aid in educational reform, as she was unable to support it on her own. She had even secured a cottage that was large enough for a school on the edge of the village. She had high hopes that she would be able to refurbish it soon and find a time when the children and even adults could come and learn despite their daily work often requiring grueling hours in the fields or factories. Her papa was also dedicated to making it so the villagers who leased and worked the lands of Englebright holdings had the time to dedicate to this endeavor. He was already looking into modernization techniques for both cultivation and animal husbandry to make it so.

Alas, it had taken her far longer to reach the village than she had planned, so she hurried on through the cobbled street that led to Nan's cottage. She was intact with no broken bones, but she was not in any better mood for not having gotten out for her run.

"Like a child needing a nap," she muttered. She gently tapped on the half door. The other half was open and letting in the fresh morning breeze. She was greeted by a busy Nan, who beckoned her in with a wave of her arm without so much as a glance to see who was there.

"Come in, come in. You're just in time to help me, m'lady." Upon actually looking up at her, Nan's mouth fell agape. Rosalind had leaves and twigs poking out of her hair, her pants were torn, and her face was smudged with dirt. She looked as though she had been mauled.

Rosalind slid through the door gracefully, pulling her pilfered morsels from her pockets. Her goodies were slightly crushed from the fall. She placed the cheese and sausages upon the rough-hewn table. Then she strode over to her host while unwrapping the last treasured nutty bun. She tore off a generous-sized piece and popped it into her own mouth, and all but shoved the remainder into Nan's gaping mouth.

"There, there, Mrs. Willoughby. Close your mouth and chew on that. You look like a trout I once caught. I am quite fine, I assure you," Rosalind said quickly in her foul temper. "I daresay when I discover the foul beast that destroyed my path, they will fare far worse. And, dear friend, how many times have I asked you not to call me 'm'lady'…so formal, really," she said as she tucked another bite of nutty bun into her mouth. "That epithet should be saved for one much more refined than I," she said as she chewed, rolling her eyes and gracelessly plopping into a chair.

"I'll stop calling you m'lady when you stop calling me Mrs. Willoughby," Nan muttered through the mouthful of pastry, obviously relieved that her friend was truly not injured, but just in a snit. She picked up a linen cloth and wiped the delicious caramel from her lips before she went back to her task.

"Oh, Nan, 'tis nothing but proper respect. Besides, I told you I would stop calling you Mrs. Willoughby when you would agree to come live in our home with me as my sister," Rosalind stated, nodding for emphasis.

"Papa adores you, more than me anyway," she declared in a pretend pout. Too bad Michael or Edmund simply does not suit you; I could have you for a real sister." Rosalind winked at her.

Nan simply rolled her eyes at her dearest friend. They had been having this same one-sided discussion for the last several months. The moment Nan had come out of mourning for her Erwin, Rosalind had started in on her with every argument in the book…it wasn't safe living alone…she would be too lonely…ruffians would abduct her…

"Those rapscallions will not suit any lady until they settle themselves and realize they are proper, gently bred men," she chided with a warm smile. In truth, she felt more a sister than a potential mate for the vivacious twins, or any of Rosalind's brothers, and Rosalind knew it.

"Speaking of refinement," Rosalind said in near awe as she rose and walked across the small room, "Nan, this latest creation is exquisite! I have never seen its equal. This ivory silk…so sheer and delicate. Like a fairy's dress!"

She admired the beautiful dress pinned to the form in Nan's eating nook. "Is it a wedding gown?"

Rosalind reached as if to caress the smooth sleeve of the dress, then saw the dirt caked on her palm and stopped short. The dress was made of cream-colored silk gauze that draped delicately over an ivory satin bodice and a heavy overskirt that had been adorned with delicate, little glass beads. They were faceted and caught the light like tiny dew drops. A crinoline was needed to make the skirt flare and sway.

Rosalind could just imagine the effect the combination would have by candlelight. The bottom edge was trimmed with silk swaths that fell like waves around the hem, reminding her of the purest cream as it was poured from the pitcher. The sleeves were three-quarters in length and flared at the elbow; it would have been perfect for one of the fabled faerie folk. More intricately woven Belgian lace tightly lined the Vshaped bodice that would allow only the gentle swell of the lady's breast to escape. There was an additional silk belt tied around the waist, which was attached with hooks that were camouflaged by a large bow. A trail of the tiniest pearl buttons marched down the back like beautiful, pale soldiers all in a row.

The entire creation had an opaque quality and seemed to nearly glow in the sunlight that filtered through the shutter. Rosalind noticed there was no embroidery on this masterpiece to mar the flowing quality of the gown, except, of course, Nan's signature crest that she carefully placed on the right sleeve of each dress she made. The tiny detail was her mother's crest. Nan had an identical silver pendant on a chain around her neck. It was her way of keeping her mother close.

Nan nodded her response as she removed pin after pin from between her lips. "Cream and white are replacing the bold colors of older styles," she stated as she continued placing the pins in the dress she was fashioning on her second dress form. It was an emerald green silk brocade with tiny red and gold flowers embroidered around the squared neckline. The sleeves were capped with just a bit of puff, and there were matching red and gold roses centered at the shoulders. It was not quite complete, but already a work of art.

Nan had an excellent eye for dress design. Recently, ladies from as far away as London had heard of her skills and had been seeking her creations. It was all because the blasted Duchess of Kent had been on a visit to some long-lost relative or another in the Northumberland countryside and had lost her entire chest of dresses to ruffians on the journey. It was said that she had fainted three times in the telling of the horrid story. It was all very dramatic. Well, a duchess does not simply run about in her chemise, so she had inquired locally of the best dressmaker in the area. The staff at her relative's estate had directed her to none other than Nan.

The rest was history, Rosalind sighed. Because of that blasted Duchess, her Nan was completely self-sufficient and would not hear of moving into Papa's manor. Of course, Rosalind was exceedingly proud of her friend, just lonely herself. Living with a house full of brothers and no sisters left no one to talk to about female things. She did have

Elsa, but she was more concerned with Rosalind's propriety and how marriageable she was.

"Well, the lady who wears that for her wedding will be the talk of the Ton. I think you have outdone yourself, yet again," Rosalind commented, dropping back into a chair and propping her chin on her hands.

"Perhaps one day, I can make your wedding dress," Nan mused with a wink at her friend. "You know you cannot put it off forever." She filled her lips with pins again and continued refining the dress.

"Blood and ashes, not you too," Rosalind grumbled, slumping farther into the comfy chair. I cannot bear the thought of being leg-shackled to some overbearing brute."

She flings the back of one hand to her brow in mock dismay. "Just yesterday, Elsa told me Papa's fête was a perfect time for me to pluck up the right man…as if they were turnips in the garden to be harvested. Can you possibly imagine any man of the Ton allowing me any liberties to get my exercise any way but by needlepoint or strolling the lawn? Much less what he would do if I accidentally spouted off some of the inelegant epithets my brothers have taught me."

Rosalind smiled and said in a very haughty voice, "A lady does not say 'blast, bloody, or bollocks,' Lady Rosalind."

"Ara, Love," Nan gasped, removing the last pin from her mouth, and turned to look her friend in the eyes. "Sincerely, your language today is abysmal," she chided. "Shall we drop the pretense? You are my dearest friend, so please let us not pretend that is the reason you do not wish to marry. I know what troubles you, and I promise, having loved and lost him, I would travel the same road over and over, knowing the sorrow at the end, just to have the love I shared with my Erwin. You know your father would do the same." Nan stared intently at her friend with a slight dampness to her eyes.

"I cannot discuss this, Nan," Rosalind stated quietly with a sadness in her voice that she knew Nan hated to hear. Rosalind hopped up from the chair, continuing more matter-of-factly, "Besides, no matter my reasoning, there are no turnips about that I would consider plucking, nor to which Papa would consent. Most are wastrels who spend too much time in the gambling houses or drinking halls. A sense of duty means little to many men of the Ton. They flitter through their inheritance like I flitter through Mrs. Mary's nutty buns…

"Few can live up to my expectations of what a man should be, none but my father and brothers…and your Erwin, of course, could ever be as dedicated to family, estate, and care for those who tend their lands…and most of the Ton are too pasty pale. Turnips may be an appropriate vegetable to describe them. Or parsnips…or some other equally unappealing food stuffs," she said, tapping her chin.

"I want a man with some vigor…a liveliness about him and color in his cheeks. Something more robust than root vegetables. I want a hearty cut of beef," Rosalind spun in a circle and continued, warming to her topic.

"Any man that fears the sun on his face can take his pale backside back to London proper. I'll have no part of him. His hands would not know hard work, or…or…bother to know how to please a woman in the ways of which the tavern girls speak!" Rosalind smiled at the look on her friend's face. Nothing like a wee bit of shock to change the topic, she thought.

"Rosalind Arabella Englebright, you should not speak such, and you know it," Nan half-heartedly rebuked. She knew her friend feared loss ever since her mother died, but also knew she had to move on. She would drop the topic for now, knowing Rosalind would just flee if she continued down this path. God willing, it would resolve itself with the right man. That was exactly what had happened with her when she met Erwin. She sighed and smiled, thinking of her sweet Erwin.

"Enough of this foul talk. Come now. I don't have much time to complete this latest commission. It must be perfect!" She picked up a damp cloth from the wash basin and scrubbed as much dirt as she could from Rosalind's face and hands, none too gently. The result was Rosalind as pink-cheeked as a newborn piglet…and scowling like a mother sow.

"Would you like a scouring brush? I think you left a bit of flesh here." Rosalind glowered, pointing to her nose.

"There now." Nan nodded decisively, tipping her friend on her nose with the cloth. "Slip off those dreadful trousers and put this on," she said, pointing to the freshly pinned dress. "Then we shall go out back to the measuring stump," ordered Nan.

Rosalind did as she was bidden and headed out the back door into the warming sunlight. The day was turning out to be glorious. Now dressed in the delicate gown, she stepped carefully onto the stump. She had removed all of the twigs she could find from her hair so as not to pull the delicate silk accidentally. She had then coiled it back atop her head loosely, so it looked more like a bird's nest than a delicate coiffure. She would be lucky if a house wren did not take up residence before they were done.

Nan looked at her and laughed. Tendrils of red locks fell around her rosy cheeks and shone in the sunlight, appearing as if her face was being licked by auburn flames. With her fiery countenance, she held out her arms dutifully like a statue so Nan could begin the poking and prodding. She had her face pointed skyward, eyes closed, and a soft smile soaking in the cleansing light.

"It really was a fortunate thing for this old elm to die, Nan. Erwin cut it to just the perfect height for us and left us this little island of perfection in the sun."

The measuring stump was the stump of an old elm tree that Erwin had chopped down and planed flat the summer before his illness. It was in a clear, sunny spot hidden from prying eyes and just happened to be the perfect height for measuring and pinning skirt hems.

Rosalind was always forced to be Nan's model for measurement. She had such a slim waistline without corseting that Nan could easily make adjustments without the bulky undergarment in the way. She had been stuck with so many pins in the last year, she thought she could have been an honorary hedgehog if she had but left them all in place. But she certainly did not mind if it meant helping her friend, who was the hardest-working woman Rosalind knew. Nan was determined to fend for herself.

"Now then, are you prepared to tell me what happened on your *walk* over?" Nan stressed the word 'walk,' knowing full well Rosalind never walked anywhere if she could help it.

"Oh, Nan! Some horrid creature has dug holes all in my path. I nearly broke my neck," she said exuberantly, turning her head to look at Nan over her shoulder.

Nan immediately gently grabbed her chin and turned her back to face forward.

"I have no idea what in the world could have done it," Rosalind continued. "And even stranger, there are holes but no corresponding piles of earth," Rosalind raised her arms in exasperation. Nan grabbed them gently and put them back straight out. "Maybe Old Maude would know something? Do you think?" Rosalind pondered, shifting from one foot to the other.

Nan laughed. "Lord, this is like trying to dress a cat. Can you please be still?" she laughed, shaking her head. "Maude would just tell you it was witches and spit upon your shoes!"

Rosalind burst into laughter. "Ouch! You are making mince pie out of my posterior, dear friend."

"Sorry, Ara," Nan said, removing the pin from Rosalind's behind.

She had called Rosalind by the same pet name her mother had used since they were young girls, which no one else was allowed to use. Nan's own mother had been a seamstress and often worked for the duchess, so Nan had grown up playing with Ara, going on whatever adventure they could cook up together. Nan never thought it odd that the estate had so much mending, as the boys were always rough on clothing, but as she got older and more observant, Nan suspected the duchess kept her mama busy because she knew what a struggle it was for women in the world when they had lost their husbands.

Most of the village folk worked the estate lands or raised livestock on them. It was a profitable village, mostly because Lord Englebright made sure to have the best equipment, made the best use of fields, and other land management instincts that Nan could not even imagine, but it was a small village. When Nan and her mama had settled there after her papa died, her mother must have surely known it could not provide enough work to keep them fed.

When she was old enough to realize her mother's choice in relocating seemed a poor one, she had asked her mother once why she had chosen this particular village. Because it's a fine one, was all she would ever say. She and Lady Anna had formed an immediate friendship after meeting. The duchess was of the kindest ilk, and Ara was just like her, Nan mused, looking at her friend as she glowed in the sun.

Wondering why Nan had stopped poking her, Rosalind looked over her shoulder at her and winked. "What are you musing about back there?" she asked. "You look completely lost in a daydream."

"I was just thinking about our mothers and what close friends they were…and what an unlikely friendship it was…and that I am ever so glad they were, because you and I have always had each other. But I still forbid you to move, Ara," she scolded, seeing her friend about to hop off the stump. "You can hug me when we are done," she laughed.

"And I shall, Nan," Rosalind beamed back at her, and then looked down at the dress to fully appreciate the beauty, and pursed her lips. "Don't you think this décolletage is a bit revealing? I am near to bursting out, and I am not overly blessed. If your patron is buxom, she might look like the prow of a ship."

Nan shook her head and bit her lip as she pinned another small pleat and responded a bit sheepishly, "No, I think it will suit its purpose just fine!" She looked up and winked at her.

"Oh," said Rosalind with a wicked grin, looking down at her friend. "It's for a doxy, is it? Well, sail on, then, prow forward."

Nan's mouth dropped open. *Oh, her papa would threaten to send her to the nunnery if he heard her talking like this. Why does she like to shock me so?* Nan just shook her head. "Hold still, Ara, or a pin might deflate your prow."

Rosalind laughed heartily at the jest. "I can't help it, Nan. This embroidery, while exquisite, is making my bosom itch. I am bare as a babe beneath it, if you will recall. I don't know how your client will tolerate it unless she only plans to wear it for but a wink, if her profession is as I suspect!" Rosalind twisted about on the stump and winked at her friend over her shoulder.

"You are incorrigible," Nan sighed. "What would your father think if he heard you speaking such?"

Rosalind just laughed.

Chapter Three

Kristoff knew he should not listen to private conversations. It was not the gentlemanly thing to do, but he had not smiled this much in ages. He could not imagine who this "Ara" was, but the language she used…he was certain her Papa would wash her mouth out with lye soap if he heard her. He could just imagine what a handful she was; likely one of the townsfolk's daughters, perhaps the innkeeper's. He simply could not resist. He just needed a little peek to satisfy his curiosity.

The lilt of her voice, husky and melodic, drew him like a siren's song. Her laugh was rich like bells, but also boisterous, not contained pretense like so many bits of fluff in the peerage. He was not sure he had ever experienced a female being as wholly herself in public or private. He was powerless to resist just a peek.

Kristoff had not intended to stop at this cottage at all, but Maude had pointed him in this direction, and then he heard voices talking about those damnable holes. All his other leads had gotten him nowhere, so why not a widow's house? It was as likely as any other. How he had gotten himself into investigating this mystery after his long trek to the end of England, he had no clue.

One minute, he was speaking with John Langdon, the local constable, inquiring if any one of the Van Lynden family surname lived hereabouts, and the next, he was being spat upon. It was as if the surname had been scrubbed from the records in England, but his last clue led him to Northumberland. Instead of completing his task, he found himself directed to a haggardly old lady with a crooked nose, warts, and wire-like hair. He had asked his questions, but then she mentioned the holes, or at least that's what he thought she said. She had not ceased spitting on his shoes since the mention of them.

Maude, as she was called, had been in the town since its inception, it was believed, and would know of any historical family names if they were to be known, Langdon had told him. But after speaking with her, it seemed she would only help him if he solved the issue with the bloody holes first. Her dialect was nearly as strong as her garlicky breath. She would make a comment and spit, make another, then cross herself and spit again.

His boots were nearly soaked through before he ferreted out what she wanted of him. It was like being in some sort of superstitious spring shower. So, here he was, searching for a dirt poacher, as no other explanation seemed to fit. There were holes, large ones, but no mounds of removed earth that he had been able to find, though granted, he had been investigating for only a couple of days. Kristoff shook his head at his task and smiled again at the outrageous statements coming from the girl's mouth. Did she really just say the word "doxy?"

Placing his back against the wall of the house, he slowly slid to the corner where the gate met the cottage wall. He had meant to steal, but a glance at the girl and the widow, who sounded much younger than he had anticipated. Then, he would go to the front door as a proper gentleman should. He just was not prepared for what he saw, which had him a bit flummoxed. What had he expected? A simple town girl and an old lady, that's what; not these exquisite creatures of grace and damnable beauty.

He knew they were sewing from their conversation, but by Heaven's gate – the mischievous one was gorgeous in that deep green silk gown, even if her hair did appear to never have been brushed. The dress perfectly contrasted the unique red shade of her…bun…was it supposed to be a bun all piled on top of her head? He was not quite sure what the desired design was meant to be, but that hair, even unkempt, appeared soft.

Tendrils had fallen free from what appeared to be more of a knot upon her head, he decided. It was long, nearly to her tiny waist, and flowed straight down her back with nary a curl to dampen the shine. In the sun, it was gilded like golden fire. Tendrils had fallen across the creamy skin of her small but lovely bosom. Each soft swell beautifully crested the square neckline of the dress. He agreed with her. It was a daring cut. He liked it. Her slender arms were held straight out like a statue awaiting a bird to land upon them. Those long arms were well-toned with gentle shadows where the muscle was taut, but with a softness of sun-kissed pink highlighting the strength.

He could imagine being encircled by them, pulled close as he tasted her rosebud lips. *Good God, man!* Kristoff thought. *Get a grip.* He shook his head. He had never, not once in his life, had this immediate a reaction to a woman.

He was just about to turn and go, but then she looked at him; her eyes like azure pools that threatened to draw him into their depths. It was not the look of those coy girls at the balls in London trying to trap a husband. This was at first inquisitive and then all too appreciative as her eyes roamed over him as if taking inventory. He could drown in those azure pools and die a happy man, he thought.

They were nothing, however, compared to those full, rosy lips he had already admired more than he ought. The tip of a pink tongue moved across them as she opened her mouth to speak. He felt himself growing stiff. *Hang it all, man, lust is a sin*, he chanted in his head to quell the brewing desire. "*Where is your discipline?*" he heard his father's voice in his head.

Never had he experienced such a wanton response to any young miss, much less one he had not even spoken to as of yet. This was ridiculous. He had to get out of here. By the look of her, she was not unaffected by his presence either. *Insanity*, he thought as he just stood there like a simpleton. He had to check himself to make sure he was not slack-jawed as he just stared back.

Rosalind could not speak. She licked her lips and sucked the edge of her bottom lip between her teeth, too distracted to even realize she was doing it until she realized he was staring at her mouth. *Dear Lord in Heaven! Who constructed this wonder of manhood!* He was tall, with sun-bronzed skin — not at all like those pasty, pale gentlemen who were constantly begging for an interview or engagement with her.

This was no turnip…no, sir…not a root vegetable at all, she thought. His shoulders…my, would they even fit through a door? she wondered. And those breeches. No man should wear breeches that tight. She was sure they would be considered indecent by any normal standard, but she had to admit, he wore them very, very well.

"Oh… Oh, my!" She blushed scarlet when she realized what exactly she had been gazing at as a pool of molten heat settled in her belly. How odd a sensation, she thought. She had once had a cup of hot chocolate so hot that it scalded her lips and warmed her painfully, as if she had swallowed a burning star.

That paled in comparison to the flames coursing through…Lord, why did she feel heat…there…Oh, dear. She broke her gaze and looked down to make sure nothing was amiss. All seemed normal except she had an odd ache she had never felt. *Am I getting ill? Surely not; I have been fine all morning. Oh, no…no, it cannot be. This…this is lust.*

"Oh, God, forgive me," she whispered, looking heavenward.

Nan, continuing to try to pin trim to the dress bodice, asked, "What in the world is wrong with you? You are as fidgety as a cat in a washtub." She looked up and only then noticed the very large, very handsome man standing at her gate.

"Oh, my," she said and then looked back at Ara, shocked to see her friend apparently mesmerized.

Trying to gain her composure, Rosalind met his eyes unapologetically. *Too late for apologies now anyway*, she thought. *He probably already thinks I am wanton.* She licked her lips to speak. The smoldering look she saw in his stormy gray eyes stopped the words at her parted lips.

"Oh, my," she whispered again. That flame in her belly flickered anew. All she could manage was to just stare back and keep biting her lip, though she was trying to stop that habit.

Kristoff stepped close as he heard her mutter a prayer. He could not imagine what was rolling through the beauty's mind. She seemed suddenly concerned with her bodice and then asked forgiveness of her maker. He knew by her blush that she was an innocent, but unlike the ladies of the Ton he was accustomed to, she did nothing to hide her desire as the blush crept all the way down to her lovely breasts. She raised her eyes back to him, meeting his gaze with an intensity that he felt pulling him yet another step closer. A siren, he thought again. He was playing with fire. Oh, but he wanted to be burned right then and there.

"Ahem!" Nan forcefully cleared her throat, looking from one to the other in complete bewilderment. "My Lord," she called brusquely, but got no response. "I say, might I help you?" she almost shouted, stressing the "I" while stepping in front of Ara with her hands thrown out as if to save her friend from a stampeding stallion.

She did not like the way he was looking at Ara as if he were about to devour her or, God forbid, take her right there on the lawn. And dear Lord, Ara was no better. She had the most intense look upon her face and was all but frozen in place, mouth partly open as if to speak, but the words were clearly stopped by some unseen force. Nan knew exactly what that force was.

Her eyes widened in disbelief. Her friend always spoke audaciously but was an innocent maiden. She looked as though she was having very un-maiden-like thoughts at the moment.

Nan grabbed her skirts in her hands and marched on the interloper. A nice settling down is what he needed. No proper gentleman wandered onto a property unannounced. By his attire, he should be proper. He was rude…and lust-filled, she determined. She stood a stone's throw from him, dropped her skirts, and pointed a stern finger at him.

"As you can plainly see, my friend is not in any proper state to be receiving visitors presently. I must insist you come back at a more gentlemanly hour, and by the front door next time!"

That caught his attention. Tearing his eyes away from the vision before him and bowing his head to the lovely widow, Nan, he had heard her called, he said contritely, "Of course, Madam. I meant no insult or intrusion. My humblest apologies. I am investigating the holes located all over the county and heard there might be some nearby to see."

"I suggest you go and see Old Maude. I am sure she can assist you with this 'hole' problem of yours! Good day!" Nan dismissed him, shooing him away as she turned to face her friend and possibly shake some sense into her.

Ara had not yet taken her eyes off the newcomer. Her blush was ever-present, and she now had a bemused look upon her face, clearly lost in a daydream.

Rosalind bit her lip as she watched Nan give the man a proper sit-down. She wanted to run her hands through his chestnut, wavy hair that was just a tad too long to be respectable, sort of like a pirate, she mused to herself. His voice held a hint of an accent she could not place, but the deep quality and tone played over her senses like an orchestral bass, resonating deep in her chest. She sighed as he smiled, nodded, and turned to go. She just continued staring at the now-empty space where he had been, unable to turn away just yet…afraid the illusion she was conjuring would disappear. No turnip, indeed.

Kristoff had to take a moment and lean on the side of the cottage. He could not believe his luck. He had managed to make it his entire eight and twenty years and not be smitten by any female. He had been back in England for exactly one month on this damnable mission for his country, and now he was investigating holes dug by a…a what…Seriously?

Now he found himself inexplicably drawn to a bawdy sprite of a girl, not even of noble blood? Now? When he was so near to completing his task? He rolled his eyes at his thoughts. His father, God rest his soul, would not have been pleased that he was apparently a lust-filled idiot. He had never been one to give in to temptation, and now would be no different. He just needed to get this done and get back home.

As he turned his head back to the lane and the present task at hand, he was met with a cackle and the overwhelming essence of garlic and ale. He was startled and reached for a sword that was not there; an ingrained action from years of training. Old Maude, who was not one step from him, found the action apparently reassuring, for she nodded in satisfaction and uttered something guttural he could not quite make out. How in the world had the old lady managed to sneak up on him so quietly or without her foul bouquet assaulting his senses? He sighed. Lust was more dangerous than an army of thieves, it seemed, distracted as he was.

Attempting to escape Maude's aroma, he retreated a few steps, only to have her follow him. Fearing he would wind up back in front of the ladies – though he would not mind that, he did suspect the fair Nan would throttle him – he stopped in his tracks and allowed Maude to approach. Trying to hold his breath without being overly obvious, he nodded in her direction and smiled.

"Hello, Lady Maude," he said genially. She giggled like a schoolgirl and blushed. Kristoff assumed she had not been called "Lady" often. She seemed to enjoy the title. He would have to remember that, he thought with a smile.

"Mebbies yee shud start in t' wood insteed iv chattin' oop wor local ladies. They seem a might bit put out with ye," she nearly guffawed. Pointing her gnarled old finger up the hill at the top of a manor that just barely peeked out like the tallest tree in the forest, she hiccupped, "Yee'll fin t' beeg ouse ye lookin fer, but I 'ave told ye, yer obliged te find the ne'er do wells causin' wer li'le village strife. 'tis no place fer Ole Maude or our Sprite in yonder wood."

Kristoff, staring somewhat blankly at the old lady, had not entirely understood exactly what she had said. Not safe for the sprites, he thought quizzically? He finally got the point of what she wanted when she attempted to shove him with her bony, little arms toward the forest and away from the manor to which she had pointed, saying, "Off with ye!" over and over.

He was happy to oblige as he needed to escape both aroma and spittle. He also thought the little twigs of arms might snap right off if he did not give in soon. Giving her one last bow befitting the queen herself, he walked in the direction she indicated, leaving her once again giggling in the street. He would have to be careful, or he would have a new suitor; he nearly laughed aloud.

Chapter Four

Mary Gowan moved about the kitchen, searching for the missing buns she surely misplaced. "I could have sworn I had more nutty buns than this just a few moments ago," she thought aloud. "Surely, our Sprite only took one this morn'.

"That Desmond!" she shouted after discovering the meat she had removed from the larder not an hour ago was also gone. "He has run off with my sausages again, and I now know where my buns have gone!" she stated, pretending outrage.

Nothing gave her greater pleasure than knowing her talent for cooking never went to waste, especially not with Lady Rosalind, she thought with a chuckle. "Hmm, now that I think of it, I suppose I know where my breakfast has run off to and with whom." She laughed at the thought of Rosalind in a full run, crushing nutty buns in her pockets. "That Sprite will have ruined Mrs. Ingrid's linens," she sighed with a smile. "She'll have both our hides."

"Well, no crying over lost sausages," she said to no one in particular. "I'll have another batch cooked up in a trice. His grace must be well fed," she clucked as she bustled around the kitchens. Mrs. Mary knew how much the duke enjoyed his leisurely breakfast. "Let's see, he'll be needing hot tea, sausages, cheeses, and fresh fruits…oh, and eggs and nutty buns. He is a hearty eater, that one. Just like our Sprite."

She got fresh sausages from the larder and began slicing them into the already hot skillet, and continued muttering to herself as she prepared the meal. "Never one to shun away a good bite or morsel even when times were dark." She never required company for a conversation.

Clucking her tongue, she reminisced. "Oh, what a dark time with the passing of the duchess," she said, dabbing tears from her eyes with the edge of her apron. "How difficult it was for him to gather for a morning feast and not yearn for his dearest love. God bless the children for pulling him out of his deep despair. Aye, the children. They have their mother's spirit," she continued to no one, nodding agreement with herself as she navigated the warm stone kitchen and continued to dab an occasional tear away.

Mary's normal morning calm was driven into disarray as Elsa stormed into the kitchens, followed closely by Ingrid, who normally did not tolerate any nonsense when there was work to be done.

"What is it, Elsa? What has you in such a fuss this beautiful morn?" asked Ingrid, as she carried in a beautiful bouquet of fresh-cut daisies that she had been trying to give to Elsa to arrange for Lady Rosalind's chamber. Instead, she had been chasing the lady's maid through the manor, trying to sort out what had her in such a state.

"Oh, Miss Ingrid, it's our Sprite. She's run off again. This time, I caught sight of her runnin' across the grounds in men's breeches, pockets stuffed full of what I am sure is your breakfast fixin's," she said, nodding at Mrs. Mary for emphasis.

"Men's clothing, I tell you. What am I to do?" Elsa cried dramatically, wringing her hands. "It's the third time this week…that I know of at least. I tell you, those breeches must be breeding like rabbits. I must have given our young Markham at least three pairs of nice tweed ones this week, but she just turns up more every day."

"Maybe she's better at needlework than she lets on." Mary smiled.

"She simply will not dress like a lady and stay put," complained Elsa. "Have you ever heard the likes of a gently bred lady sporting servant boy breeches whilst running willy-nilly all over God's green Earth? It just isn't done." She threw her hands in the air and nearly knocked the flowers from Ingrid's hands.

"I'm so sorry, Ingrid. I'm just at my wits' end. Guests will be arriving soon, and I know she wouldn't wish to disgrace her papa. I have yet to sort out how to get her to slow down so I can stuff her into one of Nan's lovely creations."

Though Mary knew she should not goad poor Elsa further, she could not help herself. "Perhaps you could tie her to your leg. At least then, you would always know where she is," she stated as she flipped the sizzling sausages. "Of course, you would have to learn to 'walk' a bit faster, I suspect."

She all but laughed aloud at the incredulous look Elsa gave her.

Mary had seen many a nanny come through these halls trying to keep up with their Sprite and had seen them drag the girl out of breeches more times than she could count. It was a wonder the stable lads did not run about half-naked. She did not envy the position that Elsa was in, but thought she had earned her right to poke a bit of fun at the lady's maid.

Besides, Duchess Anna, God bless her departed soul, was the one to blame for Sprite's preference for dress. More oft than not, she wore a split skirt fashion that allowed for more mobility. Their Sprite had just taken it a step further. She might not mind herself not worrying about skirts catching fire near the ovens, she thought wistfully as she looked down at her own woolen skirt.

"Oh, I likely know where she is," Elsa ranted. "I'm more worried about where she is not, presently. His Grace has given me the task of 'encouraging' her to find a suitable husband at the party. A bit of matchmaking is what he said. How, I pray, am I to do that if she won't even don a proper dress or stay where she is put? Like a wildling, that one is!" Elsa threw her hands in the air again in exasperation, and this time, nearly knocked the nutty buns off the counter.

"I would not let her be hearing you talk about weddings if you hope to ever have her under this roof again," said Ingrid with a sidelong look at Elsa as she steadied the platter of buns. "You know our lady has no interest in being what she calls 'leg-shackled to a brute.'"

"A good beatin' would put the gal to rights," came a gravelly voice from just beyond the kitchen door.

Everyone turned to the voice in shock. Mary looked from the wretch of a woman speaking and back at Ingrid over and over, gripping her spatula so tightly, it was near to breaking. It was Ingrid's job to manage the maids, so Mary said nothing but, oh, how she wanted to crack the woman over the head with her frying pan.

"I will remind you, Edith," Ingrid said, clenching her fists, "that your position here is temporary." She stated the temporary with emphasis. "His Grace would not take kindly to talk of beatin' his only daughter." Ingrid chastised her none too gently while starting to restack the nutty buns that were now teetering near collapse.

"I meant no disrespect, Mrs. Ingrid. But it sounds to me the chit is quite wayward and was simply…"

Everyone gasped as the words left Edith's mouth.

"And we do not refer to m'lady as a chit!" Ingrid nearly shouted, almost toppling the tower of buns she had just restacked. "She is the lady of this house since sweet Duchess Anna's passing, God rest her soul. You will be giving her the proper respect befitting her station if you are to remain in my employ…and you may call me Mrs. Nielson."

"My 'pologies, Mrs. Nielson." Edith simpered, emphasizing the Mrs. with mock respect. "I ain't had no proper schoolin' to behave better than I do," Edith stated, but not very contritely. "Could you help me keep my position? Take me under your wing, as it were? I can't afford to lose it, see. I have a sick brother countin' on me. His Grace helped me brother, before he fell ill. That's how I come to be here. Please don't give me the boot."

"Duke Englebright is an honorable man," Ingrid admonished. "He always does right by those in his employ, but you will show him and m'lady proper respect. You won't be told again."

"I'd be happy to show him some respect," Edith mumbled.

"What did you say?" Mary was not sure she liked the woman's tone.

"Only His Lordship is a fine looker, he is. He is full of vigor, that one," Edith stated tartly with a wink. "Men need their biscuits buttered from time to time. I be good at churning the butter, Cooky."

With a gasp, Mary nearly dropped her skillet of sausages when she turned abruptly. Throwing her hand towel onto the counter, she glared at Edith. "Last warning you will be getting from me, you hear? And you best be staying away from Lord Englebright. He is not that kind of man. He is devoted to the memory of his one true love, her Ladyship Anna."

There was a break in Mary's voice. "He still carries her love letters in his breast pocket. The family is known for holding on to things dearest to their hearts, and you are not one of them," she admonished as her ire at the woman rose.

With a determined look, Mary approached the woman, hot spatula in hand. "If we were not so short-handed and in dire need of help for the upcoming festivities, I would escort you out of my kitchen immediately. But His Grace deserves a wonderful party, good man that he is," she said, wielding her great weapon like a stick about to give the woman a good whack. "And you will do your job if you know what's what and stay away from the gentlemen."

"Not just letters, Mrs. Mary," the little maid Alice walked in on the tail of the conversation and said dreamily. "He keeps her treasure map, too. Did you tell her about that, Mrs. Mary? Did you? The one her Ladyship had pressed on her bosom upon her death," Alice said, staring off into space as she held her hands over her heart like she was about to recite a love sonnet.

"Bless it all, Alice." Mary turned toward the familiar voice of the sweet and simple maid, while lowering her spatula. "Stuff and nonsense. The map leads to nothing, Alice. 'twas a game, is all. We've talked about this. Now enough of this chit chat and dilly dally. We'd best be on with it, or we'll all be begging for scraps. Off with you." With that said, Mary turned about and dismissed the whole lot.

Edith, noting how simple the young maid was, pounced like a cat as she left the room behind Alice. She followed her out into the hallway. "Miss Alice, I be beggin' your pardon. What do you think that map leads to? Cooky, there, says it's nuthin' but a game."

"Oh, it is a mystery to be sure," Alice whispered dreamily, looking about her secretively and ushering Edith over to an alcove in the hall. "It was rumored that her Ladyship died with that map clutched to her bosom, she did. It had secret codes all on it. Some, like Ol' Maude down in the village, think the map holds an evil omen over the household and the manor. But others say it leads to a hidden fortune our Lordship's father buried." Alice leaned in and spoke with a wide-eyed innocence. "'tis with the love letters in her chambers, of course. His Lordship will take solace in her letters and her room on occasion…sometimes, he keeps them in his coat pocket, next to his heart," she said as she clutched her hands over her heart again and looked wistfully into the air.

Then she looked left, then right, and whispered, "The treasure map is in our departed lady's secretary. I've seen it, I have. Hidden in the secret drawer under the stationery. I can't get out of Mrs. Mary or Mrs. Ingrid, why she had it when she died." She looked a bit sheepish.

"I did try to look at the code once…but it was all a jumble of numbers and symbols. I can show you…maybe later, when our chores are done. Only don't tell Mrs. Ingrid, okay? I bet it's a treasure of untold value. Why else would she have it on her out in the woods?" Alice asked with a knowing nod, her eyes growing rounder as she spoke.

"If yer so sure, why did you not take it yerself to seek freedom from servitude?" Edith whispered with a hint of disgust.

"Why, that is dishonest. 'Tis not mine to take. And besides, I ain't no code breaker, Miss Edith." Alice started when her name was echoed in the adjoining room. "That sounds like Mrs. Ingrid. I have work to do," she said, calling back over her shoulder, "I must be off. We can talk more if'n you like, and maybe later, I will show you."

"No, no…no need, my pet. Promise me you won't meddle, though. Don't go looking for that map. I was just curious. As you say, best not to meddle and leave it be. Yer a good, honest gal. Go on with ye, or Ingrid will get us both, and I need me job." Edith smiled, remembering a time when she had been so sweet and naïve; maybe not quite as naïve as Alice, who was more childlike than her years accounted for. She sighed. Time had a way of turning a gal's heart…and time had been no gentle master with her. She had learned long ago to take what she needed when she needed.

Chapter Five

Elias Corbin, Viscount Durham, stared at the invitation he had just received from his butler. Elias tapped the envelope upon his hand thoughtfully. This could either be a fortuitous turn of events or yet another wasted effort.

"What to do?" Elias thought aloud, and would the boy agree? On the one hand, it would gain them access to a powerful family known for their far-reaching connections and have the possibility to finally gain an heir, to boot. Something Elias's lout of a brother could never have accomplished for the boy. As he stared at the letter, his personal valet, Jared, came in, took up a stance to the right of the door, and waited for Elias to address him.

"On the other hand," Elias thought aloud, "If my reserved nephew fails to woo the daughter of Umberland or worse, manages to entangle himself with a country gentry low-born who are sure to be invited, the boy will be the ruination of the Corbin name. What are your thoughts, Jared? We have spent years nurturing our family name and reputation. Would not the Duke Umberland's daughter be the pinnacle…our crown jewel, as it were? And I hear that twins run in the family. Two babes for the price of one," Elias said excitedly, staring at the valet intently.

"I think a link to that particular family would be mutually beneficial, as you say," said Jared in a bored tone. "Given how horse-mad the duke is reported to be, I think your nephew would be more amenable to such a match than that of a similar peerage to which he has been introduced. Respectfully, I admit I would also like a look into those estates. They are reported to rival Seaton Delaval Hall in both architecture and design. And if rumors are true, the duke is an avid historian with a collection of rare documents. You know how much I enjoy good architecture and history," Jared answered as he was bidden. "In addition, I hear the girl is a beauty with much resemblance to her mother."

"Seriously, Jared, how do you come by such knowledge? That estate is at least a two-hour ride from here!" Elias stated curiously.

"Servants do talk, Viscount. I simply listen," Jared said with a slight smile.

"My nephew is a reserved man. He does seem to prefer the company of horses to people. Lord, to think of all the balls and musicals I was subjected to trying to find him a suitable mate…but none of those London chits would do…not an available duke's daughter in the bunch to be had. They were quick enough to try to sequester him away…the young misses, and their mothers to boot…trying to sneak a private moment so they could call foul and claim my nephew and inheritance for their ilk. Just sickening.

"Jared, I am not even sure he has *been* with a woman, much less does he know how to woo one into the marriage bed. Horses might just be the proper motivation to gain his compliance. And this catch might actually be good enough to inherit my family name. Of course, he will do whatever he is asked," Elias said flatly, staring at the valet.

"Naturally, Viscount, Jared agreed," watching Elias as he sat thinking and tapping a long, graceful finger upon the desk. He was waiting for Elias to come to the same conclusion he had already reached; this was a sound match and had an equestrial enticement to encourage Jacob to form the connection. Jared only wanted what the viscount wanted in this, but had been in the employ long enough to know that Elias must come to the conclusion himself.

Elias was fixated on begetting an heir, and until that happened, they would continue traveling England for balls, parties, musicals, and the like. Jared missed their broader travels, which allowed him more freedom to explore his interests, but Duke Umberland's interests enticed him as well, he had to admit. This could be a rather enjoyable party.

Elias quit mulling over the problem and said matter-of-factly, "Naturally, Jacob will do what I say. It is the way of things, Jared. Go tell the stable master to prepare the crested coach. He will be leaving by noon. Have my nephew's valet prepare his things for transport. He will need attire for a ball and woman-wooing.

"I trust you can find him appropriate attire. Do not let my nephew know what you are about," he called sternly after a smirk.

"Of course…just as you say," agreed the valet.

As Jared began to leave, Elias called him back. "Jared, send Jacob to me before you set about your task."

"Of course," agreed Jared with a solicitous bow.

"Oh, for the love of St. Peter! You cannot be serious. Another ball! This is the last straw, Uncle. I will not continue to parade around with those sniveling, gold-grubbing chits to satisfy your sense of honor. I thought we had escaped that when we left London for your country estate."

With a raised eyebrow, Elias slammed both fists on the desk in one swift motion.

"You will not use such crass language in my presence! If you choose to speak to me in this manner, you will stay in the stables with the filth."

"I apologize for my poor words, but, Uncle, you have to admit that we have gotten nowhere with us attending this season's festivities," Jacob apologized and vented his frustration. "Even if I had found any of the young ladies suitable, you did not. What is the point in parading me to a flock of unmarried pigeons if you find none of them are worth putting into a pie?"

"None of those particular pigeons was the daughter of a duke. It is as if I have taught you no standards at all," Elias scoffed. "You need to always step up a level in your influence, not pilfer in the gutter with the rats, boy," he stated as if instructing a simpleton.

Jacob had been having this same conversation with Uncle Elias at least twice a week for the last year. He was always trying to shove some "festivity" down Jacob's throat in hopes of gaining an heir and to further his standing within the Ton. It almost seemed it was more important for his circle of influence to be expanded than Jacob's happiness. He knew his uncle must love him to have taken him in and made him his heir, even ensuring he had an honorific courtesy title, but by the love of all that was holy, he could not abide marrying for no more reason than getting a woman with child or because of the influence of her father, though he knew that was the way of the aristocracy. It just did not suit his nature.

As Uncle Elias held vast lands in the North, homes in the South, and even some land in the Netherlands, Scotland, and other places, it was likely his right to demand an heir to carry on his family name and take care of the holdings he had worked so hard to build. Jacob revered Uncle Elias, even though he was a stern, even harsh man. Jacob mused that Uncle had always treated him as his very own child, providing the best education with personal tutors, the best clothing, and the best horse stock. It was as if he devoted himself to trying to be a better father than Jacob's own father could have been. He had all the best intentions but lacked affection.

Jacob's life abroad had been a good life, if only a bit lonely. He had few long-term friends, no other family, and barely felt as though he was a noble citizen of England, having only finally settled into his Uncle's London home during the last year. Prior to that, they never stayed in one place too long, as Uncle Elias was always taking on new missions for his government but never sharing any details of his life with Jacob. Jacob had felt alienated most of his life, he thought. His horses and stables had become his refuge, but he had left so many well-trained steeds behind over the years that even that refuge was bittersweet. But that all changed now, it seemed. He truly felt Uncle Elias meant to stay here, which meant he could continue with his dreams, but also meant he had a new selection of women to be subjected to.

Uncle Elias wanted Jacob to marry into a family of some significant power, not because he wanted to utilize that power, but because it was the best and most prestigious. No, not just any girl would do, but if she was the daughter of a duke and had a womb, then she would do just fine, even if she had horns sprouting from her head. Just thinking about the numerous balls he had attended in London prior to retiring to their country estate made him sigh heavily. Thankfully, they had left before the full season had gotten underway.

Determined mamas and papas would stop at nothing to shackle some unsuspecting titled gent to their daughters. Frankly, most of the young ladies he had met were pleasant enough, most were lovely…but most were also in their first season, were far too young for his liking and were…well…quite dull, unless one enjoyed talking about the weather, the crush of the crowd, or God forbid the color of ribbons and toile.

He did not blame them for their lack of spark; they had been schooled from childhood to keep their individuality carefully, almost painfully, in check. He wished for someone he could actually share an interest with…build a life of at least some affection with.

Alas, Jacob knew that bloodlines must live on so estates could be secured. Though he had never gathered the courage to ask Uncle Elias why he himself had chosen not to marry, he just knew he was deeply distrustful of women; he knew his duty well enough. Yes, he had finally run out of time. He sighed in resignation.

"Jacob, are you listening to me?"

Jacob's thoughts were broken, and he wiped the look of boredom and resignation from his face and continued to pace, glancing at his uncle.

"Would you sit down?" his uncle demanded in a resonating tenor that left no room for argument. Jacob was pacing back and forth across the room, passing in front of his large desk over and over, driving him to distraction.

"You will marry a woman from a suitable station. Hang love. I need to know there will be an heir beyond you who is worthy to carry on my legacy," his uncle demanded, while running his fingers through his hair, which was wavy like Jacob's, though age had tinted his uncle's tawny locks with streaks of gray. Elias kept his hair in a longer, older style that was shockingly fashionable on the man. It accented his high cheekbones and drew attention to his piercing green eyes. He was a handsome man whom ladies often fawned over. While he was cordial to them all, he never encouraged the attention. No matter how many balls they attended, his uncle never danced, stating that frivolity was for bucks seeking a spouse, which he most definitely was not.

"I have been getting along in years and would like to meet my grandnephew before I die. There has been plenty of time to dabble and sow your oats with many a skirt, though you always prefer horses to ladies, it seems," Lord Corbin muttered under his breath, causing Jacob to sigh in exasperation.

"I have given you everything your father never could. You have had education, culture, and travel. You even have the estates here and abroad, along with my title when I am gone, which we would not have if it had not been for me. Your father certainly did nothing to protect the family legacy. You would not even have your high standing as a known thoroughbred breeder if it weren't for me."

Jacob balled his fists in his lap, controlling his anger. He could only vaguely remember his father, but all those memories had a sense of joy to them. What had gone amiss between the two brothers had never been shared, but it upset him to have the man maligned when he could not even defend himself. It was poor character to speak ill of the dead. He stilled his anger, knowing that conversation would lead to yelling.

"Uncle, we have been through this before," he said, stopping in front of his desk and leaning over, both hands braced shoulder-width apart in a stance he hoped conveyed his desire to be done with this conversation.

"I am not interested in marrying just anyone with a womb," he stated, leaning forward and banging his fist upon the desk edge, his knuckles blanched white, and the stack of papers his uncle had neatly arranged on the edge of the desk fluttered off to litter the floor.

Jacob, ashamed of his outburst, rushed to pick up the letters. His uncle jumped to his feet, nearly overturning his large leather chair, and snatched the papers out of his hands. Jacob had just barely noted they were from the British War Department. He raised a questioning eyebrow at his uncle, wondering with a sense of dread what new quest his uncle might be sent on. Uncle Elias always requested that Jacob travel with him wherever he went, and he was tired of traveling. He just wanted to raise his horses.

"No. I am done waiting for your fanciful endeavor to come to fruition. It is high time to move on," his uncle stated flatly, ignoring the questioning look on his nephew's face, while slamming his fist onto the desk, nearly dislodging the family crest emblazoned upon the front in his anger. He neatly restacked the papers and placed them in the topmost drawer and locked it.

"You will attend this celebration and find a suitable mate. You might find this particular ball to your liking," he said and quirked an unusual smile, throwing the invitation across the well-polished mahogany desk and leaning back in his chair, crossing one Hessian over his knee as he awaited his nephew's response.

Jacob picked up the invitation and looked up at his uncle in shock…or was that excitement Elias read in his eyes? Interesting, he thought. Maybe Jacob had heard of the stables and this lady as well. Maybe something different than those dullards in England would finally put some desire into him, Elias pondered, and decided to push for his compliance. He would have his way.

"Your time has expired. If you are waiting for love, you can save it for your mistress or your blasted equine. The Duke of Umberland," he said, pointing at the letter with a raised eyebrow, "has requested an early audience with you, specifically. I have prepared you well for this, and you will see it done." He stated this with a frustrated glint.

"You are to meet with him on the morrow. Let us hope he will be arranging for you to marry his daughter, Lady Rosalind." He stared at Jacob intently, looking for any sign of a reaction. but was slightly disappointed when mention of her elicited no further response.

"Once you are wed and have begotten me an heir, you can find true love with a lover. Marrying is for an heir and position," he said, shoving himself away from the desk and gaining his feet.

"Jared has prepared your conveyance and necessities sufficient for paying court to the lady. I assume you can do the rest on your own. I expect a notice of your betrothal shortly after I arrive for the festivities. I will attend the ball to see that you do not muck it up and shame me," he stated brusquely, barely catching a breath so his nephew would have no time to argue.

"It would *not* be remiss of you to…shall we say…compromise the girl, with nothing more than a kiss, of course, strategically planned for the correct persons to see, so she has no choice in the matter. I will gladly direct you in this mission should you fail by the time I arrive," his uncle offered.

Jacob stared at him, mouth agape. He could not believe his uncle's intentions, especially after they had avoided such a situation in London several times.

"Compromise the girl? Dear Lord!" he exclaimed in surprise. What had gotten into that man?

"With a kiss." Elias waved his hand dismissively as he beckoned Jared back into the study and smiled at him as the valet nodded his agreement with this plan. "You know how the papas of these girls can be. That would be enough to seal her fate. Even Jared agrees, see?"

He waves his hand in the general direction of his personal valet. "Since he rarely has an opinion on anything, you should trust us on this. I believe you have been dismissed. Go!"

He waved his hand in the direction of the door, brooking no further comment.

Jacob stood and nodded as if Jared's agreement was all the encouragement he needed. In truth, he had not been this excited to make an acquaintance in a good while, though Uncle Elias would be upset to know the true reason. Jacob well knew the stables of George Englebright, the Duke of Umberland, rivaled those of the king. With this meeting, he could finally expand his own stables and reputation in England, across the border to Scotland, and beyond. If this lady was amenable, he might consider courting her just to get Uncle off his back, but the horses…oh, the fine stock in the Englebright's stables …that was his true target. Jacob hurried off to gather his things and be on his way.

Chapter Six

The sound of the horses' hooves clip-clopping on the drive was about to drive Rosalind to complete lunacy. She was pacing in her room, occasionally staring out the window with the arrival of each well-appointed carriage. Some were more reserved, while others were in the Clarence style, complete with four ornate lanterns, one at each corner.

The house would be full to bursting with the closest of her papa's friends and various other dignitaries who were invited to enjoy the revelry. The local gentry would come to the ball only since they were all so close by, and they could come and go without the need to travel long distances in the wee hours of the morning when the festivities would end. Her papa's more distant friends would stay on for several days afterward to enjoy a good visit.

She looked out the window again and sighed as the Maxwell family exited their coach. The two young Maxwell girls were nearly bouncing in excitement, she noted with a smile. She knew she had to play the role of lady of the manor, though she felt like nothing of the sort. Her family and tutors had instructed her on what was expected of her when she became the lady of her own estate, God help them all. She had to do it well so as to not shame Papa or her brothers.

She bit her bottom lip, recognized the action, and then immediately stopped. She had not realized the habit until her encounter with a certain too-handsome gentleman. Oh, if she could think of any way to avoid the pending festivities, she would. She did not wish to hurt her father or ruin his birthday celebration, but she loathed crowds and the pretenses she oft got from the aristocracy.

The other young ladies were so refined and genteel…and often avoided her and thought her odd because she did not know the latest fashion trends or care which men were eligible. More than once, she had seen a group giggling behind their fans while looking in her direction.

And the gentlemen…oh, the gentlemen; they had no clue what to discuss with her, as she also despised city life and all its trappings…and she had no desire to discuss the country with them or her school, she sighed aloud. She had attempted once to discuss her plans for a school to educate the village children. The gentleman she had been dancing with asked her why they would even want to be educated. It was not as if it would benefit them in the fields or when tending pigs or other filthy animals. Filthy animals, which he had enjoyed devouring that night, she noted to herself.

She knew time was running out for her before she was considered "on the shelf" and an old maid before she was even old. Once that happened, none of the Ton except those seeking her dowry would have anything to do with her. That honestly suited her fine, but then there were other aspects of marriage that she could not fathom sharing with someone she cared little for.

"Turnips, the lot of them," she said aloud and sighed again. She just wanted some peace from the suffocation of these "fine" young gentlemen who wanted to talk of nothing but how fine her father's stables were, or worse, how wonderful they, themselves, were.

She sighed again and watched through her window as another crested carriage arrived. She needed a distraction, at least until her brothers arrived. Ever since she had returned to the manor the previous afternoon, Elsa had barely left her side, supposedly at her papa's request. Elsa, of course, had also been thrilled to help rid Rosalind of her offending trousers to help her in her efforts to not embarrass herself in front of her family.

Drumming her fingers on her writing desk, which was scattered in a mess of strings, needles, and a snippet of tapestry she had tried to distract herself with, a tapestry that now looked more like a rat than a dog, truth be told, she gazed out the window longingly at her lovely woods and sighed aloud. If she just stepped out for a few moments, perhaps Elsa would not notice her absence. After all, the entire staff was far too busy seeing to partygoers and should not concern themselves with her. Maybe she could even encounter a certain giant of a man who had plagued her thoughts since she laid eyes upon him at Nan's cottage. She sighed and rested her chin on her hands dreamily and bit her bottom lip again.

As she gazed into the woods through the long window of her room, she thought she saw the glint of something silver in the sunlight that shone through the trees.

"Well, that is definitely curious. That settles it," she declared as she stood and began stripping out of corsets, petticoats, and stockings, and other whatnot confinements. She grabbed her breeches, which were conveniently placed in a hidden valise under her bed, and quickly donned them and a soft linen shirt.

After tucking her hair into a woolen cap and tugging on some soft leather boots, she took a peek in the looking glass and decided she looked enough like a lad and shoved the cap a bit farther down on her head. She snuck out the door, down the hall, into the hidden door that led to the servants' stairs. At the bottom of the stair landing, she heard Elsa mention needing to run into the village for a bit to pick up some new gowns from Nan. Excellent, thought Rosalind. The ladies who were visiting had obviously heard of Nan's talents. She was excited for her friend and thrilled at the prospect of freedom for a few hours.

Instead of running across the grounds, she headed directly to the stables, pretending to be a stable hand on a mission from his master. She snuck into the large, open wooden doorway. The passage within led to a back entry that would let her out near the woods. Rosalind opened the heavy, creaking door and slipped outside without causing so much as a nicker from the horses in the back paddock, who looked up to see her and went back to grazing on the lush grass.

Just beyond the stable was the spot she thought she had seen the glint of something metal. Dashing across the short distance, she ducked under the trees. It seemed as though someone had extinguished a candle with one swift puff as she entered beneath the canopy. She moved in near silence from tree to tree in the dim light that managed to make its way through the thick mesh of leaves. Ol' Maude would be proud of her sneaking ability, she thought with a smile.

Rosalind had been walking for about ten minutes when she heard raised voices echo throughout the forest. If it had been any louder, the horses at the manor would be rearing in fright. *Professional thieves, these gentlemen are not*, she mused. She snuck up behind a large elm and squatted to watch what they were doing.

"Hit me one more time with that bloody shov'l, you eedgit, and I'll put you in that blighted 'ole," growled the largest of the three men, clearly the leader of the marauders.

"Why we diggin' for anyways, Sid? All I've seen is roots and rocks in this bloody 'ole and that bloody 'ole over there, and then the other five you had us diggin' the other day. Least ways if you throw me in, you could say we found somefink in these blighted woods," said a skinny man whose arms were no larger around than the shovel handle he was so poorly wielding.

"How much you say we being paid for this, anyways?" asked the third, portly rascal of the group.

"You get paid what and when I says and no sooner, but I was told it's a ha'penny per 'ole and anover for the dirt we bring back to prove we've been digging. If'n we find anyfink in the 'oles, root or rock, then we get a fifth of what we find," said the man named Sid.

"What we want with a fifth of old dirt, rocks, and roots?" pouted the skinny man.

"I mean, if we find a squirrel or a bit of bones, we can sell 'em to that old witch in the village at least," the portly man stated with a spit at the mention of the witch.

Rosalind nearly snickered at the thought of the man trying to sell squirrel bones to Maude. She would send him packing for sure. Rosalind was relieved, however, to know who these scoundrels were, even if she had no clue as to why they were digging on her father's land. She had seen at least one of them stumbling out of the local pub a time or two, far too early in the morning to have been stumbling, truth be told. Skinny man, she had never seen before, but assumed he was local as well, or perhaps a relative of the others. None of them had even proven to be terribly bright.

The men continued digging while discussing the merits of squirrel dung for fertilizer and whether it was worth more than a ha'penny. Movement and a slight shifting of leaves to her left drew Rosalind's attention away from them. Was it another dirt poacher, she wondered with a smile, and shifted her position as quietly as possible so she could see what or who was making the noise. Rosalind could not believe her eyes when she saw the source and had to stifle a gasp. Her breath caught, and her heart began to race like the frantic bubbling of one of Mrs. Mary's pots left over the roaring hearth too long.

For a full night and a day, Kristoff had endured the bumbling company of these three fools, though they were none the wiser to his presence. Yet, despite his persistence, he was no closer to unmasking the hand that paid them nor the motive behind their mission than when Maude had first sent him off into the woods.

The men kept a steady stream of dirt coming out of the woods, but what they were searching for he still had no clue, and they just kept piling the removed earth on the far side of the estate near this little cottage he had seen. Surely, it was not a bit of prized soil with all this secrecy, he thought as he peered on, almost laughing aloud at the inane conversation…it was more akin to the braying of donkeys than an actual conversation.

While he hated to resort to brute force, he did not have the luxury of time to waste nor the patience to continue this investigation much longer. He had a job to do for his country, and this was his last assignment before he could get on with the rest of his life. What that might hold, he thought as he watched on, well, he had yet to decide. He had promised Maude, so he would honor his word, but if he had to hear one more conversation on squirrel shite, he might lose his mind; it was time to escalate.

"Seriously, gentlemen," Kristoff said in exasperation as he stood from behind the large oak that had shielded their view of him, "how about I pay you a ha'penny each to stop speaking of squirrel dung and just tell me who employed you to dig up this estate? I grow weary of following you and listening to your asinine conversations." He nearly growled the last.

The three men stopped talking and looked at him with blankish stares. Kristoff thought he had completely confounded them, as they clearly understood very little of what he said, or perhaps they were just shocked at his sudden presence. The largest of the men – Sid, he had heard them call him – grabbed the shovel from the chap that was so thin as to be nearly transparent and said, while brandishing the shovel like a spear, "Just who you callin' an arse?"

Sighing and shaking his head, Kristoff began to approach the men while unbuttoning his overcoat and rolling up his sleeves. He knew where this would lead. Sometimes, you just couldn't reason with people.

Rosalind stood abruptly and gasped. There were three of them, and he was a mere gentleman. They would kill him for sure.

"I fear we misunderstand each other," Kristoff said, raising his hands in a conciliatory manner, swinging his gaze to include the fourth of the men, who had just revealed himself…well, boy really. The lad was too slight of build to be called a man. He assumed the boy was their lookout, but made a rather poor job of it, to be sure. He really did not wish to fight these men. He would break the twig of a man in half, and the other two smelled more of dung than he was willing to get close to; the fourth appeared barely out of nappies.

"Perhaps we can come to an agreement without someone getting hurt," he said as he partially raised his palms to them, beckoning them to see reason.

Portly man laughed. "You 'ear that, Lads? Our fine gentleman here don't want to get 'is fancy breeches dirty!"

The other two guffawed at this. The bravado of the porker was enough to encourage Sid to advance with his makeshift weapon toward the "dandy." They all leered at Kristoff as they began to surround him.

Kristoff took note of each one's position; the boy seemed frozen in place, so he did not think he needed to worry about him at all, but these three morons were going to try to teach him a lesson. This should be fun, he thought. After the last twenty-four hours he had spent in these woods following and listening to them, he was quite ready to pour out some of his frustration upon them, but he did not want to kill any of them. He would have to remember not to use full force.

Rosalind could not move. She could not decide how best to aid the gentlemen. Was he really so stupid as to take on three scoundrels at once in the woods, where no one could hear or help him? He was a gentleman, after all. They were rarely the most useful of men…except her father and brothers, of course, but they were different.

She began looking around and remembered some larger rocks on the stream bed that she could throw at them to help. She turned and ran toward the stream, listening to the grunts and sounds of fists hitting flesh. Good Lord, they were going to kill him before she got back. Was that crying she heard? Rosalind made it to the stream, scooped up as many medium-sized throwing rocks as she could easily carry in her shirt tail, and headed back to the fight.

Kristoff looked over his shoulder long enough to see the boy running away. Good, one fewer thing to worry about. His attention was diverted just a bit too long, which allowed Sid to get in one good shot with the shovel. It scraped his shoulder but thankfully missed his head.

He must be out of practice to lose focus like that, he thought as he grabbed the shovel end and, in one quick yank, had Sid off-balance and lying face-first, upside-down in the hole; his feet flopped over the edge and moved no more. The tumble appeared to have knocked him out cold. *Two down, two to go*, Kristoff thought. Portly man called to his skinny friend, "Be wary and stop your cryin'; he can't get us bof. You take the front, and I'll get his back," he directed.

Kristoff almost smiled. Skinny man was having none of that. "But that is the side wif his fists," he cried as he backed up, tripping over a root and falling into a tree stump, knocking himself out. *Three down*, Kristoff thought, shaking his head with a laugh.

Kristoff rounded on the portly man, who had apparently found a nice-sized branch as a weapon. He had already raised it high, and it was about to be brought down on Kristoff's head as he was turning to face the man. Fortunately for Kristoff, the lad had returned to help his mates by throwing rocks at their attacker. Unfortunately for the lad's mates, he had horrid aim. He hit the portly man in the temple with a fist-sized stone. The shock and pain of being struck in the head by a rock was enough to make the rotund man immediately grab at his new injury, which was leaking a rivulet of blood into the man's eyes. Apparently, the fool forgot he was holding what was nearly a log. As his hands grabbed at his head, the weapon conked him square on top, thereby knocking himself out.

Kristoff wished every band of fiends would fight themselves like this lot had. He did not get to even swing one punch, and they were all out cold except the tike now hiding behind the elm. Kristoff slowly turned, his amused gaze falling upon the boy, who he now noticed looked familiar. He just could not place him. He needed information and did not want the lad to warn his employers that his crew of miscreants had been caught. Perhaps he could scare the answers he needed out of this child before turning the entire lot of them over to the authorities.

The lad must have read the intent in his eyes, because his face drained of all color, and his mouth hung agape. He immediately dropped all the stones he had been holding, turned, and took off like a thoroughbred through the woods.

"Oh, no, you don't," shouted Kristoff and gave chase.

Rosalind had only just realized that she was dressed as a boy, skulking in the woods with ne'er-do-wells. She thought it might seem to the gentleman that she was part of their band. *Gentleman,* she thought with a smile. How had a gentleman defeated that large scoundrel with a shovel? There might be more to him than she had originally given him credit. She could not, however, let him catch her. She had no idea what he might do to get information he thought she might have. She had to disguise herself with all haste. She was closer to the village than her home now and knew just where to go.

Kristoff could not believe how quickly the boy had disappeared. The speed with which he ran had to rival that of the message carriers

Kristoff had encountered during his military service to his country. The boy was clearly very familiar with this portion of the forest to navigate his way out so quickly and with little to no sound. As well as he could, Kristoff followed the trail the runner had left, but there were very few broken branches or evidence of footfalls in the verdant forest floor. The few hints he got led him back toward the village. Perhaps he could find the lad there and question him then. But before he did that, he was going to question the thugs he had left littering the ground some distance back.

Kristoff backtracked toward the site of his "fight"; he chuckled as he recalled doing nothing of the sort. As he walked back, he noticed a woolen cap lying in a pile of leaves. He had missed this upon his first search because it blended so well with the surroundings. He picked it up and noted it had the aroma of cinnamon and something nutty. How odd, he thought. Perhaps the lad's parents were the local bakers. He tucked the hat into his coat and continued walking.

Upon reaching the site, he was shocked to find all of the men had gone, leaving nothing but a bit of parchment, a worn shovel, and a pile of dirt. He guessed they would get no ha'pennies today, and he shook his head in disgust. He grabbed the parchment and unrolled it. It was a very detailed map with what appeared to be code along the edges.

He sighed. All he needed was a bit more mystery and less time to do his actual job. He was no code breaker, but surely, it would not be that hard to sort out. He tucked the map into his coat pocket and started walking back toward the village. He had to make his way to the estate over the hill this afternoon to secure the Van Lynden signatures he had come for. The holes could wait another day.

Chapter Seven

Nan was just packaging the last dress for Elsa to take back to the manor. Rosalind was going to be shocked when she realized nearly all the dresses Nan had been commissioned to create were for her. Nan hoped Ara was somewhat prepared for the inevitability of marriage, but was not so certain it would go smoothly for anyone involved. She was such a free spirit with her own ideas and goals that only a man who supported her uniqueness would do for a mate, or more importantly, a lifelong companion and love.

If Ara had not found what she would at least consider acceptable at all the other parties, and visitors, and a very brief season in London in years past, Nan was not sure this party would make any difference. Apparently, Lord Englebright was determined, having invited the gentry from far and wide. As she folded the final dress carefully to make the wrinkles minimal and easier for the maid to remove, she glanced at Elsa. The poor dear looked harried and worn thin.

"Elsa, would you care for a cup of tea before you head to the manor?"

Elsa nodded her thanks. "That would be lovely, Nan," she said, gently sitting in the wooden chair at the well-scrubbed little dining table. "I have felt quite overwhelmed of late keeping up with My Lady."

Nan nodded knowingly as she busied herself pouring the hot water from the already warm kettle into the tiny, china cup. It was an heirloom piece from her mother, delicate and nearly transparent. She should probably worry more that it would be damaged, but it pleased her to use something of her mother's in her little cottage. She delivered the delicate cup, now steeping with a floral Earl Grey tea, and sat opposite her weary friend and offered the sugar and cream she had yet to return to the pantry from her morning meal.

Elsa nodded her thanks again as she accepted the cup and smiled for the first time since entering. "I know you are her dearest friend, and I do not wish to make disparaging remarks, for you know I love her, but she was aptly called 'Sprite' by Duchess Anna. That girl gets into more trouble."

She sighed, inhaling the fragrant tea, then added a sugar cube and a splash of the cream. "I am enjoying the quiet and calm of your cottage. You have such a calming presence, Nan."

Elsa smiled up at her, visibly relaxed against the wooden chair back, and sipped her Earl Grey. "Some days, Lady Rosalind is like a gale wind blowing all around me, and I don't know which way to go. I do not wish to see her married off to someone not of her choosing. That will break her spirit, and none of us wants that for our dear girl. We do love her so, as we did her mother."

She gently placed the fragile-looking cup upon the table.

"Lady Rosalind needs a strong man with an ample supply of patience. There are just none to be found hereabouts," Elsa sighed, shaking her head but relaxing a bit more.

She now appeared to be almost melting like warm butter into the chair, clearly releasing some of the tension of the past weeks. Nan could tell the poor dear had been strung as tight as a bow when she arrived to pick up the dresses. She was glad to see her relaxing finally.

Elsa picked up her cup of tea to take another sip of the sweet brew. He face showed the exhaustion of the last few weeks slipping from her tired limbs. As she raised the cup to her lips and inhaled deeply, the back door slammed open, banging into the wall behind, causing Elsa to slosh the tea both up her nose and all over her dress. Sputtering and coughing with tea dripping from her wet nose and chin, she jumped from the table, upsetting the chair she was sitting in with a loud bang as it hit the floor. This all happened as Lady Rosalind ran through the door, slamming it behind her, locking it soundly, and then running to Nan, gasping about how "he" was not a turnip after all. Nan just stared at her in confusion, trying to connect the pieces of conversations of past days as Ara shook her gently.

"Oh, Nan! It was him, and not only is he not a turnip, but he is not a dandy. He fought three scoundrels in the woods at once! Well, I helped some with the third, but no mind. He fought them all without gaining a single scratch on his handsome face or breaking a sweat. I just knew he would catch me. I need a dress right now!" Rosalind all but shouted while shaking her friend's shoulders and then abruptly stripping out of her trousers as she talked.

Nan had no clue how to respond to her disrobing friend. "Ara," she chided, "get a hold of yourself, girl. What in the Heavens are you talking about? What man, what scoundrels, what woods?" She tried to stop her friend from removing any more clothes, as the front half door was standing wide open. Clearly, Ara had not realized Elsa was standing there sputtering, near to choking, covered in tea.

"Take a seat and put on this dressing gown immediately," Nan told her as she handed her a garment from a stack of freshly sewn clothing and motioned for Elsa to close the door.

Nan had seen her friend excited to the point of incoherence in the past, but this…well, this was a first. Never had Ara demanded a dress. Nan sat her down and then realized Elsa was grinning like a loon. Had they both gone mad?

"You heard her, Miss Nan, let's get m'lady a dress. I would love to hear all about this gentleman she seems to find so, dare I say…suitable," she continued, grinning like a little girl who just found a shiny new penny. Nan knew Ara was in trouble now.

In a rush, Rosalind retold the story to Elsa of how the mysterious newcomer had shown up at Nan's garden gate looking like a Greek god.

"Oh, Elsa! I assumed he was a priss like all the others who have come to the manor, just a rather larger and exceedingly handsome one." She continued with a story of the bravery and pure masculinity of the forest escapade that left Elsa blushing.

Nan plopped down in the nearest chair and shook her head from side to side. She was so confused and realized that she was the one being blown around by the gale force that was "Ara."

"But Ara, why were you disrobing in my kitchen and demanding a dress? In all my years, you have never wanted to wear a dress," Nan questioned in an exasperated tone, running the back of her hand over her forehead in apparent vexation.

"Aren't you paying attention, Nan? He nearly caught me! Then, he would have put me to the question, and I couldn't answer him! What would I say to him then? I haven't got any answers? I didn't do it!"

On that note, Nan put her hands under her chin as if in prayer and stared at the rather large cross on the wall, and asked for guidance. Maybe He would give her a sign that her friend did not belong in Bedlam, and Elsa, Lord help, was still grinning like a simpleton.

"Ara, Love," Nan began again, "why does any of this mean you need a dress?" She paused and slapped her hands upon her knees as she stood. "You know…it really does not matter. Let's just get you that dress." Elsa could not stop nodding in agreement. Nan thought she might do her neck an injury with all her head bobbing.

Rosalind nodded her quick agreement as Elsa began picking the random leaves out of her charge's hair with a grin as broad as a crescent moon.

"Oh, drat!" shouted Rosalind as she flung her hands on top of her head and began to spin, looking at the floor, causing Elsa to jump and rain leaves about the room.

"My cap! What if he finds my cap, and there is hair in it? He will know," she said frantically, "he will know it was me and put me to the question."

Elsa, forgetting about the leaves she had littered upon the floor, patted her lady on the arm, comforting her. She then grabbed the dress Nan was now holding and tossed the chemise over Rosalind's spinning form as Nan tugged the skirts up over her narrow waist.

Nan could take no more. Shaking her friend by the shoulders, she nearly yelled, "What questions could he possibly ask of you because you were not wearing a dress?"

Rosalind took a deep breath and realized her friends were looking at her with fixed stares of befuddled incomprehension, as if she were speaking in a forgotten tongue. She took another deep breath and began again, pacing her words more slowly. "I was wearing breeches, following those brigands. When he saw me, he thought I was a boy and that I was with those ne'er-do-wells digging holes in our woods. He thinks I am one of those dirt poachers Maude keeps spitting over. I think he really is here to investigate them like he said when I was on the stump barely dressed."

Nan noted the smile fading from Elsa's lips as she tied the skirt into place a bit more tightly than necessary.

"He saw you in what state, My Lady? And you…" Elsa took a deep cleansing breath. "Only want a dress as a disguise, to be clear?"

"Nearly naked and exactly so, Elsa." Rosalind smiled now that her message was clear and she no longer sounded like a frightened ninny.

Nan gasped and yanked the bodice around her and began fastening buttons. "You were no more near naked than you are now. That lovely green silk you wore that day is a beauty." She sniffed.

Rosalind lifted one well-structured eyebrow at her friend and muttered, "For a lady seeking a groom, perhaps!"

"But he is a gentleman, no less, and attractive?" Elsa interrupted with some hope lingering in her thoughts. Rosalind said nothing but blushed a deep shade of red that was quite revealing. Elsa smiled and began to hum as she grabbed the last parcel from Nan and headed out to the carriage.

Rosalind just looked at Nan in fright, realizing the implications of that smile.

Chapter Eight

Nan, Elsa, and Rosalind all climbed aboard the packed carriage to set out for the short trip to the manor house. Elsa continued to hum and smile as she directed the horses down the dirt lane. The three ladies piled up onto the bench as the carriage itself was full to bursting with packages. Elsa rarely had an opportunity to take the carriage out on her own, but the stable hands had all been busy taking care of the guests' various horses and carriages. She enjoyed the task of driving a great deal, which was not at all ladylike, but she was unconcerned for such a quick jaunt to the village.

"I am so pleased you decided to return with us, Nan." Rosalind smiled at her friend. "It makes good sense because the party is only an evening away, and Papa loves having you. He says you are a calming influence on me," Rosalind laughed, wrapping her arm around her friend's shoulders and smiling broadly at her.

Rosalind's laugh was as merry as Christmas bells, and Nan smiled back at her. Rosalind had no idea her papa was the one to ask Nan to come today and help Elsa get his daughter to the party on time and dressed in the green gown he had commissioned for the occasion. She smiled to herself, knowing just what her dear friend thought of the cut of that gown's neckline.

The three ladies happily bounced along the rough road, chatting as they went about which other ladies might be in attendance, and if the dancing would be lively. Rosalind admitted to enjoying a good, vigorous dance but hated a waltz.

"Oh, to waltz with a fine gentleman," sighed Elsa.

"Oh, you shall, my friend," Rosalind simply stated. "Of course, you shall dance with all the men you please. I had Nan make you the most beautiful golden gown to match the lovely flecks in your eyes,"

Rosalind declared, grasping her maid's hand briefly. "Papa insists you attend me everywhere I go to help keep me out of trouble."

She winked.

Elsa almost groaned at the thought, but kept her smile in place, much to Rosalind's delight, if her broad smile was any indication. Elsa knew her lady really did not intentionally torment her. She just could not help being who she was.

"My Lady, you very well know I cannot attend the ball as just another girl to be swept off her feet. It wouldn't be proper," Elsa retorted as she shook the reins of the cart to get the horses to pick up the pace a bit.

"I have duties to tend to. You speak of stuff and nonsense and can tell me all about it at our morning meal the following day," Elsa told her.

Rosalind smiled at Elsa but agreed to nothing of the sort. Two could play the game she had been getting at. Elsa needed a good man to come home to at night. Rosalind could help in that department. Her father made sure to invite the local gentry, well-to-do tradesmen, and gentleman farmers from all around to his ball. He had a varied range of friends and thought very highly of them all, no matter their station by birth. Two could definitely play the matchmaking game she knew Elsa was up to.

"I believe it may rain, Ladies," Nan said, drawing their attention to the large storm clouds that were quickly gathering on the horizon, just as a bolt of lightning streaked across the sky in the distance.

Elsa encouraged the horses to trot a bit faster. She had no desire to get caught in one of England's notorious spring storms. They blew in and out in the wink of an eye, but were like Poseidon himself had unleashed his fury, only in billows of rain instead of waves. It would ruin their dresses. The horses picked up pace at the encouragement of the reins tickling their backs, until Buttercup, the tawny mare, gave a shrill snorting neigh and came to a halt, pawing the ground with her front left hoof.

"Oh, no, Buttercup appears to have injured herself," Elsa cried as she hopped off the carriage, followed by Rosalind and Nan. "I have no idea what to do for an injured animal," Elsa stated while stroking the mare to comfort her. Nan gently took the horse's hoof into her palm and tried to pull it up to take a look. The horse swished her head and nudged Nan away.

From behind, Nan heard another carriage approaching. She hoped it was someone who could help the poor animal. She continued trying to pick up the hoof so she could examine it, but Buttercup was having none of it and kept nudging her, but was now beginning to shake her leg, implying to Nan she wished to be left alone.

A smooth voice called out, "Ladies, please stand back before you are injured. An animal in pain is unpredictable and may be prone to kick."

His warning was too late; the horse caught Nan's leg in one swift kick and sent her flying. The man belonging to the voice caught her in strong arms before she hit the ground. He had her cradled against his warm chest within an instant.

"Are you injured? Where did she kick you?" he asked, concern lacing his words.

Nan was too shocked by the injury and the man's speed to comment. She looked into his hazel eyes, noticing he had a ring of green around the hazel. It was striking, reminding her of emerald reeds surrounding a meadow pond.

"I think I am uninjured," Nan said shakily, smiling up at him as Rosalind and Elsa ran to her side and stopped in their tracks when they noticed the two staring at each other.

"Might I look to ascertain the damage?" he asked, unable to pull his eyes from hers.

All Nan could do was stare in shock. He wanted to see her legs. No man had seen her legs since Erwin. Her face heated with a blush. Rosalind began to blush as well. Elsa began to smile for the second time that day. Humming a new happy tune, she rubbed her hands together. Rosalind looked at her as if she had lost all reason.

"I promise, my Lady, I just wish to ensure you are at no risk. Your modesty is safe with me."

Nan nodded briskly, feeling shy like a schoolgirl. He quickly, and rather gallantly, flung off his traveling cloak with one hand and spread it upon the ground with a flick of his wrist whilst keeping her cradled against him with his other arm. He then gently sat her upon the cloak. He did all that without so much as a grunt of straining, she noted with a deeper blush she could feel pouring over her cheeks like an overfilled cauldron of jam. She felt hotter still as he delicately took her foot into his hand and lifted her skirts to view the calf beneath her white stocking. He could not see the injury properly without rolling her stocking down. She was having none of that.

"You can ascertain the damage through my stocking, sir," she stated, glowing scarlet. She winced as he gently prodded the area that was already turning a deep purple, which could be clearly seen even through the thick, white stocking.

"I believe she just grazed you. I see no signs of a break, but it may be a lovely shade of purple by morning. May I assist you into your carriage?" he asked, looking deeply into her large, cinnamon brown eyes as he scooped her up again without permission. Her eyes were the most beguiling shade of brown he had ever seen. They nearly matched the color of her hair perfectly, except her hair had sable streaks that nearly glowed within the curls that were escaping her bun. They fell about her face, giving her a cherubic visage. He could not help but smile at her. She felt as light as a feather in his arms. Even though he should not take such liberties, he could not seem to put her down. She seemed a delicate, even fragile little thing, and she seemed near to tears. He noted she smelled of fresh lavender and tea.

"I thank you to put me down, sir," Nan said with no small amount of fear in her voice.

She sounded like a ferocious kitten about to pounce, but dear Lord, did she think he meant to harm her? Appearing a bit insulted, he set her into her carriage and inclined his head into a quick bow without saying another word.

Turning his head to the other ladies, he asked, "May I please check the horse's injury? Perhaps it is nothing serious."

"Oh, please do," pleaded Rosalind. "Poor Buttercup is nearly a family pet. I can't bear her to be in pain."

The gentleman approached the wild-eyed horse and stroked her nose and ears, speaking gently to calm her. Once she seemed to settle, he leaned over, rubbing his shoulder into hers, and ran his hand down the length of her injured leg to a spot just above the fetlock and gave it a gentle pinch.

"Do be careful," Nan called, but to her amazement, Buttercup lifted her hoof with complete ease and rubbed her muzzle atop his head as if they were the best of friends. The man looked back and smiled at her, causing a kaleidoscope of butterflies to take up residence in her belly before he turned his attention back to Buttercup.

"Ah," he stated matter-of-factly. "Here is the problem. It is nothing but a large stone lodged in her hoof. I can take care of this with but a moment." He turned and walked back to his carriage, with the ladies watching as he went.

Nan noticed his long legs made short work of the distance between the two carriages. He had a confident stride. He was muscular but not given to bulk. His hands had been so gentle on her leg and on Buttercup's. And he was so handsome. The golden highlights in his blonde hair nearly glowed in the sunlight, conjuring images of the Archangel Gabriel in her mind. Tinged with a bit of guilt for looking at any man in appreciation of his physique, she cast her gaze down to her lap. What would Erwin think if he knew she was admiring another man's form?

Rosalind, eyeing her friend's discomfort and watching the array of emotions flood through her face, must have known what her friend was thinking. She would address that later. It had been two years, after all. Nan deserved some joy, even if it was nothing more than a gentleman tending her wounds. Rosalind also finally cut her eyes at Elsa, who had not stopped elbowing her in the ribs and smiling like a goose since the gentleman had so gently touched Buttercup.

The man returned shortly and noticed his injured Lady looked forlorn, the owner of Buttercup looked thoroughly irritated, and the third lady was smiling like a giddy schoolgirl. What an odd bunch he had happened upon. He made short work of removing the stone from the horse's hoof and then proceeded to check the others. "You're set to rights, sweet Buttercup," he said, feeding the mare an apple he had procured from his pocket. She knickered happily at him and nudged his head with hers. He then confirmed all the tack was in proper order before assisting the ladies in remounting the carriage.

"My Lord," Elsa called. "What is your name, if I may be so bold?"

"But of course, how rude of me; Mr. Jacob Corbin, traveling to Englebright Manor for his Lordship's birthday celebration." He bowed low. "At your service, My Ladies." He noted by attire that it appeared to be a lady's maid making inquiries, which was odd, but country life often meant the formality of city gentry was forgone. He quite liked it, but his uncle would be appalled at her forthright manner. "And whom do I have the pleasure of rescuing this fine day?" he asked in return with a warm smile.

Giving a brief curtsey, as much as her blasted skirts and the carriage bench would allow, Rosalind said, "I am Lady Rosalind Englebright and am pleased to have made your acquaintance, as well as to have you as our rescuer, kind sir. This is my dearest friend, Nan, the widow Willoughby."

Nan's mouth popped open, and she gasped quietly at Rosalind's boldness in calling her a widow.

"And this is my lady's maid and close companion, Elsa. We owe you a debt of gratitude, it seems," she said genially with a smile as she gently rested her hand under her friend's chin and closed her mouth for her. The action was hidden from the gentleman, but Nan was no longer forlorn; she was near fuming at her apparent matchmaking ploy.

Jacob smiled back, though his stomach sank a bit at meeting Lady Englebright in such a way. His uncle would be pleased that he had ingratiated himself with Englebright's daughter and her lovely friend as well, but truth be told, he would have done it if it had been just some village girl in need. His uncle placed too much stock in station and title. He was just happy they did not get caught in the brewing storm.

"We had best be off if we are to beat this tempest," he said and nodded toward the sky. The ladies nodded in agreement, glancing at the clouds that had thickened like cold molasses in the last few minutes.

"We are nearly there, my Lord." Rosalind smiled at him. "Perhaps it would be best if my friend rode with you, as she is already injured; we would not want her soaked through as well."

Rosalind practically gleamed at her friend as the lord agreed it would be for the best. Nan could have shot daggers from her eyes at Rosalind. She did not want to ride with this man alone.

"My Lady, I believe it would be best if you all rode with me, and perhaps we should protect your packages as well, as they are exposed to the elements in your open carriage."

Before any of the ladies could disagree, he had his driver, Douglas, down and transferred their things to his carriage, which was fully enclosed and well-protected.

"My Lord, there is insufficient room for the ladies, yours and the ladies' things, and you," Douglas told him discreetly, as the ladies were moving into the interior of the carriage.

"Well then, my fine man, you shall move my things to the open carriage, and I shall drive myself to the estate. You can take the ladies," said Jacob.

Douglas peered at the darkening sky and smiled at his master in a completely unconcerned manner. "You may be soaked through before we arrive. Are these ladies lovely enough for that?" Douglas chortled. "You grow too bold, my friend! Uncle would have your hide if he heard you speaking to me with such familiarity and candor," Jacob said with a wink as he mounted the open carriage after the last of his things were in place.

"Then I guess it's a good thing your uncle ain't here," Douglas laughed.

Rosalind poked her head out the carriage window and called to Jacob, "My Lord, you will catch your death of cold. I can walk."

Jacob was taken aback that a gently bred lady thought herself more resilient than he and nearly laughed as he shook the reins, calling back, "I am not near so delicate as all that, dear Lady!"

Rosalind gaped at him in wonder. This was the second useful gentleman she had met today. She popped her head back into the carriage with her mouth wide open and stammering a bit incoherently. It was Nan's turn to pop her friend's mouth shut, and none too gently.

They heard the snap of the reins from Douglas, and they were off. Elsa began another off-key tune, which Rosalind believed she could not possibly know the lyrics to, or she would not hum it thus. Rosalind laughed and could not help but join in on the bawdy tune. Before long, she could have sworn the driver had also joined in. She laughed, and Nan glared as the sky let loose in a downpour with a clap of thunder. Rosalind, still humming, looked at her friend and winked. It was not until then that she noticed Nan's attention was focused on Elsa. Her friend appeared a bit worried for some reason. Rosalind glanced at Elsa, and her song caught in her throat. Elsa wore the most mischievous smile. Rosalind got a sudden sinking feeling.

"I believe another gale is brewing," Elsa said and winked at Nan. "What a fine day it is, indeed," she giggled, taking Rosalind's hand in hers and smiling even more broadly. "A fine day indeed," she repeated as another clap of thunder echoed in the distance.

Chapter Nine

It was the worst day Mrs. Mary could remember in quite some time. Elsa had asked her to look in on Lady Rosalind to make sure she did not disappear again. But when she went to look for her and take her the nooning meal, she was nowhere to be found. Her dress and shift were in a heap on the floor, as were her slippers. Mary knew what that meant. After all her twenty years of keeping up with her Ladyship, she had actually lost her. She was so ashamed and just knew Lord Englebright would have her hide.

Mary made her way to the study, where she knew his Lordship liked to take his nooning meals. Hopefully, he was not entertaining guests as of yet. Most liked to sleep in during these long visitations and balls, but not the Englebright family. They were frequently up at dawn to start their day. She knocked tentatively on the ornate, wooden door, hoping perhaps his Lordship had gone out. *Oh, don't be such a coward, you fool,* she thought just as she heard the familiar baritone voice call, "Enter."

She took a deep breath and opened the door and walked into the cozy study. It always smelled of leather and fresh lemon oil. The high windows behind the desk provided ample light, making the study far less foreboding than others she had seen. The room reflected the temperament of her employer rather well.

"My Lord, I am afraid I seem to have misplaced our lady…again, perhaps in the woods, my Lord…perhaps not." She coughed to cover her embarrassment, looking down at her hands, and peeking up under hooded lashes, just realizing he was not alone. She gasped.

Standing just left of the door, looking at the abundant collection of books on the shelves, was one of the largest and most handsome men she had ever laid her eyes upon. His gray eyes seemed to reflect the storm brewing outdoors. His hair was a near match in color to the warm wood tones of the bookcases in front of which he was standing. She saw concern mar that handsome forehead.

"Oh, begging your pardon, my Lord." Mary hesitated with eyes going wide. "I did not realize you were hosting presently. I am sure 'tis no matter; she will turn up when she is good and ready."

She laughed nervously.

"But there does seem to be a storm on the horizon. I would hate for her to catch a chill," she said, curtseying as she backed away toward the door, looking first from her employer then to the giant. She backed out of the door and began to close it within seconds of entering.

"Mrs. Gowan?" Lord Englebright called. "Could you please come back here? I feel I might need just a wee bit more information in order to fetch Lady Rosalind. Perhaps Lord Kristoff Van Reede would assist us in this search; apparently, finding people is his forte," he said as the woman came back in with her cheeks flaming red.

Lord Englebright inclined his head to the visitor, raised his teacup in a brief salute to the man, and smiled warmly at him.

Kristoff looked a bit taken aback at Lord Englebright's nonchalance at his daughter's disappearance.

"Of course, my Lord. I am at your disposal," he said, approaching the man with his hand outstretched. It contained a rather thick file that appeared to be full of papers.

"We are unable to conclude this business until all my sons arrive anyway, correct?" he asked. Kristoff nodded and handed him the file. "Let us go fetch my girl. Now, Mrs. Gowan," he said, "might you have any idea of where she could be?"

"Oh, Your Grace, I am sure she will turn up in a moment. You know she likes her quiet walks," Mrs. Gowan said, almost choking on the word walk.

"The storm seems fast approaching. I fear if she is outdoors, she will be at risk, sir," Kristoff stated in a worried tone, trying to intimate to the lord the danger his daughter was in. Gently-bred ladies were rarely of a sort to withstand a torrential downpour without succumbing to some sort of ailment or another. The ladies of society in London had even been known to take to their beds for weeks for having gotten caught in nothing more than the morning dew. They were oft of a weak disposition, but perhaps the country aristocracy were a bit more resilient.

With a chortle, which perplexed Kristoff even more, Lord Englebright tossed the file upon his desk, glanced at him, and said, "Please call me George or Englebright, whichever you prefer," as he headed out the door, beckoning Kristoff to follow.

A cacophonous commotion at the front steps had Lord Englebright smiling anew. He clapped his hands together, walking down the steps, and said, "Never fear, I believe she has been found."

Looking through the front door, Kristoff stopped dead in his tracks and could not believe his luck. Emerging from the large, black carriage, sporting an intricately carved crest that he did not recognize, was none other than that sprite of a girl he could not stop thinking of since he had met her days before. She seemed to have no care in the world that she was being soaked through, or that the dust settled all over her clothing was turning to mud. She even had a blotch of dirt on her nose and cheek. He almost smiled. It did little to detract from her mischievous beauty. Her bodice, he noticed, clung to her as it became damper.

Damn, but she was tempting even in her current state. He felt himself reacting to her and had to avert his attention to regain some restraint. He was sickened by his own lust. As he turned his head away to the other ladies hopping out of the carriage unassisted, he recognized the dressmaker, who looked no better for wear, especially with a slight limp to her gait. There was now a third lady following in their wake, also covered in dust turning to mud. She was smiling as if she had no cares in the world, either. In truth, her smile was a bit manic as if she had just gotten away with a mischievous crime.

A gentleman who was dripping puddles upon the drive was attempting to aid each of them in exiting the carriage, but the ladies seemed to be quite self-sufficient. Kristoff almost laughed at the near disgruntled and perplexed look upon the gentleman's face. Indeed, he had never seen such a ragged group lining the lawn of a lord's estate.

Surely, none of these girls could be Lady Englebright. They looked more akin to near-drowned pups than gently bred ladies.

Harold, the butler, seemed to think nothing of the arrival of such a higgledy-piggledy group. In fact, he looked quite resigned to the cleaning the foyer would require. Lord Englebright hurried out the door, smiling broadly at the ladies and the gentleman. Kristoff followed him closely and stopped on the landing at the bottom of the steps, trying to sort out what assistance he could possibly provide.

"Ah, my dear Sprite," Lord Englebright welcomed the beauty standing beside the carriage in a warm, one-armed embrace, apparently uncaring that she muddied his linen shirt.

Her father had called her "Sprite." Kristoff almost laughed when he heard him, for that is exactly as he had thought of her upon their first meeting. Clearly, everyone knew her demeanor and appreciated her for it, as her father did not make it sound like an admonishment. Her hair was turning from a rich auburn to a warm, ruddy brown as it was soaked in the deluge. She seemed oblivious. In all his days, he had never encountered a lady who was so wholly and unapologetically herself. And somehow, he found it completely alluring.

"What have you been up to, and whose carriage have you absconded with?" her papa asked, raising one dark eyebrow at her, then turning his head to better take in the full scene before him.

"I fear you may have been up to mischief," he added and turned his head back to her and winked.

Removing his arm from his daughter, Lorde Englebright turned to the gentleman who had clearly aided the ladies.

"Papa, allow me to introduce Mister Jacob Corbin, our rescuer this fine day," she laughed as she spread her arms and twirled in a circle as if she could not have found finer weather than the drizzling rain falling upon them all.

"Ah, the horse-whisperer himself, in the flesh," Englebright gushed over the young man. "I have been anxiously awaiting your arrival, my man! Your reputation precedes you, and I can't wait to show you our fine stock," he said as he offered a hand to Jacob to shake.

"He was a wonder with sweet Buttercup. She kicked poor Nan, Papa!" Rosalind exclaimed. "He tended to Buttercup and to Nan's wounds. He is a man of many talents, it seems!"

"Oh, dear, Nan, are you well? Harold!" he called over his shoulder as he changed direction and approached Nan. "Call the physician. He arrived a short while ago for the fête."

"No need, my Lord. 'tis but a bruise," she stated with a wan smile.

"Pish, posh. I will have you attended to. Elsa, can you assist her inside, or do you prefer one of the strapping lads carry you, my dear child?" he asked as he reached for Jacob's still outstretched hand to shake vigorously while winking at her where no one else could see.

Jacob stepped forward a bit too anxiously as if to sweep Nan into his arms once again the moment Lord Englebright released his handshake.

"A pleasure, my Lord. I would be pleased if you called me by my given name, Jacob. The ladies seemed in a bit of distress. Poor Buttercup captured a stone in her hoof. I would be more than honored to assist the Widow Willoughby to her rooms, attended with an escort, of course."

Lord Englebright smiled at him without averting his gaze. The young man met his eyes and did not turn away. That spoke volumes about a man, Lord Englebright thought. He could not help noticing that he was handsome and had a strong grip. Clearly, he was of good character for stopping to help the girls, getting soaked in the process, and he spoke the thought aloud, patting the young man on the shoulder with genuine gratitude.

"I cannot thank you enough for stopping to help my girls in their moment of distress."

Though he had a hard time ever thinking of his lovely girls as *in distress*. Even though injured, Nan seemed no worse for wear and as stubborn as ever to go it alone as always. He nodded at Jacob as if to give his approval. Nan worked too hard and needed a good man to help with her worries. He made his mind up. A bit of matchmaking was in order, it seemed. This might be the finest birthday he had seen in many a year.

"You are too kind, my boy…please do assist. It would break my heart if our dear Nan fell ill. I would happily carry her, but just this morning, I injured my arm, you see?" said Lord Englebright, rubbing at his perfectly fine shoulder and wincing for effect.

"You are injured, Papa?" Rosalind worried.

Her father gazed at her a bit sheepishly and guided her toward the door.

Jacob was not sure what to make of this man. Jacob had met his gaze, but it took a sheer act of will not to turn away. He felt very certain that Lord George Englebright missed nothing and could ascertain his very soul with one look, though he had no idea why he felt that way. He had never seen such intensity in a man's gaze except his Uncle Elias. That was a frightening thought.

The two men seemed nothing alike, though. Englebright even referred to a lady's maid as one of his girls, as if she were family instead of staff. Uncle Elias would have had apoplexy at such a raucous display. Englebright seemed to take it in stride as a normal occurrence, Jacob thought as he swept Nan into his arms yet again without asking permission.

Lord Englebright patted the young man on the back and began to direct him to the house as his other arm went back around his daughter. She was poking and prodding his arms to determine where his injury might be. He gathered her up like a hen would a wayward chick and looked at Jacob, carrying their Nan with such ease, and smiled.

As Lord Englebright turned back to his daughter, he noted that she was now staring at Nan with a gleam in her eye. She clearly had decided that his arm was well enough to divert her attention back to her friend gathered in Jacob's arms. He could not quite decide if Nan was in trouble or if the fine, young Jacob was.

Once Sprite set her mind to something, she typically stopped at nothing until her goal was achieved. He knew his daughter better than she knew herself, he often thought. Today, he was certain she was up to matchmaking. He was also certain he was up to helping. He had not failed to notice that Nan had not taken her lovely brown eyes off the newcomer. He also noticed that Kristoff was looking at his daughter in a complete stupor.

Kristoff feared his mouth had fallen completely agape as he watched what appeared to be a theatrical farce put on by the Théâtre Royal. The gentleman, Jacob Corbin, seemed to be completely enjoying the chaos, but Kristoff had never seen such a display by the peerage in all his days. Lady Rosalind was, again, so joyful and almost boisterous that he could not imagine how she got on with other ladies of the Ton. Perhaps no one had ever instructed her that a lady was to have a calming, pleasant demeanor, not participating in nonsense. He was so dumbfounded, he just stood there like a buffoon, he thought, staring at her. She was wholly and unabashedly her own person. Damn, but it was near intoxicating to watch.

Thankfully, no one seemed to notice him due to the eventful arrival of the ladies and their apparent savior, and thanks to the ever-increasing downpour that was now pelting them. Oddly, the ladies did not seem to care one bit, and now the duke had forgone all propriety to have this girl carried by a complete stranger to her bedchambers. Country folk were odd indeed. He had best act with care, or he would be married by the week's end…maybe even to old Maude. He smiled at the thought. He was not sure which would have been stranger at this point.

"Kristoff, my man, please come back inside out of this storm and properly meet the family," Lord Englebright called out as he ushered the lot of them into the foyer.

His daughter, normally quite observant, had just noticed the gentleman standing upon their stoop and had come to an abrupt halt despite the rain trickling down her face and soaking her through. Her eyes widened to near saucers as she gaped at her father, her gaze bouncing back and forth between him and the handsome devil. Her father, noticing her apparent discomfiture, looked down at his daughter quizzically

"Or perhaps you have already met?" he questioned with that handsome eyebrow quirked in her direction and then Kristoff's.

Clearing his throat with a slight guilty cough, Kristoff acknowledged, "Only in passing, my Lord, when I was down in the village being commissioned by a fine lady by the name of Old Maude."

He smiled as he made that statement and nodded toward Rosalind, meeting her gaze only and not averting his eyes to take in the rest of her. He was not sure he could withstand the temptation that another good look would cause him.

Rosalind took a deep, steadying breath, which she knew was not unnoticed by her papa. She suddenly felt seared to her toes by the intensity of that gaze and rather demurely lowered her eyes and nodded back to Kristoff. She gasped as she realized her dress was clinging to her bosom like it had been glued in place with flour paste. She flung her arms across her chest and blushed.

Still looking at her, Kristoff said, "I would be happy to formally meet these lovely ladies, my Lord," in that deep melodic baritone that hummed across her skin as he spoke. She had been thinking about that exact timbre since their first meeting in the village, and how it felt somehow rich, like it held secrets. Then she blushed scarlet again as she thought back to the conversation…or lack thereof. *Oh, Lord in Heaven, the things I said. Could he have overheard me talking to Nan?* She could not remember the entirety of the conversation, nor much of anything after his arrival. His entire countenance seemed to fill her every thought of that moment.

Lord Englebright could not fathom what had come over his daughter. She looked demure and was acting like a skittish kitten, and was now blushing the deepest red he had ever seen on his dear Sprite. Nothing ever set her this ill at ease.

"Dear me," he stated, drawing the attention away from his clearly addled daughter and desperately hoping she had done nothing to embarrass herself as deeply as that blush indicated. He diverted the topic back to what he hoped was a safe one.

"I would love to hear the story of what Old Maude might have you up to. You'd best be careful around that one," he chuckled. "She's been on the lookout for a replacement husband for the last fifty years and will spit upon your shoes as quick as a wink if she thinks something is amiss."

Turning his attention back to the ladies and Jacob, he indicated they should upstairs to don warm, dry clothes so as to not catch a chill.

"Harold, old boy, after Nan is settled with Doctor Wallace, would you mind showing Jacob to the Blue Room? I believe it is still unoccupied." He intoned to the young man, "Please make yourself at home. Cook will ring the bell for a bit of brunch with our other guests in a while." He smiled warmly as the group departed.

As Elsa mounted the first step, she turned back and winked at him. Lord Englebright was taken aback by the maid's odd behavior. He stared at her as she nodded toward Kristoff and winked again. Assessing the two gentlemen who had just arrived, he got the maid's message and nodded back at her, winking in kind, which had the maid miss a step and stumble up the stairs.

No matter, Elsa continued smiling like a crazed woman. He could not help thinking that he and the maid were of like mind. Perhaps, finally, he had found a worthy adversary for his daughter and just might see Nan settled as well. Fate had dealt him what he hoped would turn out to be a happy hand. For the second time, he thought his party might be the finest ever.

Chapter Ten

Rosalind's day could not have been worse, and it was all because of a stupid hat. And more to the point, now she had to be even more careful about her breeches and had to wear blasted dresses on a daily basis, or Lord Kristoff would catch her for sure. Not to mention, all of the fine ladies in attendance. She could not shame her father.

The day started off well enough with a beautiful sunrise after the downpour the night before. Thinking that she would just take a quick jaunt into the woods to retrieve her woolen cap lost the day before, as she wanted to leave no proof she had been running about the woods, she donned her lovely new blue day dress, which Nan had made for her, and took a leisurely stroll toward the stables to see what young Markham had left for her this week. The stable lad often helped Desmond with the tack and mounts, but also had a soft spot for Rosalind and would supply her with all the breeches her heart could desire. The two of them were of a similar size, but Elsa had confiscated all her breeches after the debacle in the woods. She blushed to think how horrendously she had behaved when she burst into Nan's cottage acting like a complete simpleton. She had never become so flustered over any male, no matter how strong, or capable, or broad-shouldered…she shook her head. Her thoughts were getting all scrambled, and it was his fault.

Rosalind opened the large stable door and went to her hidden chest in which Markham would place his outgrown breeches. In return, she would leave him bolts of soft woolen fabric that Nan would obtain for her so his dear mama could make his younger siblings new clothing. The arrangement worked out well, for his papa had died of a fever some years back, but his mama would not hear of taking charity. Rosalind would never insult her pride by offering.

As she opened the chest, she noted the breeches smelled a bit musty and were quite a bit larger than the last pair. Markham appeared to be outgrowing her. *Blast it all*, she thought. She pulled the clothes from the chest and gave them a good shake to remove any spiders or other unwanted crawly creatures. She sneezed as dust puffed in a cloud around her. She would need a bath when she was done, she thought.

She moved to the back of the stall and undid her tiny pearl buttons that were neatly lined down the front of the gown. Nan knew her well and knew she might just need to remove the dress unattended…or she liked to think that was the case, but she did wish she had not sewn quite so many of the blasted tiny buttons. They did not make for a quick costume change.

Rosalind neatly hung the dress on a wooden peg, making sure the hem was not in the straw. It was fresh straw, but she still could not stand the idea of ruining something her friend had worked so hard on for her. She had already tightened her corset around her bosom. It really was quite uncomfortable to run without the bothersome things corseted in some way. She threw a clean but rumpled work shirt over her head, tucked it into the breeches, tied her hair up in a knot, and popped on another tweed cap she had pinched from Markham.

She sniffed; the hat smelled a bit of garlic…or something she could not quite place. It was definitely a "boy" smell, she thought with a wrinkled nose. She would return it to the hook when she retrieved his other hat. The one she had lost in the woods did smell much better, though she was sure by now it smelled of dirt and leaves. After assuring she looked more like Markham than a lady, she set off out the back stable door and headed into the woods.

Kristoff was looking out his window when he saw Rosalind…or Sprite…or Ara, whatever the vixen preferred to be called, hurrying across the lawn to the stable. It was so early in the morning, he was surprised she was up and dressed, much less out and about after being nearly soaked to the bone the day before. He just knew she would be abed most of the day so as not to fall ill. He decided it was high time he properly met this lady with the colorful vocabulary of a barmaid and got over his infatuation with her.

The ladies had not come back down from above the stairs the entire previous day. He assumed they feared the vapors, or whatever malady a woman might suffer from after being merely damp, and they had been soaked through. In truth, he had been rather worried about her, though for the life of him, he could not sort out why. He did not even know this woman. She seemed no worse for wear this fine morning, and in fact, he noticed her rosy lips and cheeks from afar, as well as the sway of her narrow hips.

Thank God those blasted skirts covered her well enough. After seeing her in the soaked, clinging bodice yesterday, he was not sure how much more temptation he could take. Given that he was not prone to indulging his baser desires, he was a bit angered that he could not get this lady out of his head…or his blood, he thought.

The mere sound of her voice yesterday had heated his blood like a stallion in rut. He was disgusted with himself. She was not the type for a dalliance, and neither was he. She was an innocent, hang it all, and did not deserve to be ogled like a piece of freshly carved meat by a starving man. If he just met her, had a chat…likely about ribbons or whatnot…he knew he would be disappointed as he had in all the other ladies who had tried to garner his attention back home, and he could quell this heat.

Perhaps she was going for a morning ride. If that was the case, he could join her and perhaps even speak to her of Old Maude's assignment. He still had a debt to the woman for sending him in the proper direction to find the Van Lynden heirs. Yes, that was the only reason he found himself skipping breakfast and heading out the door.

He heard the horses nickering in the back paddock and decided to walk around the large wooden building rather than through it. He could have the stable lad saddle his mount and be ready to join her before she was off. As he broke around the back corner, he looked to the treeline and noticed the silhouette of a boy ducking under the large oaks lining the pristine lawn and leading into the forest. Rosalind was nowhere to be seen. Weighing his odds, thinking the boy was the same one he had encountered the day prior, he decided he would have to put off his encounter with Rosalind until later on that day.

Where is that boy? thought Kristoff as he stood at the treeline of the woods. He had never known a lad to move so stealthily and quickly. *Good thing I am so well-trained in tracking,* he thought as he slipped quietly under the verdant canopy. His time spent training for his government was well put to use during this latest assignment. "No slip of a boy will best me," he whispered under his breath. All he had to do was look for a sign to point him in the correct direction. He ran his hands over the leaf litter, feeling for an indentation or any sign of a footfall.

Rosalind thought she heard something on the breeze and stood as still as the grave, leaning against the trunk of a large wych elm. Its leaves, high above the forest floor, were shimmering silver and green as they waved gently in the soft wind. She closed her eyes and listened like Maude had taught her. She could hear nothing but the soft sigh of the wind. Perhaps it had been a doe or squirrel.

My, I am jumpy today. Those brigands have me on edge, she thought. Even so, she did a double-take of her surroundings to make sure she was not being followed. *A young lady can never be too careful dressed as a lad in musty breeches…* She sniffed. *Which are too big…* She adjusted the waistband that had begun slipping down her narrow hips. *Too long…* She bent over to roll the hem up a bit so she would not trip. *With a baggy shirt,* she thought, chuckling quietly to herself as she tucked the shirt in more thoroughly. She knew she looked a fright. Thank the heavens no one would see her. She sniffed at herself again and wished she had a sprig of fresh mint to stuff into the pockets.

Just as Rosalind was cutting her eyes to the left, a small, fluffy rabbit crept its way around the base of the roots of the elm tree and gently nudged her foot. Rosalind gasped in surprise, nearly causing her to kick the poor animal across the forest. Sighing, she realized that her wild and unfounded thoughts were getting out of hand. She was alone and safe.

Stepping lightly, she approached the holes the ne'er-do-wells had created in the center of her forest. These, unlike the others she had nearly fallen in on her path to Nan's, still had piles of earth scattered about. She looked into the nearest hole. It was quite deep. *What could they have been seeking?* she pondered. Shaking her head in bewilderment, she began to circumnavigate the area, looking for her lost cap. How she hoped Kristoff had not found it.

Rosalind continued searching the area for at least five minutes with no luck and lost heart. *Either a bird has decided to make a nest of it, or he has discovered it…or,* she hoped, *I am just searching in the wrong spot, perhaps.* She decided to move farther into the woods, going in the direction of Nan's, thinking that if she could just retrace her steps, she would surely stumble upon it.

Kristoff stepped silently through the crush of brambles that surrounded the area of yesterday's encounter. He noted the small footprints in a pile of earth near one of the holes and surmised that the lad had come back for the bit of parchment he had found the day before, or perhaps there was a rendezvous with the other scoundrels. If he just sat back, all would come to light before him. As he waited behind the same tree where the boy had hidden previously, he heard a twig snap a short way into the deep forest to his right, and noted the sounds of the birds ceased in that direction. He waited a few minutes more, but the din of the forest returned. Thinking he was right the first time, and that the lad was searching for what appeared to be a map, he set off in the direction where he had heard the telltale snap.

Kristoff had been trained and excelled in traveling afoot silently. It took him a few moments to catch up with the lad, who appeared to not notice his presence. The boy was cursing under his breath like a street urchin as he looked about the forest floor. The lad had a soft voice, so could not be out of leading strings yet. He was far too young to speak with such a vulgar tongue. Kristoff thought he might have already learned a new phrase or two that he had never encountered. The lad was quite creative in his expletives.

Kristoff had managed to maneuver behind the boy as the child bent over to search a pile of brush. He grabbed the little scoundrel by his waistband but realized too late that the boy's breeches were two sizes too large. The lad fell forward as Kristoff wrapped one strong arm around his waist and jerked him back toward his chest none too gently.

The boy jerked and gasped in surprise as Kristoff said in a menacing voice, "Looking for something you've dropped, are we?"

Rosalind began to struggle against his strong arms. They were so hard, they felt like boulders about her waist. The more she struggled, the more he tightened until she thought she might pass out from lack of air.

"Hold still, and I will not hurt you," he said. "You obviously have something to do with the mystery of the bloody holes, and I tire of Maude spitting upon my shoes."

It was not until then that Rosalind realized he had no clue who she was. She stilled in his arms, which proved to be a mistake. As his hands splayed flatly against her form, she felt him jerk in astonishment when he stroked the stays under her light shirt, which was now bunched under her bosom, and her pants were falling off her waistline. Just then, her cap, which had fallen over her left eye, fell to her feet, releasing a waterfall of auburn locks into his face. "Oh, hell," she said, none too quietly.

No, thought Kristoff. *Just no. This could not be Lady Rosalind. What the hell could she be thinking coming back to where those men could grab her, and what did she have to do with this bloody map…and why for the love of all that is holy, is she in men's breeches!!!*

He felt his emotions warring with him. On one side, he was both curious and enraged as to why she would put herself at such risk. On the other, he was so enchanted by this aptly named Sprite that he felt like laughing.

With a smile in his voice, for the enchanted side had won, he quickly spun her around and loosened his hold so she could breathe and better look up at him. He spun her so quickly, she nearly toppled over, making him tighten his hold again to steady her.

"I must thank you for the education in new epithets to use next time I am in a brawl." He chuckled. "I have never heard some of those phrases used in such combinations before now. Your vocabulary is quite…shall we say, creative."

He leaned his head back and let out a full-bellied laugh without letting her go.

As he looked back down at her, still with laughter rumbling in his broad chest, which was harder than his arms, she noted, she blew a wisp of hair out of her face and looked at him with the most disgruntled scowl she could muster. Laughter still gleamed in his eyes, with the most handsome little crinkles at the corners. *Handsome…handsome and infuriating is what he is.* But that voice. It washed over her like a warm caress. She felt her face heat; her belly fluttered in the glow of that caress.

Rosalind was mortified and furious at herself. How had he actually snuck up on her? She would never hear the end of it if Maude found out her star pupil had failed so dreadfully. She always prided herself on the fact that she never even allowed her brothers to capture her. She decided a different tack was needed and once again smiled demurely at him, as if nothing in the world was out of the ordinary. Yes, she would just pretend this was a normal way to find a gently bred lady. *Maybe he will think country folk just behave in such a way,* she thought. *And maybe I am the queen of France.*

One edge of his lip quirked. She looked at his mouth to see if he was about to burst into laughter again, so she could brace herself for more ridicule. That was a mistake. She could feel his heart quicken beneath her woolen shirt, and she responded in kind. She widened her eyes at the sensation he was causing in her and looked back at those gray eyes that had turned from laughter to clouded, with what, well…she could not describe. They had deepened to the gray of a stormy sky before the first break of lightning. She licked her lips and noted that his eyes were focused on her mouth, which was suddenly dry and so hot. She licked her lips again as she watched the intensity of his face. It was so mesmerizing, even in her anger at herself. She leaned in, tilting her head to the side ever so slightly for a closer look at those lovely near-black specks in his eyes. As she began to form the thought upon her lips, wondering why his eyes were changing thusly, he leaned in and sealed his lips against her partially open ones, startling her into jumping against him.

He knew he should have let her go as soon as he felt the wash of thick hair fall from that overly dusty and pungent cap. As the stench of it fell away, the scent of cinnamon and caramel had invaded his senses. Her hair was like silk upon his face and smelled divine.

The little minx had the nerve to smile at him as if she were behaving perfectly normally. Did she think he had never been in the country before, and did not know what was still considered appropriate behavior for a gently bred lady? He knew by her widened eyes that he was having an effect upon her and thanked God that he was not the only one in jeopardy of losing this battle of attraction.

When he had turned her in his arms, he felt his heart quicken. Despite his anger with even having this enthrallment, he was bewitched by both her beauty and her grit. She was nothing like any woman he had ever met. Everything about her was simply stunning, even that bawdy tongue. He smiled. He was definitely stunned by that; he nearly laughed aloud at the thought. Her glorious smile and the lick of her lips were his undoing. He felt passion winning and his good sense and anger at this temptation leaving him. He knew she could read it in his eyes.

He felt her lean in close, clearly drawn in by the same desires thrumming through him like the beat of a drum. He did something he never would have conceived of doing before with a near stranger. As his eyes shifted to her full lips, which were rounded in a gentle pucker, he claimed her mouth, giving in to both their desires. *God, she is soft*, he thought.

As his lips brushed hers, the smoldering ember of his desire for her burst into full flame, licking heat into his every nerve. He could not control his response and felt himself begin to harden against her as she responded to his touches. She felt so right in his arms. Her body was taut with lean muscle but also soft in all the right places.

Rosalind was completely taken aback by the feeling of his lips upon hers, cutting off the question she was about to ask. Though startling, it was such an alluring feeling. His lips were full and soft, and the way he had looked at her before the kiss. He made her feel beautiful even in her current state. It felt as though he accepted her for all her idiosyncrasies without judgment.

In fact, he might even find her amusing, she thought the second before she was overwhelmed by what she thought might be a wave of desire. Yes, desire is what it was. She thought it must be, though she had never really felt it before now as her heart began to thrum in her chest.

Having never been kissed, but yearning for this new adventure, she mimicked the motions of his mouth moving upon hers. She felt a warmth begin in her stomach that seemed to wander about her body, settling into her most intimate parts. It was a deliciousness, like warm caramel seeping through her veins.

She lost all sense and reason, unexpectedly succumbing to the pleasurable sensation. This was no longer a mere curiosity. She wanted to feel more, explore these sensations. She never realized one could feel a kiss all the way to her toes. She tried to move in closer as an ache, a need filled her, but she knew not what else to do except continue to press her lips against his more fervently.

As if reading her thoughts, he pulled her small form more tightly to himself and deepened the kiss, nibbling on her bottom lip gently. She sighed against his mouth, opening her lips but a bit.

Rosalind felt as though she had been coiled too tightly all her life and was finally unraveling in his arms. Her hips gently rubbed the hardness at the juncture of his muscular thighs. This was too bold. She knew she needed to stop herself, but, oh, this heat. She needed… something. It was too much. She pressed her lips to his more firmly yet again. It was terrifying to want this to continue, but the thought of letting him go, to make these sensations stop, was as unbearable as asking herself to stop breathing. She sighed against his parted lips.

Kristoff took her sigh to mean she welcomed this sweet passion. He could not keep it gentle for long. He wanted to claim her mouth completely. He needed to taste, feel, experience all that was his Sprite. He lifted his hand to brush along her cheek as his other arm pulled her up against him, sealing their bodies together as closely as possible. He had to stop her from wiggling against him like that, or God knew he would take her on the forest floor. He knew she must feel his arousal, but it was too late to worry about that.

He gently swept his tongue across her lips. She tasted of caramel and cinnamon, like warmth and home. He almost growled when she responded in kind, and he felt her tongue timidly touch his bottom lip. With gentle pressure to get her to open for him, he swept his tongue inside her mouth with a passion fiercer than any he had ever known as the flames burst through every thought of control.

Kristoff slanted his mouth over hers again, wanting to feel her tongue upon his, but knowing if he did, he might not be able to stop. Taking a deep, shuddering breath, realizing that he was compromising a lady, for the love of God, he slowed his pace and began to try to pull away from her. He just needed one last taste and nibbled her bottom lip, as his tongue swept over it and his mouth claimed hers anew. He felt her suddenly stiffen against him.

Rosalind was brought back to her senses with a start. This adventure was a bit more than she bargained for. He had put his tongue in her mouth. It had made her feel marvelous and dangerous…and suddenly like a complete fool. She was an unwedded woman, allowing a near stranger to maul her in the woods. Papa would demand marriage if he found out.

Oh, Lord, oh, Lord, oh, Lord, the thought of marriage brought her passion to an abrupt end. Coming to her senses and realizing the liberties this rogue was having with her and the damage it could do to her plans, she swiftly brought her knee to meet his crotch, that most sensitive area. Her brothers had taught her well.

Kristoff promptly crumpled to the ground in agony as he watched her hike up her breeches and take off into the woods at a dead run. He had felt the moment her passion had left and had no idea what had caused it, unless she was completely innocent. Oh, hell, that was it. He had likely just given the girl her first kiss and had nearly ravaged her. She must have been terrified when she finally overcame the passion. But she had started this when she leaned in to him. He smiled arrogantly despite the deep ache in his groin. At his feet, he noticed the tweed hat she had left behind. Now he had two bloody hats to return to their owner. He wouldn't be surprised if they belonged to the stable lad. He would be sure to pay him a visit just as soon as he could stand upright and walk at a decent pace again.

Chapter Eleven

Rosalind ran as quickly as one of the forest deer, but not nearly as silently. Her heart was nearly exploding from her chest before she had even begun her run back. She had thrown caution to the wind and defied Maude's training of never leaving a trace and dashed pell-mell back to change back into her gown, both to be ready when the other guests started to awaken and to get away from that man. *Gracious*, she thought, *are all kisses so scrumptious?* Kristoff had tasted like peppermint when his tongue briefly touched hers. Surely, that was not an acceptable way to kiss a lady. She had never heard of such. Though it startled her, she felt as though tiny lightning bolts had begun to course through her nether regions. She blushed again. He was dangerous in more ways than one.

Distractedly, she made her way to the stable, where her dress was stashed. Somehow, Buttercup had managed to make her way into the stable with a new goat companion Rosalind knew belonged in the lower paddocks. How the creature had gotten out, she did not know. But here he was. The goat continuously nudged her thigh as she tried to dress, making the job very difficult. The beast had nearly knocked her to the ground when she noticed a bit of nutty bun sticking out of its gnashing teeth. The little fiend had stolen her forgotten breakfast. Glancing at Buttercup, she noticed the horse had a bit of a nutty bun on her muzzle as well. *Traitor*, she thought. Thankfully, they had not seemed to have damaged her dress in the process. Her pockets were intact. She had to speak with Nan immediately to discuss kissing methods. If the dress had been damaged, she would have had to sneak back into the house by the rear entry to avoid any early-rising guests, of which she hoped there were none. She had avoided all her guests thus far, leaving her father to entertain, which was less than noble of her. She would have to make amends today and be a suitable hostess for the day's activities.

Rosalind nearly ran to the house, looking over her shoulder as she entered the main door. She noticed Kristoff exiting the stable with a bit of an awkward gait. Grimacing, she turned and ran into the foyer, gently closed the door, and started up the steps. Behind her, she heard a deep voice coughing a bit.

"Rosalind, my love, do you feel a bit of a draft on the stairs today?" her father asked with a mischievous grin.

"Good morning, Father," she said a bit breathlessly as she descended the stairs to give him a kiss and proper greeting. "Why would I?" she asked, blinking with curiosity.

"Did you not care for the design of this particular dress? I see you have altered it a smidgen without Nan's assistance," he chuckled as he looked in the direction of her back skirts.

Rosalind began to spin in circles, trying to get a glimpse of her rear, but could not see any issue as she spun. "Come this way, Darling. You must take a look in our foyer looking glass. You are missing the back half of your frock. I would say it was the morning meal of a farm animal. Mmmm… a goat, perhaps?"

Walking forward, Rosalind was able to see her missing skirts in the foyer mirror. Gasping in horror, she could not believe the large gaping hole in the back of her skirt. The entire back half of her dress was missing all the way down to her petticoats. "Blasted goat! He ate my beautiful frock! What will Nan say? She'll blame me for his untamed hunger. That's what I get for taking the stable boy some of Cook's lovely nutty buns. Papa, please don't mention this to Nan. I'll steal away above stairs and change before she wakes."

Her father was shaking his head but smiling. Delivering nutty buns, indeed. He was quite certain his daughter was up to nothing of the sort. She was probably out running in the woods, judging by the amount of foliage stuck in her tresses. He really should chastise her, but didn't have the heart. She reminded him too much of his sweet Anna.

"My lips are sealed, my love," he said with a warm smile. Giving her a quick kiss upon her forehead, he told her, "I will have all your brothers home by this evening. I expect you will want to entertain our guests with them, correct?"

Rosalind could not contain her excitement. "Even the twins, Papa?" she asked. "It seems ages since we have had little Michael and Edmund home…though I guess they would not appreciate me calling them little," she laughed.

"Even the twins, my dear. Andrew should arrive no later than the nooning meal. Charles is picking Michael and Edmund up from school on his way. The headmaster has given them leave for the week," he all but beamed. "All my precious babies under one roof, what more could a man want?" he said happily.

Rosalind was thrilled and knew she needed to hurry and take care of her questions and get this embarrassment over. Andrew would know something was amiss with her if she did not get this out of her system before he arrived, then Lord only knew what she might confess to him.

Rosalind hurried up the stairs to her bedchamber. Along the way, she bumped into Edith, who was stealing out of her mother's sitting room. "Beggin' yer pardon, missus, but I thinks you got a hole in yer lovely gown."

Rosalind sighed deeply. "I am aware, Edith. I fear a wayward goat made a snack of it. May I ask what you are doing in Mother's sitting room?"

"I was cleaning, I was. No one 'as touched that room in so long, the dust was near to my knees. I'll be sneezing for days, I will. Crying shame to leave the place in a shambles as your Lor'ship 'as," Edith muttered as she walked away without so much as a curtsey or nod.

Before Rosalind could scold her for speaking ill of her father, the housemaid had run off down the hall. Rosalind made a note to let Mrs. Ingrid deal with the woman. She quickly entered her room and shut the door behind her. Elsa was already there, laying out her day dress and a pair of silken slippers. Upon looking at her, Elsa nearly choked and shouted, "My Lady, your dress!"

"Yes, yes…I know. A goat ate it. Now, please do not tell Nan. I just do not have the heart to let her know her delicate needlework has been demolished. We should eat that blasted goat for dinner, but I love her cheese too much," Rosalind lamented, plopping down on the bed and falling back in a dramatic mock swoon.

"Come now, Lady Rosalind, let's get your attire repaired. Have you taken note of your hair, perchance? It seems you have a bit of forest adorning it," Elsa said cheekily as she began picking leaves from Rosalind's hair.

"I am afraid I was a bit preoccupied with my posterior being exposed," Rosalind grumbled.

She stood and allowed Elsa to remove her ruined dress. At least the delicate chemise and petticoats were still intact, she thought. The day dress that Elsa had pulled from the armoire was a soft cotton muslin of the softest green. It looked like a lime chiffon Mrs. Mary had once made for dessert. The dress made Rosalind hungry, and her stomach growled unladylike as a reminder that not only had that blasted goat eaten her dress, but it had aided Buttercup in stealing her nutty bun.

The end result meant that she would have to join the guests at the breakfast buffet. She sighed, supposing it was time to redeem her behavior in her guests' eyes. Before she could do that, she desperately needed to speak with Nan. Surely, Erwin had never done such a salacious thing to Nan. Rosalind blushed crimson as Elsa finished buttoning her gown. The thought of Kristoff kissing her brought that same warm sensation to her belly.

As Elsa turned her to straighten her skirts, she looked at Rosalind's glowing cheeks and quirked an eyebrow at her. "Is this gown too warm, my Lady? Do you have the vapours?"

Elsa nearly giggled. She knew how Lady Rosalind hated pretenses of weakness to garner attention. They often joked of vapours; that malady that could mean you suffered a chill, your corset was drawn too tight, or you just preferred to avoid someone's company. Rosalind had not been ill a day in her life, so the cause just might be of a personal nature. Elsa wished to ask, but knew it would be too impertinent, no matter how close they were. She was still the lady's maid and must behave as such. She did wonder if it had anything to do with a robust guest she had seen heading into the woods after the be-breeched Rosalind.

Elsa had no more than finished the last button on her fresh gown, then Rosalind had quickly tucked her feet into her little slippers and headed out the door again. She quickly ran to Nan's room and knocked robustly, knowing her friend might still be abed. Nan called out for her to enter, looking a bit surprised to see Rosalind, yet again, flushed scarlet and in a dress, standing in her doorway.

"Rosalind, dear, whatever is the matter? You are so flushed. Do you have the vapours?" She giggled. "Let me feel your head."

Nan smiled at her.

Closing the door, Rosalind looked at her in disbelief. Twice in less than thirty minutes, someone had mentioned that silly malady. Rosalind could not help herself and burst out laughing. Nan joined her in short order.

"Come, my friend. Tell me what has happened to bring you to my threshold at such an ungodly hour. The sun has barely touched the horizon. It looks as if you have an adventure to tell."

Rosalind did not know where to begin. The memory of his hands splaying along her back, his lips pressing against hers, the delicate touch of the tip of his tongue on her lips, the buildup of fire in her belly all came flooding back. All of a sudden, she felt shy and embarrassed about the kiss. Her cheeks turned from a rosy, wind-blown blush to a deep crimson within a matter of seconds. Rosalind looked down at her hands, trying to mask the heat radiating from her cheeks, and coughed.

Nan was beginning to grow concerned. In the span of two brief days, she had seen her friend's behavior begin to radically change. Rosalind was always unpredictably predictable in her free-spirited nature, with nothing ever seeming to embarrass or hinder her from sharing her innermost thoughts. This demure, rose-glowing girl before her was most alarming. She was having none of it.

"Enough of this! Remember who you are. You are the daughter of the spirited Anna Englebright. Ara, snap out of this. I demand it at once, Lady Rosalind Arabella Englebright!"

That seemed to do the trick. Nan never called her by her full given name. Straightening her shoulders, she rushed to the bed and sat beside her friend. "I need you to tell me the specifics of kissing and the ways of men," she demanded.

That was most definitely not what Nan was expecting. "Well, what exactly do you mean by specifics, Love?" she asked, a bit taken aback. "I mean, there are several ways of doing it, umm…depending on the intent. You see. What I mean to say is, when a man is…umm…attracted to a woman and loves her very much…"

Rosalind interrupted her abruptly, "Oh, hogwash, Nan. I know good and well that a man is not required to love a woman to kiss her. I want to know about the fire in the belly…and, well, other areas. Why do one's nethers seem to warm and moisten upon a thorough kiss? For that matter, what is considered a thorough kiss? Are tongues supposed to be involved, or is that a peculiarity by region, perhaps?"

She tapped her chin in deep thought. "That must be it…a regional nuance, you think?"

Nan was now the one to turn crimson.

"Ara! What…how…where have you heard such?" she stammered. "This is not information for an unwed lady. Did you learn this firsthand? Where have you been this morning? Oh, God…Fire in the belly. I may need a brandy. I…I might have the vapours. I need more information, Love. What happened this morning to impart such in-depth questioning?"

Rosalind proceeded to tell her friend of the morning happenings and ended with, "I am not entirely sure he knows what he is doing to be putting his tongue in someone else's mouth. That seems unsanitary, oh, but felt deliciously scandalous. I did happen to notice he is no longer walking quite upright or with such a confident stride. He even looked a bit sheepish when I saw him from a distance."

Rosalind shrugged as if she did not quite understand the degree of pain a well-placed knee could cause.

"My brothers taught me that move I had to use to break away. They told me it was effective, but I always believed they had exaggerated the whole business. Seems they were right after all. He hit the ground like a dropped sack of potatoes." She shrugged and looked at Nan to get her input.

Nan sat silently for a minute, trying to keep her mouth from falling open. She and Erwin had a loving relationship, with a great deal of intimacy. They had been each other's first and only loves. She was not quite sure whether the level of passion Rosalind was explaining was something she should discuss with her. It seemed the passion brought on by a man with a great deal more experience than her Erwin had possessed. It seemed Kristoff shared a level of intensity that her dear friend had, which had never met its equal. At the same time, they knew little of this man. He could ruin her friend and leave. Then what! Nan was so uncertain of what to do. Should she go to Ara's father? No, she thought. It would be best to be forthcoming with her friend and then keep an eye on this Kristoff. Lord Englebright seemed to hold him in high regard. Perhaps there was more that she did not know.

"Ara," she began again, "when a man and woman feel a certain connection, preferably within the confines of marriage, then there is a sense of internal …um…longing for them. To want to feel, know, touch…Well, every part of them." Nan knew she was blushing, but soldiered on. "To know them…body, heart, and soul. It is not enough to just want that from the body. It will leave you hollow, Love. That is not something you could withstand with such strong emotions. Passion should be accompanied by commitment for it to be thoroughly consuming. Without it, well…it is just a shadow of what it could be."

"Dear God, "cried Rosalind. "If this is but a shadow, then I would be devoured by the intensity and longing. I can't allow that. You know it, Nan. I will not fall into the trap of love and marriage. It makes people shells of their former selves," she nearly cried. "What if I fell in love and lost him?"

Nan's anger flared at her friend's response. "You think me a shell of my former self, do you?"

"That is not at all—"

"Enough, Ara!" Nan exclaimed, jumping to her feet. "You have no clue of what you speak. You allow fear to rule you. You, who I thought was one of the bravest women I knew. You who would face down brigands and teach children to read despite public ridicule. You who would dare to be yourself despite societal expectations of how you should behave. You who dare to dress in breeches and run wild and free through the forest and not care who sees you do so.

"I never thought to say it, but you, my friend, are a coward! I loved Erwin, and yes, I lost him. But I would take those two years with him over again and again, even if it meant the same outcome. Those two years of love and passion are enough to last me all my days. You have no clue of what you speak because you refuse to feel beyond your own comfort. So what if you happened to fall in love? Then you love, for as long as God gives you, and you are thankful for it. You love with a passion and intensity with a man that matches your own. In for a penny, in for a pound, Ara! That is what you do…and you *live*."

Nan was in hot, upset tears as she stared at her friend. "You, live, Ara…because to do less would dishonor the mother who gave you that courageous spirit. To be married is not a kiss of death. With the right man, it is embracing life itself."

Unshed tears sparkled in Rosalind's eyes. She knew her friend was right. She was a coward when it came to love. She hated change, good or bad. She was comfortable in her life. She had always been the one to make things unpredictable, fun, and a bit chaotic around her. It was fun and exciting, but she never let anyone do the same for her. She had such tight reins of control on her own life and feelings that she refused to make room for any other than those she already loved.

Now this man had come into her world and turned it topsy-turvy. She felt out of sorts and only wanted to experience the physicality of a relationship and then go back to her sense of normal, but Nan was right. That would be a shadow, the dimmest star on a dark night. She wanted to burn like the sun. She did not know how to let go of the control she'd had over herself for so long.

"Nan," she whispered as tears rolled down her cheeks and she stood. She walked to her friend and embraced her with what she hoped conveyed the thanks she felt for a friend who would speak truth to her, no matter how painful. "You are right, as usual, my wise friend. Forgive me, please, for being callous in my remarks. You are no shell of your former self, but I do still read sadness in Papa's eyes. I just can't get past the fear of what I will become if I suffer the same. I do not have your strength."

"You have strength by the bushel," Nan said, smoothing her hair. "The fact that everyone who knew her acknowledges you are so like your wonderful mother tells me that. In that spirit is the courage of a thousand warriors. Be brave and see what comes of this attraction, but do not give in to those bodily urges without love. It could ruin you or take your choices from you, dear."

Chapter Twelve

Kristoff knew he should be furious, but could only laugh about this predicament in which he had found himself. Damn that wretched witch. She had nearly changed his gender with that kick. As he approached the horse paddock, finally able to walk without grimacing, he decided he would take a look at the large expanse of stables more closely before he went into battle with Lady Rosalind again.

The stables really were quite magnificent, with large open stalls for each horse, a large runway in the center for hitching carriages out of the weather, and even a veterinarian suite for caring for injured animals. The tack room was massive and well-stocked. The fodder was in the loft with an ingenious delivery system for bringing down the horses' meals without the need to enter the fodder room.

There was a drainage channel leading from each stall out of the building, aiding in keeping the stalls clean. The floor was immaculate, with intricately worked stone and wood that was clearly well-tended. All the doors were solid wood and very sturdy, with hefty iron latching mechanisms. The walls were of hewn stone that matched the manor house. The building was a work of art, and clearly, there had been no expense spared on the beautiful structure.

As Kristoff walked past the well-lit stalls, he heard a voice speaking gently as if to a child. Peeking his head around the corner of the half door into the stall, he greeted Jacob, who was talking to his horse. Kristoff smiled. Clearly, this man was as horse-mad as Lord Englebright appeared to be.

"Good morning," Kristoff called genially. "I see you are an early bird as well."

Jacob smiled at him. "That I am. I often fear my horses will not be well-tended when away from home, but I believe the king's stables themselves are not quite as well-tended as these appear to be. That Desmond knows what he is about."

He smiled as he patted his horse and exited the stall.

"I heard he is the gardener," Kristoff laughed. "Seems that man knows his whereabouts in many trades. The gardens are also immaculate."

He and Kristoff walked slowly in comfortable silence down the length of the stable, admiring the thoroughbreds they found in each pristine stall.

As they walked, the large front door was opened wide, and a tall, broad-shouldered man walked a large chestnut mare through the opening. He was followed by a string of three large barn cats. The mare was continually nudging the owner's head in a sign of apparent affection. The man laughed and looked up as he strode closer.

"Admiring Father's hobby?" he asked, extending a hand. "Andrew Englebright, at your service, Gentlemen," he said and smiled.

The men introduced themselves, each in turn. Jacob was taken with the chestnut.

"Would you like to inspect her?" Andrew asked amiably. "Tempest is one of the finest mares I have found in Southern England," he stated, patting the mare's long neck.

"What stable did you purchase her from?" asked Jacob. "If I am not mistaken, she is the offspring of Defiance and Tramp; a fine offspring she is at that!"

"You know your horseflesh, that is for truth." Andrew looked appreciably at Jacob. "How did you know?" he asked.

"At one time, I trained her brother, Dangerous. He was a hard horse to break, but we got him in the end. I have never seen a faster stallion in all my days. He was like a flash of lightning out of the gate. Nearly broke my neck the first time I rode him at speed. He was the most beautiful shade of brown but had one small white patch just here," Jacob reminisced as he touched the horse just under her chin, where an identical white spot lay.

"You mean the same Dangerous that broke records and men's pocketbooks when he won the Derby as a longshot?" Kristoff asked with an awed look at the beautiful horse standing before him.

"The very same!"

"Has Father spoken with you about this?" Andrew asked excitedly. "He was hoping to start a breeding and training program, but was uncertain where to start. Perhaps we can chat about this over breakfast. Give me a moment to pass Tempest off to Markham, and we can make our way."

"Would Markham be a stable lad, perchance?" Kristoff asked with a quirked eyebrow. He holds his hand up to about his shoulder height. "Perhaps about yay tall, and he likes to wear baggy breeches and woolen caps like these two."

He holds up two boys' caps, one of which had some long auburn hair hanging from it.

"Ah. He would be just the one," Andrew said, shaking his head in pretend dismay. "Might I ask how you came to have that particular cap collection in your possession? That is a story I would very much like to hear."

"Perhaps we should locate this Markham together, and he can retell the story for us both. I may need to have a word with the lad," said Kristoff, dropping the hats back down to his side.

"Would you now?" Andrew asked. "If the topic might be the one of the propriety of lending clothing, I would like to know why you might want to be the one to have that discussion," he asked with a raised brow.

Jacob could not fathom what was happening in this exchange. Was this some type of code…and why was the lad's clothing something that seemed to get these men's hackles up? They had gone from amiable conversation to Andrew now looking as though he might throttle Kristoff. Did he think the man was a hat thief or worse? The hats were rather filthy, but apparently not odiferous enough to discourage the goat that had just snatched them from Kristoff's hand and begun munching away.

As the goat ran off, none other than the lad in question appeared, looking startled when he noticed the cap the goat was munching upon.

Markham knew he was in for it now. That was none other than the cap he had lent to his Ladyship the day prior. He also noted his daily work cap lying on the stones with a large tear in the side. His mother was not going to be pleased. But by the look on the faces of the beast of a man and his Lordship, Andrew, perhaps he should just pretend nothing was amiss, and get Tempest and leave as quickly as possible.

"Not so quickly, lad," Kristoff stated. "I need a word with you."

Andrew was less than pleased that this brute was trying to take his sister to task for her attire. What business was it of his how she wished to dress? It was her bloody home, and she would do what she bloody well pleased. Andrew was patient, though. He would wait to see how this played out before he escorted him aggressively off the premises. He never lost his temper, but this lout was about to try his patience, he was certain.

Kristoff leaned down and looked the boy in the eye. "I wanted to ask if you were aware of the renegades who have been roaming in the woods hereabouts. They seem a dangerous lot, willing to hurt a lad if they found *him* running about in breeches *unescorted*. In fact, it was only yesterday I was in the woods doing an errand for Maude, and I came across such a lad watching three of these ne'er-do-wells digging holes about the estate. Now, the *lad* was well-hidden and apparently able to run rather quickly, so there was no fear this time," Kristoff stated matter-of-factly.

"That might not always be the outcome. I know not what they were up to, but I intend to find out. It would be for the best if small *lads* stayed out of the wood *unescorted* until this unsavory bunch is taken in hand and their benefactor discovered. It simply is not safe, and their intentions are loathsome at best. So, perhaps you and your, shall we assume cousin, should stay out of the woods for a time. Once this is resolved, I think it will be safe again," he said with a stern look at the lad.

Markham looked abashed and sought Andrew's eyes. "I didn't know there was danger about for M'la...I mean to say, my cousin. I'll make sure he stays clear in the future. I never meant no harm, M'Lord."

Andrew lost the anger that had been simmering and felt an immediate kinship with Kristoff. He had protected Rosalind's reputation in front of Jacob and held no judgment of her attire or exercise habits. He seemed to have sought only to keep her safe.

"No worries, Markham. Your *cousin* has oft been difficult for the staff to manage. I will speak with *him* myself. But, please, for the time being, no more breeches hiding in chests until this is resolved."

"Aye, my Lord," Markham agreed quickly. But as the lad took the lead and began to walk away, the men heard him muttering, "My Lady is going to have my hide, no more breeches...how about you tell her and not me."

Though said under his breath, Andrew and Kristoff smiled at one another.

Jacob was thoroughly confused but kept his composure. Apparently, the topic was one of a delicate nature, but hang him if he could sort out why, or why Lady Rosalind would care.

Chapter Thirteen

The breakfast room was all abuzz with the excitement of ladies; ladies in lace and satin, and velvet - all talking of ribbons, dances, and the horrid weather of the prior day. Rosalind had been greeting and conversing with mamas, papas, and their lovely daughters of polite society, discussing dresses and weather to the point that she was bored out of her mind. She needed Nan.

"Toile, you say?" Rosalind smiled sweetly. "Oh, I simply love toile." What in Heaven's name was toile? She hoped it was not some dread disease for which she had just declared her love. She had never realized her own inadequacies in genteel topics more than when she was placed in the presence of what she considered true ladies of the Ton. This, in part, was why she had been avoiding them all since the arrivals began.

She needed Nan immediately, but she knew Dr. Wallace had her ensconced in her rooms with her leg elevated and a poultice on her terrible bruise. He assured them both that the stinky application would mean she could dance without care this evening at the ball. Rosalind had already disturbed her once this morning and had no intention of causing her further discomfort…*Oh, dear, Nan. What a true friend!*

As Rosalind made her way back across the room and was about to load a plate with all the delicious foods Mrs. Mary had prepared, she heard a familiar voice booming with laughter from the foyer. Without a thought for propriety, she squealed her excitement and ran out the door with plate still in hand. She shoved the plate into Kristoff's hand and all but launched herself at Andrew. He wrapped her up in his big, strong arms and twirled her in circles, laughing all the while.

Kristoff noticed Rosalind had failed to secure the door behind her, so the polite society ladies all witnessed the entire exchange and lack of formality and began whispering to each other. He moved to block their view and entered the breakfast room along with Jacob, closing the door behind him to allow the family a moment of privacy.

He bowed politely to the room at large.

"What a blessing to have a close family." He bowed low over one of the young ladies' mamas and kissed her hand gallantly. He next bowed to the father and introduced himself formally.

"Lord Kristoff Van Reede of Netherland, at your service, my good sir. Please allow me to introduce my friend, the future Viscount Durham, Mister Jacob Corbin."

As Kristoff suspected, that introduction immediately had the topic changed, as Jacob was now the highest titled, eligible gentleman in the room. The mamas all wanted an immediate introduction. That title turned him into a more-tasty dish than the nutty buns Kristoff could smell wafting from the buffet. He could feel the daggers from Jacob's eyes at the ploy, but was happy to divert the attention from his Sprite. His Sprite, he pondered. When had he started thinking of her as his Sprite? He had known the blasted woman only for a day and was fairly certain she was nearly mad as a hatter.

Jacob, being an ever-dutiful aristocrat, bowed and smiled at all the mamas and their daughters in turn. Kristoff noted he kept scanning the room as he bowed over and over, making polite conversation as he went. If he did not know better, he thought that the absence of a certain widow had left poor Jacob in dismay. The poor chap would have no peace for the remainder of the events. It was not every day that you had an opportunity to thrust your daughter in front of an eligible viscount…even if he had not yet inherited the title.

As Kristoff made his last introduction and approached the buffet to partake of all it had to offer, the doors opened wide as Lord Englebright filled the entry, followed by Andrew and Rosalind, who nearly glowed with joy. Kristoff's breath caught. She was glorious.

Lord Englebright seemed to have grown in stature with his children around him. Though he was a fit man, he now seemed to fill the room. It was with his energy, Kristoff mused. Everyone was drawn toward him. No wonder the man had people from far and wide traveling to the end of England to celebrate his birth. You simply could not be in a room with him without wanting to get a bit closer or engage him in conversation. It was as though all thoughts of breaks in decorum were washed away by his entry. The young ladies once again spoke to Rosalind as if they were long-lost friends. He heard the word "viscount" whispered over and over. Kristoff turned his attention back to the buffet. He would never understand the Ton of England and their fickleness.

"Forgiving lot, aren't they," Jacob whispered to him.

"Indeed," Kristoff agreed, passing the man a nutty bun dripping in caramel.

Chapter Fourteen

After the meal, Lord Englebright agreed to take the gentlemen in attendance to the stable for a tour as the ladies adjourned above stairs to begin their preparations for the ball or to nap prior to.

Kristoff could not imagine Rosalind ever napping. She was far too vibrant; the thought of her other brothers arriving had excited her to the point of near effervescence. She bubbled out that energy like a flute of fine champagne.

The household followed suit with the arrival of guests: ladies, gentlemen, chaperones, ladies' maids, and the like, arriving one after the other in a crush of carriages and horses. The house and stables alike were a flurry of activity in preparation for the night's ball. Most would attend the ball and return to their homes, but a small group who had traveled the farthest would stay for several days, he learned.

Kristoff walked along in the procession of men, happily speaking with each of them. He normally dreaded these soirees, but he thought this might be the first he had ever enjoyed. A certain near-giddy female was the cause, but so were the gentlemen he had met thus far. They were such a receptive and jovial lot. Most were quite interesting to speak with as well.

After only the briefest conversations with Andrew, he felt they had known each other for years. He enjoyed Jacob's company as well, but the man was a bit more reserved than the others and seemed more difficult to get to know. The man seemed a bit overwhelmed by the whole family, though he was taking it in stride. He almost seemed to mold into what was expected of him for each reaction and conversation. In truth, he seemed a regular member of the Ton, unlike the rest of this merry lot.

Kristoff had also made the acquaintance of Mister Thomas Maxwell. He had been an undersecretary to some War Department official or another for many years, and he had the most interesting stories of how they had caught various plots and criminal activities during the Napoleonic war. At first, Kristoff thought the short, overly plump man would regale him with stories of his hunts or some such at brunch when he insisted Kristoff sit next to him.

The man nearly had the whole room rolling with laughter with one tale after another of how they caught the worst band of smugglers ever known. They called themselves the *Semper Victos*, thinking it meant always victorious, when in actuality, it meant always the loser. The War Department had apparently let the farce go on for some time because they got so much intelligence from them. Kristoff smiled again as he thought of the conversation.

This entire assignment from his king had not turned out as expected. It had been one mad turn of events after another, and now, he found himself nearly smitten…nearly. Maybe fondness was a better description…yes, not smitten. He was merely fond…but not just of Rosalind. He was fond of the whole lot of them. The thought of his plans once he procured the last needed signature from the eldest son danced around his head and just seemed so incomplete and unsatisfactory now.

He planned to return to the Netherlands and begin his life anew. He loved his homeland…but what would he do there? His king had indicated he might have other assignments, traveling the world…That seemed somewhat enticing, but now, the thought of doing that without the involvement of a beautifully vivacious, breeches-wearing, red-headed sprite? Well, that thought left a pang of longing in his heart that he was not ready to explore further.

As Kristoff followed the other men in the direction of the stable yard, he saw soft green skirts brush around the corner of the tulip-lined garden wall. He knew it was Rosalind and was determined to keep her out of harm's way, even if she was determined to be in the heat of it. He could not imagine her traipsing amongst the forest in proper skirts, but he had grown to understand she did not behave as expected…

He loved that trait and smiled at the thought. She was a free spirit. He admired that she found freedom and independence when society had so many rules and expectations for unwed women. He also knew that made it exceedingly more difficult for her to involve herself with the conversations of those girls just coming out for their first seasons, or for her to find a connection and befriend them. He saw the strain of that on her face at breakfast. She did well to hide it, but he was trained to read the subtle nuances that facial expressions could reveal.

She was blessed to have Nan, who accepted her exactly as she was. No peer in London would ever understand. He knew her father wished for her to marry well, but how in Heaven was the girl to do that, behaving as if societal rules did not apply to her? She would be miserable, and that lovely spirit would be crushed in short order by a normal man of nobility. She needed an estate and a large expanse of woods, and an understanding mate who would embrace her for who she was. No, he did not envy Englebright for his task in finding just that for her; for he knew the man would settle for no less than that for his only daughter.

With a curse muttered under his breath, he broke away from the others and headed in the direction of the green skirts. Apparently, the family's madness was contagious, and he had been thoroughly infected by it.

"I wanted something that melded Georgian design with modern function," Englebright stated as he demonstrated the fodder delivery mechanism. "With this device, the stable lads can pull this lever, and the appropriate amount of grain feeds to each stall."

The men all nodded their ready approval. It was most impressive.

"I say, Englebright, this is a very modern apparatus," Jacob noted. "It can cut the time for feeding a large herd into a fraction, leaving more time for training. I have read about such a system but have not implemented it into my uncle's stables as of yet. I am happy to see it works as well as what I have read." He nodded as he rubbed his hands together like an enthusiastic schoolboy.

"Let me show you our newest addition, Mister Corbin. She is a beauty," Englebright said, cupping him on his shoulder and guiding him to the rear-most stalls. "Tempest is the offspring of some of the finest thoroughbreds in England," he informed the group at large eagerly.

"Please, my Lord, call me Jacob," Jacob requested with an amiable smile as he was led to the back of the stable.

"Just so, my man, just so," Englebright stated, slapping him upon his back in a friendly gesture. "I would like to discuss the stables and breeding program with you in more detail. You are held in quite high esteem in the field. You were a rather difficult man to track down as you seem to move about a bit. I am glad you have settled in our region. Good luck for us."

As the group of men moved farther into the stable, Andrew looked around and noted the conspicuous absence of Kristoff. He had seen the man walking back toward the garden as the rest of the entourage moved into the stable yard. He had thought Kristoff would join them shortly. He rather enjoyed his company and looked forward to learning more about how he and his father were connected. He knew his father's influence spread far and wide but knew of no certain connections to the Netherlands. Perhaps he was a descendant of his mother's family, but as she had been an only child of an only child, he was not certain how that could be possible.

Andrew left the men in the capable hands of his father and headed in the direction of the large entry door. As he was about to exit, the doors were opened wide as Earl of Derby, Edward Stanfield entered the stable. Derby was a man of short stature, with a prolific beard upon his face to match the mass of curls upon his head. He had a patrician nose and a stern look about him.

Those who did not know him would believe him in a perpetual state of deep thought, which was not far from the truth. Andrew knew his father liked and respected him immensely. Andrew did as well. Derby was the current secretary of state for war and was a powerful man with a conservative nature, but was also open to new ideas that would help the masses. That is why he had petitioned for the reform of education, which meant Rosalind fairly worshiped the man, as well.

"Derby, my good man, so good to see you out of the office. Father was uncertain you would make it. He and Rosalind will be so pleased, as am I," Andrew said, grasping the man's hand in a hearty shake. "How on earth did you manage to break away?"

"They do let me out into the light of day from time to time, my dear Andrew," Derby chortled. "And you, my boy, what have you been keeping yourself up to of late? We have a ready position for you in the colonies. Just say the word and we will have you on a ship in a fortnight."

"I think I shall keep myself on this side of the pond, if you please," Andrew replied and smiled, clapping him on the back.

The man had been trying to recruit both Andrew and his older brother, Charles, for military service since they had come of age. Their father never seemed keen on the idea, however, so neither brother pursued it with much interest.

"I have been busy designing my next ship, the *Siren*. Oh, just wait till you see it, Derby. She will have three masts and a steam engine. I am melding the design of the current warships with that of older wooden 'pirate' vessels, if you will. It may not be the most modern design, but I am a romantic at heart, Derby…She will be a beauty and a work of art. Oh, you should see our figurehead!" Andrew said excitedly.

"I imagine she is a lovely vessel, son. If you have the schematics here, I would love to look over them with you," Derby said, looking nearly as proud as if his own son were telling of his accomplishments. All of Englebright's boys were creative and successful in everything they touched, it seemed.

"Where is the old boy, Englebright? I need to speak with him about some things of some importance. I am afraid I am never far from my duties." He smiled at Andrew. "I suppose that is not a very convincing selling point in my recruitment efforts, now, is it?"

"Come, I'll take you to him," Andrew said, motioning back the way he had just come. "He is presently giving a tour of the stables to our visitors, though I suspect it is really for Jacob Corbin's benefit. Have you heard of him? He has quite a talent at breeding and training horseflesh. Father is quite sure he can bring his breeding program up to snuff in a trice."

"Corbin, you say? Yes, I am quite familiar with his uncle, Elias…who is the Viscount Durham. He was of some service to the king and country some years back. Such great service, in point of fact, that he was bequeathed a rather large holding near here. The details are all shadowed in secrecy, of course," Derby stated, waving his hand dismissively before Andrew could ask. "I assume Durham will attend the festivities now that he has settled in his estate and retired from service. I hear the man likes his connections, he does, and your father would be a prime one for his collection of acquaintances, shall we say."

"You don't seem to particularly care for the man, my Lord," Andrew noted.

"Oh, nonsense. When you have been in the War Department for as long as I, you rarely trust…and look for mischief around every corner," Derby said, waggling his considerable eyebrows at Andrew. "I am afraid it has made me a bit cynical. Come now! Take me to my old chap. It has been too long since I have spoken with him."

"Of course, sir," Andrew agreed, leading Derby on as they chatted. "Rosalind will be thrilled as duck in a new pond to see you, of course. You are quite her hero now that you have given Parliament what-for in regard to how we treat those less fortunate than ourselves. I anticipate our girl will have schools popping up all over the country. Ah, there is Father. I fear I must leave you here, Derby. I have to go fetch the lady in question now before she flees the countryside," he said in a conspiratorial whisper.

Kristoff was surprised that Rosalind could actually walk at a somewhat normal pace. He would not quite call it a stroll, but it was not a full gallop either. His long legs made short work of lessening the gap between them as she ducked into the hedge maze. It was not so tall that he could not see over the top, but she was slight enough that he could not catch a glimpse of her head as she made her way through it. He was not entirely certain why he was following her, but could not seem to stop himself. He was inexplicably drawn to wherever she was. *A siren,* he thought again and smiled. That did not mean, however, that he wanted her to know he was there.

Based on their last encounter, he would like to maintain his ability to sire children and walk upright; he grimaced. That, combined with his apparent lack of self-control around her, made it unsafe for them to be alone together again.

Most of these Georgian mazes were created such that you would find the center if you just kept going left. That is what he decided to do. He walked along quietly, stopping periodically to listen for her footfalls. He never heard a single one, nor did he note signs of movement in the gravel path. Clearly, she had some skill in not being tracked. He wondered if her brothers had taught her that trick.

As he was about to proceed to the next left, he noted a small archway to the right with a reflecting pool in the center of the opening. There were lilies of pink and white floating on the surface. He could not help going to get a better look. It was a beautiful alcove. He did not know who had designed the gardens, but they were lovely.

As he approached the pool, a gentle touch upon the back of his arm, like the brush of a butterfly, caught him off guard. He rounded, jumping to the right and assuming a defensive stance.

Rosalind rolled her eyes and crossed her arms across her bosom. "Really, sir, do I appear that dangerous?"

Kristoff relaxed his stance, letting his arms hang loosely by his sides. *How* had the blasted vixen snuck up on him? Apparently, she had been taking lessons from Old Maude. "Based upon our last encounter, I would say yes, most definitely, Madam." He smirked. "You just keep your distance, and I shall maintain mine."

"Are you insinuating that I was at fault for that little mishap?" she demanded. "I only wanted to ask why your eyes had turned that particular shade of stormy gray. The next thing I know, you are mauling me in the middle of the forest," she stated emphatically, jabbing a finger in his direction.

"I thought you were a boy…and a brigand to boot," he shouted. "How was I to know you were in the habit of running about in men's clothing? Who does that other than…well, men?"

"In the habit of kissing boys, are you!" she demanded, stepping closer still, jabbing her finger in his general direction as she shouted at him. "And who are you to decide how a lady should dress on her own properties? Oh, I spoke with Markham, all right, after I found my trunk emptied. He said no more breeches and all because of some overbearing brute of a man thinking it improper. You have no right!"

She stamped her foot.

"Woman, you twist my words. I could not care one whit about how you wish to clothe yourself, but if you had not leaned in for the kiss, I assure you it would never have happened. I am not in the habit of taking liberties that are not freely offered."

He heard her gasp at the insinuation but continued, not allowing her room to speak. He wanted to shake the young beauty until her teeth rattled for putting herself at such risk with those moron ruffians about.

"Do you have any clue what would have happened should one of those men have found you? Never mind how you were dressed. They would have done you a harm to keep you from talking. Now imagine further what would have happened if they discovered you were no boy at all. That paltry kiss would have been the least of your worries," he stated sternly and paused to allow that comment time to sink into her thick skull.

Rosalind had finally appeared as if she realized the ramifications of her actions. He saw the dawning of understanding on her face that she was in true danger. She looked completely shocked, thanks to the gods. At least that is what he believed until she opened her mouth next, as a broad smile spread across her face, and she took a step closer.

"What would you like to see me wear, Kristoff?"

He just groaned and backed away.

"I mean to say, my breeches, they do not offend your delicate, gentlemanly sensibilities, my Lord?" She advanced ever closer with a twinkle of mischief in her eyes. "And a paltry kiss is an excellent description. I am certain that with practice, you could get it correct."

Her smile was dazzling. She was sweet and demure again. He knew he was in trouble. The woman was clearly addled in the head. She stepped a bit closer. He found himself backing farther away as she advanced upon him. He was astonished. From the entire conversation, he knew the only thing she had gleaned was that he did not care how she attired herself. He would never understand the gentler sex…or at least not this one. Wait, had she said practice?

"And just how would you know about kissing?" he asked incredulously.

"Well, I um…I am certain that my observations have never included tongues, my Lord. My dearest friend was married, after all. I am certain she would have mentioned it. I think you've been misguided, or perhaps there is a different way of lovemaking in the Netherlands," she said curiously.

She was now puckering her lips in thought with a quizzical, bemused look upon her face. He could tell she was giving this more thought than was proper. He would not have been shocked if she had removed a bit of parchment and quill to document her notes on the topic. This could only lead to his downfall. He sighed, raising his hands as if to fend her off.

He began looking left and right for a mode of escape without hurting her delicate feelings. She moved ever closer, now a hair's breadth away. Those big blue eyes looked up at him with such trust, he knew he was in dire trouble and needed out of this maze immediately. God's truth, he felt himself growing hard with desire just at her approach, sickening him at his own lust, yet again.

Before he could draw his next breath, he was assaulted with a glowing warmth as she pressed the length of her body against his, reached up with both hands, and pulled his head down as she raised her lips to his. Again, the woman knew no pacing. She latched on to his lips as if her life's breath depended upon it…like he was her last bit of air before plunging into a pool of lava…like the lava now coursing through his every vein.

This was no gentle kiss. This was raw passion. Her lips were wet and oh, so soft upon his. He wanted to devour her, but knew he had to end this. He was warring with the passion building between them. She was a lady and deserved better than to have a romp in the hedges, but how he wanted her naked and writhing beneath him. That was the last coherent thought he had as she opened her lips and stroked him with her tongue.

Suddenly, he had a tidal wave of images flooding his mind of his hands cupping her naked, soft breasts as he laid kisses upon her every curve. Lord, he wanted her. His reality was nearly as nice as his imagination. She clung to him, whimpering her need. Kristoff knew this was about to escalate beyond his control if he did not end it now. God help him, he could not.

He pulled her closer, lifting her off the ground in his embrace, and slanted his mouth over hers again, licking at her soft lips, his tongue entangling with hers. She pressed her body more tightly to his, cradling his manhood in the warmth of her narrow thighs, her skirts too much of a barrier for them both. She moaned again as his tongue swept across hers. He claimed her mouth as his thoughts completely left him; he was all instinct and fire… Plunging into lava was just what he imagined as he slanted his mouth over hers, their tongues caressing, soft lips pressed together. He was hers, body and soul, unable to tear away.

His mouth left hers, and he kissed a hot trail down her neck and felt her arch her back against him. Breathing raggedly, he came to his senses, realizing how innocent she was, and that he was behaving as a rake. She was not experienced enough to understand where her kissing practice would lead if he did not cease this immediately. He gently grasped her shoulders and tried to push her away from him.

She was having none of it, and she wrapped one leg around his and rubbed her sex against his hard thigh. Ye gads, what was she trying to do to him? He abruptly pulled away from her and shook her shoulders gently.

"Rosalind!" he said in a passion-graveled voice. "This cannot happen, not here, not now. You are a lady, and I…" He breathed in deeply. "I am supposed to be a gentleman. But you are making it vastly difficult to want to leave, Love."

With passion still misty in her eyes, she could feel the tears beginning to well at his rejection. "Why are you even here?" she demanded as she pulled her arms from around his neck and looked down at the ground so he could not see the vulnerability she hated and knew was written in her eyes.

"I spoke with your father earlier about my presence here. I will be conversing with your older brothers shortly once Charles arrives. I promise that I am not here to intrude on the upcoming celebration. Once all is explained, they can decide how to proceed. To be blunt, it is not my place to inform you of my quest," he stated with a gentle squeeze upon her shoulders and let her go as he began making his way around her body back toward the entrance.

She whirled on him. "You follow me around, you take liberties you should not take, and now you just walk away. And to top it off, you had my finest breeches removed, so I can't even enjoy the forest properly. Things were fine before you came," she said as she flopped upon a bench and began hiking up her skirts to reveal boys' work boots.

He got a glimpse of one well-toned calf as she began unlacing the boots and continued shouting at him.

"You might as well take these as well, since I won't be needing them," she said, throwing the well-worn leather boots at him one by one, narrowly missing his head. "Before you, my days were normal. They were predictable. No one ravaged me in the woods or stole my clothing or my freedom."

She glared at Kristoff as he laughed aloud at that statement.

"Well, my dear Lady," he said, emphasizing the *lady*, "in the short time I have been here, I have realized that nothing with you is predictable. You are a whirlwind of confusion and chaos! And I would like to point out that you mauled me this go-round, and you can have your damnable breeches and your freedom the moment the forest is safe. Clearly, someone must protect you from yourself. I assure you, I am not volunteering for that duty. Now, if you will excuse me, I appear to have an urgent appointment with your father. You clearly do not have your good health as a priority, so perhaps he and your brothers should be aware of that. Good day."

With that last statement and upon her outraged gasp, Kristoff left Rosalind fuming in the maze. Andrew was near to rolling with laughter from his vantage point, where he had witnessed the majority of the rendezvous. He was not thrilled with witnessing his sister's wanton behavior, but thank goodness Kristoff was a true gentleman, well…mostly.

He did not have to bring out the pistols for a duel on her behalf. Truth be told, he may have to challenge his sister to keep her from compromising poor Kristoff's integrity and taking advantage of him. Apparently, he needed to have an appointment with his father as well. However, it seemed a small chat with Rosalind was first at hand as he had just noticed tears beginning to roll down her cheeks in earnest. It was worse than he thought. She never cried. He also needed to ascertain Kristoff's true feelings.

Apparently, Sprite had met her match and was falling, if not already in love with the man…love and hate walked a fine line when passion brewed this hot, he thought. Andrew sighed as he walked around the hedge, picked up her boots, and placed them on the bench beside her, then gathered his sister in his arms.

"There, there, Love. 'tis not so bad as all that," he soothed.

"Is everyone following me today?" she groaned. "This is because I am wearing a dress, isn't it? I never had these problems in breeches before that brute came. This is all his fault. I am acting like those silly chits on a husband hunt, and I don't even like him," she cried harder.

"Well, Love, that is not the impression I got from the way you were clinging to him. You did almost attack the man."

"I did no such thing," Rosalind sobbed. "I only wanted to know if that was truly the way of kissing. It was an experiment. Nothing more. I care not for the ruffian."

"You were rather…um…close to one another," Andrew noted with a gentle smile as he looked at her upturned face. "Oh, hang it all, Sprite. You do not know enough about the ways of men. You should thank your stars that Kristoff is a gentleman and stopped things before

I had to, and Father did not witness this, or you would be facing the vicar in short order…with a man…" He quirked an eyebrow at her. "You don't even like!"

"Why is everyone so insistent that I am to be married off? Am I such a burden to have about that you are all so anxious to be rid of me?" She sniffled.

Andrew tipped her nose again.

"Never. Your energy reminds me of Mama so very much. I can't imagine the estate without you." Andrew laughed gently. "Do you remember how Mama loved adventures? She would work for weeks mapping out our little scavenger hunts with riddles and such, and let us get away with things that would make the civilized world shudder. I recall, specifically, that time when we were all decked out in our finest, ready for a picnic by the lake. That stupid pig of Michael's made his way into the kitchens. Michael was so proud riding it like a horse covered in mud from head to toe."

Rosalind hiccupped on a laugh. "And Edmund led the charge using a bunch of carrots to lure it in. I thought Mrs. Mary was going to string them out on Mrs. Ingrid's laundry line. But in the end, she just sat laughing with Mama. Then she was appalled that Mama insisted on helping her to clean the mess."

She laughed again.

"And you, you, Andrew, so proud of your finery, began chasing the pig to no avail. Getting that pig out of that kitchen may have been the single most difficult challenge of our lives. The kitchens were a mess. In the end, we were all covered in mud, and Papa just picked the thing up and took it out. You know, I think he let the chaos continue just because Mama was so tickled by the whole affair," she said, laying her head on his shoulder. "I do miss her ever so much, Andrew."

"I know, Love. We all do, but do you recall what she told us that day, after all was cleaned, the pig was back home, and Mrs. Mary had rushed us out the door with a picnic basket?" Andrew looked down at her and smiled as she shook her head. "She told us the single best blessing that God had ever granted her was her family. She called us a gift," he said, resting his head on top of hers.

"And you," he said and looked down at her again and waited for her to look at him, "you are just as adventurous, as exhilarating, as compassionate and kind, and fun... You deserve to be happy, you deserve to share that same adventurous energy with a family of your own someday. That is the only reason any of us would wish you to be wed. But you need to be careful with Kristoff, Love. He is not a dandy seeking a fortune. The man has his own, I suspect. I also suspect that if he decides he wants to marry you, I think you will be left with little choice in the matter. You may have met your match," he said, kissing her atop her head.

"There will be no half measures with this one. Though I do think he believes us all a bit mad," he laughed as he nudged her arm.

Rosalind laughed as she wiped the tears from her cheeks. Andrew always knew how to make her feel better and put things back into perspective.

"I *would* like my own adventures someday…and I suppose we do appear a bit mad." She laughed again, but then groaned. "Lord, Andrew, I did almost attack the man. He will likely hide from me the rest of his stay here."

Chapter Fifteen

Harold stood in the usual spot as he surveyed the foyer and waited for the gentlemen to return from the stable. He and Mrs. Ingrid had the entire household well in hand, with the staff all handling their respective tasks like a well-oiled machine. He was inordinately pleased that all was going so well with such a large number of the Ton in attendance. He would not have his lord appear to have any shortcomings in his household. And God bless Sprite; she was putting her best foot forward for her papa. All would be well.

Harold broke from his musings as he watched the approaching gentlemen through the large leaded glass window in the door. They were leaving the stables and working their way to the main house. Lord Englebright appeared to be in high spirits. He was certainly in his element.

As Harold reached for the door, he heard a soft voice from above stairs, lightly laughing. If he was not mistaken, Mrs. Nan had finally been released from Dr. Wallace's administrations. He was quite pleased the young lady was well. He liked her company exceedingly, and she seemed the only one who could slow their dear Sprite down a wee bit. Harold smiled to himself. As he opened the door and turned back to Mrs. Nan, a cacophonous din from the back entryway let him know the twins had also arrived.

Nan walked down the stairs carefully as her leg was still a bit tender. She held the banister as instructed to ensure she did not fall as she descended the curved mahogany grand stairs. As she approached the landing, Charles, with the twins, Michael and Edmund, in tow, bounded in from the back hall. Well, the twins bounded. Charles walked like the future Duke should. Nan beamed at that. It felt like ages since she had seen the jovial bunch. The twins were definitely more of the same disposition as Ara. Nan loved their energy. They had been proposing to her in turn since the age of three. She always joked that she simply could not choose between them. Charles was looking as handsome as ever. His deep auburn hair lay in thick waves, perfectly highlighting his well-sculpted jaw. He had a broad smile on his face when he looked upon her. She smiled back just as the twins assaulted her with their normal affections.

"Mrs. Willoughby," called Michael, bowing low enough to befit the queen. "It has been far too long since I have laid eyes upon your lovely face." He smiled broadly as he reached for her arm.

"Shove off, you," called Edmund, as he shoved Michael out of the way to join Nan by her side and assist her down the stairs.

Michael was having none of that and took up her other side.

"Boys, you will tumble her down the stairs if you don't cease your affections. Can you not see the lady appears injured?" Charles asked as he cuffed them both on the head affectionately.

"Mrs. Willoughby, it *has* been too long," he said and smiled warmly as he took her hand, aiding her down the rest of the stairs, and then placed a kiss upon it, smiling at her all the while.

As he lifted his head, the foyer filled with gentlemen and the booming voice of his father.

"Sir, you had us released. How can we ever thank you enough?" Michael and Edmund stated in unison with large grins as they hugged their father exuberantly.

"Hello, Father," Charles said as he embraced his father in an affectionate hug. "By the gods, it is good to see you and be home."

Jacob's eyes darted between Charles and Nan and back again as the other gentlemen began greeting one another. Jacob noted that the future duke was a tall man, at least half a head taller than him. He was broad of shoulder with deep auburn hair that reminded him of Lady Rosalind's, but with more gold than red tones. He did appear quite muscular, probably from sport or maybe even horse riding. Jacob supposed Charles was a handsome man, though he had never really noticed such about other members of the Ton. He looked to be a larger, more robust version of Lord Englebright.

Jacob had a sudden pang of…something as he watched the comfortable nature with which Nan and Charles regarded each other…but it was not jealousy. He had no time for such, especially now, since he had just made the connection with Lord Englebright. This was his opportunity to seek out what he had come for. He could hear Uncle Elias now berating him for straying from his task. Nan was an unneeded distraction, and yet, there he was walking across the foyer, approaching the beautiful woman. He was just going to inquire about her injury. That seemed only polite, he thought.

"Mrs. Willoughby, you are well?" he inquired as he gently took her hand and kissed the air above it. He dared not risk being too forward by actually placing his lips upon her flesh. That thought made his blood begin to grow hot with a longing he had not experienced before.

Nan was shocked at the gesture and noticed the man appeared to have blushed a bit. That was odd and made her blush in kind. What could he be thinking to bring such color to his cheeks, she wondered. That thought led her mind to places it should most definitely not be going, especially in mixed company. She had noted Charles was now looking at them both, a crease forming between his green eyes.

"Nan, may I escort you to luncheon?" Charles asked politely, using her given name, which he never did. "Or would you care for a turnabout in the gardens? I would love to catch up, as it has been quite a while since we last spoke. I would love to regale you with stories of happenings in London."

Nan was thoroughly confused over all the attention she was suddenly receiving. It was a bit overwhelming to have two handsome men vying for her interest. Lord, where was Rosalind? Nan feared herself in need of a rescue for a change. She could not fathom what had gotten into Charles, who was acting like a protective brother, or worse, a jealous beau. Alas, she was saved by an unexpected source.

"You may *not* turn her about the garden or escort her," both twins piped up at once. "She owes us both a fair game of Fox and Geese," Michael noted as he took her left hand out of Charles's reach.

"Indeed, and I mean to win this time," stated Edmund as he took her right arm away from Jacob. Looking over his head at Jacob, he said none too quietly, "She cheats!"

With a mock gasp, Nan stated politely, "I do no such thing, Edmund. You simply lack the patience to make a good fox." She winked at Charles before she thought better of it. She did not wish Jacob to think her a flirt. Truth was, Charles was like a brother. She could no more think of him intimately than she could Harold, the butler. She smiled and allowed the boys to escort her to the study as she looked back over her shoulder at both men, who were just watching her be all but dragged down the hall.

"I have never heard of this game," Jacob called to them with a smile, in truth thoroughly enjoying the revelry of the family. He had never known this type of camaraderie with anyone. Uncle was more task- and duty-oriented; there was no time for the frivolity of affectionate conversation and gaming. He was suddenly very aware of what his upbringing had lacked and wanted to soak in what he was able before this came to an end.

"May I join you?" he asked.

The boys eyed him with faux wariness. "Are you her accomplice? I mean to win with my foxlike cunningness," Michael said, winking at Nan.

"Come along then, good sir," called Edmund. "We shall teach you and then take advantage of your inexperience," he laughed.

Jacob laughed heartily as he followed along.

"Mind your manners, you two," Lord Englebright called. "And no more marriage proposals, you hear." Englebright laughed aloud. "I am not planning a wedding this weekend."

Chapter Sixteen

"Father, who was that gentleman?" Charles asked.

"Oh, bless me, Charles. I am failing in my societal duties. I will properly introduce you soon enough. That lad is going to aid me in building a fine breeding program, I am sure of it," he stated excitedly, leading them all toward the library.

"Englebright," called Derby, "before we go enjoy a brandy, I need to discuss something of some importance with you."

"Always working, eh, Derby?" Lord Englebright said. "Come, man, surely it can wait till tomorrow."

"I wish that were the case, my friend. But it has to do with a certain species of bird and a boy. I think you would find this development most curious," Derby said with a knowing nod.

"I see," said Englebright. "Let us go to my private library and have this chat. Gentlemen, please make yourself comfortable. Harold will see to your every need," he said, nodding to Harold, who bowed his head in deference to his lord.

"Charles, I fear I must call on you to entertain our guests for a moment," he said, clapping his son on the back. Charles bowed his head in acquiescence but looked curiously between the men.

As Englebright and Derby headed up the grand stair, Kristoff came through the door in a hurry. Assessing his surroundings and locating Englebright, he immediately engaged him in urgent conversation as he followed up the stairs.

"My Lord, I apologize for this abrupt interruption, but I must speak with you with some haste. It is regarding boys' breeches and some rather unsavory individuals lurking in your forest." He nodded with raised eyebrows in order to convey the potential danger to the man's daughter.

"Is there somewhere private we could chat so as not to alarm your other guests?"

"It seems the bill for the day is urgent conversations," Englebright said amiably.

"Come, Kristoff, I would like Earl Derby to hear what you have to say as well. Charles, forgive me again. This is Lord Van Reed. You will meet him properly later as well. He has some business to attend to with you and me."

Kristoff shook the man's hand in greeting but turned back to Englebright. He was not certain Englebright understood his daughter's reputation was in jeopardy as more people learned of her unique habits.

"This topic might be of a delicate nature, sir," he said in a low tone.

"Of course it is," Englebright replied and smiled again, "and I have no secrets from Derby, my dearest and oldest friend, I assure you. You may speak freely of any matter in his presence, and it will not leave the room."

As they entered the comfortable study, Englebright offered both men a brandy, which they gladly accepted.

"Now then, Kristoff, tell me what this is about." Lord Englebright sat down behind his desk and invited him and Derby to have a seat in the comfortable leather-backed chairs on either side of the large stone fireplace. The room was just warm enough with a small fire suited to the spring weather.

As Kristoff relayed the tale of what he had seen in the woods, leaving out all details of Rosalind but emphasizing the appearance of a young *lad* in breeches, he ended the telling by placing the found map upon the man's desk.

"I have no idea what these men are searching for, as I have not had the opportunity to solve the code, but Maude will not release me until I have them brought to justice. She is convinced witches are about and will not cease spitting upon my shoes each time I see her," he laughed. "I either have to solve this mystery or marry the old lady, as she seems to have taken a liking to me," he laughed again in order to lighten the mood that seemed to have overshadowed Englebright's face as soon as he saw the parchment. The man was going red and looked ready to go into battle.

"Georgie," Derby called, using his given name. "Whatever is the matter? You look as if you are ready to go to war. I have not seen that look in many years, my friend. What is that parchment?"

Englebright did not answer for a moment and seemed to be gathering his calm. He stood, picked up the parchment, and walked it over to his friend.

"Take a look, Derby. Do you recognize the writing?" he asked far too calmly.

"Ah, sweet Anna. Where did they get this?" Derby inquired.

For the first time since he had met the man, Kristoff found himself wary of the lord. He feared whomever that anger was directed toward would not see the morrow if found.

In a voice that veiled Englebright's apparent fury, he stated, "From my wife's rooms, that is where! That means we have a thief amongst us, and I cannot abide a thief. Keep a close eye out, Derby. Kristoff, keep an eye on my girl, hang propriety. I'll not have her put herself in further danger."

"George, I fear this timing is rather coincidental. No more than two months past, John Proctor was killed while guarding the archive room at the department. The only thing they found to be missing were your Anna's and Janssen Haberlin's letters, but only those containing any information about the Raven. It took us nearly a month to sort out what had been removed. The thief was neat, efficient, and very skilled with a knife. The blade was left in poor Proctor's heart. There was no apparent sign of a struggle, but the blade entered with force. We believe it to have been thrown from some distance…perhaps even through the bars in the door. There was a marking upon the handle; that of a small, black bird," Derby told him emphatically. "You know what that implies."

"The Raven!" Englebright growled.

He ran out the door, leaving the two men in his wake. They quickly followed. Kristoff was unsure of what was going on, but it seemed danger was suddenly afoot. He felt he needed to be ready for anything.

"Englebright," he shouted. "Slow down, man. Where are you going?"

As realization dawned on Derby, he grabbed Kristoff's arm to stop him from following. "He is going to check the other letters to make sure they are safe. Just give him a moment, and I shall explain. You were a military man, correct? And you appear to have some affection for our dear Sprite. We may have need of your services," Derby told him as they walked back into the study. "The Raven is a formidable foe and not one to be trifled with. He is the type to target a man through those he loves. If he discovers there are more letters here, well, I feel the family may all be in danger." Derby shook his head. "During the war, the Raven traded in secrets like black marketeers traded in goods. We always suspected perhaps he could have been a double agent, because he was always a step ahead. We never caught him, though some think he might have been in the same room as they at times. He is a master of disguise and deceit, you see. We also believe he may be the reason one of our dearest friends was killed in an ambush orchestrated by lies."

"What does that map have to do with this Raven?" Kristoff asked.

"Ah, that…well…nothing at all, point of fact," Derby said, raising his hands in apparent vexation. "Our Anna loved a mystery and often created scavenger hunts for her children. She would have them running all over the estate solving her puzzles to find hidden treasures."

He smiled as he remembered the many stories and raucous dinner discussions over these intrigues.

Kristoff could not help smiling in kind, now realizing where Rosalind might have inherited her spirited nature.

"What sorts of treasures would they find?" he inquired, still smiling.

"Oh, small things; some sweets, or even fake gems." Derby laughed as he shared one particularly inventive adventure in which Anna had actually had the local smithy create doubloons with the family crest upon them. They were iron, of course, but they were painted gold. The children had been thrilled. Derby sipped his drink, looking warily at the door while awaiting his friend's return. Kristoff paced back and forth. He appeared to want to ask more questions but was holding his patience awaiting Englebright's return. Derby appreciated the silence as he thought.

A short time later, Englebright came back into the study with a look of relief upon his face. He closed and locked the door behind him. He walked to a portrait of his lovely wife and pulled on the corner of the frame. The picture swung away from the wall smoothly, revealing a small safe. He quickly opened it and placed a packet of letters that had been neatly tied with a blue ribbon into it before shutting the door and spinning the tumblers.

Kristoff noted the parchment seemed worn as if it had been read over and over, but handled with care.

Englebright picked up the snifter of brandy and tossed it back as he fell into his chair. As he began to speak, Derby interrupted him.

"That is not all, my friend." Derby hated to burden his friend further. He could tell the news had already wearied the man, and on his birthday of all days.

"If you recall, the night Janssen went missing, the nanny who cared for your Pieter was found strangled. We assumed it was French spies who had done the deed and taken the boy to ransom him, but we could not sort out how they knew who the child was." Derby leaned forward and looked straight into his friend's eyes. "You know we never got a ransom letter and assumed the worst had befallen the lad, but we now have reason to believe that was not the case."

At this bit of news, Englebright jumped out of his chair again.

"Go on, man. What have you learned?" he begged.

"We recently brought in a man for the murder of a tavern serving girl. Awful bloke…He was bragging that she was not the first wench he had done in, and that his deeds spread as far as Liège, where he had done in a lady and her son," Derby said darkly. "We went round and round with this fellow strictly off the books as the timing seemed right for our investigation. We never stopped searching because Anna asked us not to. Anyway, this man confessed to being hired by one Elsbeth Haberlin, whom he aided in kidnapping a child. This Elsbeth apparently paid the nanny to bring the child to her. Once the deed was done, our murderer was to kill the nanny and take the groats paid to her as extra for his trouble."

"Janssen had no family that we knew of," Englebright said, leaning back on his desk and running his hands through his thick hair.

"It was policy to be closed-lipped about family, to keep them out of harm's way, you see?" He directed the comment at Kristoff. "But why would Janssen have asked us to take his son if he had relatives, Derby? And why would his own sister arrange Pieter's kidnapping? It makes no sense."

Englebright began pacing about the room again. "Did the man know more, such as where they went?"

"We know there must have been false papers created, but the trail goes cold as soon as they cross the channel," Derby said, raising his hands in vexation.

"Elsbeth Haberlin disappeared without a trace on the southern shores of the channel, taking Pieter's whereabouts with her."

"My Lord, if I may," Kristoff began, "I have quite a collection of family ancestry from that area at my disposal, as you know, which is how I traced to where your Ladyship and Van Lynden heirs had relocated after the war. I have done this for many families on order of my king to return properties to rightful heirs, as you know. This is a large initiative for our king."

"If the Haberlin family lineage exists, I may have a record of it, or can at least get access to it, though it may take a few days. Most of the material is in my Newcastle office. If this Elsbeth existed," he said and nodded to them both, "she would be in my official lineage records. Not even the king himself could have the official copies removed. There might even be records of orders of protection if she was renamed to protect the child after the war, though I would think that would have been aided by your War Department as well."

"That could be just the bit of information we need," Derby said excitedly as he stood and started pacing the room as well. "We may have a record as well, if our department assisted unbeknownst to me. I have searched, but perhaps not deeply enough. If she existed, perhaps there was a husband as well. Maybe she feared for her nephew, given

Janssen's line of work, took him, and relocated to somewhere safer. Anything we could use to track her down and just make sure Pieter is well would take a load off of both of us. But Georgie, my friend, why all of this now? Why the War Department, the map gone missing, and new information on Pieter's whereabouts coming out all at once? You know how I feel about coincidence."

Englebright knew his friend was truly confounded to have used his boyhood name in front of others.

"Yes. There is no such thing, and I agree. We need more information. If you are willing, young man, we would surely appreciate your assistance," he said to Kristoff.

Kristoff nodded, looking at each man in turn. "I do not want you to leave Rosalind unprotected. I am sure you and her brothers are capable, but she is free-spirited. I worry her curiosity over this mystery in the woods will get the better of her. Until we figure out how that piece plays in, we will all need to keep a watchful eye."

"Too right. I will inform her brothers immediately of the danger, but it will take us all to keep a close watch on my girl and the twins. Once the boys discover there is a mystery afoot, it may take the entire royal guard to keep them out of the forest. Rosalind's curiosity is a trifle compared to theirs. They are far too wild, the fault of which lies with me. I would ask you to stay close to our girl's side as well. Is there someone you can send to your offices to fetch the information we need?"

When Englebright saw the look on Kristoff's face, he felt a bit sorry for the man, for he looked as if he were suffering a bout of indigestion.

Well, hell, thought Kristoff as he nodded and said, "Of course, my Lord. It would be my honor to ensure her safety. As for the documents, if you lend me a runner, I will have him fetch my clerk with the files right away. Do you have some parchment and a quill I could use?"

Englebright had already had Derby look into the young Lord Van Reede's background the minute he entered the village. For a small village without a train station, a telegraph office was not a common thing, but given his history and secret work, he had been able to finagle the installation of one. Derby had managed to procure all the needed information as efficiently as a spider weaving a web. He had let Englebright know everything he needed to upon his arrival.

Kristoff was a strong military man who had lost both mother and father to the war. He had more or less raised himself until he was old enough to join the military, where he worked his way up to becoming a rather young special forces operative. He was of good character and disposition, given the loss he had endured…and the man seemed to match his Sprite in spirit, to boot.

He also had no remaining family and seemed alone in the world with no known promises to other ladies. Englebright added efficient and honorable to his list of good qualities as he watched Kristoff draft a quick letter, sign it, and seal it with a bit of candle wax and a signet ring he wore on his left hand. Englebright could see from the first that Rosalind and Kristoff shared an attraction, which the man was obviously fighting.

There could be nothing for it. He had to keep his daughter safe from his past, and if he could use this to his advantage and play at matchmaker, he would. It was a sound match that would be good for them both, Englebright decided with a nod to himself.

As soon as Kristoff handed over the letter, Englebright grabbed the bell pull that would signal to Harold he needed him, and heard a knocking upon the door as the bell chimed in the distance.

"Father," Andrew's voice called out as the locked knob began to wiggle. "Are you well? You've been locked in that study for an hour, neglecting your guests. It is unlike you; please open the door. I need to speak with you urgently."

"'Tis the theme of the day, Son," he called tiredly as he strode to the door and unlocked it.

As Andrew looked into the room, Charles approached from behind him. Clearly, Harold had sent him up, assuming that was what was being requested; wise man, he thought.

"You've left Michael and Edmund to entertain your guests, you do realize, sir. That seems to be playing with fire," Charles laughed.

"All the ladies have retired above stairs to attend to their toilette for this evening's event. The other gents seemed to be quietly reading the Times or whatnot for now, so we should be safe enough for a moment. What is going on in here, anyway? I thought I heard running." Charles looked at the grim expressions on each face in the room. He shut the door behind him. "What is happening, Father?"

"My Lord, I will take my leave and have word sent to Newcastle at once," Kristoff said, rising and walking to the door. He paused before he left.

"I know we will have a close eye upon Lady Rosalind, but I worry this threat would put both Mrs. Willoughby and your daughter's maid at risk, even perhaps your other guests. I fear it is too late to send the guests away. Do you think this Raven will surface here after all this time? Does he have any reason to target your family?" Kristoff did not wish to overstep his boundaries, but was suddenly very concerned for his unpredictable Sprite and her companions.

"There is some chance…if he has read the letters thoroughly, he might seek Anna or me. The letters provided enough intelligence to make his life very difficult in the end. Anna's family and family name have been diminished, as you know. I fear, however, that my heirs and I are quite easy to find. Blast it all, this should never have happened," he said, pounding his fist on the desk. "The fiend was quiet for years, and now, through our inability to catch him, I have put my family at risk. The game is afoot, yet again, it seems."

"We will see it through, my Lord. You are not the guilty party in this situation," Kristoff said, patting him on the back as he headed to the door. He nodded to Andrew and Charles as he exited the library, noting both had a confused look upon their faces. He heard Englebright's tired voice speak as he closed the door.

"Sons, have a seat. There is something I need to tell you…"

Chapter Seventeen

Rosalind met Nan in her rooms with Elsa in order to prepare themselves for the evening. Nan had noted the state of poor Rosalind's eyes when she came back from her stroll in the gardens. She knew if she pressed, her friend would never tell her why she was in such a state. Oh, how she hoped Kristoff had not taken advantage of her. He seemed too much of a gentleman to do anything of the sort, but one could not always tell someone's character with such a short acquaintance.

Maybe that was why she was reserving judgment for Jacob. He had been so sweet while watching her play games with the boys. He acted as if he had never been part of this sort of revelry. In truth, the Englebright household could be a bit overwhelming if you were unaccustomed to such, but he seemed to drink it in like a parched man on a hot summer day.

The boys had kept him laughing with their antics and cheating, all the while trying to convince him of her duplicity in the game. At one point, he had laid the lightest touch upon her shoulder as he laughed and pointed out a goose that had somehow slipped back onto the board, though it had been clearly captured moments before.

Michael had distracted her with a rather boisterous story of how Edmund had stolen the headmaster's wig and then proceeded to wear it to their parliamentary procedure lecture with that very same headmaster. All the while, Edmund was placing geese back upon the board and winking at Jacob as if she could not see. It was all in good fun, and she had not laughed as much in weeks, it felt. That touch, though, had warmed her skin and resurrected feelings that had once been reserved for only Erwin. It left her feeling both guilty and exhilarated, which, of course, made no sense at all.

And then there was Charles. What had he been about with his overprotection? Perhaps it was brotherly, but somehow, it had seemed more this time. Oh, hang it all, she was losing her wits. Of course it was brotherly. Charles had never been anything but a model of decorum with her, as the future duke should be. And she was most definitely not aristocracy, no matter how she had been adopted by Ara. She was not duke-courting material, she thought as Elsa tugged her back to the present as she tightened the laces on her bodice.

"Goodness, Elsa!" she exclaimed. "Not so tight or I may not be able to breathe."

"Oh, Nan," exclaimed Rosalind, "that is the most stunning gown I have ever seen."

She gently touched the royal blue organdy over gold satin skirts. The organdy had been pulled up in loops to allow the shimmering gold satin to show. Each loop was attached at the waist with a delicate sapphire-colored glass gem that caught the candlelight in the most glorious twinkles. Loops of smaller beads dangled delicately over her hips and the pointed waistline.

The bodice was exquisite panels of royal blue satin lined with golden ribbon at each of the stays. There were matching smaller blue glass beads lining the top, with strings of them looping over the capped sleeves mimicking those at her waist. The neckline was modest and squared, as was the fashion of which both Nan and she were most fond.

"I do say, though, Elsa…you have her bosom heaving. I dare say a certain gentleman from Durham way may faint from the pure pleasure of it," she laughed at Elsa's gasp.

"M'lady, please don't speak so. It is unseemly."

"Oh, pish posh, Elsa. Allow me my fun now," Rosalind stated, with a sigh, touching her head with the back of her hand in mock vexation. "For soon I must behave with perfect decorum."

She laughed as she wiggled into her underthings.

In a more serious tone, she looked at both women in turn and said, "I will not dishonor Papa. This is his celebration, and he deserves nothing but pure joy. He shall have nothing to fear from me, I assure you. Now then, Elsa, where is my gown for the evening? I told that horrid Edith earlier that I would wear the blue brocade when she asked, but I can't do that if Nan is wearing blue. I dare say, I will pale in comparison no matter what I don."

She smiled fondly at her friend.

"Nonsense, M'lady! You both will be striking. I believe Mrs. Nan has made you just the thing for the evening. I already removed the wrinkles and laid it in your dressing room," Elsa said, winking at Nan.

"Oh! A Nan original. I cannot wait to see it! Nan knows just how I like my dresses. Not too tight in the hips, and buttons in the front in case I need to make a quick getaway," she giggled, winking at Elsa's sigh as she passed her on the way to fetch the gown.

"We'll have none of that tonight," Elsa said as she pulled the green silk out of the side dressing room.

Rosalind gasped, recognition quick as a wink, and she groaned. It was the very same dress she had been helping Nan fit. "No…Nan…you didn't! You said that was for a, a…"

"Don't you dare say what you are thinking, Ara. You will hurt my delicate feelings."

"But…" Rosalind began to protest.

"And if you recall, you did all the saying of what that dress was for. I just did a fitting," Nan said, cutting her off mid-sentence.

"Nan, Papa will have my hide if I come out in…in…*that* this evening," she sputtered, as pink crept up her face. "The bosom…well, it will be more than heaving, I can tell you that."

"Stuff and nonsense. You only saw it partially completed. There are lovely beads at the neckline with a bit of lace. That will cover you nicely," Nan stated with a mischievous grin as she brought the gown forward and raised it as if to stuff her friend in without so much as a by-your-leave.

"Besides, Ara, at some point, you will have to stop binding your bosom and accept what God graced you with, Love. Though I must say," she stated in faux concern, looking her friend over, "I may have miscalculated the amount of lace by a bit. But no matter, your father commissioned the design himself…and thought it a lovely gown. He thought all of the gowns he commissioned for you to be perfect. Why,

I am not sure I have worked on gowns for anyone else but you, me, and Elsa for weeks now."

Nan looked at her friend pointedly with that remark.

"*All* the gowns you say?" Rosalind asked as Elsa began tugging the gown over her hips and cinching the waist ties. Rosalind spun on them both, grasping her unfastened bodice to her bosom.

"You said, 'all the gowns,' Nan. All the ones in your home, then?" she asked, looking from Elsa to Nan in turn, a wide smile spreading on her face.

"When were you going to tell me you were to marry, Elsa? Who is he, then? I know you will be a beauty in the white silk, but we are friends, are we not?" Rosalind stated, taking the other woman's hands in hers.

Elsa, quite stunned, looked from Nan to Rosalind and back, flushing red. "I…I'm not to marry, M'lady."

"That blush speaks otherwise, my friend."

Rosalind nodded knowingly at her.

"You have the look of a lady in love. How have I not seen it before?" she said, gripping her friend's hands tightly and giving them a little shake. "Oh, I am so sorry, Elsa. I have been so involved in my own dramas that I neglected you."

Rosalind hugged the befuddled Elsa to her chest. "He will be a most fortunate man! Though I will miss you so. What am I to do without you…Oh, look at me! Thinking of myself again."

She beamed at Elsa. "Do I know him? I would have hoped you would have introduced me before now, but I understand you like to keep some things to yourself."

Nan interrupted the exchange with a slight cough and a gentle pat upon her friend's hand. "Ara, Love, we will be late to go below stairs if we do not hurry."

"Shall I fetch you some water first, Nan? You seem a bit choked. You're not falling ill, are you? Vapours, perhaps," she laughed.

Both Nan and Elsa stared at Rosalind with huge, round eyes, appearing the image of innocence. Seriously, did they think she was a fool? Well, she was certainly not intending on finding any wedded bliss anytime soon, though…those kisses. Those might make any clear-minded lady addled and agree to just about anything. She sighed audibly and blushed a bit, she knew.

She noted both Elsa and Nan looking at her quizzically, so she quickly averted her eyes and got back to the task of doing up her numerous tiny, green gem-like buttons. The dress really was dazzling, she thought. As she finished the last button, she turned to give them both a sweet, innocent smile. She would play along with their game and have a bit of fun in the process. She did love a bit of mischief. It was rather bold of her father to commission her a wedding dress and even bolder of Nan to agree. Yes, she would have a bit of fun this night. She smiled sweetly at them both.

One look at Rosalind was all it took to have both Nan and Elsa widen their eyes in a bit of dismay. She winked at them in response.

"Will you dance with this handsome prince of yours this evening?" Rosalind asked with a large grin, dancing in circles around her friends. "Oh, let's play a fun game. Let me guess which gentleman it is. I will be in charge of filling in your dance card, and by the end of the evening, I will have your fair betrothed picked out of the crush!"

Rosalind smiled at her again and grabbed Elsa's hands, swinging her about the room. Elsa looked suddenly terrified and began sputtering.

Elsa had been more of a friend than a lady's maid for more of her life than Rosalind could recall. Elsa's own mother had served Rosalind's mother until she passed in childbirth, not a year before Rosalind's mother's death. Elsa only had her papa now, so it would be fitting for her to have someone strong and kind to love her. If she could help her friend find the right sort of man, then that white dress would not go to waste, after all.

Her smile was now glowing as she thought her plan through. She had seen every man in the village except some of the country gentry who lived a bit beyond a day's ride. She had never seen Elsa pay any particular attention to one man or another in the village, and she most certainly would have noticed since she, herself, spent so much time in the village teaching the little ones.

Of late, she had even been spending time in the new school-to-be with local carpenters and the like, with Elsa in tow. Oh, how she could not wait to have her school complete, her thoughts diverted. Hmm…There was one carpenter, a tall, handsome man of no more than five and twenty. He went by the name of Bradford O'Leary.

He, his mama, papa, and three younger siblings had moved to the village only a few months back. His father tended a flock of sheep, and his mama was a weaver. He himself was kind and spoke gently to the children and the mothers, and she had seen him repairing homes all over the area…*and* she had seen Elsa side-eye him when she thought no one was looking.

Papa always invited every tradesman, farmer, and member of the aristocracy to his birthday ball, so she knew he had been invited. She knew just what to do now and began rubbing her hands together. When Rosalind looked up, she found both women staring at her, eyes growing ever wider.

"You two act like the cat who ate the canary," she stated with her hands on her hips. "What are you two about?" she asked.

"Us? What about you? I have seen that gleam in your eyes and that mischievous smile, Ara," Nan almost squeaked, worry marring her lovely face. "I usually see it right before you get us into a world of trouble. Like that time you put your dress on a goat and tried to convince the twins she was a long-lost princess who needed a kiss to be restored…What are *you* about?"

"Calm yourself, Nan. I would do nothing to shame Papa, and you well know it. But Elsa's husband-to-be might be here tonight, and I, for one, plan to meet him," Rosalind replied with a smile.

Elsa just continued to stare wide-eyed in shock at her friend, her mouth opening and closing, but no words seemed able to escape. She was beginning to look a bit like a trout out of water. Rosalind smiled at the thought. This was going to be a lovely evening.

Nan and Rosalind helped the still silent Elsa into a lovely, pale, yellow silk gown of a simple cut that befitted her position. Rosalind wanted to adorn her with jewels, but Elsa was having none of it, as it was not proper for her as Rosalind's chaperone and companion for the evening. She informed Rosalind that the delicate forget-me-nots embroidered around the hem in shades of oranges, reds, and pinks were enough adornment for her and provided a stunning contrast to the yellow.

Having completed their dressing, the ladies began coiffing their hair into elaborate curls. Elsa pinned Rosalind's auburn tresses into braided loops that reflected the beading upon her dress. She fashioned curls to frame her face and pinned the remainder atop her head in a delicate braided bun, then adorned it with one of the early spring roses she had gathered from the kitchen gardens. Elsa gasped as she looked upon her charge and handed her the matching green satin gloves.

"My Lady, you are fetching," the sweet maid stated in awe. It was amazing how this chance of fate in bringing two affable suitors to the estate had lightened Elsa's whole outlook on being Rosalind's maid, she thought with a smile. The daunting task of finding a match for her lady seemed more probable as the day wore on. If only she could prevent Rosalind from what she suspected was a bit of matchmaking for her, then this evening might just go off without a hitch.

"Shall we be off, then?" Nan asked nervously, wringing her hands a bit. Lord, what if Jacob asked her to dance? She was as nervous as a bride on her wedding night, she mused, and then blushed. Lord, she was beginning to think like Ara talked.

Chapter Eighteen

Rosalind, Nan, and Elsa descended the steps just as the clock struck nine. Edmund and Michael were waiting at the bottom to escort them Rosalind and Nan into the ballroom. Rosalind felt bad that there was no one waiting to escort Elsa, as Andrew had already entered the ballroom with Papa. She would rectify that soon enough, though, if she had her way about it. Her friend would dance the night away.

She looked down at her décolletage before stopping on the landing and biting her bottom lip. She would let Nan and Papa think she was none the wiser to their machinations, but goodness, if the cut of this gown did not alert her to their true intent, then the white gown certainly did. She would play along with their games and perhaps play a bit of her own, but there would be no wedding for her in the near future if she had any say in it, which she did, of course. Just because she had nearly thrown herself at a man did not mean she wanted to skip to the altar after him.

She did understand what Andrew had told her about playing with fire, and she needed significantly more time to ponder that before she decided to give in to her baser instincts again and let a man ravage her…or God forbid she do the ravaging, she thought with a blush. She had goals and would see them through…and those did not include a husband. She shook off her thoughts, held her head high, and looked at her brothers with a smile.

"My, you two are rather dashing this evening! Be careful, or you will be pursued by all the eligible ladies here this eve." She smiled at each in turn as Michael offered her his arm, and Edmund offered his to Nan, gleaming at his brother in what appeared to be pure triumph.

Michael grumbled, "Edmund won at dicing earlier, which is why you have the honor of being escorted by the more attractive twin, Sprite. Poor Nan," he said, winking at her.

Nan laughed at his cheeky comment and allowed Edmund to escort her down the hall. The ballroom was toward the back of the manor and abutted the conservatory. The clear glass windows on one side allowed the greenery in the conservatory to be viewed from the ballroom floor. She was told it was an unusual architectural choice, but had no basis for comparison, as she was not in the habit of wandering about other people's estates when the opportunity presented itself.

The ballroom was semicircular on the opposite wall and had been lined with niches that now were filled with delicate glass lanterns of every color. The colors reflected in the conservatory glass with a magical pooling of jewel tones about the room. Mirrors in the niches reflected the light even more, giving the impression of an even larger room. The light combined with the floral arrangements, and the music from the stringed quintet had the guests gasping in wonder as each was announced and allowed to enter the room. It was a truly fantastical setting. Rosalind had never imagined such a fairyland in her own home. Mrs. Ingrid and the staff had outdone themselves.

"I am so nervous," Rosalind confessed to Nan. "I feel as though every gentleman already in attendance is staring at my bosom. I need to find a dance partner who is shorter than I. What were you thinking, Nan? Really. Can I borrow a bit of your lace for a modesty panel…or perhaps I should steal a bit of ribbon from that floral arrangement and stuff it betwixt my cleavage. Perhaps we have some blind chaps in attendance."

"Stop fussing, Ara. You will draw attention. You look just as modest as all the other young misses here."

"Yes, but they are husband-hunting, and I most definitely am not," Rosalind stated as she turned her back on the room and stuffed a lace handkerchief down her bodice.

Nan smiled politely at Rosalind and promptly yanked the bit of fabric out again, making sure not to draw undue attention to her friend's perceived predicament. Having removed the offending cloth, Nan tucked it into her own glove and smiled sweetly at her friend. "I believe your first dance partner is making his way over. I suggest you prepare your dance card and stop fussing."

As Rosalind turned back to face the room, she saw a boy not much older than the twins making his way to her, her brothers following him with mischievous grins on their faces.

Edmund cleared his throat importantly and announced, "Lady Rosalind, might I introduce you to our dear friend Mr. Mycroft Hawthorne. He has been most anxious to make your acquaintance, dear sister. Mycroft, old boy, this is Lady Rosalind, our enchanting sister."

Mycroft's smile stretched across his face, which was marred with blemishes across his nose and chin. He was not an unattractive lad, but she was fair to certain when he spoke, his voice would surely squeak.

"My Lady," he said, swallowing perceptibly, glancing furtively at her face and her bosom in succession, "might I have the distinguished honor of this first dance with you?"

His voice broke on the question as beads of sweat broke across his forehead.

Curtseying properly and following decorum, she allowed him to sign his name to her card and thanked him genially, then glared at her brothers as the boy turned to go. Normally, boys of this age would not be allowed attendance, but her father had made an exception for this one celebration.

Edmund bowed to Nan and asked her the same favor. She smiled warmly and allowed him to sign her card as well. Michael, in turn, asked for the second dance.

"Boys," Elsa warned, "you know your father told you to do your duty to all the guests. Leave poor Nan alone."

Winking at her in turn, the incorrigible lads went to seek their next partners. Already, Rosalind could see a group of young girls looking at the boys and giggling. She had no doubt they would do their duty to the guests, indeed. Hopefully, Papa had warned them not to cause a scandal. They already had a reputation for causing mischief while away at school. There was no telling what they could do with a room full of ladies and desperate mamas. Rosalind thought it was silly that she was the one with a chaperone when the twins were the ones who clearly needed constant supervision.

Just as Rosalind's musings digressed with thoughts of the boys' possible antics, a stunning sight caught the corner of her eye. He was almost unrecognizable from this morning, but nonetheless, it was Kristoff, looking as delicious as a dark chocolate bonbon, she thought, and immediately dreaded. She was always hungry, it seemed. He was dressed in a superfine black dress coat and vest that spanned his broad shoulders and opened at the front of his chest to reveal a delicately pleated white, crisp shirt and a simple, yet elegant styled cravat. His pants were a matching black and had a snug fit in all the areas to make an innocent maid blush. His glossy boots contrasted with his pants. He was adorned with simple studs for his sleeve links, which made the entire ensemble a trap for her imagination and wandering eyes.

Oh, God, I am blushing again. I need to leave, thought Rosalind. Instead of running, she plastered a smile upon her face and thought of her papa. She would make it through this night for him.

With long, slow strides, Kristoff was making his way straight toward her and Nan. His approach was almost predatory as he weaved his way through the crowd. He was all feline grace in his movements. He looked like he wanted to throttle her. What had she done now, she pondered. Jacob was following him, having no problem at all keeping up.

"Well, look who's coming to join us: our valiant rescuer from this morning, accompanied by none other than your Kristoff. They are surely dashing in their evening attire, wouldn't you say?" commented Nan.

Nan could not take her eyes off Jacob. Those golden locks of his gleamed in the candlelight. He was a handsome man, to be sure, and so jovial, if not a bit reserved when he spoke with her. His eyes were intent upon her. It warmed her to the tip of her toes to be the recipient of that look.

Before the gentlemen could approach, Charles was magically standing before Rosalind and Nan.

Rosalind started. "Good Heavens, Charles! Where on Earth did you pop up from? I swore I saw you but a moment ago on the other side of the room with Papa, Lady Maxwell, and her lovely daughter. Persephone is her name, I believe. A lovely girl who enjoys toile, if memory serves me well enough."

Charles nodded to his sister with the quirk of a grin that showed his adorable dimple.

"Do you have an inkling of what toile actually is, Ros?" he asked merrily. "But to answer your question, yes. I was with Father and the young Lady Maxwell. She is a sweet child. No doubt she will make a fine wife for someone someday."

Turning to Nan, he inclined his head in a slight bow. "Nan, might I have the pleasure of taking a turn on the dance floor with you this evening?"

Nan was taken aback. She had danced with Charles before, but only during country dances and with Erwin's approval.

"Of, of course, my Lord," she stammered. "I would be honored, but do not wish to take you away from more important guests."

"Nonsense," he replied and smiled, "who could possibly be more important than Rosalind's dearest friend?"

He signed her dance card for the third slot, behind the twins, and raised a brow at her. She delicately shrugged and smiled. He nodded to her again, the picture of propriety, then turned to greet Kristoff and Jacob as they approached.

"Gentlemen," he said with an acknowledging nod at Kristoff and offered both gentlemen his hand in turn.

"A pleasure to see you this evening. I leave the ladies in your care," he said as he strolled away, leaving Nan dumbfounded in his wake.

"My Lady, might I have the pleasure of a dance with you this evening?" Jacob asked Rosalind as he took her offered hand and kissed the air above it as was proper.

"Of course, my Lord." She smiled warmly at him. "How could I deny our brave rescuer? You did, after all, slay a thunderstorm in our honor. I believe our Dear Nan owes you her dance card as well in appreciation of your valor.

She took the dance card from Nan's hand and offered it to him as she turned to look at Kristoff. It was completely improper of her to insinuate the man owed Nan anything, much less to demand he dance with her, but Kristoff's presence had her so flustered, she feared she would make a fool of herself in short order if she did not get away from him. She scanned the room for any distraction.

Her eyes lit upon a certain carpenter whom Elsa had also noticed. She looked up and started to say, "Excuse me," but Kristoff being so near seemed to have turned her thoughts to molasses. She suddenly had no idea what she was about to do.

"Lady Rosalind, Lady Nan," Kristoff stated, sparing but a polite glance for Nan. "Might I have the pleasure of a dance, my Lady?"

His rich baritone washed over her like chocolate on a decadent cake. She was so drawn to him and leaned in closer as she offered her dance card for him to sign, noticing his scowl as he looked upon the card.

"Who is Mycroft?" he asked with an undercurrent of what sounded like a threat instead of a question.

"He is my first dance partner of the evening," she said a bit haughtily, offering no more explanation as she licked her lips and stared into his eyes with a challenge.

He looked back and then let his eyes roam over her as she had done to him on that first meeting in Nan's gardens. He smiled when she flushed pink. *Ye gads*, he thought. *How am I supposed to survive this night without being this innocent's undoing?* He had never been so ill-disciplined in all his days. What was it about this woman, this inexplicable pull toward her? He felt drawn too tight when in her presence, like a bow string about to pop.

Elsa stifled a giggle. "You let Mr. Hawthorne claim your first dance? I thought he was still away at school."

"I see," said Kristoff with a cough to cover his laugh. "Until then, my Lady," he said, bowing over her hand and brushing his lips actually upon her glove, not taking his eyes from hers. He let go of her hand but did not move away.

Rosalind bit her lip as she continued to gaze at him and felt her heartbeat quicken at his boldness.

Jacob cleared his throat as if to clear the tension that was brewing like a storm on the horizon between the two. Good Lord, he felt like he was intruding on an intimate moment. This thought made him blush again. Why was he always doing that in Miss Willoughby's presence? She surely thought him a simpleton. He cleared his throat and found his nerve.

"Mrs. Willoughby, might I have the honor to lead you upon the dance floor this evening? A waltz, perhaps," he asked as he tentatively looked into her eyes. He knew this request was too bold, but could not help himself. The waltz was the most intimate of dances, and that was what he wished to share with her before his uncle's arrival. He knew that might change his choices significantly.

Nan smiled demurely, a faint pink rising upon her cheeks at the intimacy of the request. "I would be honored, my Lord," she agreed again, dumbfounded that not one, but now two of the Ton seemed more than casually interested in her attentions. What should she do, she wondered.

"Excellent, if you will excuse me, I wish to greet our host. Kristoff, care to join me?" It was clear Kristoff wished to do nothing of the like. He was still staring intently at Lady Englebright, who was giving back as good as she got.

"Of course," he said, bowing to both ladies in turn. "My manners seem to be bewitched by our lovely companions. Until we dance…my Sprite."

He whispered the last for only her ears.

Rosalind's breath caught. He had said the last in a whisper, but she knew she heard him correctly. He called her his Sprite. Panic at the insinuation began to build. She turned to see if Nan had heard him as well, for they were nearly side by side, but then noted the same look on her friend's face as she stared at Jacob. Rosalind, seeing the growing distress, smiled at Nan and inwardly chided herself. Nan looked near to bolting. This must be so difficult for her. She had not attended a dance since before Erwin's passing.

"You will enjoy the evening, Nan. 'tis but a dance. Erwin would not begrudge you a bit of joy and frivolity, nor your happiness. Enjoy the evening and stop fretting at the 'whys' in your head," she said knowingly as she squeezed Nan's hand.

Nan smiled at her gratefully, so glad her friend could read her thoughts and know just what to say to comfort her. Even if she was often a whirlwind, Ara always had her best interests at heart.

If you will excuse Elsa and me for a moment, Nan, I have to discuss some carpentry with that gentleman, just there." She pointed at Mr. Bradford O'Leary, glanced at her maid, and smiled when she noted the blush on Elsa's cheeks. *Good,* she thought, and tugged her maid across the room for a proper introduction. He and his father had attended together, while his siblings and mother were away visiting his grandmother, it seemed. Both men were quite handsome, with Bradford being a younger clone of his father. The older Mr. O'Leary sported older-fashioned mutton chops down his cheeks. His blond hair was coursed through with wisps of silver. He was quite dashing and charming.

"Look here, my boy, the loveliest flowers in the whole of England have sought us out, save for my own Darla, of course," he beamed at both girls. "Is my boy doing right by you, Lady Englebright? All his building is up to snuff? And who is this darlin' beauty with you? A vision in gold, she is. Isn't that right, my boy?" he said, nudging his son, who he had just noted could not take his eyes off Lady Englebright's companion.

"Forgive me, sir. This is my friend and companion, Elsa. I believe she has been in the proximity of your son but has yet to formally meet him. We are ever so glad you could attend this evening," Rosalind said, bowing her head to both men.

"Your father is a fine man, m'lady. Before we located hereabouts, I had never heard of tradesmen being invited to a fancy ball as if we were equals. And he knows what's what about his land, he does. My sheep are getting so fat on the lush grasses, they may be rolling to the shearing house before long instead of walking," he told her with a wink.

Both Rosalind and Elsa laughed at the image that conjured.

"Miss Elsa, might I have the honor of a dance?" Bradford asked politely, but with such confidence, Elsa found herself saying yes before even asking Rosalind if it might be all right. She looked at Rosalind, who beamed a huge smile and produced a dance card from her glove.

"Ah, I have her dance card, just here," she said, smiling at Elsa. Elsa stared at her a bit open-mouthed as he signed her dance card.

"And of course, I would love to dance with you as well, Lady Englebright, if I am not being too forward?"

"Of course." Rosalind smiled and handed him her dance card as well.

"Well, I leave you young ones to it," Mr. O'Leary said, smiling at them. Think I will go and search out some of those lovely treats I saw in the dining hall," he said, rubbing his hands together as if he were about to go on a conquest. The group laughed again as he departed.

Nan, Rosalind, and Elsa continued to have gentlemen, young and old, request their hand upon the dance floor until their cards were filled. Elsa, who originally thought she had no dance card at all due to her role as companion, did not realize that Rosalind had created one for her until she handed it to Bradford O'Leary…Rosalind had made sure to fill the card with her relatives until the slot for the waltz, so she was sure to share the intimate dance with the handsome carpenter. Elsa looked at the card, confused, and nearly choked on the bit of punch she was drinking when she realized what Rosalind had done. Rosalind just smiled at her and patted her back as if to ease her choking.

In turn, all of Rosalind's brothers, her father, and Lord Derby had requested a dance with her. Her card was nearly overflowing with family, which suited her just fine. That gave little chance for the other gentlemen and dandies to have an opportunity to leer at her bosom.

"I do find it odd that my entire family has requested a dance with me. Perhaps Papa has given up his quest to find me a proper suitor this evening," she commented with a smile. If he had truly been interested in his cause, he would have cautioned her brothers away. Oh, well, perhaps he had a change of heart and, just perhaps, she thought, this party was not going to be as bad as she had feared.

Chapter Nineteen

The composer, Josef Lanner, did not have Mr. Mycroft Hawthorne in mind when he composed his quadrille played at these festivities. It was the longest, most grueling dance Rosalind had ever endured. This was all because of Mr. Mycroft Hawthorne, of course. He was a salacious twit, and he turned this popular spin into agony. At the tender age of ten and five, he had no more of the gentlemanly notions than the goat that had eaten her dress earlier that day.

Indeed, she had determined the goat likely drooled less upon her destroyed frock than the boy was now trying to place upon this one. He simply could not look her in the eyes because he was too busy looking at her breasts. She would likely need her handkerchief back from Nan when the dance was done. She had tried her best to be civil and carry on a proper conversation with the lad, but it was pointless. He squeaked responses that indicated he had no interest in conversation.

The dance ended with him making a bit of a fool of himself and proposing a hastily squeaked offer of marriage. Kristoff had been dancing with Madame Maxwell but staring at young Mycroft as if he might do the boy harm.

As Mycroft led her off the dance floor to her next partner, he was clearly awaiting a response to his proposal. He stopped a few steps shy of Jacob and looked at her with large, anxious eyes. "Perhaps, you should follow proper decorum, Sir, and speak with the Duke Umberland. He might have a thought on your request. I see him just there," she said and gestured, "standing beside my brothers, Charles and Andrew. They might have a thought on the topic as well." She smiled serenely at him. "Best you seek approval from them all," she stated gently, prodding him in their direction, and then turned to glare at the twins, who were most pointedly not looking at her.

Kristoff approached her with a grin. He was quite impressed at the way in which she had handled the situation. He wanted to drag the fool boy off the dance floor and give him a beating for treating a lady with such scandalous behavior.

"I see your intimidation tactics are as effective as your fighting skills," he said with a smirk. "Poor Hawthorne ran in the opposite direction from your family. Did you see? He nearly took out a potted shrubbery on his way."

His laugh was a rich sound that made her smile in kind despite her anger toward him.

"Ah, my Lady Englebright. Are you prepared for a twirl about the room?" Jacob smiled at her warmly, approaching them and interrupting the conversation. "I must say, I am not sure when last I had such a jolly-good time with such good company."

Rosalind could not help noting that his gaze wandered toward Nan as he made that declaration. He was such a pleasure to be around, unlike some other gentlemen in attendance. She hoped her friend would not let her reservations cause her a missed opportunity. She would have to make sure that was not the case, she thought as she turned her attention away from Kristoff back to Jacob.

"I am yours to lead, my good sir. Shall we?" she said, offering him her hand.

Chapter Twenty

Viscount Durham, Elias Corbin, was finally going to have the connection of the century through his nephew, then nearly all he had worked toward would be complete. If they could get the banns posted within the month, then it would be possible to have a babe within the year. He stepped down from his black carriage with the aid of his driver, placed his top hat upon his head, and grabbed the silver knobbed cane from his valet within.

He liked to think he struck an imposing figure as he walked across the drive and up the entryway stairs. He had seen this manor many times, but only from afar, never quite figuring out the best way to gain entry or an introduction to Umberland and potentially the heir of the century if his nephew could just do as he was told.

Elias had heard Umberland preferred to be called by his surname, Englebright, even by local gentry, which was just too common a thing to be allowed, thought the Viscount. These country folk seemed to forget their station, which meant the local townsfolk would forget theirs as well. Everyone should know their place in the world, he thought; a motto he hoped he had instilled in his nephew as well. If Jared was correct, Englebright was known to invite the low-borns to his balls, which was galling, to say the least. With the potential of what were essentially country peasants in attendance, his nephew would once again be the target of fortune seekers. He shook his head as he admired the massive estate before him.

He could see the grandeur of the manor now that he was in closer proximity. He had not thought it large enough to house a ballroom of any significance, but he could now see he was mistaken. The opulence of the home was apparent in every detail. The marble stairs had even been engraved with scrollwork upon the risers. No expense had been spared in the décor for the celebration either. Hothouse flowers adorned the entry doors and the marble lions guarding the front walkway. The lions had garlands of greenery and roses, of all things, upon their heads like halos.

"Whimsical as well as horse-mad, it seems," he said to Jared, who followed and was directing two smaller boys with his trunk.

Luminaries, just now visible in the waning sunlight, had been lit all along the length of the drive and paths leading into the garden beyond. The grand oak doors were lined with cut glass sidelights and transom windows, throwing small rainbows out at him from the candelabra light beyond. Through the sidelight windows, he could see a massive grand stairway leading to a second-floor landing that was also lined with delicate luminaries and more hothouse flowers.

"Again, roses," he said in disgust. He hated roses. Their smell was too cloying and put him forcefully in mind of the heavy perfumes favored by old dowagers who prowled the ballrooms husband-hunting – but to have so many delivered this early in the season was quite impressive. As he approached the door, a rather elderly butler opened it to allow him entry and bowed. Without a word, Elias handed the servant his card, hat, and cane and walked in, awaiting his formal announcement.

Harold noted the air of superiority of this Viscount Durham, but had no recollection of ever having heard the man's name. He must be of some import to have such an austere demeanor. He led the man to the ballroom entry for immediate announcement.

He called out in a loud, clear voice, "The Honorable Viscount Durham."

As Elias entered the ballroom, he took in the scene in a single glance, as was his nature and innate ability. He was inordinately pleased to see his nephew dancing with the most beautiful lady in the room. The way Umberland looked upon the girl, he assumed that she was Lady Rosalind Englebright. He inquired as much from the wizened old serving man.

"You man, who is that lady in the green dress dancing just there?" he asked, waving his hand in their general direction.

"That is M'lady, my Lord. She is the daughter of His Grace, Duke Umberland, and your host. He is coming your way now. Shall I leave you to it, my Lord, or would you like me to fetch you a refreshment after your long ride?"

"Ah, a man who knows his business, are you? Off with you. I can make my own way," he said with a dismissive wave of his hand and set out to meet his host.

"Very good, my Lord," said Harold as he departed the room with a sniff.

"Durham, at last we finally meet," said his host as he extended a hand and gave Elias's hand a hearty shake. "That nephew of yours is quite the master when it comes to stables. We have enjoyed a grand discussion most of this day on how we can mutually benefit from mixing my Arabian stock with his. With his training, our combined stables would be the talk of all Europe. We may have come to an accord on that account, I do believe."

He smiled kindly at Elias as he led him deeper into the room. "You must be very proud of him," he said, looking back at the young man and his smiling daughter dancing.

"I am happy to hear that mutually beneficial arrangements could be made, Umberland. I see my nephew has made the acquaintance of your lovely daughter. Could one hope for arrangements beyond those of your stables, perhaps?" Elias asked with the raise of an eyebrow as he looked at the young couple smiling and conversing easily upon the dance floor.

Taken a bit aback by the forwardness of the viscount, Lord Englebright decided to reserve judgment on the man. He likely just wanted what was best for his nephew. Who could fault an aging lord for that? He, himself, wished to see his children beneficially wed, but only if that meant happily as well. "Ah, well. My Rosalind is a bit like my dear Anna. She has a mind of her own when it comes to love, I fear.

I would not press the girl into a decision that is not of her own making."
Lord Englebright laughed amiably as he eyed the viscount.

"Just so, Umberland. Just so," Elias said, but his dismissive tone
seemed he was inclined to disagree.

"I do say, I know this is our first meeting, but you do look familiar.
Have you perchance been to this area before…or perhaps I have seen
you in London?" Englebright questioned.

"No, no. Can't say that we have met, old boy. But sadly, I have
been told I have one of those faces that seems familiar to so many." He
smiled wanly. "I suppose my lack of characteristic features lends to
such. I fear I have been a bit of a recluse for some years now. Dear
Jacob is the one who has been the traveler, building his reputation as
an expert in horseflesh and all that rot."

He looked back at his nephew as he escorted the lady from the
floor and bowed over her hand.

"Do you get to London often? That is quite a distance from here,"
he noted, never taking his eyes off his nephew.

Damn it, Elias thought. Jacob had placed a kiss above her hand as
he led the woman to her next dance partner, who was a beast of a man
who stood at least half a head taller than Jacob. He could only hope the
brute frightened the poor chit back into his Jacob's arms. His nephew
should have been bolder, he thought, and placed his lips on the girl's
hand. Clearly, he would have to intervene if this was to go to plan.

Turning back to Englebright, he continued, "As I said, I am a bit
reclusive of late. I am more interested in history and ancient tomes and
puzzles of ancient times, I fear. I am a bit boring for most. But yes,
Jacob has done well with his little hobby. He is steadfast and
dedicated…fine stock, he is," Durham said to him, nodding.

Englebright realized the insinuation the second the man made it.
He appeared quite intent on an understanding between his Sprite and
the man's nephew. 'Little hobby,' he had called his nephew's
accomplishments. He would think the man was at least a bit proud of
what the young man had done.

"Well, by my reckoning, Jacob has made a name for himself, that
is to be certain." Englebright smiled at the man.

"Just so, Umberland," the viscount stated. "Will you excuse me, Your Grace? I would like to have a word with my nephew before the next song begins. We are not accustomed to being absent from one another. I fear I am a doting old uncle and grew lonely in his absence."

Elias realized Englebright was clearly a sentimentalist. Perhaps he could use that to his advantage. The man would surely empathize with one of his own class, he thought. He did not wish to seem rude as he had just met the duke, but his nephew needed guidance, apparently urgently. He was now approaching what appeared to be a simple town girl in a rather plain, yellow dress. It would not do.

Englebright smiled at his guest and inclined his head. "Of course, Durham. Take your time. I would like to introduce you to Lord Derby as well, and perhaps show you my collection on the ancient Egyptians in my library. I actually acquired a bit of papyrus from the area some years back. It was a gift from my Anna. If interest in history and ancient tomes makes one a bore, I fear I am guilty as charged. Would you like to see it?"

That comment captured his attention, Englebright noted, happy to find common ground with this man.

"That sounds like an invitation I'll call upon. Shall we say in an hour, good man?" inquired the viscount.

"Indeed! I'll meet you by the conservatory double doors. It will be a jolly, good show. It's been years since I've dusted off those old parchments. It'll be grand to pull them out from under the special display case where I keep all my historical knick-knacks. There might be a bit of early civilization statues you would enjoy as well." With a nod and a slow smile, the viscount turned to fetch his nephew.

As the viscount walked across the floor toward Jacob, Englebright noted the young man did not seem thrilled with his uncle's arrival. Odd, he thought, considering Durham spoke the words of a doting uncle.

"Uncle, I see you have finally arrived," Jacob said, inclining his head in deference. "Might I introduce you to Lady Englebright and her companion, Elsa? I fear I have to deliver this lovely lady to her next partner, but…I have most enjoyed our twirl about the room."

Rosalind curtseyed deeply in recognition of the viscount's position and extended her hand. The viscount took it and kissed the air above it.

"It is a pleasure, my Lord," Rosalind commented. "Welcome to our home. I hope you do enjoy your stay. I must say, my companions and I have enjoyed your nephew's company. He is of a quick wit and fine humor. I do hope this is the first of many visits."

Rosalind curtseyed again as she and Elsa turned and walked toward their next partners. Elias looped his arm through his nephew's and pulled him away from the prying ears, smiling at him proudly.

"Well, well, my boy, it seems you have done it on your own," he said, clapping Jacob on the back. "When can I expect you to seal the deal with Umberland? The man seems to hold you in high regard already."

Jacob was taken aback by his uncle's obtuse comments about Lady Rosalind. Although he had known her only for a short amount of time, he was embracing the openness and cordial ways of the family. It was a new perspective that he had never witnessed before. With that in mind, all he could say was…"Sir, please. I have known the girl for a few days. I think you mistake her kindness for more than it is intended. There has been no understanding made, nor have I discussed such with her father. I have not decided to pursue her in that manner."

"You dolt!" he hissed, never removing the smile from his face. "You are in the perfect position to get everything we have worked so hard to obtain. Just think what a position in this household could mean for me, for you…for the Corbin name. You will do exactly as we planned, no excuses. If the girl does not hold you in her sights for husband, then we will compromise her so she has no choice in the matter. Oh, don't look at me like that. I am no beast," he said as Jacob's mouth fell agape incredulously. "These simple, country Ton will send her off packing for nothing more than a stolen kiss. It's not as if I wish you to bed the chit on the garden green."

Jacob blushed in reaction to his uncle's crass words, looking around to ensure they had not been overheard. "Sir, I am engaged for this next dance. I will take your comments under advisement," he said with a scowl as he turned and began walking away without so much as a by-your-leave. As he turned, Elias grabbed his arm and whispered, "Remember your duty. I have given you everything your father never could, boy. You will obey me. This is the final piece. I am meeting her father in the library in an hour. I expect you to have her there alone. A simple kiss…I ask for no more unless you fail me in this!"

Jacob was sickened by this man's resolve to find a womb with no regard for the chosen lady's thoughts. He simply could not understand the man's insistence on having an heir so urgently. Why had they not stayed in London if that had been his goal, rather than running off to the country with limited prospects?

As he walked away, he could see Uncle Elias sneer in his direction. What must the other guests think? This was no way to make an impression. For the first time, he was ashamed by his uncle's behavior. He turned and smiled at his uncle tightly so anyone watching would think nothing amiss, and went to find his next dance partner, a lovely girl by the name of Charity Glasswell. Had her father not approached him for an introduction, he would not have requested the dance at all.

He would much rather dance with Nan, but more than one dance would cause gossip…and he knew for sure his uncle would demand they return to London if something as "untoward" as his association with a seamstress was mentioned even in passing. *I mean to stay here, Uncle,* Jacob thought. *If you are so interested in an heir, perhaps you should marry the lady and leave me be.* He sighed to himself, slapped a smile upon his face, and held his hand out to the waiting girl. "Shall we?"

Chapter Twenty-One

Rosalind had no eyes for any other than her dance partner and noticed nothing else in the room. She felt as though her palms were growing moist at the prospect of dancing with Kristoff.

Kristoff, she noted, did not seem as intent on her. She glanced over her shoulder to see what had him so interested. It just appeared to be Jacob preparing to dance with Miss Glasswell. Perhaps she had been wrong about a mutual attraction. She blushed thinking of how she had all but forced herself upon the man. What if it had been unwanted affection? Andrew said he walked away because he was a gentleman, but what if it was because he really was not interested in her like that, and it had been completely unwanted affection? Lord, she had even called kissing him an experiment. Well…all the better if he was not interested in her. One fewer thing to worry about, she thought.

"I believe this next dance is the long scarf," Kristoff said as he took Rosalind's elbow, startling her as she stared back over her shoulder at Charity and Jacob. "Do you know the steps, or shall we sit this out?"

"I am familiar with it, my Lord," she said hesitantly. Turning her head to the side, she murmured barely audibly, "Perhaps they have a spare scarf that I can stuff into my bodice."

Smirking, he replied, "I'm sorry, my Lady, I did not quite catch your comment." He had heard her clearly enough and realized how uncomfortable she was with so much flesh exposed, which was not the impression he got from other ladies in her position. He thought he might finally start to understand some of her nature. She really was uncomfortable in formal attire but was striving to please her father and make sure the crush was none the wiser to her discomfiture. He already knew she was unique. He had far too quickly grown to appreciate those differences.

"I suppose we shall see how we fare then, my dear," he said in a near whisper, sweeping her onto the dance floor as he took the offered length of fabric that would serve as the scarf in the dance.

The dance director handed out the remainder of the scarves as the music began; the women lined up on one side of the floor across from the men, who lined up on the other, with scarves stretched across to form an alleyway. The leading lady was to twirl into the scarf, meeting her partner, waltz under the remaining partners' scarves, and then unwrap again, raising their extended scarf for the next couple to dance under. It was a simple dance, but it could be quite intimate.

The melody was slower than she had anticipated for this particular dance, which was normally accompanied by a jaunty tune. Rosalind began the slow winding of the fabric around her waist as she twirled closer to Kristoff, then felt his arm slide gently around to place his hand into the small of her back. His other hand held the scarf a bit tighter than was customary, drawing her closer than propriety likely would permit. Rosalind began to breathe more deeply, enjoying the feel of his warm touch more than she knew she should.

"Your dress is quite stunning, Rosalind." He said her name in a low whisper near her ear as he waltzed her under the scarf alleyway.

Hearing her given name upon his lips felt like a caress, sending shivers down to her toes. Beneath the heavy sweep of her lashes, she cast a glance upward, her eyes betraying a hunger she could scarcely identify. It was a feverish longing for him to desire to kiss her as much as she wanted to kiss him. As the dance pulled them apart, she began a slow, almost torturous unwinding, her gaze anchored to his with every rhythmic revolution. Even as she drifted toward the line of other ladies, her world narrowed until the crowded ballroom dissolved into nothingness; there was only him.

She loved the way the candlelight caught the sun-darkened hue of his skin; the shadows seemed to trace the provocative curve of his mouth. Her focus snagged upon that singular, shallow indentation just beneath his lower lip, a mark that lent his smile a dangerous, but alluring quality. His lips were full and soft, and the feel of them had been like the caress of something decadent across her mouth. A shameful heat flooded her chest as she imagined the sensation of her tongue against that roughened, whiskered flesh.

Caught in the throes of a silent, scandalous inventory, she caught her own lip between her teeth, her mind venturing into territories that could well end all her plans for herself, but only if she acted upon them. As long as her vivid wanderings across his flesh remained her secret, she was safe enough. She let her mind settle back into the memory of what his lips had felt like on hers, on the sensation as his tongue had gently flicked over the delicate span of her neck, causing a heat to blossom in her secret places and suffuse throughout her entire body.

She felt a scarlet flush deepening across her cheeks as she forced her mind back to the present. She knew it was a testament of her want for him, yet she refused to break this spell on her senses as she stared into his stormy eyes. Then, as the violins rose in a frantic, soaring crescendo, she was swept back toward him. The tempo quickened, the air grew thin, and as she spun back into the waiting heat of his embrace, her breath caught at the first scorching touch upon her again. From that one point of contact, she nearly forgot that he had been speaking to her seconds before.

"Thank you, my Lord, I am glad you like it. It is a Nan creation," she stated breathily as she neared him, coiling herself ever closer to his strong arms.

As he laid his hand upon her back again, she felt a jolt of energy dancing up and down her spine, and again she recalled his hands upon her face as his lips claimed hers in the woods and maze. She was breathing faster in time with his steps. She knew Nan was right about being intimate without love, but she wanted to burn like the sun with this man. She wanted to feel all that his bold look promised. When she looked into his eyes, she knew he read the desire she was trying to mask and failing. She heard a low growl in his throat as she began to unwind and wanted to cry out in the absence of his warmth.

As he loosened his hold, he knew he had to take control of this situation or, by God, they would be wed by morning just so he could bed her. As she slowly unwound, he commented to her conversationally across the floor, "It does bring a word to mind."

She looked at him quizzically, but her eyes still smoldered with what he could only describe as an invitation. He could not tear his gaze from her as they awaited their next turn.

Rosalind felt as though his eyes were able to see into her very soul. She felt a delicious sensation each time her turn neared. Her breath was quickening again, which she knew only added to her bosom rising and falling. She saw him glance upon the pale mounds as if he wanted to devour them. Her breasts felt heavy and warm, just as she warmed in other areas that a lady should not be considering on the dance floor. Maybe she could forgive him for his cruel rejection earlier. God help her, she wanted to kiss the man again and see where it might lead. So much for being glad he might not be interested in her.

As the music slowed for her last intertwining, she slowly wound herself next to him and asked in a voice that sounded nothing like her own, "And what word would that be, my Lord?"

He leaned in close enough for her to smell the peppermint on his breath. He gently sighed a warm breeze down her ear.

"Doxy." A low laugh rumbled from him at the shock of her final twirl away from him as the music ended.

She gasped as she realized the implication of the word. Unwinding further, reaching the end of the scarf, she heard his laughter. He appeared the perfect picture of merriment, as if this were the most enjoyable dance to be invented. But she knew…oh, that man. He had listened to her and Nan's entire conversation that day when she was on the stump.

Lord, what else had she said, she thought as she tried to search her mind, but her lustful wonderings combined with the shame that she had failed her papa had thrown her mind into a scattered torrent. She did not need to worry about dishonoring her father this night, for she had already done it with her unhinged tongue that day, and then being caught in the stable lad's breeches.

Mortified, she knew she had to escape the room for but a brief respite. She felt tears begin, and damn it all, she never cried; now twice in one day. How she wished she had her breeches. Blast this ridiculous dress, these horrid slippers, and blast that beast of a man. What would

Papa think? She had been trying so hard, she thought as her cheeks began to glow. Propriety required that she allow Kristoff to escort her from the dance floor. She bowed to him without another word and exited the ballroom without a second glance in his direction or to see who might be watching the exchange. She knew her face glowed. She would just feign heat exhaustion…or better, the vapours.

Chapter Twenty-Two

Sir Mycroft Hawthorne had not failed to note the hasty departure of his newfound love. He thought he might have to call the brute out for upsetting his lady, but decided it might be best to follow her and comfort her instead. Perhaps if he were lucky, he could steal a kiss as well. At a near run, he exited the ballroom in pursuit of his Lady Rosalind.

Edmund had just escorted the enchanting Nan from the floor when he noticed that his fool of a friend, Mycroft, had taken off after Rosalind in a near run as she exited the ballroom. The boy had no hope of catching her, of course, but Edmund thought it best to head him off before he made a complete nuisance of himself. This was his and Michael's fault, after all. Ros was going to strangle them both.

"Mrs. Willoughby, I thank you for the finest dance of my evening," Edmund said gallantly as he kissed her hand. "I fear for now, I must rescue Ros from a predicament of our making," he said, as Michael joined him with a worried look upon his face.

"Oh, dear, Edmund. This sounds dire. Shall I follow and offer assistance?" she asked, knowing what the twins were capable of.

"No need to vex yourself, my fine Lady," Michael stated with a bow. "I shall attend to my brother to resolve this minor inconvenience," he stated as he grabbed Edmund's arm and pulled him from the room quickly.

Nan was immediately concerned, if not a little suspicious, and thought to seek out Lord Englebright for urgent assistance. She worried about what the boys might have done to poor Rosalind. Dear Lord, she hoped this had nothing to do with that wretch of a boy, Mycroft. The child had stared at poor Rosalind's décolletage for their entire dance and had not stopped leering at her since. Nan thought she had seen

Lord Englebright near the conservatory doors with Charles, Lord Derby, and another gentleman whom she believed to be Viscount Durham. Oh, but if she made it across the room and then told his Lordship her concerns, it might be too late for whatever mischief the twins had concocted. She decided to head them off instead and made her way out the door.

Elias had not missed that the Lady Englebright had left the ballroom in some haste, apparently upset at something her dance partner had said. *Good*, he thought. This was the opportunity that Jacob needed. If he could intercept the chit, then he could set things in motion. Surely, he could manage a kiss so it would be seen, even if he had to help the boy a bit. He sought his nephew's blond head and saw him leave the room in a bit of a rush. His nephew had clearly heeded his warning and taken things in hand. *He will need a ready witness, however*, he thought.

"Shall we go take a look at those scrolls, Umberland? I must admit, I am anxious to see them," Elias said.

"Certainly, Durham. I have a fine, well-aged scotch in the library I've been trying to share with Derby for weeks as well. Charles, do you mind playing host in my absence?" Englebright asked, patting his son upon his shoulder as he began to lead Durham and Derby from the room, but was stopped by guest after guest telling him what a fine time they were having.

Observing the shadow of discontent that had settled upon Durham's features, Englebright chose a more winding, secluded path through the throngs to expedite their exit from the ballroom. He mused inwardly whether the man possessed a genuine, scholarly passion for ancient parchments, or if he was simply possessed of that peculiar arrogance that rendered conversation with a mere man of trade a loathsome chore.

Englebright was well aware of the haughty delusions harbored by many of the Ton—those who fancied themselves incapable of true rudeness toward the untitled, believing instead that their social inferiors found comfort in being reminded of their place. They were to be a silent, but necessary fixture - an invisible asset in the machinery of high society to be used but not appreciated. It was a philosophy Englebright found utterly preposterous.

He had detected none of the loathsome behavior in Jacob's treatment of the staff or others in his short stay at the manor, and wondered how in the world the young man had escaped harboring such feelings when it was clear as the crystal chandeliers above that Elias moved through the world draped in a gilded cloak of his own self-importance. He would suffer the one man for the sake of the other, he supposed as they left through the conservatory to make their way to the library.

Miss Persephone Maxwell was in love. Edmund was such a handsome and well-mannered gentleman. He was from good stock, a marvelous dancer, and had such hopes and aspirations for when he was done with his studies. She sighed dreamily to herself as she watched him walk away. He had kissed her hand, she thought with a blush. She had only dreamt of a night such as this.

The romantic music and ambiance of the evening were too much. Oh, how she wished she could convince him to take her for a stroll amongst the luminaries in the conservatory. She might even let him kiss her lips, she thought, turning a bit rosier. As she continued staring at his well-dressed back walking away, she saw him approach that Nan woman from the village and his brother, Michael. Nan was low-born but had such a beautiful face and a kindly personality. In that gorgeous sapphire bespoke gown, the woman could be mistaken for nobility. She knew both twins favored her. She did worry that perhaps they fancied her more than they could care for a young miss such as her.

As her fears were getting the best of her, she saw both Edmund and his brother exit the room rather quickly without Mrs. Willoughby and relaxed. In truth, she could not tell them apart from their looks this far away, but just knew she could if she spoke to them. Just maybe she could sneak a moment with Edmund. "Mama, I must be away to the necessary," she whispered discreetly. Gaining her mother's permission to take the short walk down the hall in visibility of the servants, she left the ballroom in pursuit of her true love.

Kristoff had followed the moment he realized Rosalind was vacating the ballroom. He felt like a heel for having treated her so unkindly, calling attention to her bold ways and causing her embarrassment yet again. He was not given to romantic notions, but damn it…he had grown to care about the blasted woman. She was unpredictable, unconventional, and a bit of a female renegade – and the daughter of a blasted duke.

None of these things would have been what he asked for in a mate had anyone thought to ask him before he had met her – well, being the daughter of a duke was irrelevant. She did not exactly behave as one, though she did seem to be trying very hard tonight, except perhaps while they were dancing. After the way she had been looking at him during their dance, as if he were the last bonbon on a platter of sweets, it had taken a sheer act of will to quell his heated blood so he did not throw her over his shoulder like a brute and take her to the nearest possible bed in all haste. If he stayed in this place any longer, he feared he would never wish to leave. Damn it, he had to complete his task and return home…and did not intend to do it with a wife, especially not the wildling creature Lord Englebright had reared.

He did not give a damn about Maude's holes or his vow to her. Come morning, he would gain the signatures he required from Charles and Andrew and leave this madhouse before he debauched the beautiful maiden. He sighed and ran his hands through his hair as he looked one way down the hall and then the other, sighing in frustration. He knew he could not leave, no matter how much he wanted. He had to wait for his messenger to return from Newcastle with the records Englebright needed to solve his mystery…all he needed was yet another mystery. Englebright had been more than hospitable, but Kristoff could not help wondering if the man had not placed him in the position of guard in order to gain a son-in-law. Surely, he knew his daughter was mad, though. She could marry one of those gents in the ballroom who were far more suited to taking a wife such as her in hand. Odd, but that thought made him scowl. He could only imagine what a member of the Ton would do to her free-spirited nature. She really *was* quite perfect.

Dear God, he thought, the water in the blasted village must be infected with madness if he was beginning to think *that* way of the blasted woman and her breeches — and, apparently, the damned woman was no slower in a skirt than she was in trousers. He had been no more than a few seconds behind her, but she was nowhere to be seen. Shaking his head and smiling, he decided he was indeed infected with madness.

Since he had met her, she had been a storm of energy around him, making him question everything he ever thought he wanted. His dream of a quiet life in the country was slowly being rewritten on the pages of his mind. Pictures of his own children traipsing through the wilds after a red-haired nymph leading them on a hunt for treasure, just as her mother had done for her, now illustrated the new story he was writing for his future. He shook his head, knowing he was done for but smiling at the prospect. Yes, he was good and truly mad.

He decided to once again go left and see if he could come upon her. As he turned at the end of the long corridor, he heard the most God-awful raucous tones coming from the library. A cacophony of cats would have been more pleasing to the ears.

He slowly opened the door and peeked in and found Rosalind seated at the ornate baby grand piano, her green gloves thrown onto the floor and her green slippers lying beside them. She was swinging her stockinged feet freely with each additional stab on the piano keys. She was banging out the most incongruous tune he had ever heard. Clearly, musicales were not in her future, he thought and smiled to himself as he clicked the door closed behind him.

She glanced up with a look of consternation and weariness on her face.

"Come to further insult me, my Lord?" she asked with no inflection, indeed no feeling at all in her voice. "Perhaps you enjoy the word 'tart?'"

She banged out another harsh note.

"'Harlot?'"

Bang.

"Or even 'hussy?'"

Bang, bang, bang.

"That is a robust-sounding word…hussy." She drawled the word out again as she banged another few notes on the poor, abused instrument.

Kristoff smiled at her word choices as he slowly sauntered over and sat beside her. He placed his hands upon the keys and began quietly playing Mozart's Sonata No. 11 with perfection.

Rosalind took a deep breath, trying to cool her anger, and looked at him. He was watching her…not even looking at his hands as he played perfectly. She scowled, annoyed anew. "Is there anything you do poorly, sir?"

He stopped playing, dropped his hands, and cocked one well-turned eyebrow at her.

"Leaving you alone," he said huskily. "I have tried and have it not in my power. You are like a will-o'-wisp, drawing me ever closer to your flame," he said, tracing a long, rough finger over the top of her hand. "I know I should retreat, but you, madam, are a unique creation the likes of which I have never met – and God help me, I am ensnared."

He placed his hand upon her cheek and smiled gently at her as he laid a delicate kiss upon her forehead.

Rosalind was stunned into silence. Fear warred with this new feeling of excitement. Her insides were humming with some unknown force. Her anger slipped away like the mist of a summer morning, but the fear…that was hers to hold, wasn't it? She had nurtured it, swaddled and kept it close like a precious thing that protected her heart. She was so confused, but this felt right, and there was no harm in this moment…just feeling for this moment, was there? It did not mean she yielded her heart to him. She tentatively placed her hand upon his thigh, which was pressed against her own. Such a contrast, she thought. She then laid her head upon his shoulder with a sigh, her mind in a tumult.

He accepted her as she was. How could that be? This perfect Greek god, with his strength and honor; a nearly perfect gentleman. She smiled…not a turnip, but a robust man who could let her live as she preferred, it seemed. Could she share with him all of that which Nan spoke about? Could she let go of all her fears? She just did not know if she could allow it, but…

Heavens, just being with him felt like …well, like stepping into the sun after a winter's storm…all warmth and near to blinding brightness. He accepted her, this man who was not family or a lifelong friend. With that acceptance came an exhilarating freedom. She was a fledgling jumping out of the nest for the first time. Oh, Lord, but she was falling, not flying.

That realization nearly knocked her off the bench. She refused to think beyond here and now. Tomorrow would come soon enough; for now, she was basking in his acceptance. She relaxed into his side and placed her hand upon his, acceptance for acceptance, she thought, but could not yet meet his eyes.

As he raised her hand to his lips, taking her small surrender as the gift he realized it to be, the door burst open – none other than Mycroft Hawthorne stood there with a sword, which by the looks of it, had been pulled from the decorative armor in the hall.

"Avast, you scoundrel! Unhand my lady. I challenge you," he half-shouted, half-squeaked.

Rosalind jumped up and groaned as she saw the fool followed by no fewer than half a dozen others, including the twins, who looked from Rosalind to Kristoff and then to their father. In the span of a wink, they paled, mouths agape. Miss Maxwell, on the other hand, peeked from around Michael and looked exhilarated by a bit of new gossip as she looked from them to the twins.

Nan looked at her friend and grimaced with a look of resigned acceptance as Elsa beamed and almost clapped her hands in apparent delight. Jacob looked like someone had kicked his prized stud, for some odd reason, as he looked from his uncle to them. Lord Derby, who just wanted the scotch she had certainly overturned in her haste to remove herself as far as possible from Kristoff, stared at the amber puddle on the floor and looked as if he would cry.

Lord Durham was oddly red-faced, like he had been personally offended, worse even. He looked furious and glared at his nephew. But the worst thing she saw was Papa's head drop in disappointment. He just sighed, shoved young Mycroft out of his way, and looked pointedly at Kristoff.

"Sir, I believe we need to have a conversation," he stated, shaking his head as he extended his hand to the man to guide him from his daughter's presence.

Rosalind sank to the floor in bewilderment as Nan shooed the men out and closed the door behind them.

"Dearest," Nan soothed as she gathered her friend up in a comforting embrace. Poor Rosalind's face had drained completely of color. Her friend looked as if she had just been sentenced to the gallows.

"What will Papa do?" she asked faintly, not looking up.

Nan squeezed her shoulders gently. "What he must, Love. What he must…"

Chapter Twenty-Three

"A wedding! Papa, you cannot be serious!" Rosalind pleaded like a woman on her way to the gallows.

It was nearly three in the morning, and the guests had finally settled down from the rumblings of the evening's excitement. Nan had soothed her and led her to her papa's study so Rosalind might try talking sense into him and Kristoff. She was failing miserably. She had found the matter already decided amongst the men. Papa and Lord Derby seemed oddly pleased with the situation. Poor Kristoff simply seemed resigned to his fate and expected her to accept the same, by the look he gave her. She could not believe this. The whole scene in the library had been so much of a debacle that a court jester from King Arthur's era could not have done it justice.

"Avast!" Really, Mycroft, she thought as she shook her head. She was surprised the idiot didn't charge and use a haymaker punch while he was at it. What a mess, she sighed at the thought.

Lord Englebright just stared back at her, his expression set as if carved in stone. One look at him, and she knew it was hopeless. Her papa never made decisions without much deliberation. Once his decision was made, it was made. She groaned inwardly, squared her shoulders, and vowed she would just have to change his mind.

"I am sorry, Sprite, but there must be a wedding. Too many peers witnessed the show. The rumors are already spreading like wildfire among the guests and staff. I have Elsa spinning a tale of undying love to those who are stirring now. I cannot have your reputation ruined. I know you care little for propriety, but hang it all, Rosalind, there is too much at stake."

"What does that mean, Papa? What could possibly be at stake if I stay in the country and continue with life as before? The Ton will go back to their happy lives, and I can go back to my projects. The rumor mill will find some other poor victims before long. Tell him, Lord Derby, please. Kristoff, what man in his right mind would ever wish to marry me? Tell them this is not necessary."

Derby grimaced at her, clearly uncomfortable as he started to rise. Englebright waved him back to his seat and nearly growled at his daughter.

"Damn it, Rosalind," he said to her sternly. "I will have you safe. This opportunity has presented itself to see you married to a good man and safely away from here." He ran his hands through his thick, graying hair and looked at her, his expression set with determination.

"Papa," she demanded, "what are you talking about? Why would you want me to go away? What about my plans…my school and the children," she cried, looking to Derby for his support.

"I fail to see how I am so suddenly unsafe," she commented incredulously, cocking her head at him with a skeptical look upon her face. "What has happened? We just had a ball, and all seemed well enough."

He had never raised his voice to her nor cursed in front of her. She was growing concerned and knew it showed upon her face. What in the world was happening? His response was completely out of proportion with the scene found in the library. Kristoff had not even been kissing her or anything that lacked propriety at the time they were discovered. She knew the Ton loved a good intrigue, but this was madness – and now, Kristoff was eyeing her as if he just understood something significant, nodding as if agreeing with his own internal thoughts. Shifting in her seat in discomfort, she turned her eyes back to her father.

Lord Englebright took a deep breath and captured her stare with his own. Then he began to explain a past he had hoped to forget and had hoped she never needed to know. When she discovered her brothers already knew, there would be hell to pay. He had hoped to spare her. Oh, hang it all, he had hoped to spare himself the looks of accusation she would give for not having explained sooner. He sighed and bowed his head.

"Please understand, I would be loath to force you into anything against your will, but I'm afraid I've already put you at risk. You see, this…" He extended his arms as if to encompass her and Kristoff. "Is all my fault."

Dropping his arms, he walked over to the whisky console, pulled out a goblet and decanter, and poured himself a large helping of the amber liquid within. He stood in front of the fireplace; the light danced across the worry mapped in each crease of his face and made his scotch glow in the crystal glass. He swirled the liquid as he gathered his thoughts.

He looked over his shoulder to his right for support from his dear friend, Derby, who continued to sip his scotch with a furrowed brow and looked as comfortable as a rabbit caught in a snare. He was eyeing Rosalind and Kristoff as they sat next to one another on the soft leather sofa adjacent to the massive mahogany desk.

The poor girl had plopped rather inelegantly onto the settee and looked bewildered, as if she had been caught in a hurricane and was trying to make sense of the storm now surrounding her. Kristoff, on the other hand, sat quietly, with his arm resting on the back of the sofa. Every once in a while, he would gently stroke the back of Rosalind's neck with his fingertips, as if to give her small reassurances that he was still present and attentive.

"Papa, I don't understand. How is this your fault? You did not order Kristoff to follow me into the library. That buffoon, Mycroft, truly made a fiasco of the whole affair," commented Rosalind.

Lord Englebright blew out a long breath and finally sat down in his wingback chair. "In fact, my dear…I did."

He smiled wanly at her. He glanced over at Derby, giving a silent signal that only the two of them understood. Speaking up, Derby began slowly.

"There has been a bit of trouble, my dear, that may have inadvertently put you at risk. You see…well, your father and mother had quite the adventures before they were wed. They were not always who you knew them to be. They are not simply members of England's elite. They have a colorful past that helped put away many of this country's enemies," he said, looking up at her to see how she was taking the news. She continued to look bewildered.

"It was in the ending year of the Napoleonic War that your mother and father helped alert our armies about brigands, treasonous behavior, and the movements of Napoleon's forces within the current Netherlands, your mother's homeland. The country can never repay them, even though we have tried. Your father keeps refusing any extension of gratitude. Stubborn man, if I do say so myself." Derby smiled at his old friend.

Clearing his throat, Derby continued. "That's how we met, Georgie and I, and others, of course. We all grew close, like a small family, as the year went on. Most of them were recruited straight out of university or sooner. Some were sent abroad, such as me and our dear friend Janssen, or remained within the confines of England to decipher code, such as your father. We were all working in the field in some fashion. Your mother, dear one, was a liaison in the Netherlands, an area of greatest danger, even though it was near her family seat, which is now part of Belgium," he said, nodding to Kristoff.

"Her missives were masterpieces of deception, veiled in the tender language of a lady's devotion, yet beneath the ink lay warnings of the darkest treachery. She alerted us to every illicit cargo — clandestine shipments of steel, weapons, and even stolen gems intended to fill the coffers of the Bonaparte cause. Through these 'love letters,' she unmasked the vipers in our midst: French agents and those false patriots who swore fealty to the Crown while sharpening daggers for its heart. It was a nasty business."

He shook his head and took a sip of his drink. "To the world, your parents were merely a pair of lovers lost in a whirlwind courtship; in truth, every endearment was a cipher, and every vow a strike for England's survival."

"The love letters," Rosalind whispered under her breath as understanding dawned. Tears began to stream down her face as she looked at her father, whose silence was as damning as if he had given her a written confession of his secrets.

Kristoff wrapped his arm around her shoulder and began stroking it. They could all see her trembling from Derby's explanation. Kristoff's action was not lost on either of the elder gentlemen. Lord Englebright just kept nodding as if to say he knew this was a sound match. It was just a matter of trying to convince his beloved Sprite that things would work out with Kristoff.

"But, you see, my dearest, the love letters turned into true letters of endearment as we worked together through those turbulent years. We fell deeply in love, your mother and I," her father said, smiling sadly.

"That love has never faltered to this day. I have all of the correspondence between your mother and me locked away in the safe since the duplicate copies have been recently stolen from the War Department. Stolen, we believe, by a ruthless operative known only by the name 'Raven.'"

He raked his hands through his hair, worry creasing his brow. "I never thought the letters would lead to my family's danger."

"If there is danger for you, then I will not leave you. How could you even think it of me? We can face this trial together!" Rosalind's voice had grown fierce with her conviction to stay and aid her father. "If it is so treacherous, why not send the guests away? Why continue with this party? Is it not dangerous for everyone?"

"Sentries have been stationed all about the estate and manor. By the time we sorted that there might be an interconnection between the missing letters and the happenings here, it was too late to call off the festivities without tipping our hand to the Raven. He was not one to sully his hands, but he was always singularly minded in his treachery, likely even now that his network of spies has withered. He always relied on others for the truly vicious work. He was just the ringleader…the intelligence gatherer.

"We thought that if we continued as if we were none the wiser, we might draw him out. Oh, blast…this is a foolish endeavor!" he said, rubbing his face with his hands. "I just needed to see if we could find Pieter for Anna, and in doing so, I put you all at risk."

Her father's voice faltered, but with a sharp cough and a nod, he gestured for Derby to continue the thread of the story before she could utter a word of protest.

Derby resumed the tale as his dear friend was overwrought, but with a darker turn to the story than mere spywork. "There remains another mystery that claimed the life of our most trusted companion, and we fear for his son, Pieter. There was an ambush orchestrated by the villainous Raven, who hunted down our friend, murdered him, and stole his son away into the shadows."

Rosalind gasped as the story of a stolen, possibly murdered child unfolded. Who could be so cruel!

"All these years, we thought Pieter was dead until recently, when I discovered a possible lead on Pieter's whereabouts. You see, we believe he may be here, in England. God help us if he is in cahoots with the fiend. We also believe that the Raven is on the prowl again, looking for the letters. The letters have some damning information about the Raven and clues to his true identity, we are certain. It would send him to the gallows for treason, for sure, if we could find the blasted fiend.

"I am sure the Raven has surfaced and is looking for them, but that means he may be looking for anyone connected to the letters as well. So, your father may be in danger. I am afraid, my dear, that also means you are at risk. Raven would stop at nothing or no one to get what he desires.

"The problem was always that his behavior was seemingly erratic and very unpredictable. We could never sort out his true intent, but know there was always a larger game afoot. He killed, or had killed, many along the way and seemed to enjoy it. His murderous ways came into the light as recently as last month in the death of a War Department guard," Derby said, shaking his head in sorrow. "He was a good man…a family man. It just sickens me."

"And that is why I asked Kristoff to keep an eye on you," Lord Englebright interjected. "I was worried about the Raven, and then those blasted holes started worrying the locals. I could not dismiss that either, though I am certain one has nothing to do with the other, but who is to truly say what the Raven might be about? There were too many ruffians popping up for untold purposes. I have to admit that I am getting too old for this kind of intrigue. So, you see, Sprite, it is my fault; Kristoff *was* chasing you about under my directive. It was all I could think to do to keep an eye on you without hindering your freedom. You know that poor Elsa could not keep up with you. Bless her soul, she is lucky to keep your pace on your idea of a gentle stroll."

Lord Englebright paused and took a long swallow of his drink, then looked intently at his daughter.

She sat silently during his tale, only blinking occasionally in disbelief. She knew the shock was written on her face. Her father and mother had led a second life of mystery and intrigue that she knew nothing of. She wondered if she was the only one in the dark, or if her brothers also knew nothing of this former activity of their parents. She looked at her lap. She understood why her parents wanted this secrecy, but she was also a bit hurt that her father had not trusted her enough to share this detail of this life with her now that she was older.

It had taken a threat from the War Department to get him to come clean. Though she knew he had her best interest at heart, intermingled with the hurt was a brewing anger. He had placed her in the position to be compromised, albeit accidentally. This also put into question the conversation Kristoff had with her in the library. Had he meant any of it, or was it just to keep her under his guard a bit longer?

Looking around from Derby to Englebright, Kristoff cleared his throat and commented as he felt her tense against him. "Why now? After all these years? It just seems odd. I wonder what has changed to make him seek out the letters again." He looked at Rosalind to see how she was handling the news. He could sense a well of frustration and tension building as she drew away from him a bit and squared her shoulders.

Lifting his shoulders, Derby said with a grimace, "I don't know. Maybe the old coot is dying and wants the letters before he kicks off. Maybe it is some smaller part of a larger game he is playing again. All I know is that your father and I promised your mother we would find Pieter and take care of this Raven, and we have failed." He stood, taking one last gulp of his scotch as he added, "Whatever the case, I believe we need to be on the lookout for more threats."

"The Raven has a talent for passing unnoticed," Englebright told Kristoff. "More than once he stood among us without drawing the slightest suspicion. By the time anyone even thought to look for him, he was already gone. His is masterfully skilled in disguise. Do we know when the Newcastle office will send their report on the Haberlin lineage? I hope it arrives soon. We've chased this matter for far too long, and I intend to resolve it—for Anna's sake, and for Janssen's."

He turns to Rosalind. "In the meantime, please lock your sleeping chamber doors at all times. Knowing the fiend, the sooner you are wed, the better, then Kristoff will be at your side day and night to aid in keeping you safe. I can obtain the special license in three days. I know just the man who happens to owe me a favor and will send for it immediately. I suggest in the meantime, we all get some rest."

Derby chimed in, "My men, all well-trusted, are on watch. The next few days may prove a challenge. We cannot send the guests away for fear it may spook Raven if he is about. We can't let him know we are on to him. This may be our last chance to end this."

"I want to help right this wrong for Mother's sake. Even if I am wed…which I am not agreeing to," she said, looking at them all in turn, "I am not leaving. If we continue as if we are none the wiser that he may be about, perhaps we can mention the letters' location and use them as bait to catch this villain. If he thinks his chore will be easy, then no one should be in harm's way. That, and Derby's men should keep everyone safe."

Derby nodded. "It is a sound idea, I think."

"Are you sure that is wise?" George asked him. "There are a great number of guests who will want to stay on for the pre-wedding festivities. We have to ensure the safety of all."

"I think the plan has merit," said Derby, warming to the idea. "I can bring on a few more chaps from the Department who are acquainted with undercover work. They can pose as additional guests to help maintain order." He nodded to George. "Only my most trusted men, mind you," he affirmed.

"Fortunately, we are well-decorated for a celebration, thus we can assure no other strangers need be on the grounds. Nan has already created the most beautiful gown for the occasion, as well." Clapping his hands together in excitement as he warmed to the subject, Englebright looked at Derby. "We should be all set in three days. This is coming together swimmingly. I know it is not proper, but shall we have Kristoff begin staying with her immediately?"

Rosalind flushed at his bluntness and grew angrier by the moment. They were planning her future and her wedding, all while a murderer might be about. Granted, she had never had aspirations of being wed, but knew the day must come at some point. She had assumed she would have some say in some detail of the happenings. Blast it all, she did not even get to choose her décor…or her dress…or her location, or the blasted groom.

She scowled at them all and then sighed. In all honesty, she could not imagine a better groom, but that did not mean she wanted to have the man immediately take up residence in her chambers. She had not even had time to become accustomed to the thought of a fiancé, and certainly not the man warming her bed linens before they had even had their nuptials. What could Papa be thinking?

"He will do no such thing," she nearly shouted. She wanted to throw something at her supposed fiancé. He was nearly doubled over laughing at the entire situation. She had no idea what he found so amusing.

"If I must bring on a roommate, it will be Nan or Andrew or Edmund. Kristoff can sleep in the stables, for all I care. And just what, sir, do you find so amusing about this situation?" She turned on Kristoff, with her hands planted firmly on her hips. "You can't possibly deign it preferable to take me to wed. I will make you a most miserable wife."

She smiled at him sweetly as if in challenge.

"Shall I take up residence with your goat, Madam?" He could not resist goading her further. "Mayhap you have another riding habit I can feed to it to help befriend the beast." This whole situation had gotten completely out of hand. She was in a near rage, and he could not fault her. Not only were they dictating all conditions of her wedding day to her, but they were now discussing rather intimate choices as if she were not even in the room. He now understood why she was such a loon at times. Clearly, it ran in the family, but since it would soon be his duty to comfort his…could he bear to say it…wife…he might as well start now trying to calm her. She looked ready to do battle. Her face was nearly the color of her vivid locks.

"Perhaps, my Lord, if I may be so bold as to ask, is there a room across the hall from your daughter's in which I can reside? I am a light sleeper and would hear if anyone attempted to enter her chambers. This seems a reasonable compromise and will keep your daughter's honor intact as we await the wedding. I would not have her reputation tarnished further by my actions, as I am certain, nor would you. Fear for our loved ones oft makes us prone to quick, sometimes rash decisions," he said as he looked at Rosalind with pleading eyes.

"And, perhaps, my Lady, we can use these three days to become more familiar with one another," he said as he took her hands in his. "I would court you properly if you allow it."

Rosalind lost some of her anger. This was no more his fault than hers, really. She had no idea why he had come to the estate, but certainly, it was not to obtain a reckless bride. What man would want that unless he was completely daft? Taking a deep breath, she slowly nodded in acquiescence. She would make the best of it. Though a whirlwind, the courtship would at least be a grand event. If nothing else, it would ensure Mrs. Mary performed her best meals, and Rosalind would be well-fed, even if miserable.

"I will make you a most miserable wife, sir, but since all seems to be settled to everyone's satisfaction, fine! Court away. I wish you well in your endeavor." Yes, she would be courted, though as to the topic of betrothal…well, she wished him luck, as she had no such plans.

Chapter Twenty-Four

Morning came with the bustle of a busy household, but no room in the manor was busier than the kitchens. The evening meal was always a grand feast at the Englebright household and often took the entire day to prepare. Mrs. Mary was the conductor of a fine symphony of endless entrées that the guests would gush about for the entire season.

She no doubt knew how to set the stage that no one could compare. Many a time, Lord Englebright would hear the ladies whisper, "This is nothing like what I tasted at Englebright Manor." He would come back with a congratulatory bouquet and plenty of accolades for Mrs. Mary to beam over until the next go around.

In addition, his Lordship made sure she had the finest and latest devices to make her tasks all the easier. He was a lover of fine architecture, as was evident throughout the manor, but not displayed anywhere as prevalently as it was in the kitchens and stables. It reflected upon what he loved the most…his fine horses and delectable cuisine. Like the stables, the kitchens reflected Lord Englebright's love for advancing new tastes and culinary techniques.

He spared no expense with the design to make Mrs. Mary's life easier in her gastronomical masteries and quests. It was a wonder that the man was not rotund as well, but his work in the fields with his tenants kept him fit as a fiddle.

Mrs. Mary had rotating spice racks, steam-powered spits, jelly molds, and the finest pots and pans at her fingertips. Lord Englebright would occasionally come and assist with the meal preparation to show her the proper way to utilize her "new gadgets," but Mary knew he just liked to tinker with his new toys.

Once, she had requested to be taught a new style of cooking, so his Lordship had brought in both a notable French and Italian chef to teach her their secrets. She was now famous amongst the Ton for her French and Italian mélange in Victorian cuisine. Some dishes usually could be quite bland and unappetizing, but Mary had a way of spinning sauces, spices, and sugars that made the food come to life with an elaborate taste that not even the pickiest of eaters could resist.

Ahhh…this was her time to shine: here at the manor among Lord Englebright's peers. She could not be prouder or more alive. There would be elaborate courses of soup, roast meats and seafood, vegetables, puddings, crusted pies, and sweets. To cleanse the palate at the end of each meal, the guests were offered cheese and liquor.

The dining table was to be adorned with sweet Anna's favorite china, Sunnyside, with etched glass stemware glittering alongside each plate. The staff took great care in setting the silverware on the table, as well as the beautiful table decorations of flowers, foliage, and candle lights. It would be a sight of true wonder. What could possibly go wrong?

She should have known that something was awry the moment Lady Rosalind did not sneak in for her normal morning pilfering. Why, she had left a stack of nutty buns right by the back door and left for a good fifteen minutes to allow their dear girl time to grab and run. She had not shown up yet.

Instead, Elsa had bustled in all abuzz with the news of sweet Rosalind's betrothal. Mary dabbed her eyes over and over as Elsa told her the news. It was all so romantic. Apparently, no fewer than eight of the partygoers had witnessed his request for her hand, though there was some controversy or some such over the fact that he had shrugged tradition and proposed prior to asking his Lordship's approval, but surely that meant it was a love match.

Mary was not one for gossip, though, so she had no time for speculation. She continued dabbing at her eyes all morning as she bustled about, preparing for the day's meals. This was an important day for feasting…possibly the most important day of her career in the household.

Everything must be perfect for the days to come prior to the wedding, as well. Of course, only the closest family friends would stay on while the special license was procured. Her sweet Sprite had finally found a match, and such a fine one as well, she thought as she stacked nutty buns in a pile. She hoped the lass would be in soon to perform her morning pilfering; she chuckled to herself as she dabbed at her weepy eyes again with the edge of a pristinely white apron.

The gentleman who had asked her hand the eve before was of fine stock and such a looker. Mary had not met the fellow, but took it on Elsa's good word of him that he was a fine fit for her girl. Oh, but how they would miss her something fierce. She dabbed at her eyes more as Elsa spun a magical tale of all that had happened.

Oh, she wished she could have seen it herself; the gentleman went down on one knee after dancing the night away with Sprite. The way Elsa told the tale, after one particularly intimate dance, Sprite was all flustered and fled the room, but Lord Kristoff was having none of it. He was determined to have her hand before the eve was up. Elsa could see the determination in his eyes, she had told them.

"Oh, run on with ye, Elsa. I have to change the menu for the day. How can I serve succulent lamb stew while M'lady is in love? And here I thought she might be ill, as she has not come for her mornin' pilferin'."

Mary left poor Elsa staring after her as she bustled into the drying room to start planning afresh. With an exclamation of delight, she waddled back out with an arm full of truffles that Sprite herself had found in the woods the week prior. How the girl had done so without a pig, she would never ask. Best not to know if her lady had been crawling about like a vagabond. She was so proud, but it was best to check for false truffles, as it was her first time foraging for them.

"The main courses for this evening will now contain truffles. I think my special seared scallops in black truffle beurre blanc sauce will be the first entree," she proudly announced to Elsa, who was now eyeing the pile of nutty buns. It was a fine dish that paired the rich, savory butter from one of the local farmers with French cuisine and Victorian sauce. The pièce de résistance was, of course, the delicate, thinly sliced truffles adorning the top of each seared scallop.

As was her custom, she had all of the newly procured ingredients lined up on the large hardwood table for the main entrée for this evening. Behind the table, a dresser, open at the top and with cupboard doors and drawers, held Mary's cooking equipment to easily grab as she wheeled her magic with butters and sauces. She also had a small bed tucked away for her long hours in the kitchens.

On days of preparations for parties like these, it was common for Mary to sleep in the kitchen, even though his Lordship was not happy about it. It made her happy, so he let it be. She would wake before the earliest of staff members and be the last to go to bed. It was a tiring time for her, but one she loved. To the left of the table was a smaller side room. This was where salted meat hung, other spices, and the precious truffles for this evening meal were allowed to dry and rest.

"The creamy beurre sauce will be studded with gratings of the manor's finest black truffles," she commented as she moved about the room gathering cutting boards and herbs.

It was a tricky dish with the timing and regulating the heat under the pan. Cook was the only one in charge of cooking the sauce. Today, her main concentration was, of course, the truffle dishes. It was going to be a hectic day, but with her in command of the kitchen and the guests all enjoying the gardens, she should have no interruptions.

"She's not come down for her nutty buns, you say? Oh, mercy, I'd best be off, Mrs. Mary. Perhaps m'lady slept in, but that would be a first. I'd best go and find her." Elsa grabbed a nutty bun on her way out and headed up the servants' stairs.

Chapter Twenty-Five

The canopy above Rosalind's bed was made of fine English oak. It was stained a deep mahogany color with intricate carvings around the edges. Four long poles featuring a whimsical curved design that almost resembled mermaid tails with a bit of scroll work at the top supported the overhead canopy.

There was a fine, opaque netting draped elegantly over the canopy frame. The netting allowed light to peek through as the sun rose each morning if Elsa had not pulled the drapes the night prior. At the edge of the netting, a beautiful scroll design was embroidered with golden thread imported from France. Papa would never tell where it came from exactly. It was always his "little secret." In light of the discussion from last night, Rosalind wondered. Everything had changed. Within less than a few hours, her life was turned upside-down. It was unbelievable.

She sat up abruptly. She had been staring at her canopy since they left the library last night. There was not a wink of sleep for her. Though she was up until the early morning due to the evening's events, she was still slipping from her warm coverlet before the sun rose.

Donning a simple dress Nan had conveniently styled with pearl buttons in the front, she slipped it over her head and dressed herself. After having such a well-deserved sit-down about putting herself in danger, she knew it was unsafe and foolish to run about in a lad's clothing.

As she slipped into the simple, blue woolen shift, she was lost in her thoughts of all that had occurred over the last several hours and what she had learned of her parents' past lives. She was just astonished at all her father had shared. And now, he could be in danger. It would destroy her if any harm came to him. She could also not believe how foolishly she had behaved, putting herself at risk of being caught by hooligans in the woods.

Even if there was no other danger, her being caught in the woods and being discovered to be a female could have proven catastrophic. Now, instead of being captured by ne'er-do-wells, she had been snared quite neatly by one extremely handsome and dually unfortunate, stubborn, fool of a man. She supposed she could not say she was snared; rather, he had been. She knew her fate would eventually catch up to her, as women had few choices in life when they were of noble blood.

Her duty was to marry and produce heirs to both secure the bloodline and safeguard her husband's family properties. She knew this, no matter how frequently she attempted to deny it. She honestly just could never make herself give it more thought than she had.

Now, poor Kristoff, out of stubborn nobility, would be forever shackled to her. He must be as miserable as she felt this morning. But that was not what was most important, nor at the forefront of her thoughts. Her father's safety was a priority…and… if he happened to be safe within three days, then there would be no need for a wedding. Kristoff could be free from her. Yes, a great deal could happen in three days.

Pacing back and forth from the window to the bed, then the doorway to the window, and back, she was starting to make tracks on the carpets. She needed to make plans to keep her father safe. He said it himself that he was no longer up for such intrigues. She needed Andrew and some fresh air. With that thought in mind, she quietly stole from her rooms and went down the hall to Andrew's chamber. She did not even bother knocking, but opened the door and let herself in.

Kristoff heard the moment Rosalind's door opened, and she quietly padded down the hall. He also heard the adjacent door open and close, followed by Andrew's sleepy growl.

"Dammit, Rosalind, I know that's you. Why are you not abed? Go away! It is not even dawn, you brat," he growled as he threw a heavy, feather pillow in her general direction. Andrew heard it thud against the door and then the pillow fall to the floor. "And toss me my pillow on your way out!"

Rosalind picked up the pillow and completely ignored his command to leave. She threw the heavy pillow at his head and plopped down beside him. "Wake up! Papa's in danger, and we only have three days to solve this!"

Andrew propped himself up on one elbow and squinted at her in the dark room. He could not even make out her silhouette; the room was so dark. She seemed to have no such issues, as she picked the pillow up again and plunked him in the head anew as if to emphasize her statement. "Get up!"

"Father is in no immediate danger. There are men stationed all around the house and with the servants. Go back to bed…now," he demanded with a loud yawn, yanking her fluffy weapon from her before she could smack him again.

"You knew? Does everyone but me know the happenings in this house?" she demanded, outraged and now in a tug of war over the pillow. She lost.

Having jerked his pillow back from her, he placed it firmly over his head. His muffled voice was barely audible as he said, "Well, you did not know and the twins, and maybe some of the servants…but yes. Now go away." He produced a large yawn as he rolled over, dismissing her with the lump of his back.

"You are no help at all, sir, and quite a disappointment," she huffed as she left the bed and moved to the door. Yanking the door open, she looked back at her brother and huffed again before turning and running directly into a hard chest.

Andrew laughed. He had heard the squeak of footsteps as he had been trying to shoo Rosalind away. He had no doubt that Kristoff was waiting in the wings to intercept her from some foolery. He obviously had learned in a short time that she was going to put some plan into place unbeknownst to anyone.

The man had taken the "watchful eye" to heart. It was wise that he had taken up Charles's old room in order to help keep an eye on Rosalind while they sorted this mess out. Andrew knew as soon as he heard his sister's squeak of surprise what had happened. She was in for the ride of her life with that one. He laughed, closed his eyes, and then immediately sat bolt upright. "Wait…what happens in three days, Sprite?" His question was left unanswered, but he heard a distinct, disgruntled masculine sigh as the door closed.

Chapter Twenty-Six

"What do you think you are about, sir?" Rosalind whispered.

"Exactly what I said I would be about, m'lady," he whispered back as he directed her toward her chamber. His hot breath in her ear sent tingles down her spine. Even this early in the morning, he could become a distraction. She needed some fresh air to think things through and devise a thorough plan. *Away from this…this…man…*Rosalind sighed as she stood before her bedchamber door, which was just adjacent to his.

"Are you going to accompany me to my bedchamber as I acquire my slippers and cloak? I believe I need to go outside for some air. I need to have a think. A stroll in the gardens would do nicely."

As she looked into his eyes, she noticed they had gone dark and stormy as they had before the first time he kissed her. That thought had her licking her lips in remembrance as she glanced at his mouth, one corner turned up in a smirk as if he knew her thoughts, the cad.

Taking a step toward her, he could see her begin to shiver in anticipation of what might happen next. Maybe it was from lack of sleep or just the softness of her lips, but whatever the case, Kristoff could not resist being so close and not touching or feeling her soft skin beneath his calloused fingertips.

He reached up and gently slid his index finger along her jawline, then up to her cheek. She leaned into his palm like a kitten begging to be stroked.

"You've had a go of it, Love," he whispered, as he slowly leaned his head down to place a kiss upon her brow.

"Why don't you go back inside and try to get some sleep? Sleep always clears my head after a trying night," he whispered huskily as he moved his lips down the side of her cheek to place a gentle kiss upon her jaw line. He needed her to go back into her room. He felt his discipline slipping, which was unnerving. He never lost control, not even the few times he had shared his bed with another.

He caught a tear as it slipped down her cheek, and he knew what that tear cost her. In the short time he had known her, he knew her to be proud and controlled, even if life seemed a cacophony of activity around her. A single tear was his undoing. Rosalind began shaking her head and mouthed "no sleep."

Kristoff cupped the back of her head and brought his lips to trace the path of the tear. He shifted her to his door and then twisted the knob into his bedchamber. He guided her into his rooms as his other hand dropped to the small of her back and pulled her against him.

Closing the door behind them, he kissed her with near savage force, breathing in her scent. She still smelled as delicious as last night when they sat next to each other on the piano bench. Everything about her beckoned him to her…to want more and to give her all he had never given to another.

She was his absolute, blessed ruin; she had unmade him entirely; all the things he knew or thought of himself were undone. She had scattered the very fragments of his soul, only to forge them into something new, finer, and more attuned to nothing but her. He could only see her in her imperfect perfection, and he wanted all of her. Again and again, he slanted his mouth over hers as his hands caressed her back and round, taut bottom while pulling her up and against him, leaving her toes barely touching the floor.

He supported her full weight with one arm as the other kneaded through her tangled locks, knotting her hair into his fist and tilting her head back for better access to her neck.

Rosalind gasped. She could not help herself. His kisses felt so wonderful and reassuring, though near animalistic, like she was his last breath before plunging into a dark, forbidden pool. After all that had happened, the guilt of trapping him, the desire to free him and protect her father…all she could wish in this moment was for him to devour her with this ecstasy. She needed this…nay, she desired this beyond any want she had ever felt.

The mixture of emotions coursing through her veins was making it difficult to stand, but Kristoff had that in hand. His strong arm cupped her bottom and pulled it into his masculine length. She felt the familiar hardness there that she had felt in the garden. It heated her to her very core like embers on dry leaves; she burned for something, but knew not what.

Forgetting the tiredness she had felt only moments before, she gave in to her desires, reached for his head, and pulled his mouth back to hers. She felt him growl against her lips, clearly pleased with her boldness as she stroked his tongue with hers. An unexplainable ache was building in her. She needed more…she couldn't think, wouldn't think. She just wanted this man, here and now. She wanted the dark desires she knew a lady should not, even if she did not know exactly what those were.

Kristoff tore his lips from hers and moved his kisses to her ear and neck…nibbling gently with his teeth. He had yet to let go of her hair, but in truth, she loved the feel of him overwhelming all of her senses, locking her to him, being possessed by him.

He was gently unfastening the buttons at the front of her dress. With one quick jerk, her bodice was open and exposing her chemise and the crest of her breasts. She knew he would cup them gently with his hands as he had her buttocks.

She waited, anticipating the feel of his warm hands on her delicate flesh. She was neither embarrassed nor ashamed, only anxious to feel all he would offer her. She refused to think or to try to stop this sweet torment building to some crescendo.

The ache…no, yearning in her nethers was growing. She felt moisture there and fleetingly was embarrassed, but could not care. She continued savoring each caress of his lips on her neck, breath catching, as she waited for the next sensation with which he would assault her senses.

Kristoff knew exactly how to touch her and what was right. And by the gods, this felt right, so very right. Her breath quickened as his hands began to explore her breasts…she had no idea they were so sensitive.

Kristoff pulled her to his hard chest while cradling her breast. He could feel that her nipple was already reacting to the pressure of his hand. *Oh, God! She is the perfect size for my hand.* His lips came down onto hers again. Her mouth was already open and willing. Her sweet tongue was waiting for him to explore and stroke. That was all the encouragement he needed.

He picked her up, cradling her in his arms while his mouth never left hers. His long legs made quick work of reaching the bed as he gathered her skirts in his arms. The bed was a jumble of linens from his brief tossing and turning in the morning hours as he waited for the moment he could see her again.

He sat her upon the edge of the bed and sat back on the floor on his knees, spreading her legs to either side of his hips, tossing her skirts up, and pulling her undergarments above her knees to expose her alabaster thighs. Sitting there on his knees, Kristoff pulled her toward him and began to place kisses along her collarbone, dipping down toward the exposed globes of her breasts.

She gasped and leaned her head back as he captured her breast once again with a warm hand and lifted the weight of it above her chemise, exposing the rose bud of her nipple, then he took it into his mouth. His tongue flicked over her sensitive flesh, which was ripened and hard from his touch. He took the bud into his mouth and sucked upon it, sending another surge of delight and need through her entire body all the way to her toes.

She had no idea a man kissed a woman in such a way, and she arched her back so he would do it again. It felt decadent. He began to loosen the front of her chemise, exposing her breasts completely. He cupped them both and kissed one, then the other, sucking and nipping gently on the swollen nipples. She gasped and nearly cried out with each touch as a bolt of sensation soared through her, gathering at a spot between her legs that seemed to pulse with each lick of his tongue. She arched her back in response to the sweetness melding over her body. Not thinking, she raised her legs and wrapped them around his hips, wanting to feel pressure on that spot that was growing hot and aching.

This love-play was creating a yearning ache low in her belly and all her feminine parts that had been wholly hers until this man had so overwhelmed her senses. His large hands were so gentle as he demanded more and more response from her. She had never felt the likes, but each time there was pressure to her most intimate parts, it made her want more. It was building to a near-frantic intensity.

There was no denying their need for each other. Kristoff's manhood was swollen, frighteningly so, larger than she imagined it could be. She could feel it rub against her leg as she began to squeeze him with her thighs, pulling her mound closer to him so she could feel the hardness of him against that most private part of her body. She felt a hollowness there.

As he kissed her, she began to rub back and forth, nearly writhing in his arms like some wild thing. His hands moved from her breasts to her bottom again and stilled her motion as he continued lapping at her nipples and trailing kisses back to her wanton mouth. She thrust her tongue into his mouth as she rubbed her hips into his hardness, clearly wishing there were no barriers between them.

She would not be denied his most intimate touch. She thrust her hips into his, sending surges of tiny lightning bolts through her belly and down, leaving her nearly panting. She knew she should feel ashamed for behaving so wantonly, but refused to allow thought to intrude any further. She wanted him to take her, push her over this cliff of pleasure, and let her fall. She pushed harder into him, begging without words for what she desired. She felt singed by every kiss and wanted him to feel the same. She wanted to push him over the edge, so he was so driven by need that there was no recourse but to possess her fully, taking the decision from her.

She ran her hands up to his luscious hair, firmly grasping at it to pull him more fully to her as she lifted herself and moved so there was no space between their bodies, save clothing. She knew a little of the love act from listening to the town women when they did not know she was there, but they never mentioned this ache. She was almost in pain. She needed something…just his touch through the thin silk was bringing her to the brink of something exquisite. She had to reach it.

Kristoff growled in both desire and frustration. She knew no control, no pacing. At this rate, he would have her naked and writhing beneath him in a few seconds, taking her as his own with reckless abandon and damn the consequences.

"Slow down, Love," he whispered against her open mouth. His voice was husky. "There is a lifetime of pleasure I will give you, but we don't have to experience it all at once."

He smiled against her mouth, teasing her lip with his teeth. He felt her whimper into his mouth as she moved her hips against the length of him. God, but she would be his undoing.

He had never taken a woman to his bed without her spoken consent, but she had him strongly contemplating it. Every fiber of him, every nerve, strained to feel more of her. He wanted to be buried deep inside her and have her moaning his name with every thrust of his hips.

Dear Lord, he had to stop this. He said he would court her, but this was not what he had in mind. He wanted to give her pleasure, to let her know what it could be like between them. He was going to Hell…yes…straight to Hell for the sin of lust, he thought, and for what he was about to do, but he wanted to see her passionate, glazed eyes longing for no one but him. He wanted her to want this like he did…but not just the physicality of it. It meant more. He raised himself from the floor, scooped her up, and laid her upon the bed, pinning her beneath his firm body.

A soft gasp escaped from Rosalind's lips as Kristoff started his assault of pleasure anew. She loved the feel of his crisp shirt upon her bared breasts, but she wanted to feel his flesh upon hers. She reached between them and began to unfasten the buttons on the placket of his shirt. He leaned up and pulled his shirt over his head, and covered her body with his, propping himself on one arm so he did not crush her.

He pinned her thigh beneath his well-muscled leg and then began to pull her skirts up to give himself better access. All the while, he kissed and stroked her breast, her neck, her lips. With each passing moment, she was becoming more and more uninhibited. He knew he was walking a dangerous line, but frankly, he was ready to throw caution to the wind for this sprite of a girl, for his betrothed.

Rosalind's senses were overwhelmed. The hair tickling her nipples and his hand roaming the length of her sent shivers down her core, making her more and more damp with each touch. She was unsure why she was so moist, but could not care. Somehow, he had managed to undo her skirts and pull them down over her hips. He ran his hand down the length of her firm belly, stroking her into a blaze of wildfires all over her body. All of her nerves were on fire, everywhere he touched.

She moaned again, snapping Kristoff's senses back to the vixen lying beneath him. His hands moved to explore the split in her silken drawers. There, he found her legs parted and ready for him. Her silky, private curls were so damp and slick. He could feel she was ready for him with a gentle stroke of his middle finger. Kristoff looked into Rosalind's eyes. They were hazy with passion, but he could also read the trust in them.

She was allowing him liberties no gentleman should take, but he could not stop stroking her. He began to trace the outline of silky womanhood with his finger and slowly eased in the tip. He pulled it away and then began to ease it inside her, little by little, easing deeper and deeper until she could take the length of his finger. She clenched tightly around him as he withdrew his finger, as if she were drawing it back in…so soft, so warm.

"Kris, I need you. I need…I need…I don't know what I need, but it's something…Oh, God, what are you doing to me?"

"I know, my Rose. I want us to both have it after we are properly wed. I just can't…"

He groaned as he eased his finger back out and in again. Once he started the movements, he couldn't stop. Rosalind was so infatuating to watch. She was a vision, with her vibrant merlot locks splayed in a halo about her head and face, her cheeks and chest flushed rouge with her ecstasy. Her eyes were glazed over with passion.

His movements were getting faster and faster as he allowed his thumb to stroke her sensitive nub. Her hips rose off the bed as he touched the most delicate part of her, and she moaned. He sealed his lips over hers to stifle her cries of release and continued delving into her until he felt a tightness. She arched her back with the coming tide and bit his shoulder to keep from shouting. He growled with pleasure at her boldness, sought her mouth, and seared her with a deep kiss, his tongue tangling with hers. He felt her quivering around his stilled hand.

God, she was still coming apart in his arms even after he had stilled his love play. She had a passion that he had never known. Kristoff knew she found her pleasure. He always wanted to please his partner, but this was the first time he had nearly found release watching his lover find hers. He noticed how her chest was dappled with red flowers that had blossomed across her breasts. As she lay there catching her breath, he leaned over and began kissing each red spot, only to stop at her nipple to suckle an extra second or two.

She moaned again.

"My Rose, you are the most beautiful creature I have ever seen. Your passion is like my own personal drug. I fear I could watch you come apart in my arms every day for a lifetime and never have enough. I am counting the days that we can do this properly in a proper wedding bed and truly be joined as mates."

Rosalind looked up at Kristoff. If she had not still been quivering and wanting more, she might have cringed at his mention of being wed. She reached and grasped the back of his head and pulled him back to her. "I want whatever more you speak of now, Kris. Please. We need not speak of tomorrow. Just now, ok?" she pleaded.

He grasped her legs and gently removed them from around him. She cried out in frustration. He kissed her again and then looked into her eyes. "Tell me you want me," he demanded, "now and forever." He struggled as she was trying to pull his mouth back to her lips. "Tell me, Rosalind, now and forever. I know you ache for me to end this torment for both of us. Tell me, now!"

It took Rosalind a moment to rise out of her passionate haze to understand what he was asking of her. He wanted her consent for whatever else a man and woman shared. No, this was all wrong; he was supposed to be overwhelmed and just "take" her like she had overheard the village women speaking of. She knew enough to know it had something to do with that large protrusion of his that seemed to grow like magic and made her feel hot in her private area. She had heard it said that once that appeared, a man lost his senses.

Kristoff seemed to not realize he was supposed to lose control. Then they could both blame passion when this was all done. He could leave with no strings, and she would have this memory etched into her mind like so many words on parchment for a lifetime. She nearly cried with her need for him, this man who was like no other she had ever encountered. Perfect in every way except one…his blasted honor. She never should have eavesdropped on those women. Clearly, they did not know what they were talking about.

Kristoff saw the passion clear from her eyes, and confusion fall upon the lines now knitted into her brow. Her expression then changed again…was that anger, or just tension begging for release?

"Just take what you will from me." She hated the way her voice sounded as if she were begging.

He sighed, stilling himself and propping his forehead against hers, closing his eyes to regain some measure of control.

"I promise I will take all that you offer and give you all of me in return, my sweet Rose, but it is either forever or nothing. There will never be half measures between us. I cannot give your body pleasure and then leave you as if it meant nothing to me." He leaned back and looked into her eyes. "This means something to me. Tell me it means something to you."

He held her gaze, waiting for her response. God, how he wanted her, all of her…mind, heart, body.

Rosalind was terrified by the intensity of his gaze and his words. What was he saying…did he love her? Surely not; they had known each other only a short time, but he was the most remarkable man she had ever met. And if she was being truthful with herself, she wanted all he seemed to offer, but not at the risk of losing who she was. "I want this, Kristoff. I want this moment, I want you, but…"

Just then, they both were snapped back to reality as rapid footsteps came down the hall, followed by a knock upon Rosalind's bedchamber door. Kristoff and Rosalind could faintly hear Elsa opening the curtains and saying none too quietly, "M'lady, are you up?" directly followed by a much louder muttering, "Here we go again. Cripes, where is that girl!" That outrage was followed by Elsa's quickly retreating steps down the hall.

Rosalind was horrified at the thought of being discovered in a truly compromising position. Thank the Maker they had gone into Kristoff's room and not hers. Father would not even await the special license if he had any inkling what had just occurred. They would be married within the hour. God, she was such a fool. Hadn't he already proven he was a true gentleman…though she supposed she had pushed that test to the limits. What had she been thinking to allow such liberties…to be ruled by lust?

"I must go," she said as she scrambled away from him, grabbing her skirts as she went. She deftly redid her attire, peeked out the door, and left, closing the door softly before Kristoff could finish donning his shirt.

Chapter Twenty-Seven

Elsa ran back into the kitchen in a complete panic. "Where is M'lady? I cannot find her anywhere. Do you think she has run off into the woods again? She promised me she would stay in her rooms this morning so I could don her dress for a walk with her new fiancé. Lord help me," she begged, looking heavenward.

"Well, Love, she's not hiding in the copper pots, so you can just move along. Perhaps you should ask Nan. I'm sure she may know her whereabouts," she stated as she shooed the frantic woman back out of her kitchen.

Mary was surveying the ingredients lined up on the table, double-counting the scallops and black truffles. She gently picked up each black truffle and smelled and inspected it carefully to ensure it was fresh and did not have the pungent smell of a false truffle. She knew those mistaken truffles could cause serious harm, including vomiting or perhaps death if eaten. When she discovered a false truffle, she cast it aside and continued her careful inspection. It was a painstaking process, but an absolute must when preparing this delicacy. The truffle dish was decadent and would be the talk of the Ton for the rest of the season.

"'Ello. Mrs. Gowan. Can I 'elp ye in the kitchens today?" asked Edith, the upstairs maid. "I know you're a busy lady down in the kitchens, an' I've already done me cleaning…just waiting for those fancy folks to stop sluggin' about abed so I can finish the rest of my job today."

"Well…that would be very nice, Edith. How good are you with a knife? I could use someone to chop up these truffles into small bits, like this," Mary said as she demonstrated a small bite-sized truffle chop.

"This pile over here, don't cut up; these are for toppin' off the scallops. We'll work with those later. And this pile here…"

She pointed to the false truffles. "Just go on and throw out. They are false truffles. If you eat them, you could have a serious case of bad blood; it might even kill you dead as a doornail," she said, eyeing her with seriousness.

"Very good, Missus. I can be quite good with a knife, I can," said Edith, while she started her task.

The smell of the kitchens began to swirl with spices mingled with the fresh lemon oils used on the woodwork and the fresh flowers that adorned every shelf and table. It was a mouthwatering cacophony of aromas. It wafted through the air out of the kitchens and toward the stables, calling young Markham. He could not resist. He had to go discover what Mrs. Mary had concocted in the kitchens today.

"I'm sure Cookie would give me a small morsel," he said as he trekked across the back gardens and up to the manor.

He could feel his stomach starting to rumble in anticipation as he knocked on the back door and slightly pushed it open. He noticed a small black and white barn cat had followed him.

"You thinkin' the same ways I am, Puss," he mused as the cat started making figure eights between his legs.

"Ah, Markham, I am so glad you popped in. I need some help with the kitchen fires. Go get me some more wood from the wood pile so I can start cooking the butter sauce," instructed Cook. "I'll give you a morsel in a bit. I need your help with the fires first," she directed, pointing back out the door with her wooden ladle as she noticed the cat for the first time.

The simple, black and white scrawny barn cat poked around the kitchens looking for a bit of cream and nibbles, then he looked Mary straight in the eyes as if pleading for food. She could not turn anyone away from a hearty meal, even a blasted barn cat.

"You're in luck, little kitty. I am in a fine mood as our lady is in love." She sighed happily. "It's a beautiful day, and I need a little taster to see how I am doing. Let's get you a bit of breakfast, shall we?"

Mary thought she would give the poor creature a bit of the meat and truffle sauce she was preparing for the evening meal…just a nibble or two.

"Here, puss, puss! Try a little of this here morsel of truffle sauce with these scallops. Take a bite and let me know what you think," Mary coaxed the little cat.

He purred in anticipation of the rich, creamy dish and approached, licking his whiskers in anticipation and meowed loudly. The cat sniffed the saucer of scallop and sauce, sneezed then happily lapped up the feast.

"Ah, that will make your other furry friends jealous. Don't you go and tell them of how nice ol' Cook is now," Mary crooned to the cat as she shuffled away, leaving him to finish.

Elsa marched back into the kitchens as the beurre sauce was bubbling on the stove. The aroma of the savory mix floated through the air, wrapping her in a savory hug.

"May I have a cuppa, Mrs. Mary?" she sighed. "I cannot find that girl. She is nowhere in the house, and I don't have the patience today to chase her through the woods or to venture down to Nan's cottage to see if she is hiding out there, even though Nan is here. Why does she have to wander off so? Our lady is turning my hair gray. I hope this new man of hers can keep up with her. I need some rest,

"You know, she tried to matchmake me last evening? With that handsome carpenter from town. My, can that man dance!" Elsa sighed as she walked about the room sniffing the pots that were bubbling on the stove.

A small steeping cup of lavender tea with a sprig of mint was placed in front of her. Mary patted her hand and gave her a knowing smile.

"Well, wouldn't that be nice, dear. A man of your own…and a strapping one at that. And soon enough, our lady will be married and moving on to her new home. Then you'll have no one to chase."

Mary wiped a tear from her cheek. She had heard Elsa complain about Rosalind and her escapades since the girl could walk. The upcoming nuptials would no doubt cause endless tears for everyone, but especially Elsa. Elsa would miss her deeply. But for now, a wee bit of griping and lavender tea would cure what ailed her, Mary thought.

As Elsa sipped her tea and relaxed, she began to take in the hustle and bustle of the busy kitchen. She had been so consumed with finding Lady Rosalind that she completely forgot how overwhelmed Mary would be today of all days. Scully maids were running around preparing the nooning picnic that would be held on the south fields near the chalk stream.

Pots and pans clicked and clanged against each other as another maid rattled them in preparations for another dish that was to accompany the feast. Several other maids and valets were sitting at the long table, darning hosiery and socks and the like as their charges had not yet awakened. Elsa wondered briefly what that must be like. Lady Rosalind was always up before dawn on some adventure or another. But poor Mrs. Mary and Mrs. Ingrid, there was a flurry of demands and commotion that was very overwhelming under the calm and quietness of the above stairs.

"Oh, Mrs. Mary! I must apologize for bothering you with my petty worries. You are a busy bee. The kitchens smell divine. I know our Lordship will be oh-so pleased with your creation tonight. How you can change plans so quickly, I will never understand. You are a wonder," Elsa complimented while gingerly sipping her tea. "Tell me about these truffles you were so excited about, and I will get out of your hair."

Mary looked up from the saucepan that she was stirring.

"It's called seared scallops in black truffle beurre blanc sauce. The tricky part is the timing of adding the delicately roasted truffles to the sauce. I don't want the sauce to curdle with the butter. Where is that Markham?" Mary added offhandedly. "I need more wood for the stove."

She continued talking about her dish, warming to the topic as she looked about for the stable lad. It clearly excited her to share her expertise.

"It's all about the temperature, ye see. The hard part is done thanks to Edith's help in chopping. I have already added some small bits of truffle to the sauce. The rest, I am roasting to enhance the earthy flavor before I add those, too. Then, all it has to do is simmer on a very low setting for the day with a bit of wine added every now and again as it cooks down. It is the long simmering, adding more and more cream and wine over the day as it reduces, that makes a rich, highly flavored gravy, you would call it. When the time arrives, I will sear the scallops, ladle the sauce on them, give them a fresh little truffle hat, and serve them hot."

Elsa was always amazed at how Mary could jump around the kitchen, pull a few jars of this spice or that, twirl this way and that…a pinch here, a dash there…never missing a step, then voilà, a masterpiece of culinary art to the palate. She could watch Mary weave in and out with her dishes all day.

Mary had just ladled up a spoonful to taste the flavor as Markham burst into the room and scared the wits right out of both women. Mary threw the spoon into the air in fright as he rushed toward her. Sauce covered poor Elsa from forehead to chin.

"Cook!" he shouted, grabbing her arm at the same time as his other hand snatched the flying ladle from mid-air just before it smacked poor Elsa on the head.

"You've got to throw out the stew. It's bad, I say. Did you eat it? The cat…he's got the vomits! Everywhere in the yard. Poor lad can't stop retching up what you gave him. It's something awful. Mrs. Mary, please tell me you didn't take any. I hope the poor critter doesn't meet his maker. Such a good mouser, that one." Markham worried, shaking Mary's arm like a windmill as he rushed in toward the large preparation table, dragging her behind him. He was near to tears.

Both Mary and Elsa froze.

"How could this have happened?" thought Mary aloud as she visibly blanched.

She always took great care with the preparation of each meal. Walking over to the main counter, she surveyed where the truffles had been prepared and chopped. She noticed that there was no pile of false truffles. Clearly, Edith had tossed them as she was instructed. She ran to the refuse bin…no truffles…not false, or otherwise…Mary started to feel sick to her stomach.

Edith!" Where is that blasted wench?" Mary shouted as Elsa gasped, clearly shocked by her crass language. But Edith was nowhere to be seen. She had already fled the kitchens.

Quick as a wink, Mary ran over to the saucepan and started dumping the contents into the trash bin. Turning abruptly, with tears streaming down her cheeks, she stated matter-of-factly, "Markham, you bring that cat into the kitchen immediately. You are going to stay by Truffles' side and nurse him all night until he is better. If we have to get his Lordship's personal physician to make him well, then I will. That cat was sent from the Lord Almighty, he was. He saved the household. If it weren't for that scrawny barn cat, we could all be suffering his same fate later tonight. We will *not* be having seared scallops in black truffle beurre blanc sauce tonight. The sauce was tainted, likely by that hussy, Edith."

With a quick look into the drying room, she noticed a newly butchered pig.

"We will be having seared scallops and thinly sliced…uh…bacon," she declared and nodded as she made the split decision. "Elsa, can you please go tell Mr. Harold and Mrs. Ingrid to be on the lookout for that vixen. I have to inform his Lordship of this issue and discuss a concern I have with a certain maid."

She gives an emphatic nod and marched off to the drying room to fetch the bacon to start for a third time for the evening meal.

Elsa hurried out of the kitchen toward the servants' stairs as Rosalind stole in the main entry, snagged a tray of nutty buns, and ran back out again, balancing her booty so as not to topple the delectable pile of treats. Everyone was so busy that no one noticed her come or go.

Chapter Twenty-Eight

Lord Englebright was already in his library enjoying his morning coffee before the sun rose, as was his custom. He had slept little the night before after he had confessed his past to Rosalind and his sons. So much had changed for them so quickly. He saw the hurt in Rosalind's eyes when she realized he was not the man she thought he was.

No, that was not what had caused the hurt. She would love him no matter his past. His secrecy had hurt her. They had always shared openly with each other in the family. He felt as though he had failed them all with the secrecy, but it was for their protection. Andrew and Charles had both looked a bit abashed at his confession as well. They understood his reasons for secrecy, but the hurt was written on their expressions.

A gentle tap upon the door brought him out of his dark thoughts. "Enter," he called, assuming it was Harold bringing him fresh tea.

He was pleasantly surprised to see Rosalind peeking around a stack of nutty buns on a silver platter. She looked at him sheepishly and gave him a short curtsey before hurrying in and closing the door behind her. He smiled at her warmly, hoping this was a sign she had forgiven him.

"Good morning, Papa," she said, setting the platter on the desk and giving him a quick peck on his cheek. "I fear I have troubling news."

She nodded at his quizzical look.

"It seems that horrid Edith may have been a spy with nefarious intent, but thankfully was not very bright. She managed to poison a poor kitten with this evening's meal. The kitten will recover with Markham's aid, but Edith has run off," she said, wringing her hands. Lowering her voice, she questioned, "Do you think it is connected…I mean, perhaps there is some link with our discussion from last night. Do you think she is an *imposter*?"

She mouthed the last word, not saying it aloud.

Her father was clearly taken aback as he leaned back in his chair, teacup midway to his mouth.

"Are you certain it was not an accident?" he asked, setting the cup back upon his desk.

"I think not, Papa. I found her coming out of Mama's study a few days ago. She said she had been cleaning, but now, I am not so sure. I looked in, but nothing seemed amiss, and it has been dusted thoroughly. And Mrs. Mary seems to think she is capable of shady doings. She believes the woman purposely added the false truffles to the pile with the good ones. Mrs. Mary swears she pointed them out to her and specifically told her to throw them out, but when they looked in the rubbish bin after the poor cat fell ill, they were nowhere to be found. She sabotaged the meal intentionally." She nodded her affirmation.

"Could she be the one you were looking for?" Rosalind shivered at the thought that her father's enemy could have been so close. "Lord Derby said that the Raven was a master of disguise. Could he have pretended to be a woman?"

Her father looked at her as he thought about it. They had never known all the disguises the Raven had taken on. "I suppose it could be possible. In truth, I am not sure any of us ever considered him to disguise himself as a woman. For that matter, who is to say that he was not a woman all along?"

He stared at the steaming teacup held in his hands as he thought about the possible implications.

"But Edith was hired by me personally as a favor to her ailing brother. We must find this woman and question her," he said as he went to the bell pull and rang for Harold. Before he could even half tug the pull, there was another knock upon the door.

"Apologies for the delay in refreshing your tea tray, My Lord. There appears to be a delay in the kitchens, something about an ill feline," Harold said as he brought a tray of fresh tea into the room.

"Just the man I wished to see," Lord Englebright said. I fear that we need a bit of a manhunt to search out this servant, Edith."

"I do believe she was the culprit implicated in the cat's current health issues, my Lord. I fear I took liberties and have young Markham raising a bit of a posse with the stable hands, if it suits?" Harold asked.

"Very good, Harold. Efficient as always. Once she is found, please take her to the tack room in the stables…No need to alarm the guests. I need to speak with her. Oh, and wake Lord Derby, if you would. Please apologize on my behalf, but I fear he will be needed for the questioning."

"Very good, my Lord," Harold said in his normal, dry voice as he closed the door.

Rising from his desk and clasping his daughter about her shoulders, he looked into her eyes, pointedly.

"Rosalind, my Sprite, please return to your room until we find her. I can't bear the thought of you being in harm's way. You will grant your papa this request, yes?" He slid his hand down her arm to her hand and grasped it as if she were a toddler in need of guidance, and pulled her toward the door. "Here, let me walk with you, my dear, and check your rooms before we secure you away."

Rosalind was having none of it and turned to face him as she closed her free hand over his. "I beg your forgiveness, Papa, but I would rather go with you. If she is in the woods, no one knows them better than I, and none in this household is a better tracker. Give me a pistol, and I will be safe enough."

"And what if she is with those armed ruffians you encountered, my sweet, capable girl? Besides, I expect Edith to be long gone. You promised no more dangerous situations. Kristoff would not think kindly of losing his betrothed, I am certain," he said, gently patting her hand to gentle his rebuke. "Nor would I risk you." He smiled softly at her.

At the mention of betrothal, Rosalind bristled, her face heating to a crimson stain.

Her father, being ever observant, wondered at the color now spreading over his daughter's face. Was she now excited about the prospect of marrying, or was she furious, or was that blush something else entirely? Lord help, perhaps he needed them married sooner than he thought. Normally, he had no issue reading his daughter. In fact, she typically was an open book, the thoughts of which were open for anyone willing to peruse. She shared her every notion or reflection with him. How much had changed in such a short time. He sighed, looking at her flaming face. Perhaps there were some things a father did not need to know, he internally grimaced.

Despite her argument, he opened the door to lead his daughter out and nearly ran into a rather bedraggled-looking Derby.

Chapter Twenty-Nine

Elias was awoken in the morning's wee hours by the chaotic household's hustle and bustle. Clearly, Englebright did not manage his staff properly and with firmness. Staff should never be seen or heard, but the staff here seemed to think it was their place to advise, direct, and otherwise interfere with the workings of the family. The Englebrights might have the titles and breeding, but they clearly lacked understanding of how titled individuals should treat their staff. He rose from his bed and stretched his arms above his head. The mattress was not as comfortable as those in his home.

He was still furious at his nephew for foiling the plan to wed Lady Englebright, but not all was lost. Surely, Englebright himself would prefer a future viscount to some foreigner. If he could dissuade this Van Reede from this path, that would surely open the way for this beneficial connection between noble blood. What could be more important than that for a daughter, after all?

He demanded that Jared, his loyal valet, stay in his rooms when traveling so he would be available for his every beck and call, should need arise, which it often did. Of course, Jared would never complain. He was loyal, discreet, and irreplaceable, as far as Elias was concerned.

"Jared! Wake up, man," Elias called. "How can you sleep with this chaos?"

Jared arose and looked at Elias in a disgruntled haze of sleepiness.

"Apologies, my Lord," he said, shaking the sleep from his head as his aged, yet impressively muscled chest expanded with an inelegant yawn. "Please allow me a moment, and I will be at your aid."

Jared stepped into the washroom and slipped out of his nightshirt while Elias stood in the door, tapping his foot while surveying the man as he dressed quickly. Jared turned and smiled at him, noticing his lord's impatience. He quickly brushed his thick, silver and black hair with a bit of hair oil, glanced into the looking glass, and turned to do his master's bidding.

"How might I be of assistance, my Lord?" he asked, bowing his head in deference but staring into his master's eyes as he did so. "Are we not scheduled for a ride about the grounds and a picnic this afternoon? Shall I prepare a carriage for you?"

"Do not be presumptuous, man. I tell you what things I want and when, not the other way round. Carriages are for the weaker sex. I will ride my own steed. I will see to that myself. I need you to listen to the goings-on of the household servants. I want to know the repercussions of our little setback from last eve. Is Englebright set on a marriage with a foreigner? God help us if that is what noble blood has come to." He shook his head in disgust.

Jared approached his master with his overcoat and helped him don it, turning him to face him. He straightened his cravat and smiled warmly at him. "There, my Lord, now you look the perfect viscount of the noblest breeding."

Elias sniffed at the compliment, grabbed the lapels of his overcoat, gently brushed Jared's hands from the fabric, and gave the man a slight, quick smile as he turned to go.

Elias headed straight to the stables without encountering any of the guests or household. He was shocked that most of the stable hands were nowhere to be found.

"You there?" he called to a lad mucking out a stall. "Where is the stable master? I need my mount prepared."

The boy looked startled. "Beggin' yer pardon, M'Lord. Everyone went ter find that Edith woman who tried ter kill the barn tabby. I can saddle yer mount, M'Lord, if'n you like. Jes, tell me which one it is."

The boy nodded vigorously at him, eager to please.

"She tried to kill a common barn cat, you say? Why on earth would that trigger a manhunt? From time to time, one must depopulate the vermin, or they would overtake the barn," Elias said, throwing his arms in the air.

"Well, m'Lord. They say she poisoned m'Lordship's evenin' meal. She would've killed him dead, she would've. But little Truffles got it in the end. 'tis a sad day when yer barn tabby's not even safe, m'Lord."

Elias said nothing more to the boy, but pointed out his stallion in the finely appointed stable. This was one thing Englebright did well, he decided. "Ready him quick as a wink, you hear?"

The boy nodded and began saddling the large, black horse, cooing to the beast the entire time. As he finished, he led the impressive animal back to the waiting gentleman. "I would avoid the wood, m'Lord. There's 'oles in them woods, but no one knows why. Ol' Maude says it might be witches, she does." The boy spat upon the ground with that declaration. "Wouldn't want someone as finely dressed as you to run upon a witch." He spat again.

"That is a disgusting habit," Elias stated with disdain on his face. "Do you have writing implements here?" Elias asked, shaking his head in disgust.

The boy pointed him to the office. "There be parchment and ink pots just there, m'Lord."

Elias quickly scribbled a note upon a piece of parchment and folded it neatly. He handed it to the boy. "Deliver this immediately to my valet, you hear me, boy?"

"Yes, m'Lord, but what is his name?" the boy inquired.

"I am Lord Durham. Tell the butler you need to see my valet. Let no one else deliver this missive," he said, flipping the boy a copper.

The lad's eyes grew large as he ran off to the house, and Elias smirked, thinking how easily manipulated peasants could be.

Chapter Thirty

"Derby, old boy, I think the game is afoot…and these bones are too old for this nonsense," Englebright called to him as he opened the library door wide and allowed him in. Derby's hair was a bit mussed and his cravat askew, and it appeared he could use a few more hours of sleep.

"I came here for an uneventful birthday party, Georgie. So far, we have witches digging holes in the blasted woods or dirt poachers. Take your pick. A cat near death due to poisoning, if rumors are true, and a surprise betrothal. What other exhilarating enjoyment do you have for me, old friend?" Derby smiled jovially, if not tiredly, at his host. As he entered, Harold followed with a fresh pot of hot tea, coffee, and a breakfast tray.

"Ah, good man, Harold," Derby called as he took a nutty bun and stuffed it in his mouth. He waved his hand at Rosalind to come back in just as a small lad covered in what appeared to be bits of straw and horse manure came running to the door, waving a bit of parchment.

"Mr. 'arold, sir. I have a missive for Lord Durham's valet. He tol' me no one but me should deliver it and gave me a copper ter see it done, sir. Can you point me to 'im?" he said, then realizing he had run into his Lordship's private study uninvited, he bowed low and stammered, "Beggin me pardon, m'Lord. He said 'tis urgent."

"No worries, lad," Englebright said, patting the boy on the back. "Harold will see it done. Why don't you go see Mrs. Mary in the kitchens? I am certain she has more buns she would be happy to share."

The boy's smile was from one ear to the other. "You sure are a kind one, sir," he said, handing the butler the letter and running off for his treat.

George smiled as he shut the door. "Well, Derby. My brilliant daughter has placed an idea in my head that I am ashamed to admit I never thought of before. Do you think the Raven could have been a woman? You see, we had this new maid, and it could just be a coincidence, but I find I am disliking that notion immensely of late…you see, she intentionally tried to poison the evening meal. We can think of no reason why she would have done so." He raised his arms in a shrug.

"George, I can see how a woman, slight of build, could resemble a boy, perhaps," he said, looking pointedly at Rosalind. "However, how would a woman imitate the physique of a grown man? Would that not have required the aid of many? How could that secret have been held for so long? No, my friend, I do not think the Raven was a woman."

He looks at Rosalind apologetically. "But it is this kind of thinking we need to solve this. What we do know is that he was immensely connected and well-educated. He had to have spoken at least three languages, we know of, fluently, and could move about large amounts of smuggled goods.

I think that it would take some strength of body, which a normal woman would not possess. And if he only directed others to do the work, it might have raised suspicion. You know how distrustful the whole lot of spies and smugglers we ever captured were. They wanted everyone to get their hands dirty, so they either all went down with the ship, or no one did. It was a sort of honor code, if you remember. I will not discredit the thought entirely, but do think it unlikely.

"Now, this woman, Edith. How long has she been in your employ, and where is she now?" he asked. "I think some rather stern questioning is in order since she saw fit to disrupt my restful holiday."

"Now, now…Derby," Englebright said. "I have men out searching for Edith as we speak, and intend for you to aid in questioning her. When they find her, they are to bring her to the stables. In fact, we shall venture down once you've finished up your morning meal, but there is nothing to be done until she is located. As for how long she has been in my employ…well, approximately a month, give or take. Her brother lives in our neighboring village and is a rather sickly man. She needed a good job to help him. I suppose we did not do as good a job of obtaining references as we should have, but she seemed desperate and to have few prospects."

"Just so, Georgie. Just so. You have always been a compassionate man. But enough of this nonsense and intrigue for a moment. It will give me indigestion. Let us turn to a brighter subject." Motioning his fork in the air and turning his full gaze upon Rosalind, Derby looked inquisitively at her. "Tell me about your school down in the village. I am eager to hear how you are transforming that old grain house. I have just bent the ear of an upcoming local lord about education reform. The news of the reform is spreading throughout London like wildfire. It's quite new-age in thinking. Not all are as excited about it as I am, but they will come around. There are those who are so stodgy in their thinking, they cannot see beyond their own noses,"

Continuing with the topic at hand, Derby spoke between bites of his sausage.

"The reform would allow anyone, regardless of rank, title, or creed, to be educated in reading and mathematics. A schoolhouse would be set up in the local village and in orphanages…you know what abysmal places they can be," he said, shaking his head in disgust. "Each would have government funding to hire an instructor for the children. Your schoolhouse would be the first of many. How avant-garde of you!"

He waggled his eyebrows at her. Rosalind smiled in response to his compliments and his support of her new endeavor. Eyeing her father with a raised eyebrow, she stated bluntly, "You realize that if I were to marry, I would be forced to move away, and my dream of educating the little ones will die…with my vows."

Rolling his eyes, her father leaned toward her, propping his elbows on the desk and resting his chin upon his upturned hands. "Have you even discussed this matter with your intended, or do you just assume he is a barbarian incapable of caring about the needs of others?"

Rosalind's rebuttal was precluded by a rapping on the door. Without waiting for permission to enter, Harold opened the door and let himself in. Rosalind was relieved not to have to answer her father. In truth, she assumed Kristoff was like every other man who had ever attempted to court her. It was easier to think the worst of him than face the possibility that he might agree with her plans to stay. Then she would have no reason not to wed him in the eyes of her father and her brothers, and that would make things complicated for her. She was already too drawn to the man as it was.

"My Lord," Harold interjected in the paused conversation, "it seems an adjustment to the afternoon's activities may be required. You may need to come down to the carriage house and see the miraculous transformation for yourself. It is rather inconvenient, but the carriages seem to now be boats, sir. Shall I have them ready for a tour around the reflecting pond?"

He quirked a grin at his lord, who looked somewhat perplexed.

Chapter Thirty-One

"Boats, you say, Harold? I fear your humor confounds me. How are the carriages now boats?" remarked Englebright. Harold's humor was dry as a bone, so George was not quite sure what to make of this joke.

"I mean to say your carriages no longer have wheels, my Lord. It appears someone has seen fit to remove them."

"All of them, you say. Surely not? It would take some effort and time to remove all the bolts and wheels," Englebright said, laughing at his butler's apparent farce.

"Not if they saw fit to cut them all off, my Lord. That method seems to have been quite efficient. However, there do appear to be a few wheels that have yet to fall off completely, though I would suggest you not put your guests in those if you value them."

"Good Lord, man," Englebright exclaimed. "They would need to have been at it all night. Go and wake my sons, Kristoff, and Jacob. We need to check the horses. If this fiend, whoever it is, has injured my horses, so help me, I will see them hanged. Derby, sorry, old boy, but you can add sabotage to your list of exhilarating activities for your holiday, it seems. What in the world is going on here!"

Rosalind, her father, and Derby made their way to the stables and attached carriage house to assess the damage. Just as Harold had reported, each of the wheels had been neatly sawn. Some had been completely removed, while others had only been partially damaged, but significantly enough that, should they have attempted to go for a ride, it surely would have ended in catastrophe. Someone could have been killed.

"Father," called Charles as he entered the stable, followed by Andrew, Kristoff, and Harold. "Surely, Harold was pulling our legs with his latest jest. Who could have removed all the carriage wheels in such a short amount of time, and why? It makes no sense. If you were the target, then why damage all of the carriages? There would be no way to determine who could have been injured. I think there must be more to this than meets the eye. Kristoff, you check the carriages, and I will look outside to see what can be ascertained. Andrew, please help Kristoff," he called, taking charge as he headed out the rear stable door.

"My Lord, if I may have a word before Lord Corbin joins us," requested Harold, motioning for his master to follow him to the far stall. Englebright followed him with a look of dread on his face.

"What is it now? Are the kitchens aflame?" he asked, only half jesting.

"No, sir, but the day is young. I did, however, take the liberty of viewing Viscount Corbin's note to his butler. It contained a series of scribbles that could have been mistaken for text to an uneducated eye. But I assure you," Harold told him flatly, "it was nothing more than flourishes with no real lettering. It appears he wished to empty the stables, though that is a speculation and perhaps a coincidence, but I know how you feel about those, my Lord. I thought you might like to know. I am just pleased most of our guests left last night after the ball, though our ne'er-do-wells would have had a significantly more difficult task had they not."

"Perhaps, but this devilry would have taken hours for multiple parties to complete. There is no way Corbin could have done it himself in such a short time," Lord Englebright said, scratching his head as he looked around. "Have you seen Jacob acting in any way that you find suspicious, Harold? You know every time a door or drawer is opened on this property. Is there anything in his manner to make you suspect him of foulness?"

"Not at all, my Lord. I have found the younger Lord Corbin amiable, courteous, and proper in all behavior. He has not wandered where he was uninvited, nor has he taken liberties with our Nan, though I know he has affection for her. He has been in every way a gentleman. The viscount, on the other hand, is an odious fellow, my Lord. I apologize for my bluntness, but you did ask. This does not imply he is in any way responsible, as he has also not been where he should not be, save for the coincidence that he was in the stable this morning. He is just an unpleasant man and is quite stern with his nephew, even harsh. Alas, that does not make him a criminal," Harold stated as he looked up to see Jacob entering the carriage house.

"Though his valet seems to hold him in the highest regard," he added as an afterthought. "We should keep a wary eye on both the Corbins, I believe."

"Englebright, I heard you needed my services. What is it? None of the horses is injured, I hope. Good Lord, what happened to the carriages!" Jacob nearly shouted, coming to an abrupt stop as he approached the group in the carriage house.

"It seems the wheels decided to revolt, sir," Rosalind said, shaking her head as she looked around her at the chaos of wheels lying about the causeway.

Jacob smiled as he thought she was surely jesting.

"Cut clean through, Englebright," Kristoff called. "All of them, save this last one, which is only partially damaged. It seems perhaps the culprits were interrupted in their work. There are three saws here, so I am guessing there were at least three responsible. Perhaps the three ruffians I found in the woods earlier. What I can't fathom is what those blasted holes and, now this, have in common."

Jacob, with a look of sudden urgency on his face, ran to the stable stalls and began examining the horses one by one.

"Andrew," he called. "Can you check the tack, please? Check each buckle, halter, and saddle. Anywhere it may touch a horse's flesh. Look for metal burrs or bits of glass that may irritate or damage the animal and cause it to rear or bolt. Someone is clearly up to no good. God in Heaven, someone could have been killed."

After each man had performed his task, they thankfully reported that there was nothing else amiss.

"Andrew," called his papa, beckoning him to come to the back stall. "When we leave, please recheck the horses and tack discreetly and make sure nothing was missed."

Andrew looked at his father, puzzled by the request, but immediately agreed.

"Father," called Charles as he had just returned from the back stable door. "There appear to be fresh horse tracks skirting the edge of the woods, I would say within the last hour, maybe more."

"Those are likely the viscount's tracks as his horse is missing, and the stable lad let us know he prepared his mount for him earlier this morning," Andrew called.

Charles continued, "I also found that Rosalind's trail into the woods is newly trampled with large-sized boot prints. Shall we pursue?"

"Georgie, if I may," said Derby. "It appears we have done all we can at the moment. We already have one hunt in effect. Another would only trim our resources. I will send that young lad to fetch the coachmen so repairs can begin immediately. We will also post additional guards here and at each house door and check with my men to see if anything was amiss in the night,"

He shook his head. "Something is definitely amiss, but perhaps we can get some answers when Edith is apprehended. In the meantime, I do suggest we speak of this to no one save those in this room."

"Yes, Derby, that is a sound plan. Rosalind, my dear, can you please go with Andrew and inform Mrs. Mary and Mrs. Ingrid of the change in plans? It seems we will have no carriages today for the picnic. Perhaps Mrs. Mary can alter the menu, and Mrs. Ingrid can have the maids assist in setting up some lovely blankets for the picnic. Oh, brother, Mary is going to be ready to take to her bed if any more alterations to her meals are required," he said, shaking his head.

"I have a lovely idea, Papa. We will have a picnic in the formal garden, and I will prepare a scavenger hunt for our guests in the hedge maze." She was nearly bubbling over with her excitement. "It will be just like Mama used to do," she beamed at them all.

"An excellent suggestion, my dear. Kristoff, can you please attend to Rosalind and Andrew and perhaps help with this task? Perhaps Nan would wish to help also when she awakens." He smiled warmly at his daughter, his sweet girl, so much like her mother.

"Sir, I would be happy to assist as well, if necessary. In truth, I have never been on a scavenger hunt. It sounds intriguing. And, if I may be so bold, if there are ruffians about, perhaps the more able bodies with the ladies, the better for their protection," Jacob volunteered as they exited the stables to return to the house.

As they approached the entryway, Andrew ran out of the stables to catch up. He discreetly shook his head at his father, and they all went in and headed toward the breakfast room.

Chapter Thirty-Two

Miss Persephone Maxwell was thrilled to hear they would participate in a partnered scavenger hunt. Oh, how she hoped she would be paired with Edmund. Even though she would require a chaperone, spending time with him would be the thrill of her life. She had dreamt of how he had whisked her about the dance floor, and just knew if she could have one kiss, she would die a happy girl.

Perhaps she could steal away with him behind the hedges. She had dressed carefully in her mint green day dress that had a beautiful bit of French lace at the bodice. The green complemented the unusual shade of her eyes. She had once hated the color, but then Edmund had commented on how it reminded him of a warm summer's day. She sighed as her maid curled her blonde locks in preparation to pin them atop her head. The waist-length mass was quite heavy, but her maid, Heather, could do wonders with the waves of tendrils like no other lady's maid she had ever encountered.

She could barely contain her excitement. She was near vibrating with it. She knew what a champagne glass must feel like with all those lovely bubbles popping all inside it. She felt that way, too.

"Hurry, Heather. I only have fifteen minutes before I am to be downstairs and receive my partner and first clue. I am so nervous. What if I don't solve a single riddle?" She frowned at the thought.

"Stop that now, Miss. You put a smile on that pretty face. You'll be paired with a fine lad, I am certain of it. He will help you." Heather smiled at her as she pinned the last curl in place. "Let me dab a bit of this rose water behind your ear, in case Lord Edmund gets that close."

Both girls giggled at the thought.

Mycroft adjusted his tie for the fifteenth time. He wanted to wear a sword but thought it might be a bit too much. He had placed wedges in his shoes so he would be a bit taller, and had dabbed a bit of his mama's powder upon the blotches on his face. It covered them quite nicely, he thought. Puffing his chest out, he looked at himself one last time in the looking glass.

He already felt as though he had aged enough to draw sweet Rosalind into his warm embrace. He would woo her, he just knew it…or challenge that foreign rogue who was attempting to steal her away. What did that Kristoff offer that he could not best? He smiled at himself in the mirror once again and headed toward the door. His mama would swoon when he won the hand of the lady. He met Michael as he headed out.

"Mycroft, have you grown overnight? Yesterday you were nose to nose with me, and now I can't help noticing we are now nose to eye. Have you been consorting with witches?" Michael laughed. "Did you get a visit from Maude in the night?"

Mycroft turned beet red, except for large spots all over his face.

"I say, friend, what have you done to your face? You've gone all red except for large circles about your cheeks. They are bone white," he said, leaning in to inspect them more closely. "Are you feeling all right? Do you have pox? Shall I fetch the doctor?"

"Shut it," squeaked Mycroft as his voice cracked around the words, and he shoved Michael toward the wall and stormed past him down the hall.

"Mycroft, wait, I'm only jesting. You look quite dapper. Really," he yelled after him as Mycroft ran down the hall, the back of his shoes flapping over his heels.

Michael cocked his head to one side, trying to figure out what his friend had done to his feet. He supposed whatever it was might be the reason for the change in height. Oh, poor Mycroft. He was going to be sorely disappointed if he tried to court Rosalind. Michael supposed he had best go stop him before he made a complete arse of himself.

"Oy! Why are you shouting at Mycroft? And what has he done to his feet?" Edmund asked as he approached his brother, watching their friend run down the long hall. "Shall we stop him before he tumbles down the stairs?"

"I suppose we should. After all, it is our fault he thought Ros might consider him." Michael said after a sigh and glanced at his brother. "I never thought he would take us seriously. I heard he challenged Kristoff to a duel…with an ornamental sword, no less. Pulled it right off the wall, he did. Then charged in like he was one of King Arthur's finest. If it weren't for him, Sprite might not be in the predicament she is in. So…in a way, if it weren't for us…"

He grimaced, looking at Edmund.

"She would not be in this predicament," sighed Edmund, finishing his twin's sentence. "She's never going to forgive us if she finds out, is she?"

"Nope! Definitely not. So, best we keep this between you and me," Michael said with a wink. "And best we stop that fool from any more chivalrous actions. Let's go catch him, shall we?"

"I know a nice broom closet we could stuff him in," Edmund stated and smiled mischievously.

"Say, do you think Ros will pair me with Miss Maxwell?" Michael asked.

"No clue, Mate. But if she pairs her with me, I will gladly swap, even if you are paired with Maude."

"Seriously, Edmund. She is beautiful with those summer green eyes and smells like cake. You know how I like cake," he said, smiling and shoving his brother into the wall.

Edmund looked at his brother and shook his head in disbelief. "As I live and breathe, my brother has become a simpleton over a skirt. I wish you well in your downfall, Mate. The 'cake' is all yours."

Chapter Thirty-Three

The formal garden had been transformed into a fairyland of blues, pinks, reds, and lavenders as the confetti of various blankets had been sprinkled about the lawn adjacent to the reflecting pool. Mrs. Ingrid had laid parasols of various sizes, from small to tent-like, amongst the blankets as well, to provide some protection from the sun for delicate skin. The whole scene reminded Rosalind of Christmas dinner. It appeared as if an enormous Christmas cracker had popped over the lawn to magical effect. She could not have been more thrilled. That was not even the best part.

Baskets were overflowing like Greek cornucopias, as if Zeus himself were expected to dine. Grapes, pastries, cured meats, and pies could be seen amidst the contents. Bottles of sparkling champagne and fruited waters were set on trays beside the baskets. The delicate spring daisies had been clipped from the nearby field and placed neatly in the middle of each blanket, arranged in a mist of baby's breath.

Small boats adorned with tea candles had been placed on the reflecting pond. The regatta was ready to launch the moment the sun began to fade. Even if no one remained to view it, the attention to every fine detail had been attended to. "If only Mama could see," thought Rosalind, aloud, clasping her hands together and getting a bit teary-eyed.

She had prepared the maps and riddles, and with the aid of Nan had copied them for each pair of guests, then she alone…well, followed by Derby's men…had laid the trail of faux gems and other trinkets for each team to find. Most of the remaining guests had been local and left as soon as they had broken their fast, so there were not so many teams to prepare for. Thanks be to the heavens that the issue with the carriages had been discovered so early. With the aid of some of the village craftsmen, the immediately necessary conveyances had all been repaired. She was just left with five teams who were to participate in the picnic and scavenger hunt.

She laughed to think of the looks on their faces as she announced their pairings. Of course, each unwed lady had to be accompanied by a chaperone, and she was expected to pair with Kristoff. Elsa was her companion. Rosalind would not participate in clue solving, but was quite anxious to see how Kristoff and Elsa fared in the game.

Poor Mycroft had gone near apoplectic when he learned he was paired with the younger Maxwell daughter, Little Melanie, as her family called her. The beautiful girl was only twelve but already seemed more mature than Mycroft. The child had been thrilled to be paired with an older boy and clapped her hands in delight as she viewed the first riddle with him. Apparently, the happy girl beaming smiles of sunlight and joy, accompanied by a riddle to solve, was enough to dissuade the young man from raising further protest. Her mama looked less than thrilled with the pairing, but bore the ordeal with grace. She, her husband, and the two would be a team.

Michael, at his near begging the moment he found out there was to be a paired game, was matched with the lovely Miss Persephone, who continued to call him Edmund. He seemed not to be fazed and just corrected her with a smile. The poor girl could not keep the brothers straight, which Rosalind could understand for someone who had not lived with them their entire lives. Michael, however, had one striking difference. His left eye was ever-so-slightly a deeper shade of stormy gray than the right and had blue flecks amidst the haze of gray.

Edmund did not have this feature of heterochromia, as it was known. It was a rarity, per their family doctor. Surely, any girl who had gazed into his eyes, as Rosalind had overheard the young miss touting to her mama, would have noticed. Alas, Michael would set her straight in the end, no doubt. He seemed completely taken with her. Her lady's maid, Heather, would be her chaperone.

Rosalind had placed Jacob with Nan, much to her dismay. But not having sufficient ladies for the pairings, Charles had stepped up and volunteered to attend their team. Rosalind knew he did it to aid in keeping an eye out for her friend, but it did appear rather suspicious, as he kept staring pointedly at Jacob as if he could will him to disappear with a glance. She would have a discussion with him later to sort out what in the world was the matter with him. He had been acting rather like a mother bear protecting its cub, and poor Nan was the cub. He had never paid her this much notice, which was making Nan even more nervous than the prospect of sharing some private time with the handsome Lord Corbin.

The older viscount had decided not to play, begging off due to the aches of age in his joints. He was seated at the winner's table to watch the frivolity, a bit of a scowl marring his otherwise pleasant face. That scowl had been firmly in place ever since he returned from his morning ride.

He had not been unpleasant to her father all the evening before, but seemed greatly put out since the discovery of her and Kristoff in their ridiculous, compromising position. She supposed he was disappointed that her father allowed such a thing to have happened to his only daughter. The man clearly thought less of Kristoff and kept glaring at him when he thought no one was looking.

Andrew was more intrigued by the thrill of the game than the lovely ladies. So, to give him a reprieve, Rosalind paired him with Edmund. They both were more strategic in nature and had snuck away, already whispering about their strategy for victory. She could see Edmund looking over their opponents, and then nodding back at Andrew, and commencing whispering again. Michael had slowly meandered toward them to listen in, which resulted in Edmund jovially pushing him away. "Shove off, you. Victory shall be ours this fine day," Edmund declared with laughter in his eyes.

The general excitement and joy of the event were contagious. All of their guests, young and wise in years, were anxious to begin. It was as if her mother had joined them in spirit. Her father smiled at Rosalind over the tops of the guests' bobbing heads. She knew he felt it too.

"Gather round, everyone, please," Rosalind called to the various teams, beckoning them to circle her. The younger attendees were almost bouncing on their toes as they readied themselves to be off.

"Here are the rules of the game. Each team will solve the clues one at a time in order. I have started each of you on a different clue, which will eventually lead you back to the starting point. Once you have solved the first clue, you will collect the item identified by the clue at the location where it leads, and then gather your next riddle," she said, clapping her hands.

"You are only allowed to take one riddle per location," she directed, looking pointedly at the twins, one after the other. "No cheating!"

She laughed at the incredulous look upon their faces, as did everyone else. Persephone just continued to stare at Michael in admiration. Rosalind doubted the sweet thing had heard one thing she had said.

"Once you have solved all the riddles and have collected the five designated items, you will return to this table, where your host will determine the winner," she said, pointing to the table and Papa in turn. "The prize…" She paused for dramatic effect. "…is that you will be the guest of honor at dinner, seated at the head of the table and…" She paused again. "Lead the first dance of the evening."

Oohs and aahs swept across all in attendance, but none seemed more thrilled or determined than Little Melanie Maxwell. Rosalind thought that if the child had a war horse in her possession, she would have trampled them all in her determination to win. Due to her age, she had not been allowed to attend the formal dinners, nor the dances.

Mycroft, Rosalind noticed, seemed just as excited. A little too excited, she noted as he stared longingly at her. She decided to clarify one important point.

"Your dance partner, of course, will be your current paired partner." Mycroft's face fell dramatically, but Little Melanie did not seem to care one whit as she continued to rub her hands in anticipation. Rosalind laughed at Edmund as he bowed to Andrew and offered him his arm.

"Sorry, Edmund, Andrew," she called, with amused laughter in her voice, "but you are assured a skilled dance partner at least." She laughed aloud. The rest of the crowd followed suit as Andrew twirled Edmund in a circle.

"One last note," she called. "As many of you have not had the privilege of committing our lovely hedge maze to memory, I would like to inform you that there are cherubs located throughout with various fountains at strategic points. Much to my family's dismay, I have had the darling cherubs rearranged for this event to make it fair for all. Lord Derby will be circling the outer ring of the maze to put you to rights should you lose your way.

"Upon my mark," she called, withdrawing the tiniest pistol from her pocket. It had been a gift from her mama and papa for her eighth birthday and had been imported from the Wild West of the United States. She raised the delicate, mother-of-pearl-handled gun above her head and pulled the trigger. A small "pop" signaled the rivalry to begin.

Michael grabbed Miss Persephone's hand boldly and pulled her into the maze. Her lady's maid, Heather, trotted a safe distance behind as the two raced ahead. Michael directed her left, then right, and right again, to a small niche that was out of the main flow of the path. "The first clue," he said as he began to read it aloud in a whisper, her head leaning in toward his to hear what his low voice was saying, "states the following:

'Roses are red, daisies are white, cherub's cheeks glow in the noon-day light.

"I think that means the center of the maze, where the sun shines directly down," he said to her conspiratorially, lowering his voice again so she had no choice but to grow closer to him to hear what he said.

Persephone sighed. He had stared into her eyes and held her captive with the intensity of the look he gave her. She was helplessly trapped, imprisoned by his long lashes, his perfectly arched brow…he was just beautiful, she thought as she sighed again. She could not make herself turn away, but just stared into his beautiful eyes.

"And I, my beautiful Persephone," he said, looking deeply into her eyes and taking her hand in his with a little nod, "am Michael, not Edmund. Look into my eyes, and you will remember."

He paused and lowered his voice to barely a whisper, leaning in a bit closer.

"But in case you think to forget, Persephone…" He said her name like a gentle caress as he quickly brushed his lips across hers in a brief, tender kiss. "Perhaps that will help you remember."

"Oh," was all she could manage to say as Heather ran around the corner to join them.

Stepping back to a more respectable distance, so as not to wind up in the same state his sister was in, Michael smiled at both girls. "Shall we be away to the center of the maze, then?" he asked, wiggling his eyebrows with boyish charm. Persephone blushed and giggled as she grabbed his hand boldly and followed him.

Nan stood a bit dazed as she looked at the tall, handsome gentlemen she found herself flanked by; she did not know which arm to take. She inexplicably found herself feeling tiny, as if she had wandered into a forest of very tall and majestic trees – if trees could be well-muscled and handsome, she thought with a sigh. Finally, she offered her arm to both gentlemen, raised a perfectly sculpted brow.

"Shall we be off then?"

Smiling back at her, Jacob stated excitedly, "Indeed, I think this first clue leads us to the outer walls of the maze. Charles, Nan, what do you think?"

"Let us see," she said, taking the paper and reading the clue aloud.

I am brown and smooth, but can be broken, but if I am, you will find something golden. But this hunt is not for the gold!

"It does seem as if we are to look to the 'shell' of the maze. Good job, Jacob!" she said, beaming at him. She felt her heart flutter when he smiled, showing perfectly white teeth behind those full lips. Heavens, that smile would make Venus herself take a second glance.

"Shall we?" she asked, her voice catching a bit and her heart flipping again as he took her arm in his.

She felt her cheeks going pink and quickly turned to look at Charles. *Oh goodness*, she thought. The intensity with which Charles was looking at her made her cheeks flush even more. At this rate, she feared she would spontaneously burst into flames before they could find the first treasure. She quickly cleared her throat to help her gather what semblance of wits she had left so she could concentrate on the game.

Nan had enough of Charles's intense scrutiny of late. What had come over him, she had no idea. When she could get him alone, she would certainly give him a piece of her mind. The way he looked at her as if she were both a tasty treat and a naughty child in need of scolding made her want to pop him over the head with one of the lovely parasols. Perhaps that would knock some sense back into him.

Jacob continued to lead them forward toward the east side of the maze, close to where the gardens met the treeline that led into the woods. Charles gazed at the wooded area with suspicion as movement caught his eye. He could have sworn he saw a figure, but when he glanced into the woods, there was nothing there. Letting go of Nan's arm, he told the two he would join them momentarily. Jacob eyed him warily, but Charles just gave him an assuring nod and stepped into the edge of the wooded area.

"Where is he going?" asked Nan as Jacob led her away from Charles.

Jacob did not wish to alarm her with his suspicion that something was definitely amiss, what with the sabotage of the carriages and whatnot. He looked down at her and just smiled.

"Ummm," he stalled as he led her farther away from the treeline, "perhaps a call of nature?" He grimaced and could not believe he had said such a crass thing to a lady.

Nan quirked an eyebrow at him. She was trying very hard not to burst into laughter. The strain surely made her look nearly as appalled as he did. He actually looked as though he swallowed a lemon.

He shook his head and apologized. "Oh, Nan. I am so sorry; I should never have said something so vulgar and inelegant. I mean to say, you are so refined and genteel. I am ashamed to have offended you so. Can you forgive me for my poor choice of words?" he asked, as he stopped to search her face for signs she was disgusted with him. Lord, but she was lovely. Those brown eyes of hers beckoned him in like a tide finding the shoreline. He was drawn to her sweet demeanor, her wit, her spirit. She seemed so reserved and controlled. But he could feel almost a hum thrumming through her hand. There was something bubbling just beneath the surface of that controlled exterior like a tightly coiled spring in need of release.

Jacob had not expected her response. His tightly coiled Nan burst into laughter and nearly doubled over as she looked at him. He was so sincere, but she could not stop laughing. He had seriously said Charles was using the woods as his personal necessary. She had tears rolling down her cheeks as she grabbed his arm, pulled him to her side, and headed on toward their clue.

"Oh, you are a contradiction, my good sir," she giggled. "I think I could spend a lifetime getting to know you and never expect to hear something such as that come from your lips."

She chuckled again. He stopped and turned her to face him.

"A lifetime, you say? An interesting proposition." His smile held hidden promise as he looked at her.

Now that she had said it, he could not help thinking how that might just be a wonderful thing, spending a lifetime getting to know this enchanting woman. The pink attire she had chosen for the afternoon's gathering accentuated her rosy cheeks, along with her chestnut tendrils and eyes. Those lovely eyes turned upward at the edges ever so slightly, like almonds atop her silken complexion. She was such a fetching sight that he could not stop gazing at her.

Since the afternoon of gaming with the twins, she had haunted his thoughts. Her every action…her bright outlook and jovial demeanor…had been seared into his memory, like a hot coal ready to be rekindled at the slightest provocation, warming him and reminding him of things he had not yearned for until she…well, this family…the whole lot of them, had made him realize they were absent in his lonely life.

He knew without a doubt that the day would be forever etched on his mind as if an artist had rendered it there permanently. She was such a contrast to his upbringing with Uncle Elias. It was a nice respite. Returning to his everyday life would be difficult when the festivities were over, Jacob realized. His uncle would likely disown him if he courted what he would consider a commoner.

Nan breathed in deeply and looked at his full lips. She noted he suddenly seemed lost in thought, and his eyes and smile had turned a bit sad. She wondered what it might be like to have him kiss her and see if that would break the cloud that had overcast his mood suddenly. Oh, Lord, she thought. She could actually imagine how soft and warm his lips would feel on hers.

She had to get a hold of herself. She knew she was glowing red yet again. These men, she thought. They would be the death of her. She shook her head and walked on as Charles walked up and took her other arm again, startling her. She jumped and fell into Jacob's side with a little cry of surprise. Charles's gaze swept over her glowing cheeks, rosy, yet again from her wayward thoughts. He smiled at her.

As Charles looked at her, he was shocked to realize he had never noticed how fetching their Nan was. She looked absolutely bewitching in her lovely pink walking dress. The front of the bodice was simple and delicate, just like her. It was trimmed with bobbin lace, topped with a complementing lace fichu. The matching skirts were loose so that she could sit on the blankets and tuck her feet gracefully under them with ease.

The front panel of the outskirts was lined with three small bows. It was topped with a wide ribbon belt, making it functional as well, so that it was easy to tuck the fichu into it. The belt itself sat just above her natural waistline, accentuating her feminine curves, showing that a man's hand could easily span her narrow waist. Her sleeves were slightly puffed, which went against the fashion of the day of larger-sized puffs or even double puffs that made a lady look as if she would topple over with a gentle waft of wind.

Clearly, this was her own design made to fit her style. She had accessorized the entire ensemble with a matching wrap. He assumed that was just in case there was a brisk breeze about the gardens.

He had never really noticed Nan in the same light as he had recently, and he wondered why that was. The moment he had noted Jacob's obvious affection for her, he had felt pangs of…hmmm…surely not jealousy, but what? He thought. Was it brotherly protectiveness? Surely, that was it.

He had seen Nan raised from a gangly child into this beauty. He had never been jealous of Erwin and shared an amiable relationship with the man, though he always thought him a bit too tame for Nan. Though she did not show it much, she was nearly as spirited as Sprite when she felt fiercely about something. The rest of the time, she was a perfect calming balance to Rosalind's apparent chaos. Jacob had come along and started sniffing around, giving her nearly love-sick glances, and he just did not like it because he wanted to protect her. Cutting his eyes toward the back of Jacob's head, Charles was unsure if this chap should even be trusted to escort dear, sweet Nan.

"It's here! Look, gentlemen…I see the prize, but it is just beyond my reach. Can you get it?" Nan requested, eyes jumping back and forth between Jacob and Charles.

There was a blue cloth molded into the shape of a perfect bird's nest propped in the niche where two branches met. Nan knew Rosalind had climbed the blasted tree to put it there. What on Earth had she been thinking? How would Little Melanie and Mycroft get the thing? It would not be considered proper behavior for the young miss or a young gentleman to climb a tree… well in mixed company. She and Rosalind had done it often enough in their younger years.

"I think I can jar it with this stick," said Charles as he grabbed hold of the narrow branch since he was the tallest of the crew. Charles began gently poking the nest. "I think I've almost got it."

He gritted his teeth and made one last jab. "Jacob, my man, catch…"

One egg toppled down and hit Charles right on the head. The loud "thump" sound let the other two know that the egg was definitely made of wood.

"Ouch, Dammit, Ros! Pardon, Nan, but that did not feel nice," he exclaimed with a grimace.

Nan hurried over to him, stretched up on her toes, and began running her hands over his hair to feel if there was damage. "Are you quite well, Charles? Are you bleeding? I say, that did not go as planned!"

He reached up and gently took both her hands in his. "I am well enough." He smiled as he released her hands.

Nan blushed again. Heavens, she was certainly sick of blushing for the day. Men!

"I am climbing the tree. Jacob, please hoist me up there, and I will retrieve the remainder of the eggs and look to see if there is another clue. Stuff and nonsense poking at it with a stick."

Nan grabbed his hand in a no-nonsense manner and pulled him toward the tree. As she got closer to the tree, she looked directly into Jacob's hazel eyes, without flinching. "I need you to intertwine your fingers like this so that I can step into them. Charles, you will help steady me as I push myself up to retrieve the nest. Understand?"
Both gentlemen stood there dumbfounded over the simple explanation.

"Are you with me? Or are you both going to stand there gaping all morning? Time is wasting, and I truly cannot bear the thought of losing another competition to one of the twins. They keep saying I cheat. Charles, you are well aware, it is those rascals who are the tricksters. So, let's get on with it."

Charles was surprised by Nan's abruptness and, frankly, he rather liked it. His sister must finally be rubbing off on her. He questioned why she had this change in assertiveness. Could it be Jacob, he pondered. Was the man bringing out a side of her that Charles had not seen before? The thought did not sit well with him as he scrutinized the man beginning to squat near the tree. "I am sure there is another hint in the nest that will lead us on our merry way," he called to Nan. "You know, Rosalind, she thrives on the thrill of ..."

He stopped in mid-sentence as Jacob smoothly hoisted Nan up the tree by bracing his legs and extending his arms upward in one fluid motion. She was anchored firmly by his two hands around her narrow waist. It was obvious that he was a strong fellow. He hid it well under his cordial demeanor and pristine attire. His shoulders were broad, but he was not given to bulk. He was a fellow who was not all what he seemed. He definitely needed to be watched, especially considering his familiarity with Nan and the chaos going on around them.

"Here is the next clue," Nan cried in delight as she waved her newly found parchment in the air. It was tacked to a small, blue pysanky egg. "It is specific to where we started our hunt. We are supposed to choose the blue egg. Hmm…there are other colored eggs labeled 'from the lyre' or 'from the sundial.' I wonder where those will lead. You can lower me now, Jacob."

Jacob, with extreme care, slowly lowered her to the ground. He did not seem eager to make swift work of it. Instead, his touch lingered on her waist far longer than Charles thought necessary as he watched on.

As Jacob released her, she stumbled backward on an exposed root. She fell ever so slightly backward into his warm arms, her back pressing against his broad chest. Upon instinct, Jacob enveloped her waist in his arms, protecting her and slightly lifting her against any possible harm that could occur if she were to fall.

"We shan't have another injury, shall we?" Jacob whispered into her ear. The warmth from his breath spread from her sensitive ear toward her inner core.

The intensity of her response to him sent quivers of desire, the likes of which she thought long dead. Something was alluring about Jacob that caused her to put propriety aside and to forget her audience. Turning completely as he held her steady, Nan adjusted herself so that she was nose to nose with him. Her lips could brush his if she but stretched up on her toes. Her pulse accelerated with his proximity. There was a connection between them that could not be denied. Nan could not pull herself from his gaze.

"Ahem!" Charles cleared his throat rather loudly.

The spell was quickly broken between them. Charles was suddenly standing next to the couple with a look Nan had never seen before. His eyes had turned as dark as a tempest about to break open the skies. She realized that she had nearly kissed Jacob right in front of him. Oh, goodness. What was coming over her! Charles surely thought her morals had taken a holiday. No wonder he looked as if he wished to throttle them both.

Charles looked askance at Jacob, grabbed Nan's elbow, and pulled her abruptly, yet gently, toward the hedge. "So, what is the next clue? Let's see that parchment. As you stated, we need to get a move on it; otherwise, those twins will turn the tables on us. They can be quite devious. It reads: '*Roses are red…* "

At the entry to the maze, Kristoff stood surveying the couples as they dispersed in various directions. The most odd-looking pair was, of course, the clodhopper of a lad, Mycroft, with the trailblazer, Melanie. Her parents were trailing them at a snail's pace. They obviously were not accustomed to this type of intrigue or jaunts about the gardens. They did have a certain paleness about them.

"Are you coming, Mama?" Melanie called a good ten paces ahead of the lagging pair.

This young lady was determined to win regardless of the odds against her. Just to be sporting, Kristoff thought he would help tip the scales in her direction.

Upon reflection of the past several days, Kristoff had to admit this was the most fun he had had in a long time, minus the hag spitting on his shoes, poisoning, and carriage sabotage. Those were just small nuisances in the grand scheme of things. When his patron commissioned him for "one last service to the king" to deliver the land deeds to misplaced nobility and rightful heirs, how would he have known that his life would take such a drastic turn, a quick turnaround as it were?

It was supposed to be an easy delivery of papers, then an honorable decommission, then, perhaps, a small plot of land to start a life in the countryside away from chaos and tension. He had accumulated a tidy living along with his noble title and had contemplated tucking himself away and living in quiet solitude. Perhaps he would have bought some sheep, or other livestock, and become a gentleman farmer. He really had no clue what the future would hold.

With the stroke of luck and the blaze of auburn hair, every thought of any plans had been laid to rest. He had an inclination that a quiet life would never come to fruition, and he would always be on another adventure with his lovely Sprite. He had to admit that this was more appealing than a life alone in the country with a herd of sheep.

Gathering his thoughts, Kristoff eyed Elsa and, with a tilt of his head, beckoned her to approach him. He was trying to formulate a plan to help the young Melanie. Mycroft would reap the reward in tow. Elsa would know the grounds better than anyone. With her collaboration, they would make a fine conniving pair; one to decipher and one to guide and help with the lay of the gardens.

The young couple would need more than determination to pull off a win with this competitive crowd, especially Edmund and Andrew. He feared they would be the hardest competitors to overcome. Michael was so smitten with Persephone, Kristoff would not have been surprised if the twin had not found a small bush with his lovely partner to steal a kiss. The rest of the pairings were not a concern.

Rosalind could not miss the glint in Kristoff's eyes as he scanned the partners. When his gaze finally lingered on Melanie and Mycroft, she knew he was up to something. She was not sure if she should be concerned if there was a rift between the two, seeing how Mycroft had challenged him to a duel with a decorative sword the previous night. She assumed that in the eyes of Kristoff, Mycroft was an annoyance who needed to be managed so that he could finish his assignment.

When Elsa joined him over on the side of the garden and began in heavy discussion, Rosalind's interest piqued, indeed. She was going to follow him regardless, but now she was determined to join him and Elsa on the adventurous hunt. Then the corners of his lips turned up ever so slightly, the smile reaching deep into his eyes, turning them a deeper stormy gray.

His smile and his eyes were dancing in mirth as he made eye contact with her. That gray, she mused, that beautiful gray reminded her of the passion they had shared and of what he had demanded of her before he would share more. He made it seem as if he had grown to care for her and wanted the same in return.

Oh, God, she did care for him…more than care. For the briefest of seconds, she could not breathe. It was as if her heart stopped. It was a feeling that made her want to toss up her lovely nutty buns from this morning. *How could a man make me feel desirable and nauseated at the same time? Oh, God, he is such a cad!* she thought. This whole mess was his fault again. He just had to go and accept her for who she was. *How is a girl supposed to resist that?* she fumed. Then they would marry, and he would die, leaving her all alone in a crumpled heap of brokenness. No…she simply could not have it. She would not have it.

"Then it's agreed upon? We are to go to the left of the hedges and follow ten paces behind the young pair; that way, we can determine when we need to intervene to assist them, making sure not to be seen," commented Kristoff in a gentle tone with a wink. Elsa was nodding conspiratorially, rubbing her hands together like an eager little girl as Kristoff finished up his strategy. "Off with you, Miss Elsa, I'll join you in a moment."

"Ah, my darling Rosalind. How is everything faring? Miss Elsa and I would love for you to join us as we demonstrate our superior strategies in finding our bounty," Kristoff said with a wink, nodding in the direction of where Elsa had strolled off.

While taking her hand in his, he gingerly pulled her into his side as he began to stroke her palm ever so slightly with his fingertips. Warmth bonded them with a simple touch.

"My Love, are you feeling okay? I noticed a moment earlier that you became pale, as if your breakfast did not settle so well for you this morning. You did not taste some of the dish that the cat nibbled?" Kristoff added in a hushed tone and a close eye on Rosalind, concern etched across his brow.

Aghast at his keen observation skills, Rosalind shook her head slightly and mumbled, "I'm fine. I did not partake of the dish. If you recall, I was with you." She said this as scarlet crept up her cheeks. She surmised she would have to do better at disguising her feelings. He missed nothing.

Sighing with relief, Kristoff squeezed her hand, raised it to his lips, and kissed it gently as he looked into her eyes. There was a promise in his look of something more to come, smoldering hot between them. He released her hand, adjusted his to the small of her back, and ushered Rosalind into the maze following Elsa's lead. They looked at each other and smiled as they heard a loud chorus of name-calling. It sounded oddly like one of the twins, followed by laughter ringing out over the hedge.

"You have the most enchanting family." Kristoff smiled at her and meant it.

Melanie, after having read her first clue, charged on alone, Mycroft running in her wake, his shoes flopping like a fish that had inexplicably found itself on dry land. He called for her to wait, but she charged on like a wee locomotive and disappeared into the maze just ahead of Kristoff, Elsa, and Rosalind.

"Oy, Andrew! What are you doing with your head in the shrubbery?!! That's not going to work with the clue. Come over here and look over this again," Edmund bellowed over the hedges. "We have to hurry," he said and then shouted, "You know Nan cheats!"

From somewhere outside the maze, Rosalind heard Nan gasp aloud and then laugh. "I heard that, Edmund."

Rosalind could not stifle a giggle. She was thrilled that everyone was having such fun.

Michael and Persephone had made it to the middle of the maze with Heather in their wake. There, they found a sweet little cherub playing a lyre. The cherub was on a small, stone dais that was adorned with five rolled parchments. Each parchment was tied with a different colored ribbon with instructions on which color to take, depending on the team's last location. Michael smiled and realized he could outwit them all with a bit of subterfuge.

"Would you prefer green to match those lovely eyes of yours, my Lady?" Michael asked Persephone. He winked at her, and she blushed. My, he did love that particular shade of pink on her cheeks. She was just so charming.

"That would be lovely, or we could choose the blue to match that feather wisp of blue/gray in yours," she said, fluttering her eyelashes at him. Her heart fluttered like a butterfly when he winked at her. She longed to get him to kiss her again, but knew that was not proper. He would think her a wanton woman, and heavens, she did not even know what that even meant, but Mama always told her it was very bad and not to be flirtatious. She could not seem to help herself. She felt a bit silly, but her eyelashes just would not behave themselves when he was near.

Michael picked up the scroll and untied the green, silken ribbon. He handed the parchment to her, and then boldly took her wrist and tied the ribbon around it into a neat little bow. "There," he said, gently rubbing the inner part of her wrist. "Shall you read the clue aloud?"

She could barely catch her thoughts. She giggled as she drew her hand away from his. "Let's see," she said, unrolling the parchment. As she did, a small green gemstone fell out of the center. "Oh!" she said eagerly, handing it to him. "Look, we have a jewel. The clue says,

"'*Your gem is green, as is a lime, but go quickly. You are short on time.'*

"Is there a clock cherub or a lime tree? Perhaps something of the like in your maze, Michael?" she asked, letting his name roll off her tongue as if it were a delicious treat she was savoring.

Michael loved that she now had him and Edmund effectively sorted out. He smiled broadly at her and could not help sweeping a quick kiss above her gloved hand, and was thrilled to see her cheeks pink up yet again. "Beautiful and intelligent," he proclaimed to the air, drawing yet another radiant smile from Persephone.

"Indeed, we do have a sundial on a pedestal that normally sits right here in the center of the maze. If the lyre cherub is here, then the sundial must be in the eastern corner. I know the way." He outstretched his hand to see if she would take it. "We had best hurry. I can hear Ed and Andrew. Their shouting is getting closer. I say, I am not sure what Ros was thinking putting those two together. They never agree on anything," he laughed as he pulled her along and plunged back into the maze.

Michael, with Persephone and Heather in tow, had just made their way to the niche where the sundial cherub now stood as Melanie and Mycroft took off past them out of the niche. They were waving what appeared to be a golden arrow with a bit of parchment tied to it. Melanie was giggling as she ran off. Her poor mother was breathing heavily and leaning against the dial, waving her husband on to catch the two. She smiled warmly at Persephone and then scowled as she saw Michael release her daughter's hand.

Kristoff, Elsa, and Rosalind entered the alcove as well. It was getting quite crowded.

"Madam, are you well?" asked Rosalind with concern apparent in her voice. Rosalind had noted the woman's deep scowl and wondered what in the world Michael had done to deserve it, as it was directed at him.

Clearly, Michael had sensed the lady's mood as well. *That rascal,* Rosalind thought, as she watched her brother bow low enough to befit a queen and ask if he could have the privilege of escorting such a beautiful creature back to the refreshment table. He even winked at her. Dear Lord, what was he thinking! To Rosalind's amusement, Mrs. Maxwell blushed at his flirtation and actually batted her eyelashes at him…she batted them…at which point, Michael kissed her hand.

"Oh, go on with you, lad," she said and smiled at him. "I'll not steal you away from a far fairer catch."

She nodded at Persephone, who was looking rather perplexed by Michael's behavior.

Michael smiled broadly at her. "The apple does not fall far from the tree, Madam." He winked at her again, let go of her hand, and turned back to Persephone.

Rosalind and Elsa both stifled a giggle as Madam Maxwell literally sashayed out of the niche.

After that, however, the game was afoot again. Kristoff grabbed a golden arrow and handed Elsa the parchment. Persephone did the same, handing Michael her parchment to read. The two groups huddled in secrecy as they deciphered the next clue. Michael and Persephone seemed to solve it faster and stormed out of the niche. Michael began to whistle as he took Persephone's hand in his again and disappeared around a corner.

"He is quite the charmer, that one," Elsa commented and smiled, handing the arrow to Rosalind. "Where are we off to next?"

Rosalind tucked the arrow shaft into her skirt pocket as Kristoff unrolled the next clue.

After reading the clue aloud, Kristoff decided they were to go to the outer edge of the maze.

"I just happen to know a shortcut, my Lord," Elsa told him.

"Lead on, Miss Elsa. I shall happily follow."

Chapter Thirty-Four

Nan read the next clue, which led them to the center of the maze. As she looked up from the parchment, she discovered that the men were peculiarly eyeing each other. It was as if they were sizing each other up…Charles was brooding, and Jacob was looking at Charles through narrowed eyes. *This is truly uncomfortable,* thought Nan.

"Uhh…umm, gentlemen, the clue points us in that direction. Over there somewhere. Charles, do you remember where you had a sundial or something for telling the time?"

"Ah, yes, my dear Nan, it should be just over here to the right. If you will lead the way, and Jacob can take up the rear. Excuse me, my dear man."

Charles shouldered his way past Jacob as he escorted Nan toward the clue's hint.

The threesome approached the designated spot. There was only one parchment left in sight. Their team was lagging, if the parchment was any indication of the ranking system of the race.

"What is next on the list?" asked Charles. "We'd better get moving if we are to move up in the ranks. This is one of my sister's insane games, and she will have us going in circles if I am not the wiser. I'm sure we will just end up where we started. It's all about the chase, indeed! She is so much like Mama," Charles said with a longing smile.

Nan unrolled the last parchment and pocketed the gem as proof that they had completed this leg of the riddle. Dutifully, she began to read the clue aloud. Jacob and Charles hovered over the parchment in order to ponder the next riddle.

"What has a neck but no head?
You will find a parchment inside me if you were not misled."

There is but one, so be the first to find it, or you will dread.
Then to the winner's table, if you are wise to flee,
You will find a final gem with the lord of the manor, which he will give to
thee."

"Well, Mrs. Willoughby, that must be the oddest riddle I have ever read. What do you make of it? Can you decipher such a riddle?" implored Jacob.

With a dainty shrug, Nan gazed toward Jacob. Then she gasped as an idea popped into her mind.

"Is it a bottle, perhaps? The neck with no head…the neck of a bottle. Is that what Rosalind was referring to in this riddle?"

Charles began nodding in agreement.

"I do believe that you are onto something. Bottles…where did I see some bottles lined up neatly before we started this insane game?"

Jacob piped in with enthusiasm, "I saw them at the beginning, where your father was standing."

The threesome quickly rushed toward the maze entrance, but as they exited, they discovered they were last in line. Little Melanie looked as if she were about to bubble over like the champagne bottles they were picking up and setting aside in turn.

Nan laughed, "We will all be covered in champagne before this is done. Surely, there are empty bottles about, and not the ones within the picnic baskets. Look, Kristoff is even searching poor Lord Corbin's open bottle of brandy. See how Rosalind is smiling. She knows it is not there. Sneaky girl!"

Jacob pointed excitedly at a single bottle propped on the edge of the reflecting pool wall. Unfortunately, Melanie saw it at the same time, and she took off like a cat whose tail had been stepped upon and snatched it up, squealing in delight. She turned and skipped toward the winner's table.

From a distance, Edmund was in a full run toward the poor child, yelling, "Oy, give me my bottle. I lost it yesterday, seriously! That's my bottle. It has no clue. Come on, let's have it!"

Melanie glared at him and took off in a run again. She was so fast, poor Edmund never had a chance. She slammed the bottle on the table with a loud "crack" in front of Lord Englebright. Barely breathless, she bowed low and requested her final jewel, her smile as broad as could be.

As Melanie slammed the bottle down upon the table, Rosalind jumped with a start. She had not expected the girl to be quite so aggressive. Her adrenaline surged at the sudden noise, and she felt a pull in her shoulder. She shook it off and smiled warmly at Melanie.

Rosalind smiled at the girl and laid her hand on Kristoff's arm so he would stop searching in the viscount's brandy. She could not help laughing aloud. She had finally sorted out what he and Elsa had been up to. He was trying to help Melanie win the contest. He was being completely ridiculous, though, searching a full bottle and taking a nip or two to confirm it held no clue.

"Congratulations, Miss Melanie," Rosalind said as she pulled the final gemstone from her pocket and held it out to the beaming girl. Mycroft and the others circled, congratulating her as well. As Rosalind reached out to hand the stone to the girl, she noted that her shoulder stung quite a bit. She would need to put some liniment on the muscle later.

Persephone approached her with a look of concern on her face. She looked rather pale.

"Persephone, are you quite well?" Rosalind asked. "You look as if you might swoon. Father, come quickly. Persephone is not feeling well."

Michael ran to her aid immediately. "What is it, Miss? Can I help? Do you need a cool drink of water? Edmund, get Persephone some water immediately," Michael shouted.

Everyone was gathering around the poor girl when Rosalind's father took control. "Give the girl some air. Michael, go fetch a chair. My dear, did you overtax yourself?" he asked as he assisted the girl into a chair. She was looking more frantic with each additional question.

"Your daughter," she croaked out, looking as though she might be sick. "Lady Rosalind…" She pointed over and over, growing more and more frantic.

Lord Englebright looked at Rosalind, perplexed, and shrugged. "Yes, my dear?" he asked.

"She is bleeding profusely, my Lord," she all but shouted as she pointed at Rosalind, who looked completely dumbfounded and began looking at her arms and hands in confusion. Persephone then turned ghost white and fainted.

Chapter Thirty-Five

Desmond simply could not believe the damage that had been done to all the carriages while he was in the woods searching for that hag who had poisoned the cat. He could not fathom how some culprit could have gotten in, done the deed, and then gotten back out again with no one noticing, unless they did so in the dead of the night.

"Where is Markham and that wee lad brother of his?" he called to the farrier, Richard, who had also been recruited to aid in the repairs.

"I need someone to fetch some additional wood from the loft. We need grease, too. Thanks be to the Maker that we had spare wheels for at least a few of these carriages. The carriage maker in Newcastle should be here any moment with the rest," he called over his shoulder as he headed up the loft ladder, muttering to himself.

"A fine bounty he has reaped this day, that is to be sure," he sighed. "Six fine carriages were completely incapacitated, and two more nearly done so. Markham! Lad, are you up here?"

He lit the lantern on the hook near the ladder and took it in hand so he could throw open the loft door to the outside and allow some sunlight to pour into the space. This done, he set about searching for the needed axle wood, all the while calling down to the farrier a constant stream of chatter.

"I know I put those supplies up here somewhere last winter. Confound it, I cannot seem to recall exactly where."

He rummaged about the loft, which had been divided into separate storage areas. There were the grain bin and grain feeding system that connected to the stables, a storage nook for extra supplies for the smithy, some leather straps and halters, and a hay storage area to keep the supply dry and protected from the seasonal rains. There was also a scraggly old barn tabby that whiled his days away up here, assuring the mice population was kept at bay. They called him Mouse.

"'Ello, Mouse," Desmond called as he leaned to scratch the cat behind his ears. "What are you looking at so intently, my friend?"

The cat was staring into the corner where the hay was stored, but seemed to not want to go any closer. "Trapped yerself a morsel in there, have ye?" Desmond chuckled as he looked into the shadowed corner, but it was not a mouse or rat that he noted.

"What's this, then?" he asked aloud as he moved into the corner. He had seen a bit of material protruding from behind the neat stacks of straw.

"Blimey!" he shouted. "Richard, go fetch his Lordship. That hag we've been searching for is up 'ere dead as a doornail, she is. Been whacked all hard like over the head, it seems. Run quick," he said as he saw Richard poke his head up through the ladder hole and quickly disappear again.

Chapter Thirty-Six

Rosalind looked at Persephone's limp form as Michael supported her to keep the girl from falling to the ground. She then looked at her own front up and down, spinning slightly to see if she could ascertain what had the girl in a panic.

"I think I would know if I were bleeding profusely," she called to no one in particular. They all seemed intent on aiding the little miss and were ignoring her, with the exception of Kristoff.

"Hold still," he commanded as he examined her front and then back to look for injuries. "Ah," he said as he sucked in a breath. "I think I have found the source of Miss Persephone's swoon. You seem to have cut your arm during our hunt, love. Clearly, it does not pain you, since you took no note of it, but it is bleeding quite a bit."

He pulled his handkerchief from his pocket and placed it upon the cut, which was not deep, but did not seem inclined to stop bleeding either.

"Do you become faint at the sight of blood?" he asked and then smiled at the outraged look upon her face. Of course, she did not. Not much other than the thought of marriage seemed to cause Rosalind to become out of sorts. "I apologize, my dear. I did not mean to offend. Other delicate ladies would take to a swoon and then their beds for a fortnight over such an injury. You," he said, leaning in to take a closer look, breathing into her ear, "are more passion and storm than delicate flower."

The statement made so seductively in her ear made Rosalind weak in the knees. Did the man not realize he was supposed to fawn over her, sweep her into his arms, and whisk her away to the doctor? She would have hated every moment of it, but instead of doing the expected and treating her like a piece of bone china, he sounded as if he would like nothing more than to strip her bare and make her forget her wound in an entirely different manner.

She felt her heartbeat quicken again, and it made her want to throw caution to the wind and kiss him until they were both dizzy with the same passion he had kindled earlier that day. Always, Kristoff astounded her by not behaving as a gently bred man should. It always made her want him to do to her, she knew not what, but was certain the lawn was not the place for it.

Having seen the passionate dip of her eyelids as she looked at his lips while he dabbed at the injury, he felt his resolve leave him yet again. He reached beneath her legs and scooped her into his arms, calling to her father and yet never taking his eyes from hers, "My Lord, it appears your daughter has a minor injury. I will take her in and have Mrs. Gowan attend to it. Seems to be no more than a scratch."

He finally tore his gaze away from Rosalind's to look at her father, but damn it all, could tell he failed to hide the passion she had aroused in him. Lord Englebright looked knowingly at them both, nodded his agreement after a moment's hesitation, and returned to waving a fan in young Persephone's face as they awaited the smelling salts to do their trick.

"Best to get her away from Persephone, in case she sees the blood again once she awakens," Englebright called to him and Rosalind, but they were already halfway to the manor, Kristoff in a near run.

"Oh, how romantic," cried Madam Maxwell. "He is so fearful for her, he is in a near run. How rare a love match is," she said, dabbing at the corners of her eyes with a lace handkerchief.

Chapter Thirty-Seven

Kristoff could not get to the house quickly enough. His gait was purposeful and efficient. He wanted to tear her clothes off and bury his face in her amber hair as he kissed every inch of her firm body. She was so slight of form and yet had a strength of both body and mind that he could not get enough of. Her response from their earlier interlude had his muscles coiled and taut. He wanted her like nothing he had ever wanted in his life. He wanted all of her, not just her body, but her mind and her heart.

Rosalind had wrapped her arms around his neck as his long strides moved and flexed the muscles of his well-toned chest and arms against her soft form. It made heat pool in her belly and secret places to be carried so intimately. Kristoff did not go into the side door to see Cook as she anticipated, but slid around the manor house to the conservatory door.

He opened it with a flick of his wrist, never letting his hold on her falter. They slipped inside. The moment he was assured that they were alone, he lowered her and pinned her against the wall with his large form. He quickly tied the handkerchief in place after checking that the bleeding had stalled, and then he overtook her mouth like a hungry man feasting for the first time. He slanted his head so he could deepen the kiss.

"Open for me, Rose," he growled against her lip.

She did. She loved the taste of him; always mint, and heat. She swept her tongue over his, holding nothing back. She clung to him, forgetting the sting in her arm, wrapping her hands behind his neck to make sure he could not stop this passionate assault. She heard whimpering noises. Goodness, she was making those but could not stop.

He reached down and cupped her bottom and lifted her to cradle the very core of his manhood. He was so hard beneath her skirts. She was not sure of the full act of lovemaking, but the feel of him both excited and terrified her. He dipped his head to kiss a trail along her neck, nipping at her deliciously with his teeth. She boldly reached down to get a better feel of the hard planes of his chest, hands dipping lower to feel the very heat of him, which seemed to throb beneath her hand. It made her gasp and smile to have such power over him. He groaned.

"I cannot ravage you on the garden wall," he growled, frustration apparent in his voice, his breathing ragged.

"Please, Kristoff," she begged him to continue the sensual torment, tugging on his hair and drawing his lips back to hers. She licked his bottom lip and nipped it lightly with her teeth, mimicking the kisses he had placed upon her neck.

"Please," she whispered again, and again, upon his open mouth as they kissed.

He slowly lowered her so her slippers were once again resting upon the floor and held her against him, allowing his labored breathing to slow. He had nearly done it…had nearly taken her right then and there. Dammit, but she deserved a proper wedding night, not to be ravaged on a stone floor. He felt like a complete cad, but was also inordinately pleased with the passion they shared.

"My beautiful Rose," he said, kissing her hair and stroking her shoulders, still supporting her because she seemed to have gone rather weak-kneed with his love play.

"When we are wed, we will take each other in body, in spirit, in heart," he said meaningfully, looking into her passion-hazed eyes. He dipped his head and brushed his lips across hers again, more gently than before. "I want you to remember our first lovemaking as it should be. Not that I ravaged you in pure passion in the conservatory," he said, resting his chin upon the top of her head.

"What of my school?" she asked accusingly. He was taken aback by the swift change in topics. "If you whisk me away, Papa will be unprotected, in addition to all that I have worked for washing away in years of marriage, my dreams never being fulfilled. What of the village children I have taught?" she whispered. "How can I give those things up? Why can we not have this moment of passion and go back to our normal lives?" she pleaded with him, her hands on his lapels, shaking him a bit.

Placing his hands on top of hers, Kristoff began to strum his fingers on the back of her hands. "I am confused, my Rose. What of your schooling? Do you wish to attend university? I am supportive of those seeking more education. Do you want to pursue something in the sciences or perhaps a foreign language?

"As for the children in the village, I have a tidy living for us. We can build them a school in the village if they do not already have one. I am not up to date with education reform laws within England. I know not all villages have schools, and many children work the farms and have no time for a traditional classroom setting. It is, however, my belief that all should have access to education. I know it is not a popular idea among the Ton. Is that what you meant? Do you wish to build a school? That is a noble cause."

The more he spoke, the more upset she appeared and began shaking her head at him. He was so confused. He was uncertain what was causing her the most distress. Was he reading her so wrong as to think she was disapproving of educating the poorer class?

"Just stop talking," she nearly cried. He could see the tears pooling in her eyes. "I must go see Mrs. Gowan; my arm pains me." With that declaration, she fled from under his arm and ran from the room. Kristoff was left standing, arms propped against the wall, completely confused as to what he had said wrong. Perhaps her father could help him sort this mystery. Shaking his head, he left the conservatory to seek out his counsel and check on the welfare of the Maxwell girl.

Chapter Thirty-Eight

Derby ran as fast as he could to the manor after having found nothing in the woods near the maze. He knew someone had been shot when he heard the gunshot as he was moving back from behind the maze to rejoin the gathering. Then he heard a girl scream and saw the glint of metal in the woods. He immediately gave chase, but only caught a glimpse of the ruffians as they ran. There were three of them. He noted one with a large black eye. He was a short, portly man, but managed to run quickly through the woods, gain a mount, and was gone before Derby could get close enough for a shot of his own.

He burst into the front door and nearly ran Harold over. Gasping for breath and clutching Harold's arm, he shouted, "Where is George?"

"Sir, are you quite well?" Harold asked, holding the man up a bit. He was red-faced and appeared about to succumb to some overtaxation. "M'lord is in the study with Lord Van Reede. Is there mischief afoot?"

Harold was certain Lord Derby was not in danger of apoplexy.

"Is everyone else well? Tell me, man!" Derby all but shook the slender man as he questioned him.

Harold's eyes opened wider at the man's behavior.

"Well, sir, the poor young Miss Maxwell did have a swoon. You know the young and how excitable they can be at the sight of a bit of blood. She seems to have recovered well enough, and M'lady Rosalind's scratch is being tended to by Mrs. Gowan," he said as he gently removed the man's hands from his lapels, as he had nearly shaken him senseless.

"A scratch, you say?" Derby said with some relief. "I fear it may be worse than all that. Best you ready some fresh brandy. I have news to share that George will not take well at all," Derby said calmly. "I need to tell your lord that there was no scratch. His daughter has been shot."

Harold was stunned silent, and motionless for a split second. "Shot, you say? A nip or two might be just the thing," he said and walked away to do as he was asked.

Derby, having regained his breath, marched on to the study and flung open the doors without so much as a by-your-leave.

"George, sit down and brace yourself. This holiday of mine only seems to be getting worse. I need a drink, Kristoff. Do you mind doing the honors? Might be best to get us all a bit of the strong stuff."

He shared with them both what he had heard and seen in the woods. "Georgie, someone tried to shoot one of you, and it sounds as if they may have gotten Sprite."

Englebright roared just as Harold arrived with a fresh decanter full of a warm, brown liquid. Desmond followed in his wake. "M'Lord, you best be sittin'. I have bad news. You may want that nip Harold has before I tell ye," Desmond advised.

All three of the men in unison downed their glasses and handed them over to Harold for a refill, knowing the news did not seem to be getting any better with each new visitor to the study.

"We found that old hag, Edith, who tried to poison the household. Stone cold dead, she is. Head stoved in like a split cabbage up in the carriage house loft, sir. No clues I could see about who might have done her in. I feel like the guests should be sent on their merry way, but who's to say one of them is not involved, plus only a few carriages have wheels as of this moment. Should we call the constable, or shall Lord Derby take on this investigation?"

Derby looked at George with an exasperated but resigned look on his face.

"Well, hell's bells, man, why not?" he said as he threw his hands up. Eyeing Kristoff, he said, "I might need an assistant, you know. I nearly fell out from heart failure trying to catch those ruffians. I am getting too old for this nonsense. All of you, speak to no one of any of these goings on, but those in this room. We have a murderer to catch, perhaps in our midst…though that seems unlikely."

Kristoff just looked at the ceiling and shook his head in disbelief at what he had walked into when he came to this sleepy little village for his last bloody assignment.

George, in fact, did not take the news well. "Harold, assemble my children. We are having a family meeting immediately. Let Mrs. Gowan know there will be a wedding tomorrow with the nooning tea, with or without a vicar or special license. Kristoff will be staying within my daughter's rooms until this insanity is resolved."

Turning to Kristoff, he extended his hand and said, "Son, welcome to the family."

Chapter Thirty-Nine

Mrs. Ingrid had outdone herself with such short notice. She had talked Lord Englebright into postponing the wedding until at least four o'clock so that she and the kitchens would have time to prepare all that needed to be done for the occasion. He had grudgingly agreed, murmuring something about giving Sprite more time to bolt. The poor dear had the wedding jitters.

Ingrid had all the flowers from the birthday party repurposed and refreshed for the wedding. The beautiful yellow and white roses had been intermixed with fresh daisies from the surrounding fields. They were Rosalind's favorite. The wedding would take place in the large ballroom, rather than the village chapel, since it was on such short notice and at his Lordship's insistence. It was also already festooned with the blooming citrus trees from the orangery and more roses and daisies, so not much was needed to create a magical setting for the event. The delicate smell of the orange blossoms wafted through the house with the gentle breeze that blew in through the open windows.

She dabbed at the happy tears in her eyes intermittently as she worked; oh, the thought of their little Sprite marrying such a fine man. The special license had arrived all the way from Newcastle just that morning, along with a gift from the bishop himself. He was feeling a bit under the weather, she had heard, so was unable to perform the ceremony. The local priest, Father Tom, who had received the bishop's high praises, was to wed the happy couple in his stead. She knew it would be such a joyous event as her lady was so in love with the handsome Kristoff. It was a sound, love match, she thought, letting the tears flow down her cheeks as she dusted each little niche and placed new tapers into each candle holder.

Mrs. Gowan could not have been more thrilled than she was today. She was making a wedding feast for their sweet Lady Sprite, well, actually repurposing the feast for his Lordship to an even happier purpose. She had immediately sent away for reinforcements with the local townsfolk she knew could be trusted with this undertaking.

Many of the women were happy for the respite from the daily grind of their chores. They all had such a fondness and respect for the family, and especially Lady Rosalind, for all she had done for their children, that they were more honored to return some of her kindness. Their husbands and children were invited to the wedding as well, though many would not come, feeling out of place with the other members of the elite who were already in attendance at the manor. They were honored to have been invited.

The meal itself was an easy preparation, as it had been planned for weeks for Lord Englebright's continued festivities. They would have roasted early root vegetables seasoned in an herbed butter sauce for the first course. The second course would be a cool vichyssoise made of leeks, finely chopped potatoes, and cream, cooked and blended until velvety smooth, then chilled in the icehouse until wintry cold. The soup would be garnished with a bit of Indian curry just before serving, which helped give the feeling of warmth as the creamy soup was eaten. The piece de resistance would be whole roasted suckling pigs with an apple stuffed into each piglet's mouth.

Dessert was the more troubling course, as instead of a grand birthday cake, she now needed to prepare both a birthday and a wedding cake to combine the celebrations. Rosalind demanded to have it no other way if she was to be wed during her father's special celebration

In order to do so, Mary decided to make a two-tiered English plum cake piped with delicate royal icing, featuring intricate loops, basket weaves along the sides, and sugared daisies and candied rose petals sprinkled about the top layer. The cake filling would be Rosalind's favorite nutty buns mixed with cream sauce until the mixture made a sort of pudding. The flavor was simply divine. The whole atmosphere in the kitchens was a happy one, full of laughter and merriment as the work continued.

Rosalind was a wreck. She had tried every way possible to talk her father out of this insanity, but he would hear none of it. He had told her that Kristoff would be sleeping in her chamber from this night on, wed or not. She could not believe his audacity. One little bullet mishap, and they had all lost their minds. She was so worried about her father and just knew that bullet was intended for him and not her. Who would protect him?

She had gone to Andrew, Charles, and Derby in turn to have them swear they would not leave his side and to convince him to cancel the wedding. It was just too dangerous having that many people milling about the estate. They all smiled at her, assured her they would protect her father, all the while patting her hand as if she were some dotty old woman in need of consoling, and leading her back to her room. As a last resort, she turned to Nan to speak sense to them all.

"Nan, this is madness. Surely, you agree with me. We have a dead woman in the hay loft, a gunshot that nearly took my father out of this world. How would marrying today correct any of this or protect my father? Can they not see he is in danger?" she demanded, pacing around the room.

"Ara, love…*you* were shot, not your father, dear."

"Do not speak to me as if I am a fool. I am well aware of this paltry scratch upon my arm, but assure you they were aiming for father."

"Dearest, your father is sure that if they had been meaning to hit him, they would have. He believes it to be a warning to him, but of what, no one seems to understand, nor why. This all does seem rather odd and horrifying. When I think that you were shot…well, I cannot fathom life without you. We would have you safe. It is safe to assume that when Kristoff is with you, you are better protected."

"Oh, stuff and nonsense. He was with me already, and I was shot. You sound like the rest of them. There must be another way. Perhaps if I were to go to the woods, I could find these ruffians and dispatch them with my lovely little derringer." She nodded to herself as she paced back and forth in front of Nan's bed.

She looked deep in thought as she paced. Nan was getting a bit dizzy watching her.

"Do you know he told me he would use his considerable funds to build a village school," she said as almost an afterthought. "But then I am sure he plans to wed me, bed me, and run off with me, leaving my dream behind." Rosalind dramatically threw herself upon Nan's bed and sighed. "Perhaps I could sneak off to Mama's cottage and have a think for a moment…away from all this?" she questioned, peering over at Nan to see if she could garner her friend's aid in sneaking away.

"Do you wish me to call Elsa in here so we may sit upon you until it is time to dress your hair?" Nan said matter-of-factly. "How could you even think to leave when you could be in such danger! This is not a game, Rosalind. These people have killed and would have done so again. Kill you!!! You, my dearest friend. Do you really think to run off and risk that?"

Rosalind sighed again. "I am only expressing my frustration with this situation. You know I would not do that to you, nor Papa…nor my brothers…"

"But what of Kristoff?" asked Nan. "You know he cares for you. Everyone can see it clearly upon his face every time he is near you."

"It is like an illness of the stomach," Rosalind stated, closing her eyes tightly as if to shut out the world entirely. "It will pass."

"The man said he would build you a school, you have made note he is no dandy like the others who have courted you, and he is strong of both character and body. Dear me, he is built like Adonis…and you still find fault with him. What is the real issue, Ara? Surely, you are not still scared. We have discussed this until I am nearly nauseated with the topic. You give me the vapours, my friend."

"I have no desire to be stifled. We think we know this man, but what do we really know? Perhaps he is the infamous spy. You know, the Raven," Rosalind said as she jumped up and whirled to face Nan.

"He seems to say all the correct things now, do all the correct things, seems to be my dream come true. His passion is real enough, but once things cannot be undone, then it is too late. I do not want to love him, but feel like I am falling into a chasm where all my waking thoughts are of him. How can anyone live like that? How will I ever accomplish my goals if all I can think of is him?"

"Ah," said Nan. "It is not a kiss of death, you know? This is a new beginning, and an exciting new adventure. You love adventure. Let Kristoff *be* your new adventure if you are brave enough. I feel he will not disappoint you. He loves you," she said, poking Rosalind in the shoulder.

"I will make you a deal," she said, looking at Rosalind as seriously as she could. "If you marry him, and he becomes a brute, I will help you do him in and hide the evidence. I am sure we can find a pig farmer." She smiled sweetly at her friend, and then both burst into laughter.

"Truly, Nan. That is the most gruesome thing you have ever said," she laughed again.

Though Nan saw some of the tension leave her friend's face, she suspected this discussion was far from over. Best to get her dressed, shove her in front of Father Tom, and get it done before she could bolt.

Chapter Forty

George could not help tearing up when he saw his beautiful daughter escorted down the steps by both her older brothers. She was a vision in the lovely gown Nan had made for her. It flowed around her and made her look like an ethereal fairy, otherworldly and simply stunning. Her grandmother's Belgian lace veil trailed her. He knew Kristoff's breath would be taken with one glance.

She smiled nervously at her father as she approached and took his arm. "Don't let me fall, Papa," she whispered shyly as he embraced her and kissed her upon her head.

Elsa had intertwined daisies into her braid, along with small crystal pins that held her mass of curled locks into place. He turned her around to face away from him and clasped a necklace around her neck.

"I gave this to your mother upon our first anniversary. I would like you to have it now. It is a way to have both your mother and your grandmother with you for the day, my sweet girl." The pendant was a beautiful marquise cut sapphire that was so blue, it was nearly black unless the light played upon it just right.

"Oh, Papa!" she exclaimed. "It is truly lovely. Thank you." She almost cried as she hugged him tightly.

Nan then came to her and placed a small silver bracelet upon her wrist. It had a delicate little crest dangling from the clasp.

"And this I would have you wear as a symbol of our friendship and for hope. It was left to me by my father. I wore it on my wedding day as well. I would be honored if you wore it today." Nan gently secured the bracelet upon Rosalind's wrist.

"Oh, Nan, my sister at heart. Of course, I will wear it and take the utmost care to keep it secure and safe for the day," she said as she admired the dainty silver charm. Emotions swept over the friends as

Rosalind hugged Nan. "I am so happy you are here with me and will be my matron of honor. You mean the world to me," she said earnestly, looking into Nan's eyes. "Thank you for always talking sense into me, my dearest friend." She smiled again and squeezed Nan's hand as her brothers approached her.

"You clean up right nicely, Sprite," the twins said in unison. "Here is a sixpence to put into your shoe from each of us, so you always have good luck. We figure two is better than one, though Elsa told us one was enough. Seems a bit cheap to us, so…well, you got two. You can put one in each shoe." Both twins leaned in conspiratorially and whispered, "That way, if you do run, you will be well-balanced and can make a cleaner getaway." They both waggled their eyebrows at her and moved off so Andrew and Charles could give her their gifts next.

"You trust me, Sprite, do you not?" asked Andrew. She nodded her agreement immediately. "You know he is *truly* a good man. Give him a chance to show you," he said, tipping her gently under the chin with his finger. He then gave her the most beautifully embroidered handkerchief to tuck into her hidden pocket. "May this only receive tears of joy on your next adventure, Sprite. I love you and wish you all the happiness the world has to offer." He picked her up and swung her around.

Charles had tears in his eyes as he approached her. "You remind me so much of Mother; her beauty, her spirit, her joie de vivre, my sweet sister. No one can ever crush that. You are too strong. He loves you. Allow yourself the freedom to love him, too," he said as he handed her a beautiful bouquet. Tucked inside, she found a little bit of parchment wrapped tightly and tied with a ribbon. She looked at him quizzically.

He smiled and said, "For your first adventure as a married couple. Open it later when you two are alone."

He winked at her and kissed her upon her cheek and then raised her hands and admired the delicate bracelet Nan had placed upon her wrist. The small circle of silver had three tiny wasps above a crest containing a shield and a thistle.

Rosalind sighed as she steeled herself for the next steps. She placed her hand upon her papa's just as the stringed quartet began to play *Ode to Joy*. Charles, looking so handsome in formal attire, took Nan's arm and began to escort her down the aisle. Each of her other brothers then walked in one by one to stand in support of Kristoff since he had no family present.

Little Melanie had been denied the first dance, since it was now a wedding event, and thus, they requested that she be the flower attendant. She looked adorable in a pale blue satin gown and simply glowed with happiness as she sprinkled the rose petals upon the aisle between the guests.

The quartet then began to play *Canon in D*, which was her father's signal to escort her in. "Papa, please hold tight," she whispered. "Don't let me run, please."

"I've got you, Sprite. Always," he said and kissed her on her hand, then escorted her to her intended.

Kristoff's stance relaxed when he finally saw her. She was a vision. She looked up at him through her lace veil. He wanted to tear the thing away so he could see her eyes; see if the fear was still there. He prayed she would see they could have a wonderful life together. He would do all in his power to make her happy.

Rosalind was touched by the look Kristoff was giving her. He looked at her as if there was no one else in the room. She felt cherished and seen for who she was. For the first time, it felt right, like it would all be ok. She took a deep breath and took his arm and faced the priest.

The vows seemed to be done and over with so quickly that Rosalind was a bit dumbfounded as Kristoff was informed he could lift her veil and give her the first kiss as a married couple. The kiss was sweet and gentle, but far too brief for her liking, or for his, if the look he gave her was any indication. It held forbidden promises.

As quickly as that, they were swept off into the crush of well-wishers. Friends and family alike were hugging them both and patting each upon the back. They were then whisked into the dining room, where a feast was ready to be laid before them. She could not wait.

"I'm starving," she said and smiled at Kristoff. His gray eyes stared back as he leaned down and whispered, "As am I." For some reason, she did not think he meant food. Again, that hot feeling began to build in her belly.

"You know, Kristoff," she whispered, "we are now properly wed." She leaned in as if she were sharing a secret and nibbled his ear instead. She heard him inhale deeply as he shuddered ever so slightly.

"You little minx, are you trying to be my undoing before we even reach the dinner table? You are going to make this damned uncomfortable if you do not behave." He grasped her chin and leaned in for a quick kiss, flicking her lip quickly and pulling away before anyone noticed the intimacy. Her eyes widened in surprise that she enjoyed this flirtatious game.

They sat down for the feast in deference to their guests, as no one could eat until they were seated and the toasts were made. Rosalind began to stroke his thigh as her brothers began the toasting. Each wished them well. The twins had even composed a ballad for them, much to their father's dismay. All the while, Rosalind was growing bolder with each sip of champagne, her hand inching up his thigh. He curled his hand around her wandering fingers and began to trace circles in her palm. He stroked the length of each finger, gently, as he never took his eyes off each new well-wisher.

For Rosalind, the meal unfolded at a pace that made it feel as if the clock has just stopped. The food was phenomenal, as usual, but she was so anxious for what was to come, she barely ate more than a bite or two of each dish.

"Cook would be very upset with me if she knew I was only slightly sampling the fare tonight."

Kristoff laughed. He had actually never seen a more delicate creature eat as much as his petite bride. Smiling at her, he said, "I am not sure even the twins ate as much."

She grinned and shrugged.

"I have it under good authority that I will require a great deal of strength and vigor for the evening's continued activities." She actually winked at him. "Dancing, you know, can be quite exhausting."

"Ah, I see. And pray, M'lady, who counseled you on these activities? Do I need to have a serious exchange with the wee Mycroft? He is rather taken with you. I do believe he may have a pistol hidden in his trousers this eve in order to do me harm. He may actually challenge me to a duel once the wedding celebration is completed," he leaned in and whispered. "I shall ever be on my guard."

Kristoff gently poked her in the rib, causing Rosalind to jump and giggle in response to the jab.

She glanced at Mycroft, who did look a bit put out, but she believed it was due to the animated conversation that Jacob was having with Nan.

"Mycroft seems to have had a shift in his affections." She raised her champagne flute to Nan and smiled. Nan had only just realized the boy was glaring at Jacob. In short order, however, Michael and Edmund had pulled their friend from his chair, shoving him into the midst of a conversation with some local boys and girls more his age.

The meal ended, and the serving staff were clearing away the dishes. The ballroom was being cleared of chairs as well so the dancing could begin. The newly wedded couple was slowly making their way to their first dance, thanking additional well-wishers as they went.

"I know we must follow decorum," Kristoff leaned down and murmured into her ear, "but I simply cannot wait to help you out of this dress. It looks much too confining. Can you even breathe in that corset?"

He ran his finger along the satin top of the bodice, just brushing the skin beneath. He smiled at the blush that rose to her cheeks. He could not resist the urge to brush his lips across hers in a brief whisper of a kiss. She sighed at his touch.

Watching from across the room, her father could not have been more pleased. Rosalind seemed truly happy. It was all he had ever wanted for her, and he knew Kristoff would treat her well and encourage her dreams. He was also confident he could keep her safe.

A series of stringed notes reached the dining hall as the musicians began to warm up their delicate instruments; a signal to the couple that they should retire to the ballroom. It was obvious that the staff had quickly and meticulously cleared out the chairs and floral archway from the ceremony to accommodate the dancers. Luminaries of various sizes were sprinkled about the room, casting shadows and reflections on the walls. Rosalind always loved it when Mrs. Ingrid integrated them into the decor. It made her think of the summer fireflies dancing in the woods. Mrs. Ingrid was always so considerate of bringing the outside into the manor. The night could not get any better.

"Shall we, my love?" Kristoff beckoned her as he gently placed his hand on the small of her back and swept her around into his arms.

Their first dance would be a waltz, intimate and close. All eyes were giving them admiring looks. A few of the older ladies were even dabbing their misty eyes as they smiled at the loving couple. He held her far closer than was proper and kissed her upon her head as the onlooking ladies cooed at the obvious love they shared. There was no question for any of the guests now that this was indeed a love match.

Kristoff was confident all thoughts of scandal would be washed away. The only person who looked displeased was Lord Durham. He had a scowl as deep as a plowed row of earth. Kristoff suspected that the man was so adverse to being near a scandal that he could not just enjoy the evening.

As the first measure began, he looked at her deep blue eyes. "Ah, the Little Doves Waltz. This seems fitting for you, my graceful bride. You look as lovely as a dove."

She smiled at him and allowed him to expertly twirl her about the room, picking her up off the floor for the more sweeping curls. She was pressed into him tightly enough to feel the span of his muscled chest upon hers. His breathing was becoming ragged, as they spun and spun, not with exertion, but with his need to feel more of her, all of her. As the music faded, the crowd began to clap in approval. He leaned over her and kissed her right in front of everyone. The kiss was short but held the promise of all they would share this night. She was exhilarated by those promises, unspoken and yet shared so clearly.

"I have a gift for you in the library. Will you attend me for a moment?" he asked, watching her intently.

Her blue eyes were like pools of ocean. He could see the waves of passion in them and knew if Rosalind and he were to be alone, he would have to control the tempest brewing between them. She matched his passion, which had been like a blazing fire between them since their first meeting. Her gaze fell to his lips, and he knew she was thinking of their kisses again. He felt the heat growing in his trousers. It took all his self-control not to scoop her into his arms and take her to a bedroom right then. He needed to get some things said to her before he let their control slip into oblivion.

"Come, my beautiful bride." He grasped her hand and gently pulled her from the room.

"Is this a ploy to get me alone for a moment?" she accused with a teasing tone. "I assure you, I am quite willing to steal your kisses."

"When the moment is right, my dear, I will freely give you all the kisses your heart can desire…and more," he replied and winked knowingly at her, and squeezed her hand. Her indrawn breath pleased him immensely. Their shared passion might just do them both in.

He drew her in through the library door and shut it with a soft click behind her. He turned the key in the lock so they would not be interrupted this time. He noted she upturned her face to his as if to receive a kiss. It took his complete resolve to deny pressing his lips to her willing ones, but he needed to tell her some things. He felt as though his heart would hammer out of his chest, and he had never been this nervous even before his first battle.

He took her hand in his and looked about the room. This was where it all began. His feelings had, in this very room, melted from affection and amusement to something more profound. He had never believed in love at first sight until it all but knocked him on the head. He moved to the piano and pulled a package from the bench. It was wrapped plainly, with minimal adornment. He thought that best suited her personality. He handed her the package and waited for her to open it.

She looked down at it. The package itself was a simply wrapped parcel with a narrow piece of twine holding the paper together. Examining the package in her hands, she looked up at Kristoff.

"Shall we sit?" she asked, motioning to the small settee.

"By all means," he agreed and escorted her over.

Settling beside her, he seemed incredibly uncomfortable and nervous. For such a large and confident man, this seemed to contrast with his typical nature that she had been drawn toward. Butterflies in the pit of her stomach began to swirl anew, having nothing to do with their earlier intimacy. She began to fret. With furrowed brows, Rosalind pulled at the twine.

The parchment fell open in her lap. Lying there before her was a bit of what appeared to be clothing constructed of sturdy linen. Kristoff nervously grabbed the cloth and held it up for her to examine more closely. It was a pair of breeches that appeared to have been constructed with her curves in mind. She could see Nan's insignia on the hem of the left pant leg.

"I had them commissioned for you after our first visit to this library. I was fearful she was not going to have time to construct them, but she is a marvel, that Nan."

He continued babbling on nervously. "I want you to understand that I accept you as you are, for all you are and have been before our marriage and will continue to be as my wife."

He searched her face for any response. She just looked dumbstruck and began to tear up. He felt his confidence bolstered by her response. He took her hands in his and placed them over his heart, and waited for her to look into his eyes. "Can you not see how so very much you have come to mean to me? You have captured all of me; my body, my thoughts, my heart. I am yours. My love is yours, Arabella Rosalind Van Reede, and will be until the day I die."

With this last declaration, Rosalind's face went pale. He waited for her response, acknowledgment…anything except the panic he read on her face. He would have loved her matched declaration, but knew it was unlikely he would gain such as yet. He surmised it would take her time, but damn it all, did she not realize this was no easier for him to speak his feelings?

"Say something, Rose…anything."

As she opened her mouth, a quick rapping sounded upon the door. "I…" She paused. "I had better get that. It could be Father," was all she could manage to squeak out to him. He dropped the cloth onto his lap in frustration.

She quickly ran to the door, unlocked it, and flung it open to find her father smiling at her warmly, but his face quickly fell when he saw how pale she was. "Are you well, darling?" he asked.

"Of course, Papa," she said, slapping a smile upon her face. "Only I have failed to give you the customary turn about the dance floor. Shall we?"

"Certainly, my dear," he said, pausing to look from her to Kristoff. "Give me but a moment of your husband's time, and I will meet you there." He noted that she flinched a bit when he said the word "husband."

Rosalind smiled at him, but it failed to reach her eyes. "Of course, Papa." With that, she stepped out and started to close the door.

He grabbed her wrist before she could shut the door completely. "And dear," he said to her knowingly, "do not leave the manor. You know it is still unsafe, even with Derby's men stationed all about the estate. I mean it, Rosalind."

Again, she said blankly, "Of course, Papa."

She then closed the door and began to immediately run toward the rear entry.

Chapter Forty-One

Michael was ever the gentleman. He was attentive toward Miss Maxwell. He had been somewhat concerned about the swooning event and how pasty she appeared directly afterward. It was quite alarming. He was delighted to see that color had returned to her beautiful face. She had chosen a lovely lavender gown bejeweled with light blue crystals along the hemline. The lavender accented her summer-green eyes. She was such sunshine in this darkened ballroom, no offense intended to the bride, of course.

Edmund had been long shot of him and his pining away for the lovely Miss Maxwell. Exasperated with hearing how lovely she was, he had left Michael to the wooing of the "cake" as he now called her, and went in search of Nan to see if she would be amenable to taking a turn about the floor with him.

To continue with his "wooing" and "charming," Michael also extended his caring hand toward Persephone's mother. She was a pleasant surprise with a quick wit once one spent some time with her. She had a quick smile for him and eagerly laughed at his jokes. He happily placed his name on Lady Maxwell's dance card. She was as delighted to accept as her husband was more interested in drinking in the gaming room than twirling on the dance floor.

Michael then added his name to Persephone's card for the next waltz. His plan was to win over the mother so she would not be quite so scandalized at him dancing the intimate dance with her daughter. Persephone had blushed her lovely shade of rose at him and curtsied shyly when it was her turn to dance. As he spun her about the floor, he gathered her closely in his arms, but not so close that it would cause the girl to be the target of gossip. He enjoyed the soft timbre of her voice as she answered his series of seemingly ridiculous questions. He had so many things he wanted to know about her.

There was a mischievousness about him that Persephone found endearing. Michael had been asking her questions of the likes of her favorite type of cloud, and what her preferred pet was, if she could choose any animal in the world. His was a hedgehog. She had laughed aloud at that declaration. His questioning never seemed to cease, and yet she found herself pouring out her preferences, dreams, even some that would be considered progressive and not at all heard of in a typical lady.

He twirled her again and asked in a hushed tone, "What kind of cake do you like?"

"Cake?" She smiled at his latest inquiry. "I must say, I am rather fond of *queen cakes*, heart-shaped, of course. Why?"

"Why? Well, Miss Maxwell," he continued, "you smell as delicious as cake…all vanilla and some sort of spice I cannot quite place, but it reminds me of the kitchens when Mrs. Mary, our cook, is making plum cake. I want to know which cake I am to partake of and think of you. In fact, shall we return to the gathering area to enjoy some…cake, that is?" He winked at her and was delighted to see her blush nearly scarlet.

"Oh, Michael," she gushed, accepting his arm and giving it a light squeeze. "You are so romantic. Cake? I smell of cake?" She laughed lightly. "How could I have ever mistaken you for Edmund?" Persephone sighed as she pondered the question aloud, as she allowed him to escort her to the cake table.

As they passed the open doors that led to the hall, Michael noticed Rosalind fleeing toward the outer doors. He sighed heavily as he smiled at Persephone.

"I am afraid I must leave you for a moment, but never fear, I can never resist a lovely cake for long." He kissed the air above her hand and went on a hunt for Kristoff to alert him to catch his bride before she made it too far.

Chapter Forty-Two

"Father, she has made a run for it," Michael said cheerily. "Edmund owes me a quid."

His father glowered at him. "Do you not think this is serious? We have scoundrels about, and your sister is running, Lord knows where, with them out there."

"Scoundrels? Oh, you mean those dirt poachers. Right! I am sorry, Father, I forgot about that." Michael felt like a cad. He had been so caught up in the fun, he failed to think about Rosalind's safety.

"I'll fetch Derby and the rest to go look for her through the house and gardens."

"Stay together in at least pairs of two. Do not disobey me in this."

"Yes, sir," he called while leaving the room.

Kristoff could not believe she had run from him after he had opened his heart to her. He stood there dumbfounded and just looked at his new father-in-law, not sure of what to do or where to start looking.

"The cottage…I bet she made for Anna's cottage," Englebright said, nodding at Kristoff.

"That will keep her safe enough. It is quite well-hidden."

"You mean the cottage on the east side of the wood, where I saw those three scoundrels? I hardly think her safe, my Lord. Quickly tell me the most direct route there. You and her brothers search the house, but stay together. This could give our enemy the opening they need. Damn it all, why did she run?" he nearly yelled as he ran his hands through his hair, waiting to be told how to get to the cottage.

"She is fearful of love and death since her mother's passing. That is why she never wished to marry. She could not bear the thought of finding and losing love. Take care with her, Kristoff, be easy, or she will keep running. I have tried for years to allay her fears, to no avail."

Kristoff nodded, now understanding where he had gone wrong. Damn it all. Why did he have to say, "until the day I die?" She did love him. She had to. She just didn't know it yet. He would have sighed in relief if he did not fear for her safety. He ran out the door and made for the entry, praying he could head her off before someone else did.

Chapter Forty-Three

Kristoff scanned the line of trees where Lord Englebright had directed him. There, a path led into the woods and eventually came out at the cottage, he was told. He just saw the glimmer of her jeweled gown disappear into the tree row. How in the heavens she ran so fast in such a heavy gown, he could not fathom. He smiled. She was quite determined to escape him. Unfortunately for her, he was just as determined to catch her. What would he do then? Well, he was not quite sure.

He knew what her father said to be true. The moment he had mentioned he would love her until the day he died, her face had grown ashen. He was a fool and thought her fear was of love all along. She feared loss. How in the bloody hell he was supposed to overcome that, he did not know. Loss was inevitable in life, but so were joy and happiness. He just had to figure out how to show her those things were worth the risk.

He ducked into the woods as she turned a curve in the path a good distance ahead of him. He smiled as he heard her curse rather loudly and tug the dress free from a shrub. It whipped back and slapped her upon her behind. He almost laughed aloud as she cursed again. Some of her language would have made a barmaid blush. He probably shouldn't be so amused by it, but he was.

He continued following and stifled another laugh as he saw her scream at a tree. She jumped back and took a boxer's stance. He was near to tears in silent laughter as she declared to the offending tree that she was no schoolgirl. Apparently, that would fend it off, he thought with a chuckle.

He slowed his pace. She was safe enough. He had seen Derby's men roaming the treeline and one trailing her, hidden from her sight.

Kristoff nodded at the man, stopped, and quickly whispered for him to make way directly for the cottage and make sure the path was clear, but to not let her see him. Kristoff would trail her and keep her safe.

He was suddenly glad he had sent the man off, as she was apparently determined to run naked through the trees. What was that fool woman doing? Her skirt had snagged upon another shrub, and that, it seemed, was her last straw. She began tugging and ripping at the beautiful skirts Nan had created for her. Every tear was followed by another rather unladylike curse. He just stood back and watched, but then noted her long, toned legs near to glowing in the pale moonlight. He felt himself growing hard as he watched her. The fog was crawling up those beautiful legs, and he suddenly wished he could be made of fog as well, just to caress her without her trying to escape. His blood began to warm…

Deuces and Devils…that was a new one. He was not even sure what the phrase meant, but it seemed to make her feel better.

She took off again at a full pace, but in a different direction from the trail, looking behind her as she went. Every few steps, she stopped and looked behind her again and switched directions, zigzagging across the trail. Kristoff just shook his head. Did she really think to obscure her trail by backtracking over it again and again, cursing loudly as she went? She really must be addled by his declaration. That stung a bit, but at least now, he understood. As she ran, white daisies and crystal pins rained upon the forest floor. That beautiful hair of hers was tumbling down her back in a moonlit waterfall of reds and gold. He smiled as he saw the twigs sticking out. That did seem to be a problem she had frequently, he thought and smiled.

Kristoff picked up her discarded skirts and headed to the cottage. He figured it would take her a bit to get there since she seemed intent on making the trip four times longer than it should have been. He went to find Derby's man and make sure all was well.

"My Lord, all is right as rain hereabouts. I had Charlie check the surrounding wood, and I ain't seen hide nor hair of them scoundrels. My, but that gal of yours is making a racket. I ain't never heard a gently bred lady speak such. She is surely in a snit, she is. I don't envy you the wooin' this night, sir."

"Too bold, man, but indeed." He smiled. "It does seem she is in a bit of a state. I fear I may be the cause. Kindly speak nothing of the words you have heard her mutter. Her brothers were in need of a stern talking to, that's to be sure. I think they have taught her some phrases a sailor would be embarrassed to mutter. I think you can return to the post Derby had you assigned to. Oh, and thank you."

Kristoff held out his hand to shake.

The hired man was taken aback. Handshakes from the elite were saved for the elite. No man of breeding in London proper would lower himself enough to proffer a hand to a low-born. This was a fine gentleman, indeed. "Carmichael, m'Lord." He took the offered hand and shook. "And I do wish you as pleasant a night as can be had, sir," he said with a wink. "She's a fine one, that Lady Englebright. I think you suit her well, if you don't mind me sayin'." He turned and left, shaking his head, muttering about what a fine lady she was.

As Carmichael disappeared into the trees, Kristoff heard the rustle of leaves in the opposite direction of the path. The fool lady had gone off-trail the entire trip, it seemed. He went into the cottage and waited for her patiently, and was quickly rewarded by the most lovely sight. She walked into the cottage, clad in nothing but her sheer stockings, bloomers, short chemise, and top corset. Her breast heaved beautifully, he thought as she all but melted against the door. God, how he loved this blasted minx.

Stepping out of the darkness holding her sparkling skirts aloft, he asked her, "Forget something, my love?" and could not help smiling wickedly at the look on her face as she jumped and fell flat on the floor.

Chapter Forty-Four

Rosalind stretched languidly, with little recognition of her surroundings. It was dark and warm, but where was she? Slowly, memory returned, and she gasped as she realized she was stretched out on a feather mattress and no longer wearing the confining corset. She was in nothing but her underthings and stockings. She could see him standing beside the fireplace, the embers from the fire he had built creating a halo of orange around his powerful form. His cravat lay crumpled on the chaise beside him, and his shirt had been unbuttoned so that she could see the golden, velvety hair of his chest just peeking out. He had removed his vest and waistcoat and tossed those aside as well. She watched him, not moving so he would not realize she had awoken.

Dear Lord, she had actually swooned. The brute had made her swoon, or was it all that running while in a corset? Either way, it was his fault. If he had not spoken those words to her in the library, none of this would have happened. What was he thinking? And why was he smiling now? As she remembered their first kiss, her skin began to heat. She closed her eyes and remembered the feel of his lips on hers. He tasted of peppermint and a hint of scotch, delicious and warm. She wondered what he would taste like now. She slowly licked her lips, trying to recall how *his* tongue had done the same.

Rosalind opened her eyes and looked across the room to help bolster her mental picture of his strong muscles while she tried to remember what it had felt like to be entwined in his arms. He had told her he would build her a school. Damn it, she could not think of life without him now. She was by no means ready to declare anything to him, but perhaps…just perhaps, this night could be the beginning of something new and exciting. Maybe it would be ok like Nan said. He was strong and healthy…so very healthy by the look of those breeches.

Surely, he could survive a nice, long life with her. For now, she just needed to survive the night.

He was looking at her body, his gaze slowly traveling the length of her. So, she did the same to him. Two could have that boldness, she thought. Her breath caught when her eyes fell upon his midsection. His breeches were pulled taut against that thick protrusion, which seemed to have grown further in the last few minutes. She was not quite sure what he thought to do with *that*, but it brought a warm feeling to her belly just looking upon it. She was blushing, she knew, but she could be just as brazen as he was. He started this with a kiss, and by God, she was going to finish it to her satisfaction; all traces of her previous fear were gone.

She slowly lowered her feet to the floor and stood, raising her hands to the ties of her chemise. She took one string in her hand and gave it a slow, gentle tug until it came free. Her eyes never left his. She then pulled the laces loose and let the garment begin to drop from her shoulders. *Good gracious, can I do this?*

Kristoff could not believe the transformation. She went from praying and swooning to becoming a brazen she-devil. Was she trying to drive him over the edge? It was working, whatever her intent. His breeches were near to ripping as his engorged sex strained against the seams. They were damned uncomfortable, that was for sure.

As her chemise dropped to the floor, she stood and then untied her pantalettes and let them drop as well. They caught on the swell of her rounded bottom, so she shimmied a little to cause them to fall free. She stood before him in nothing but her lace-topped stockings, giving him a view of her body, which was now in full blush from head to toe.

She would not back down now. *In for a penny, in for a pound*, indeed, she thought.

Kristoff thought he might die right then and there. His pulse was racing like a virgin on his wedding night, but he was no innocent, thank God. She was so deliciously beautiful. He did not want to hurt her by losing his composure and rutting into her like some feral beast, and he vowed to cool his blood as he reclaimed his composure. He took his time looking her up and down, taking inventory of each sensual dip, each taut muscle, each peak and valley along the landscape that was his wife's glorious body. He attempted to quell his arousal to something controllable as his eyes roamed over the puff of flame-red hair at the juncture of her thighs. She was perfection.

Her hips were narrow, with a bit of swell as they rounded into her taut bottom. She was toned everywhere but not so much as to hide the soft swell of one delicate curve as it merged into the next. Her body was an artistry like a finely crafted violin tuned just for him. Each span of delicate flesh was flushed pink with her embarrassment, but she continued to gaze at him as he continued committing her body to memory.

He wanted to feel every taut muscle quiver under his touch as he kissed his way across the pink skin and down as belly melded into that flaming triangle of red hair. He was beginning to slip into full instinct and had to slow down. Hell's bells, he wanted her naked and writhing in passion right then and there on the floor, bed, table…it did not matter. He needed to be inside her slick folds as she wrapped her legs around him. He needed her to be fully his. He prowled toward her like a predator about to seize its prey as he began to unfasten the remaining buttons on his shirt.

"It is customary for the bride to undress her groom on the wedding night, but pray continue, if you must."

Rosalind's voice was a husky whisper as she threw his words back at him and looked him up and down, appraisingly. He could see her eyes glazed with passion. He had not even laid a hand on her yet, but he could tell she yearned for his touch. It was his undoing. He reached her in one long stride as he ripped the shirt off, then scooped her into his arms.

She gasped at the first touch of his soft hair on her bare nipples. His chest and shoulders, arms…All of him was muscled. The strength he possessed made her feel weak but also protected as she stroked her hands down each ripple of flesh, until her hands rested upon his lower back just above the swell of his buttocks. She whimpered low in her throat and ached for something — she knew not what, just felt a hollowness that needed him. He crushed his mouth to hers as he lowered her onto the bed and covered her completely with his body, one of his powerful thighs pushing her softer thighs apart.

She arched her back and rubbed her most feminine parts against the hard muscle of his leg, and she moaned in delight as the jolts of fire ignited when one small spot rubbed against him. She repeated the motion, exploring the sensations it was spreading from that little nub toward her belly. Her breasts suddenly felt swollen, and she wanted him to caress them as well.

He was not moving quickly enough for her liking. He sucked her bottom lip into his mouth and bit gently as his free hand caressed the rosebud of her breast. He kissed a trail from her lips to her nipple. The touch nearly burned her to the core. Her primal moans begged him for more of his touch. Her hands could not be stilled either. She raked her nails on the length of his back as she arched into him over and over.

"Please," she begged as he sucked one pert nipple into his mouth and then the other.

"I need," she gasped, unable to speak further as his teeth grazed the sensitive bud and his hand lowered to the soft curls protecting her sex. She was slick with moisture, so hot and ready for him with the barest of touches. He slid his fingers through the wet folds and gently played along the petals, spreading the liquid that seemed to be coming from her all around the folds and that spot that sent shivers of fire through her.

He let his thumb flick over it once, twice, and a third time as he slid one of his long fingers into the entrance of her sex. He continued the torture, flicking, gently plunging a finger in and out as he sucked upon one breast and then the other. Then he would stop and kiss her deeply again as he started the motions over again. She was growing so hot, and that moisture was spreading from her so her inner thighs were slick with it. He flicked his thumb over the bud again, and she felt something building. Delicious and slick and achingly sweet. She moaned his name into his mouth as he kissed her again.

Kristoff was loving her every response to him. She was so tight upon his finger that he feared they would not fit well, but he wanted her to experience every bit of pleasure there was before he had to hurt her by taking her maidenhead. He kissed her lips and circled her tongue with his as he made love to her with his hand. Her response to the intrusion was to beg for more.

"I want this," she cried against his lips. "I need all of you. Show me," she moaned as his lips clasped onto her breast again. He slid in a second finger, stretching her for his arousal. She arched against his hand, wanting to experience all he had to offer her.

"I want you to take me now, Kris," she pleaded. "The pain can be nothing compared to this ache. Fix this now!"

"Not quite yet, my love. I intend to feast upon every sweet curve of yours first," he said as he trailed kisses down the length of her firm belly, feeling the little muscles flutter as he caressed her.

He circled her navel with his tongue as he slid his finger into her silken folds again. She nearly came off the bed and tried to drag him back for a kiss. He would have none of it and continued his journey until he was kissing the very heat of her. His tongue flicked gently over the outer petals of her sex as his fingers stilled inside her.

"This…this. I never heard of such kisses," she gasped as she ran her fingers through his hair.

He laughed with little puffs of hot breath onto her most sensitive nub.

"I would hope not; it is my pleasure to teach you all that a husband and wife may do for each other." He said each word with a little lick to the nub and began moving his fingers, sliding them out just a bit and then gently back in, rubbing the back side of her most sensitive spot.

He groaned with desire as she gasped and called his name over and over. He knew she would come apart soon and wanted to be ready for her.

He quickly stood and began to remove his breeches, which he could not seem to do fast enough. He carefully released his member, which was so engorged, it ached as much as Rosalind seemed to be. He had just pulled one leg free and leaned over to lick her soft folds again as she reached for him tentatively.

"This is a pleasure I may show you as well?" Rosalind was flushed and hot and so wanted to taste him, but was aching for him to continue his sweet torture.

"Perhaps I can taste you whilst you kiss me…there." Her blush deepened to near crimson as she pulled him to her and looked into his eyes as she tentatively ran her tongue across the tip of his erection.

Kristoff knew he had died and gone to Heaven. Her passion may be the death of him, but he was certain he would die a sated man. He sucked in a breath as her tongue flicked across his member. She was gentle and blessedly inexperienced, which heated him to near a molten state. He would be her first everything and wanted to make it all perfect for her. He needed to slow her so that they might savor each minute of this. By the gods, if her tongue touched him again, it might all be over before she found her satisfaction.

He pulled away from her and knelt to kiss her. "You have made me mad with my need for you. We shall save your tantalizing idea for another time. I want to kiss you, feel you, give you the pleasures I have been aching to give you and take from you since I first saw you."

He sucked her tongue into his mouth and kissed her slowly and deeply. He had to slow down, but she would have none of it. She rose to sitting with her thighs straddling his as he knelt there. She slowly raised her hips until his manhood rested at the entrance to her body. She was so wet, he felt the heated liquid slide down his shaft as she moved even closer.

"You fit inside me here, like your fingers, yes?" she asked, nearly panting.

He lowered her back onto the bed and braced himself over her as he took her nipple back into his mouth and sucked at it as if he had all the time in the world. She moaned his name and bit his shoulder.

"That is exactly where I will fit," he growled in a dark promise. "That is why you are so slick and wet. Your body knows this is meant to be and is readying itself for me. This," he said, running his fingers along her furrow and spreading the moisture around and over and in her, "will make it easier for us to slide together."

"End this ache," she demanded on a gasp as his finger slid into her again.

"I fear I may cause a worse pain if you are not ready."

He smiled at her outraged gasp and flicked his tongue across her other nipple, teasing her into another frenzy of sensation. God, how he loved her responsiveness. All timidity and fear were long washed away, one kiss at a time, as he smiled and tickled the flesh around her nub. She cried out.

"I love how your body responds to me. I could kiss you all night. Here," he said as he sucked her nipple back into his mouth. "And here," he said as he played with her silken entry.

"Now, Kris. Please. Whatever will make this ache ease. I want it. I feel all empty inside. Fill me."

Dear Lord, that last statement was his undoing. He laid her back upon the bed and centered himself between her thighs. She opened for him anxiously. He slowly began to caress the opening with the tip of his manhood, ever so gently as to not hurt her. It may kill him, but he would be gentle…no matter what she seemed to desire.

He ran the head and length of his shaft along her folds to cover himself with her dampness to ease their union. He centered himself again at her entrance and nearly jumped off the bed at a sudden banging upon the cottage door. He reached for a gun he did not have. Rosalind yelped and grasped the discarded coverlet to cover her body.

Lord Englebright's booming voice, yelling for his daughter, cut through all the passion either of them had left. Damn that man's timing. Kristoff groaned and collected his breeches and yanked them back on as well as he could over his quickly deflating shaft.

"We will revisit this, my Rose," he growled, leaning down and kissing her upon her love-swollen lips, sealing the statement as a promise. "I hope you have some garments here about to change into."

He looked at her beautiful naked body again with a groan of disappointment and stomped toward the door. "You need to get dressed, it seems."

Chapter Forty-Five

Kristoff threw open the door, his bulk protecting the view of his naked bride. He was still bare-chested, but that had no impact on Lord Englebright. Kristoff could see the concern on the man's face.

"So, you found her?" he asked, clearly relieved.

"I did, my Lord," Kristoff said, exasperated but deferential as he indicated his state of undress.

Why else would the man find him barely dressed in his late wife's cottage? Damn it all, his new father-in-law had told him where to find his bride after she ran off. It took Kristoff a moment to notice a perceptible orange glow about the sky in the direction of the manor.

"My Lord, what has happened?" he asked as he pulled his shirt back over his long arms and began to refasten buttons, noting that some were simply gone, apparently lost in his earlier haste to touch his bride. He groaned again. Why was everything so difficult with this family?

Lord Englebright had finally taken in the full scene before him, as he attempted to peek around the massive chest of his son-in-law to see if Rosalind was, in fact, well. Kristoff shifted in the direction of his gaze to block the man's line of sight.

"Oh…oh, dear, well, yes, then I see you have indeed found her. I …well, that is…I am quite sorry, my dear boy, but I must…umm…intrude. You see, the stables. Er, yes, the stables."

Lord Englebright shook his head, one hand raking through the graying hair at his temples as he came to his senses. Dear God, he had interrupted their consummation. He looked at Kristoff a bit sheepishly and shrugged.

"Someone has lit the stables afire, I am afraid, and I had feared the worst. If someone used Rosalind to get to me," he whispered, not wanting to alarm his daughter, "I…well, I could not live with myself. I needed to make sure she was here."

"As you can see, Father, I am well." Rosiland peeked around her new husband, blushing scarlet, clutching the blankets tightly from head to foot so that not a bit of flesh was revealed.

He thought she resembled a mummy he had once seen on a trip to Egypt. She was clearly mortified and was looking at her husband as if he had sold her prized cat.

Damn that Kristoff, this was all his fault, she thought. How mortifying for her father to find her like this. That damn near kiss in the damn library would haunt her for all of her damn days. And now he had her thinking like a common barmaid.

"Well, umm, carry on, then, yes…yes, carry on," George said as he flushed beet-red and turned to go.

"Father, you cannot mean to go back there alone," Rosalind implored. "Kristoff, stop him. He is in danger."

Groaning, Kristoff caught the man by the arm and gave him a meaningful look with one eyebrow raised.

"She is right, my Lord, there is still danger potentially even to Rose. We cannot stay here while you go back alone. Love, get dressed," he called over his shoulder as he closed the door in her face.

"My Lord, I think you might have this all wrong. I believe Rosalind is the target of these attacks. The wagon wheels, poisoned meals, gunshot…yes, could have been targeted at any one of us, but the gunshot barely missed *her*. This Raven would not have missed his target if he is still as fit as he was in your day. I think it was a warning shot. Not meant to kill…yet. She will not leave this investigation into these blasted holes alone, though what that has to do with anything, damned if I know. I fear she may have unearthed something more nefarious than poachers, as she believes."

"None of this makes any sense. The Raven was meticulous," Englebright said, clasping his hands in frustration as he stared at the clear night sky.

"This is just a bit of messy, unorganized chaos. Or maybe that is the brilliance of it. Who knows! Our attacker does not seem to be the brightest, but maybe that is the intent. What if he is after something else, and these events are just meant as distractions while he implements his higher plan? Or he is toying with us? Damn it all, I just can't wrap my head around this. And if it is not the Raven, then what is this about? The letters from the War Department missing, my Anna's map, then the holes, and now this complete chaos…so, what does that mean, or is it unrelated? I still think it all has something to do with my past. Until we know for sure, she must be kept close to the manor. I cannot risk her."

"Nor I, my Lord." Kristoff looked grim as he turned back to get his bride from the cottage.

With one hand on the door handle, he looked back over his shoulder. "There is a fire we must tend to, sir."

Chapter Forty-Six

It took them three hours to put the fire out with everyone helping. The stables had been all but ruined; so burnt that nothing but the stone walls remained. Fortunately, all the carriages had been moved to the long drive earlier that day to keep them fully visible after the wheels had all been repaired.

"Thanks to my maker, the horses were freed in time. Jacob, I cannot thank you enough for your quick thinking, but you could have been injured. I am so thankful you are safe as well, my boy."

Jacob smiled awkwardly at him as Lord Englebright patted his shoulder over and over and stared at the smoking remains of his once beautiful building. He was unaccustomed to such praise and affection.

Jacob glanced around at the devastation. They were all covered in soot, including the ladies who had been part of the bucket brigade trying to get the fire under control before it spread to the surrounding paddock and woods. Everyone appeared exhausted. The normally vigilant butler was even sitting upon the manor steps, his hair in tousled disarray. Jacob had never seen him looking this out of sorts. Rosalind and Nan sat beside him, holding each other's hands. The look of sadness on Nan's face as she gazed at where the stables once stood caused his breath to catch. Rosalind's attention was on the horses. They grazed on the far side of the field, skittish but seeming otherwise unharmed.

"Do you mind if I inspect the herd, sir? I want to make sure none were injured during the excitement."

Englebright nodded his agreement to Jacob and handed him the torch he had been holding, and watched him swiftly walk to the horses.

"Georgie," Derby called, pointing to the woods as torchlight broke through the treeline. Derby's men were dragging three rather rough-looking figures. He could tell there had been quite a tussle to get them here. Derby immediately recognized them as the ruffians who tried to shoot their Sprite.

"We found these three hiding out near the edge of the estate," said Carmichael as he and his men dragged the lot toward Derby.

"This portly git here had a gun in his pocket; a right pretty piece of work I ain't seen the likes of in some years," Carmichael said as he handed Derby a small double-barreled flintlock pistol.

"But that's a Napoleonic weapon. And look at that barrel. That's custom work. A bit ornate for these louts," Derby said, looking at the gun more closely.

The louts in question scowled at them all.

"George, see here!" Derby shouted excitedly, thrusting the gun under his friend's nose.

"Do you see that, just there on the side of the barrel?"

"Is that a Raven? Jacob," Englebright called across the paddock, "can you bring that torch closer? Carmichael, yours too, if you will?"

"Certainly, my Lord. What have you found?" Jacob quickly joined the men to see what was amiss.

Kristoff walked between the groups and eyed the captured men as the others investigated the weapon more closely.

"I believe I met this lot in the woods but a few days ago, my Lord. I believe you have also found our dirt poachers," he called over his shoulder. "Old Maude will be so pleased."

The three scoundrels tried to back away from the intense gaze of the large man, clearly recalling their last unfortunate encounter with him.

Jacob stared perplexed at the gun Derby was examining.

"That's Uncle's gun. Did you find it in the ashes?" he asked, looking from one man to the other.

"He had mentioned he keeps it in his carriage when he travels, but feared it might be stolen when the carriages were brought out. I thought he had sent his man to fetch it. That's his insignia, just there, the family Corbin, you see," he said, pointing to the small bird engraved on the barrel.

Englebright and Derby looked at each other, perplexed. "A corbin, you say?" asked Derby.

"Yes, it's a large black bird. In Latin, it is Corvus corax. The story Uncle always told me was that we are descendants of this Welsh god, Bran the Blessed, who is supposed to be a guardian of Britain and whose totem was a Corbie, hence our surname, Corbin."

Jacob looked worriedly at them both. "Did our miscreant friends happen to steal it? Dear Lord, this is not the weapon that shot Lady Englebright…er…I mean Van Reede, is it? Uncle would be furious if he knew his weapon was used to harm her."

Englebright sighed and looked at Derby quizzically…"Not a Raven, a Corbie?" he questioned.

"Well, they are the same thing, aren't they?" Jacob added. "Legend has it that Bran's head was buried beneath Tower Hill, at the Tower of London. The presence of ravens at the tower is an echo of this legend. If that is the case, I suppose they are considered one and the same. I never really gave it much thought."

He looked around at the men, who were now looking grim.

"Is that im…important, sir?" He was uncertain what had come over them all. His host had a creased brow so deep, it looked like a corduroy road. He and Derby were looking at the weapon with a most puzzled expression on their faces.

Coming to some decision, Englebright looked at them all in turn. "Perhaps it is best if we take this conversation somewhere a bit more private and get the questioning of these three done with." He motioned toward the men, who were doing their level best to break free.

"Yes! I fear there is more to this story than any of us has thought." Derby motioned for his men to take the three captives toward the manor.

"The wine cellar will do," Lord Englebright called as he continued looking at the gun, turning it over and over in his hand.

"Harold, we will need the viscount as well, since his weapon was used in this chaos. Can you fetch him, please? We need to sort out when it went missing," Englebright called to his butler while biting at his lower lip in thought.

"Father, we will tend to the guests and get everyone settled," Charles said, taking charge, nodding at Andrew, who was so soot-covered, he was nearly unrecognizable

"Come on, men, off with you."

Derby shoved the skinny man and followed the threesome closely, prodding them along, but then paused as he heard more shouting from farther up the long drive. It appeared more of his men had stopped a rider who was coming at a breakneck pace.

"What now?" he wondered aloud as he motioned Carmichael to keep going with the motley crew. "Do you think something else has happened at the department, George?"

He spoke softly as the man dismounted, worn leather satchel in hand.

"I need Lord Van Reede," the man shouted as he approached the group, looking at the bedraggled men with some concern. "He bade me come with all haste."

Kristoff, recognizing the courier from his New Castle offices, ran quickly to retrieve what he hoped were the needed documents to at least clear up one part of this mystery: what had happened to Pieter. This whole seemingly unconnected mess might actually be coming full circle.

Chapter Forty-Seven

The stone cellar was well lit, but smelled of earth and root vegetables, and was quite chilly. The three miscreants were seated in stiff-backed chairs in the middle of a room that was otherwise occupied by Derby, Englebright, Kristoff, Carmichael, and wall shelves of potatoes, beets, onions, and the like. The lantern light playing off the stone walls made it seem much like a cell in Newgate prison. Kristoff thought it was a perfect setting for an interrogation and planned to use it to their advantage.

"Where did you get this gun?" Englebright asked the rather unfortunate-looking man named Sid as he shoved him back into a chair between the other ruffians. He had so many scars upon his face that it appeared someone had mapped London proper on it. The candlelight in the cellars played off the walls, highlighting each deep mark so it stood out in stark contrast to the deep tan and soot on the rest of the man's skin. They were an unsavory-looking lot.

"Did you steal it from one of the carriages in the barn when you dismantled the wheels?"

"Stole it and used it to try to kill Lady Rosalind." Derby shook with his rage.

"We ain't stole nuffink and ain't kilt no one. It was given to us fair and square-like along with that map you stole from us. That man there is the thief. We are just poor, innocent blokes trying to make a way in this ol' world," the short, round man said, pointing one sausage-like finger at Kristoff.

"When was the gun given to you and by whom? Speak truth now and you may avoid the gallows." Englebright needed his suspicions confirmed that these men were hired by the Raven before he acted further.

"Gallows…for diggin 'oles?" skinny man asked.

"Shut it, Sticks," Sid called. "We won't get paid if'n we give these blokes the goose."

"If payment is all you seek, then I shall double your current offer," Kristoff said in a bored tone. He was leaning against the cellar wall, glowering at each man in turn. He had grown weary of this nonsense that was delaying his wedding night.

"You give us a 'ole penny each for all that dirt?" Sticks asked, flabbergasted.

Sid kicked him hard in his skinny leg. "He means the gun, you fool, and I already tol' you to shut it, or I'll be shuttin' it for yer…permanent like."

"How much you willin' to pay?" portly man asked Kristoff as he stood and scooted his chair far enough away so Sid could not reach him.

"I'm warnin' you, Gus. Keep yer mouf shut. Money won't be worf nuffink if yer dead like that ole hag what gave us the map. You know what he will do to you if'n you talk."

"So, that answers one question," Kristoff noted, looking directly at Sid with a bored glint in his eye.

He acted like he had all the time in the world to chat with them, and he looked down to examine his fingernails and said casually,

"You're dead any way; the gallows, the gent, or me. Take your pick. At least with me, I may go easy on you if you come clean. But you did shoot my wife." His face hardened, and both Gus and Sticks gulped. Sid just stared at him, not fazed.

"She warnt yer wife all propper like when we did it, so you shouldn't be so mad, right, Gus? Tell 'im," Sticks said, like it made all the difference in the world. "We weren't trying to shoot 'er noways…see? We was trying to shoot you."

Sticks smiled broadly as if this should be good news to Kristoff.

Kristoff just shook his head at them and went on with his questioning. "We now know who gave you the map. Did she also give you the gun? And if you didn't kill her, who did and why? Or perhaps that is just a ruse, and we should hang you here and now with the sacks of potatoes. This cell does seem fitting for the lot of you. And lastly, why would you want to shoot me?"

"She said the map led to a big ol' treasure in them woods," Gus shouted, looking at Sid nervously, still hopping his chair farther away from him. "She give it to us days and days ago. Said she nicked it out the missus' rooms when she fount it. And that her boss…she says…her boss says we can look for the treasure until he needs us."

Sticks picked up his story from there as Sid was side-eyeing Gus.

"Tol' us her boss would give us the loot if'n we helped her wif her job. At first, she didn't have no jobs…just wait and watch. She says…but then a day or so ago, she got new orders. She was supposed to find some letters in that big 'ouse, but no one left her 'lone long enuff to do more than clean. That map is gold, she says, but her boss don't want it." He shook his head in disbelief.

"All that loot and wants none of it. Must be a rich bloke, I says. He threw it back in her face, he did …then gives her a smack hard-like against her noggin, she says! So, we did what Edif tol' us the gent wanted done. We dig 'oles while she finds the letters. We started diggin' but found nuffink. Then that bloke…" He pointed in Kristoff's direction. "…came an' beat us for no good reason. Got a bump on me 'ead and a 'eadache to boot."

Englebright gave a knowing look at Derby, then back at Gus with a piercing gaze. Gus started to sweat and shift uneasily as he stared at the vicious look on Sid's face.

"Do you know what these letters were about?" Derby questioned.

"I'm gonna give you a'nover bump if you don't shut yer trap," Sid said in a low, cold tone as he tried to wrestle away from Derby's man holding him in the chair. He was slammed back firmly in place and glowered at his captor.

Gus moved back and started shouting out facts as quickly as he could. "Then that gent bloke met us in the woods, yonder." Gus pointed toward the woods. "Tol' us to keep that mean bloke there from marrying that one's gal," he said, pointing from Kristoff to Englebright.

"What gent told you this?" Kristoff asked, sliding away from the wall and slowly approaching the man. "Someone at the party, perhaps, or someone from town?"

The menacing look on the man, Kristoff's face, had Gus near to wetting his pants. "I…I don't know 'is name, and that's the God's honest troof, it is. He was tall, he was. Wore fine breeches and a shirt so crisp, it would have sliced me finger plum off ifn I'd touched it…not that he would get close enuff for that. Held a hanky right in fron' of 'is nose like we were odiferous, he did…and wouldn't touch us when he gave us an advance on our fee. Just tossed it to the ground like we was pigs he was sloppin'.

"He said if'n we know what's good fer us, we would do as we was tol'. Ediff 'ad said he done beat her up good cause she didn't do like she was tol'. And we believed her, too. She had a right big lump on her 'ead and bruises, she said, all about 'er body. He tol' us to stop foolin' with that treasure nonsense, and that Ediff 'ad left, and we did what he said an' only what he said if'n we wanted the rest of our fee. All he wanted was them blasted letters. Wanted 'em real bad. He must've been at the party, I s'pose. How else would he 'ave come and gone without you lot seein' 'im? Had a funny sort of way of speaking…like he weren't from here. It sounded…"

"I done tol' you, Gus," Sid said as he jumped up and grabbed the chair he had been sitting in, swinging it like a cricket bat across his back. Gus crumpled like a wadded-up piece of parchment, blood pouring from a gash in his head. "I would shut yer mouf for yer if'n you didn't shut it yerself."

Kristoff grabbed the man, picked him up, and slammed him to the floor with one hand around his neck. The crack of his skull on the cellar floor knocked him out cold. Then Kristoff turned that menacing stare upon Sticks.

"You have exactly one chance to answer my questions. After that, we will send you straight to jail to await your trial and the gallows if I let you get that far. Rest assured, if you do not answer, you will die, eyes bulging, and you gasping for air. You have already committed at least three crimes punishable by death. Give me what I need, and perhaps we can ask for leniency for you.”

Stick swallowed hard as he looked from Kristoff to Sid. That Kristoff bloke had picked Sid up with one hand…and Sid was large. What would he do to him if'n he refused, he thought. Damn that blasted hag and damned that blasted gent, he thought as words flowed like a torrent from his mouth so fast, they barely made sense.

“The gent, he didn't want you to marry the gal, and he wanted them letters Gus done tol' you about. He didn't tell me why, and I didn't care. I just needed to feed me mum. She's been deffly ill.” He began to cry.

“That hag, Ediff gives us the map and says dig 'oles til yer fin' the treasure. So, we digs the 'oles. Then she says her boss wants us to stop diggin' 'oles and to stop yer weddin',” he said, pointing at Kristoff.

“Ediff was supposed to 'elp us. Instead, she tried to kill everyone wif them bad mushrooms. I knew we was in trouble then. She weren't too bright, that ole hag. The gent met wif us all and said to only kill you,” he said and pointed to Kristoff, “and not the missus.”

Sticks wiped his dripping nose on his sleeve and continued his story with tears still streaming down his face.

“Said he'd get them letters 'imself if'n we could give 'im the time by causin' a ruckus. Said he would make it worf our while in'f we did. I 'ave to 'elp me mum, see.” He cried, looking from one man to the other.

“Then Sid said if we messed with the carriages, then maybe it would toss you in a ditch, and then you wouldn't be able ter marry…cause of yer being addled in the head and all, you know. I tells him, I do, that's seems like it might get the little lady, too, but he wouldn't listen. And Sid did find that gun in the carriage wif a bird on the side and pinched it pretty as you please. He took it just in case 'is plan didn't work, see? Which, of course, it didn't cause Sid's got some marbles loose in his ole skull. Not too bright, see,” he said, tapping his own head. He cried all the harder, “jus like me cause I got meself mixed up with that lot, and now Mum's gonna starve to def.”

“Calm yourself, man. I would never let an elderly woman in our village starve.”

This proclamation seemed to shock Sticks into silence, and he started in again, sniffing and crying so loudly that the room echoed his wailing to a near-deafening crescendo. "She's only thir'y-four," he wailed. His declarations shocked them all. She had either been an incredibly young mother, or Sticks had aged far too rapidly from a hard life.

Englebright felt sorry for the boy, who clearly fell in with the wrong crowd. "Give me her name, and I will see she gets the best physician and is well-tended, perhaps even employed with a good employer if she needs and is well enough. Now quit fretting and finish this tale."

Kristoff smiled. He now knew where Ros got her tender heart.

"You truly are as kind as they say, my Lord." Sticks sniffled and began his story anew, bolstered by a promise he knew the fine Duke Umberland, George Englebright, would keep.

"So, we go to the edge of that fancy maze, and we waits fer just the right time. I tol' 'im I did not sign on fer no killin'. But Sid…he said he would shoot me first if'n I didn't shut my trap…and then he'd go shoot me mum. And he is mean enough to do it, too. So, I headed back into the woods and leave 'im and Gus to it. But he can't see too right after he was hit in the 'ead, so he shoots the little lady instead. Next fing I know, that one there is giving chase through the wood," he said, pointing at Derby.

"Then we hear that Ediff is bashed in the head…and I know the gent done it, cause we didn't kill 'er. That makes me fink we might be next. Maybe he killed her cause she didn't get them letters. I tells Gus, here," he cried, pointing at the crumpled plump body on the floor,"we best do what we was tol' and why not just stop the wedding and all instead of trying to off anyone. We can cause a ruckus so he can get them letters *and* we stops the weddin' like we was tol' so the gent don't off us. So, we set them stables on fire.

"Only, it was a little late, seein' as the deed was already done and the vicar said 'man and wife.' I tell the boys, it's ok because I figure, can't be married if'n *you* don't, you know, do the deed," he said, waggling his eyebrows with extreme exaggeration at Kristoff. "And wif them stables ablaze, it would take the 'ol 'ouse to puts it out, so no 'usbandly deed could be done."

He waggled his eyebrows again at Kristoff. "So, up goes them stables, and out comes all the people."

He smiled at Kristoff and winked at him. "Did you do the deed or did my plan work?"

Sticks leaned forward with earnestness, awaiting the answer and nodding at Kristoff as one long strand of snot running from his nose swayed like a grotesque pendulum.

"It worked, didn't it?" Sticks asked again, looking as if he just won a prize pig. He wiped his nose on the back of his grungy sleeve and then slapped his own knee out of excitement for his successful plan.

A left hook from nowhere sent Sticks into a sound sleep.

Derby looked at Kristoff, who now had a deep glower on his face. Derby sighed, shaking his head. "I guess that is all the questions for this evening. Did anyone make heads or tails of this chaos from that story? I think we should adjourn above stairs for a brandy to sort out the rest of this mess. Hopefully, Viscount Durham is cleaned up and awake so we can question him further about this gun, though it seems like these blokes simply stole it. Carmichael, will you manage this lot? And get a doctor to see to that man, Gus, so he does not die on the floor."

"With pleasure," Carmichael said as he began to tie up the unconscious trio.

Chapter Forty-Eight

Derby took a long drink of the hot tea Mrs. Ingrid had brought up on a tray. Derby watched George pull the stack of letters from his safe. Kristoff had already spread the papers from his courier all over the desk and was poring over them as a distraction until Viscount Durham arrived and they could question him further on the weapon and insignia. They needed to close all the loops to tighten the noose on the culprit. It was taking the man far longer than they expected to put himself to rights. Kristoff scanned the pages, looking for any signs of the name Haberlin, and was starting to lose faith, but then…

"Ah ha," he declared.

Derby ran over to join him, followed by Charles and Andrew, who had just entered the study. Kristoff looked up to see the two looking a bit disheveled and in apparent disbelief at the sight that lay before them. They were looking from one pile of books and papers to the next. He supposed the room was a bit of a mess.

Charles shook his head. "Mrs. Ingrid will be appalled if she comes in here now, fair warning," he said, looking at Kristoff. There were piles of papers, maps, and books strewn about the entire room, especially the top of the mahogany desk.

Some of the parchments were meticulously stacked, while others littered the desktop. Lord Englebright sat on the settee, leaning over a worn parchment, scanning the intricate penmanship for some clue to clarify the mystery of the evening. He was surrounded by several large, leather-bound books that appeared to be more historical records. He was holding a blue silken ribbon in his hand, caressing it between his fingers absentmindedly.

"What have you found, Kristoff?" Andrew asked after glancing worriedly at his father and then at Charles.

Charles walked over to his father and touched him upon the shoulder to get his attention. "Father, everyone seems to be abed. Derby's men are stationed at all entrances. The ladies and twins are all well-protected. The Maxwell family, as well as the remaining gentry, will be leaving upon the morrow. I do believe Lady Maxwell has thoroughly enjoyed the chaos and can't wait to tell her friends of the happenings here." He shook his head in dismay.

"I suspect it will be a while before anyone forgets your birthday or nuptial celebrations." Andrew smiled as he moved a pile of papers over and hopped upon the desk beside where Kristoff was reading. "Now then, what was that 'ah ha' for, Kristoff? What have you found?"

"It appears one Elsbeth Haberlin was, in fact, the sister of Janssen Haberlin. Apparently, there was a stillborn child when she was…my goodness…barely fifteen years old. There is no mention of a husband. Both their parents died shortly after the stillbirth. It appears the girl stayed in the family estate until her death in…hmm, that is odd. Her death is shortly after her parents'. But according to Derby, that would have been five years before she showed up to kidnap the boy. How does a dead woman steal a child? This makes no sense," Kristoff mused.

"As for protection papers or name changes, or anything of the like, I will have to do more digging in those other folders, there," he said, pointing to another large bound book sitting on the settee.

"I thought perhaps the War Department has a record as well," Derby announced. "I sent one of Carmichael's men to fetch the appropriate books, so we can examine those when he arrives. The office keeps duplicates of everything, so I told him to bring them here and tell no one what he was about. If we still have a double agent about, I want no knowledge of the happenings here spreading until this mystery is solved."

Kristoff closed the folder he had been examining and motioned to Charles to hand him the book from the settee. As he flipped through the pages, he looked up and asked, "Is it just me, or is this still as clear as muddy water to anyone else? I think I may need to sleep on what all this means. It has been a rather long day."

He continued flipping pages to find the appropriate years that might contain the information they needed. Slowly, he stood and handed Andrew the books he had been perusing.

"Here, Andrew. Start on this page. It is organized by year and last name. You should be able to find what you are looking for if it is there. As for me, Gentlemen, I am off to bed. This remains to be the worst wedding night in the history of weddings." He laughed, shaking his head, and closing the door softly behind him.

Chapter Forty-Nine

"It appears that no one of the Haberlin name was granted protection of re-identification in the years in question," Andrew announced as he hunched over the binders, flipping page after page. "Let me look five years back to when our Elsbeth died," he said, flipping more pages. "Nothing here either." Frustrated, he drummed his fingers on the desk. "Hmm, when was your Pieter born, Father?"

"The same year as you, Andrew. You are of an age."

"That would be the very same year Elsbeth died, would it not?" Andrew asked. "Quite a coincidence, I suppose…Mother, Elsbeth, and Janssen's wife are all in confinement at the same time. Strange, that." He flipped back to the same year. "Pieter Haberlin…yes, here he is. His mother died in childbirth in Liege?" he asked, looking up at Derby.

"Yes," Derby answered. "Janssen was crushed after that. He was never quite the same and became quite paranoid that something would happen to him or his son. He made Anna and George promise over and over to raise the boy as their own if anything should happen to him. It was quite a sad affair…and then he was killed a few short years after. By then, the war was over, but some of the more skilled field operatives were ferreting out the last vestiges of Napoleon's supporters, who were wreaking havoc more than doing real harm at the time. They were a thorn in the side of the new monarchy in the Netherlands, so as a gesture of united forces, England allowed certain operatives to stay and give the house a thorough sweeping, as it were. Janssen was one such agent.

"George, if I recall, he had only just sent his letter of resignation the week before he was killed and had planned on relocating to England with Pieter. You see, Kristoff, lands that had fallen into escheat — meaning the family line died with no heir — were often given in recognition to war heroes. That is how Durham Hall and associated lands were handed over to Elias Corbin," Derby explained. "Though his deeds are well secured. I do not even have the clearance to know what great act he performed for king and country. Janssen was to be awarded an estate and title as well, though this was not yet decided, and then he died, and little Pieter was gone."

"What I cannot figure out is why he never mentioned a sister," Englebright said. "He never mentioned his past much, but I knew of his parents' passing. It just seems odd that he would not mention his loss of a sister as well, a short time later. It had to be devastating to lose all family connection."

Derby scratched his head. "There are too many coincidences for my liking." Motioning with his fingers, he began to count on them while pacing about the room.

"One: The duplicate letters in the War Department go missing while Edith and this 'gent' are searching for them here. Two: The insignia on the knife in the poor nightguard's death is very similar to the crest on the gun that attempted to do Kristoff in. Three: The gun belonged to our dear Viscount Durham. Four: Anna, Elsbeth, and Janssen's wife, Nora, are with child at the same time; was to be a happy year.

"Five: The existence of Elsbeth is hush-hush as well as the death of the infant…which I suppose is to be expected, given there was no husband listed…one can only assume it was an unplanned happening. Six: Anna, George, Jannsen, and I worked in the War Department as did Durham. Seven: Elsbeth makes a miraculous recovery from death, three years later in order to kidnap her nephew, the very same week her brother dies at the hands of the Raven. Lord, I think I'm going to run out of fingers!"

"Andrew, does that book state where the Haberlin family estate was?" Englebright called as he continued to read the letters one by one.

"It was in Liege, Father."

"Eight: Ah, Liege is the center of all this misfortune, during the war effort. Nine: Elsbeth Haberlin disappears without a trace after her recovery, as does Pieter. Do we know when Durham received his honorifics?" he asked the room at large.

"The question is, what does that man have to do with any of this, if anything at all. By the way, where is he? How long does it take to wash a bit of soot off?"

A knock at the door interrupted the brainstorming session. "Ah, there he is now," Derby exclaimed. "Come in."

Much to everyone's surprise, Jacob entered the room with an ashen hue to his face.

"My Lord," he said, looking at Englebright. "It appears that my uncle has left the property with his valet in tow. I am not quite sure of the reason for this hasty departure. He left this missive in his stead. It is addressed to you, Lord Englebright." Jacob walked toward the sofa, where the duke was perched among endless papers and books.

With a furrowed brow, Lord Englebright took the missive and broke the seal, which was also in the form of a corbie, it seemed. He shook his head at yet another coincidence. Silence filled the room as he scanned the contents of the letter.

"Humph," grumbled Englebright. "My friends…"

Glancing at Jacob, he said flatly, "Pardon my candor, Jacob, but Lord Durham left on account of the chaos that has ensued from the activities surrounding this situation, a great deal of which I would very much like to discuss with him."

"Ten!" Derby shouted. "The corbie has flown the coop!"

Chapter Fifty

Kristoff slowly opened the door to his wife's bedchamber and pulled it closed behind him, clicking the lock in place. He began to pull the soot-stained shirt over his head and washed his face and hands with her cinnamon-scented soap. It made him smile and react physically as he was reminded of his little minx's behavior in the cottage. Lord, how he hoped she was finally over her fears for good, though he was so tired, all he wanted to do was climb into bed, gather her in his arms, and sleep for a week.

Kristoff stripped out of the rest of his clothes, finished washing, and then crawled into bed with his bride. Ever so gently, he pulled her toward him, careful not to wake her. He smiled when she instinctively curled into him, throwing one naked leg over his. Her chemise had ridden up to above her sweet little backside. Sleep began to elude him as he gazed at his beautiful wife. How strange this entire assignment had been, but he was glad he had accepted it.

He ran his warm hand down the length of her side, loving how her waist dipped low before the swell of her hips made the most alluring little hilltop. As his hand caressed her, she sighed and moved closer to him, one hand splayed across his chest. She rolled closer and was nearly on top of him before sleep started to lazily leave her.

Images of her response to him at the cottage just a few hours earlier had him swelling to full attention. He gently kissed her neck, nuzzling in the sweet smell of her as his hand lightly brushed across the taut skin of her backside. She whimpered in response.

Slowly, Kristoff kissed a trail down her neck and across her breasts, taking each nipple into his mouth in turn as he kneaded her bottom with his free hand. She responded by grasping his hair in her hands and tugging him up for a proper kiss. She was fully awake and savaged his mouth, all the while tugging on his hair to demand more of what she wanted.

His tongue swept into her mouth as he covered her with his body. He had somehow managed to rip her chemise free without her notice. She arched into him to feel more of his bare chest against her breasts. She felt the heat building to a crescendo with an intensity that frightened her. She thought her body might shatter if he did not do something to ease the ache that had only slightly eased since their parting.

"Kris," she whimpered against his mouth, "this ache is too much. Fix it," she demanded as she raked her nails across his back and arched her pelvis against the very heat of his manhood.

That motion felt so intense, so good…like all her body was made of tiny stars about to explode into their own universe. She exhaled sharply and sought his mouth again.

Kristoff was near climax as she rubbed against him. He needed to end this torment for them both. He knew she would feel pain the moment he entered her fully, and he wanted her complete surrender before.

"Slowly, Love. We have a lifetime," he whispered across her flesh as his mouth moved ever lower until he was kissing and playing with the delicate petals of her sex.

He grasped her thighs and pulled her firmly to his mouth. He was not as gentle as he had intended, but she was so wet and so responsive, he was nearly to a peak just from tasting her. He licked and sucked in just the right places to shatter her into total bliss. She cried out as the first spasms of release took control.

He smiled smugly as he lowered her hips back to the bed and covered her body with his again, centering his length between her thighs. They were slick with the moisture from her climax. He stroked his shaft against her inner folds, sliding back and forth to cover himself with that moisture for a second time. She cried out with each stroke across her sensitive flesh.

"Wrap your legs around me, Love," he said as he kissed a hot path down her neck and seized her lips again, thrusting his tongue into her mouth, mimicking the love play about to come.

Chapter Fifty-One

Jacob, startled by Derby's shout, jumped slightly and looked at the man.

"What do you mean, Uncle has flown the coop?" he asked, confused.

"Surely, you do not think him responsible for any of this mayhem. I assure you, sir, Uncle Elias is the most unlikely man to act outside the rules of decorum you will ever meet."

Englebright looked at him kindly. "Jacob, what has your uncle told you of your past…not the crest origin, but your origin; about your parents, where you are originally from? I understand that Durham was given title and lands for his work for our government. Do you recall what that work was exactly for which he was awarded, or perhaps he mentioned the name Raven to you? Please understand, I mean no disrespect," he told him, raising his hands as if in defense.

"We just have unanswered questions, and things don't add up," commented Derby.

Jacob sat in one of the leather chairs flanking the fireplace. He was so weary. His time with this family had made it clear what he had missed in his own childhood. Slowly, he began to reminisce about the night his life changed forever.

Jacob started with how he was torn from his bed in the dead of night by his nanny.

"That was the night my father was killed, but I know not how. Nanny told me I was to go live with my Uncle Elias, whom I had never met. I was, naturally, frightened but trusted Nanny. She said she would go with me, but that Father would not. I did not know he was dead at the time, you see, and not sure I would have fully understood at that age. I am surprised I remember all that I do. She delivered me to Uncle. He and I hopped a small skiff and traveled to London. That was the last I ever saw of Nanny. Uncle told me he had sworn to Father to protect me and raise me as his own when he became suspicious of the government he had so nobly served, and that Father was dead. He did not allow me to cry or show my grief in any way that day or any other following. What is done is done. Uncle frowned upon discussing Father or his adventures. He took personal offense at my mentioning him or any happy memories. It was an insult to the manner in which he chose to raise me, he believed – and a slight on his character, which was quite noble for taking me in. I could not disagree then or now…he did raise me as his own son." Jacob shrugged sadly.

"In truth, sir, I was not permitted to speak of Father, and I cannot even recall his actual name. As for my mother, I am told she died in childbirth. I have no recollection or mementoes of her or her family, though it has been suggested by Uncle Elias that she was low-born and a disgrace to my father. I am unsure of her surname even." Jacob finished in a matter-of-fact manner, blushing a bit in embarrassment but refusing to avert his gaze from the onlookers, all of whom now were looking at him with the deepest sympathy in their eyes. He took a deep breath and continued.

"I fear I know little of my own lineage beyond Uncle Elias. I did not know my grandparents, as they died some years before my father. As I did not know my mother's surname, I have been unable to trace her lineage as well. Even if I had known, Uncle would likely have tried to stop me from pursuing such a course, fearing that a low-born connection would tarnish the Corbin name. As for the name Raven, unless it is related to the family crest, I know no more than I have already stated.

"I do recall that my father was a jovial man, though often worried about my safety." He smiled weakly at the memory.

"He frequently mentioned he had safeguarded my future with people he trusted, in case the time ever came that such was needed. I did not know he meant my uncle, but assume that to be his meaning. I have one keepsake from him that Uncle does not know of. In truth, I told Uncle I had purchased it from a street vendor, as I feared he might take it away if he knew it was Father's. It is a compass. Father told me that should I ever lose my way, it would set me back to rights. He told me this so often, that I admit, as a child, I often thought it to have some mystical power." He smiled sadly and pulled the small brass compass out of his pocket, offering it to be examined, turning it in his hand contemplatively.

The room had been quiet as he told his story. No one knew how to proceed once he finished his tale. Jacob had grown more distant, dropping all emotion from his features as he gave what he seemed to consider a confession.

"Suffice it to say, sir," he said, staring Englebright in the eyes, as if he could find understanding there, "I have never wanted for anything material. I am well-dressed, well-educated, and well-traveled. I will not malign the man who gave me his name and the resources to grow my interests and reputation as a horseman, and has made me heir to his holdings. Whatever he may lack in emotion, he exceeds in other areas."

Jacob sighed, shoulders sagging as if years of a heavy burden had been lifted. "I am of no noble blood."

They all knew how deficient and unworthy he truly was now. Uncle would be furious. He looked back at the compass in his hand, letting it anchor him.

"Forgive me, son, for insinuating insult. But I will speak plainly as you have." Englebright smiled warmly at him as he rose to approach him and placed his hand over the compass that Jacob presented. He picked it up and turned it over and over in his hand as tears began to well in his eyes.

"You have persevered in a difficult life and come out the better man, more capable of strong emotional ties and far better than your uncle, it would seem. He is a cold one, but you seem to be quite amiable and jovial, fitting right into our revelry. We hold you no ill will for not knowing your heritage. It is through no fault of your own…and if your mother was low-born, what of it? Hang what the Ton might say. Many an unhappy marriage has resulted in children who are unloved. Marriage should not be nothing more than a way to beget heirs. If your father's marriage was a happy one, who is to say it should not have been? It is certainly not your uncle's right."

Englebright then manipulated the back of the compass, popped open a secret compartment, and handed it back to the man.

Jacob looked at the compass, astonished that he had not ever discovered the secrets it held.

"Son, I would have you read that inscription," Englebright said, tears now streaming down his face. "I told your father the same when my wife and I gave it to him and your mother on their wedding day. She was as fine a lady as I have ever met."

Jacob was so confused, as were Andrew and Charles. Derby fell into his chair knowingly. They had found their lost Pieter, but who was Elias Corbin?

Chapter Fifty-Two

"Ros, come on…open the door. Something is happening," Michael whispered loudly as he tapped on his sister's door.

As he was grabbing the knob to wiggle it again, he looked at Edmund as they heard what sounded like cursing and a near roar from inside the chamber.

"Umm, maybe we should consider coming back later, Michael. Maybe she is b-u-s-y," Edmund mouthed with a knowing grimace. Kristoff was going to kill them; he just knew it.

Before the boys could flee, Kristoff, only half dressed, yanked the door open, almost ripping it off the hinges, and had both of them by the scruff of their necks.

They both yelped and began talking at the same time, tripping over blaming the other for the intrusion.

"I told Ed this was a bad idea, but we have information."

"Yeah," said Edmund. "Something is happening in the study. Father is crying and in a rage because someone took our pieter…"

"What in the blazes of hell is a pieter?" both twins asked at once.

"And Jacob…man, did we think we had it rough sometimes. That uncle of his is a piece of work, let me tell you," Edmund said, nodding.

Michael took over the story, looking at Kristoff shaking his head as if he could not believe or understand what they had heard. "Then Jacob yelled that he doesn't even seem to know who he or his uncle even is! He shouted so loudly. And well…we thought you were in there with them, Kristoff, so we were going to get Ros to explain what in the blazes is going on before everyone left us here none the wiser."

Rosalind, now covered head to toe in her dressing gown, poked her head out the door and asked Kristoff to stop choking her brothers.

"Did you say your father has found Pieter, boys?"

"Yes," they shouted in unison while nodding.

"But who is Pieter, and why has he been lost for so long? There is something more afoot here, and no one will tell us what is going on," Michael said, frustrated.

Rosalind looked at Kristoff, eyes widening. "They found him? I must go to Papa if he is so upset," she said as she tried to move past the boys.

Kristoff grabbed her hand gently to stop her. "I will explain some of this, boys, but I fear your father must explain the rest. All I can tell you is that Pieter is the son of your parents' dearest friend, Janssen. When Janssen died during the war effort, your parents were to take Pieter and raise him as their own, but he went missing. They have been searching for him for years. Beyond that, your father must explain. It is not my tale to tell."

"You can't go to him anyway, Ros. They all ran out the study door about three minutes ago. I think they are headed to Durham Hall to confront some bloke called Raven. Well, father and Durham are chasing Jacob, who took off like a madman. Father ordered Charles and Andrew to stay here and keep an eye on things.

"Only…it's just, well…Father sounded like there would be trouble, so if Kristoff is in here…and Andrew and Charles have been ordered to stay…and Jacob and that horrid viscount are not who they say they are…we don't want him going it alone. Old Derby is not what he once was," Edmund said, point of fact.

"The hell they are going without me!" she yelled as she ran back into her room to get dressed.

Kristoff frowned at both boys.

"Well, now you've gone and done it," he sighed, slamming the door in their faces, mumbling under his breath.

"Did he mumble something about never getting a wedding night," Michael looked at Ed and asked, confused. Both boys blanched at the same time, realizing what they had interrupted.

Nan, looking quite tired, peered out her door to see both of the twins looking rather ill.

"What in the heavens is happening this eve; doors slamming, you lot yelling. One would think no one is meant to sleep tonight," she said with a loud yawn.

Kristoff opened the door, Rosalind in tow. He knew if he did not take the two women, they would just show up in his wake anyway. Better to have them safe with him than making their own way in secret, which he knew they would do the minute he left.

"Nan, would you mind getting dressed? Or you are welcome to stay here. It appears we will be going to Durham Hall. It is a two-hour ride astride. I can't risk you ladies riding side-saddle. The track is too dangerous. Can you ladies make that?"

They both looked at him, rather insulted, and refused to answer. He smiled. Of course, they could ride two hours astride.

"Boys," he said, diverting his attention to the twins, "go back to bed."

The yelling immediately started anew as the twins argued that they should not be left behind. They could provide some assistance in watching over the lovely Nan. In the end, Kristoff nodded his acceptance and proceeded to lock them in their rooms when they went to dress for the ride.

"Harold," he greeted as the butler appeared seemingly out of nowhere with one of Derby's men in his wake. He was about to give him direction to keep the boys locked in, but as usual, the man was two steps ahead of them all.

"I presume the young masters are to stay put, my Lord? I believe Derby's man can make that happen," he said, nodding deferentially at the large, rough-looking man who had followed him in.

"Nothin' to it, M'Lord. I'll be happy to keep the chaps occupied right here. I got my other man, Lawson, under their window as well. I've seen these two in action this week, sir," he said as he winked at the ladies. "I believe Lords Charles and Andrew are making short work of directing the rest of the men in shoring up protections here to keep the guests and these lovely ladies safe."

Kristoff nodded his appreciation to the group. "Be sure to tell them I have these two with me. They will understand why."

The group then left for the paddock, Rosalind filling Nan in on the details she knew as they went.

Chapter Fifty-Three

Elsbeth had been waiting in the study for at least an hour…waiting and waiting to rip him apart for his idiocy. She had already sent all the staff away and told them not to return until morning. She did not wish for them to witness this unraveling of their world *she* had built. He had been no more than two hours behind her, she had thought. What was taking him so long?

She paced and paced and periodically slammed her hands on the door, screaming her frustration until he finally came in, likely to scold her for this fit, but she did not care.

"You fool, how could you have left the gun inside the carriage?" Elsbeth cried as he walked casually through the stone archway that led into the study of Durham Hall.

"You could very well have ruined everything…*everything* we have worked so hard to achieve. The lands, the titles, the reputation," she screamed, pulling her black gloves off and throwing them at him one at a time.

She ran at him, hand raised to smack him across his smug face. The fool. How could he do this to her, after all they had been through, all she had sacrificed for him? If anyone ever found out the extent of her treachery, he *knew* she would be hanged. They both would. Did he not care? No…that was one thing she was certain of; his love was unquestionable.

He caught her hand mid-swing, none too gently, and yanked her to him. His taut chest sent a thrill of anticipation through her that just made her rage even more. Damn his effect on her.

"Have I not done all you asked of me all these years?" she screamed, pounding his chest as the tears began to stream down her face.

She was appalled at her own behavior. She had not cried a single tear for Mother, Father, or her brother…not since she lost her own child all those years ago, and they locked her away like so much refuse. She swore she would never love again, and then he came and ruined her anew. He broke all the walls she had built; shattered them into a million pieces with one plan. The plan to give her back the son she had lost. And where had that gotten them now?

"Stop this," he said as he brushed his lips over her hair, then kissed the tears from her cheeks, his blood heated by the feminine weakness she was showing.

He had never seen her like this, and it aroused him all the more. His cock swelled at the thought of taking her in such a weakened state.

"Have I not always given you what you asked of *me*? Have I not put plans into motion to give you your dreams?" he said as he began to unbutton the shirt covering her underthings, his blood near to boiling with his need to take her. He kissed a trail down the exposed skin. His hands found her corset and roughly began to loosen the laces and expose her breasts.

"My plans are still unfolding, Love. You will have an heir of the finest stock. Even now, that Kristoff is being taken care of. I left explicit instructions with my associate. The gun is of no concern. You and I are not there, so there is no implicating us in any wrongdoing."

He roughly cupped her breast he had just freed from the stays. She gasped at the feeling of his warm hand as he growled his need for her and squeezed her soft flesh harder.

"You will have your babe to hold as soon as we get the boy married to Lady Rosalind and her with child, even if I have to do it myself," he said as his head dipped, and his teeth caught at the tip of her nipple. He bit and sucked the bud into his mouth. She moaned even as she struggled against him.

"But we ran away…and the gun. Those fools you hired had the gun and nearly shot Lady Rosalind. They can't be trusted to get this right."

She gasped as he bit her nipple again and then lathed it with his tongue as if to soothe his rough treatment. Her core was becoming molten with every wet lick, and her struggling was ebbing as she gave in to her desire. She had missed his touch these past days, but with servants coming and going at all hours, it just had not been possible for them to partake of one another.

He stopped his caresses and looked her in the eyes. "They were just a bit of fun, a distraction while the real plan unfolded. I said the gun is of no consequence, and thus it is not."

He knew his tone was clipped in anger but did not care. That fool Jacob had almost undone them all with his unwillingness to compromise the girl before that foreigner, Kristoff, could.

"Do you not trust me? Do you not love me?" he asked, pinching her nipple between forefinger and thumb as if to punish her, but he knew she loved his harsh treatment of her body. She longed for it.

"You have *my* love now and always," he said in an accusing tone as his other hand dipped into her undergarments between her thighs, and he stroked until wetness covered his fingers.

He smiled smugly as she cried out. He knew not if her cry was from anger or passion, and he did not care.

"Have I not earned your undying trust and love?" he growled, anger finally starting to war with his passion. She needed a bit of a reminder, it seemed, of who had created this world for them. "You know the role I have played all along, and how I have enjoyed the subterfuge, but every man has his breaking point, Love. Just as does every woman."

He withdrew his hands from her.

"That is enough for you for now. In *this* moment, you will give me what I need, what I desire. I have had to watch you all week from afar, not touching you like I have wanted, not heard you scream my name as I take you. You will scream my name before this night is done, over and over, you will scream it," he said as he dipped and bit her lip.

"You know the name I wish to hear on your lips. Say it! If you want me to touch you again this night. Say it now!" he demanded as he pushed his hand between her thighs again and roughly thrust one finger inside her and bit at her neck.

"Raven, my Raven!" she moaned. As a reward, he slid another finger inside the hot entrance to her body.

"Not good enough," he said as he stroked her harder, deeper, and thrust in yet another finger, his thumb stroking her delicate nub at a fevered pace. She began to climax, her inner muscles almost pulling his fingers deeper as she came undone in his arms.

"My Raven!" she screamed. "I am nothing without you."

"That is right," he said. "Only I love you, I made you, I take you as I will, when I will," he groaned, needing to embed his engorged sex into her. She still wore too much clothing to make that possible.

"Strip for me, now," he demanded. She immediately complied and began to unbutton her sleeves so she could remove her shirt, angry tears still streaming down her face and her breasts heaving above her corset with each sensual gasp. When she looked up to meet his gaze, she cried out and clasped her shirt to her bosom as she saw movement over his shoulder.

"No…no, no, no," she screamed again and again. "This cannot be!"

Jacob stood in the doorway, mouth agape in horror as he took in the scene before him. Uncle Elias stood, clasping a man's shirt to a tightly corseted chest, ample breasts heaving over the tops. Elias had breasts…no, that was wrong, Jacob thought, confused. Elias was a woman…a woman…and had screamed the name Raven for Jared, his…no, her valet.

"Aunt Elsbeth?" asked Jacob.

Chapter Fifty-Four

Jared spun as he pulled a gun from his pocket, grasped Elsbeth around the waist, and shoved her in front of him. The gun was pointed at her side. It appeared to be identical to the one they had found on the ruffians back at Englebright Manor.

"Don't make me take the one thing from you that has been a constant in your life, boy. Your aunt has given up her identity, her life for you, just you."

Jacob looked at his uncle…no, aunt…and quickly looked at the floor as she buttoned the shirt to cover herself. "Why?" Jacob asked, confusion and hurt roiling through him. He looked back at Elias…or whatever the bloody hell this person wished to be called. "Why the subterfuge…all these years…Why!" he now shouted, demanding to be answered.

Lies…all lies. Jacob…Pieter, he did not even know who he was…could not wrap his head around why Elias would do this to him. Englebright had explained all he knew before they left. How he should have been raised in a loving family. That was not fair. Elias had loved him in his own way, given him everything…which apparently included *her* identity. He felt like such a fool. How had he never suspected? They had played their ruse well, indeed.

"Why this farce, why the lies? What did you hope to gain?" shouted Jacob, demanding they answer him, some of his anger ebbing as he saw the angst and regret and what looked like a feral wildness in Elsbeth's wide eyes he had never seen before. It was unsettling.

"My son back!" Elsbeth screamed. She could not stop the flow of tears she had held in for so many years. She felt as if a dam were finally breaking…all the lies, the hurt…years of isolation and her baby…gone, gone, gone. And then she was found by her Raven.

"It was bad enough that I had been taken advantage of by a traveling soldier. He spoke of all the wonderful places he would take me…take me away from the war, from the home that had become a prison because of spies and intrigue. Instead of taking me away from it all, he left me. He used me and left me; left me unwed with a child growing in my belly.

"Father never forgave me, even though it was not my fault. He locked me away. When I labored, he refused to call the doctor. For hours, I screamed for him or Mother to help me. He refused and would not allow her to come to me. Then my baby died, nearly taking me with him. I tried for years after that. I tried and tried to have my son. They all died, over and over." She moaned in sad agony.

"I was not allowed to speak of it to anyone, but Janssen's wife had a baby, and that Anna had one too," she sobbed. "I read all the letters. They all got my baby. I just wanted him back."

She implored him with her hands reaching toward him as if that would make him understand.

"When I learned your father was dead, I knew I could take you away and raise you like my child should have been raised. I knew I was the better parent for you, but with no husband and no male heir, I had no choice. Raven had found me, led me…gave me options of what to do. I…"

"I believe he gets the point, Elsbeth. Be silent." Jared jerked her up hard against him, causing her to let out a little yelp as the gun dug into her ribs just as Derby and Englebright ran into the room.

"Stop," Derby said, catching his breath as he rushed in. Englebright was just behind him. Taking the scene in, Derby leveled his gun at the valet's head as that seemed to be the only threat in the room. Elias was the man's target.

"Raven tried to give me what I wanted. In turn, I gave him the secrets my brother and that fool's wife discovered," Elsbeth cried, pointing at Englebright as he attempted to catch his breath.

"I said be silent, woman!" Jared said and shifted his arm from her waist to her neck and began to squeeze, none too gently.

Derby and Englebright looked at each other in shock and disbelief. Elias was a woman?

Looking back toward Jacob, Elsbeth exclaimed, "I sold England's secrets for you…for my baby, for my love," she said, reaching back to caress the face of her Raven, who now held a gun to her.

She had done no wrong, just a bit of trickery so she could afford to raise her heirs and give them their just rights. "A woman in this world is nothing without a man. We don't even own our identities. The one purpose I could have was to bring my child into this world, but even that was taken from me. I became what I needed, what the government needed…"

"Enough!" Jared called out, cocking the gun to gain her silence. As she had been speaking, he was slowly moving them toward the back of the room. He was scanning like a cornered rat; he knew…just a bit more subterfuge for them to think that he was caught. Fools.

"The ruse is over; we know who you are, Jared, or should I call you Raven?" Derby said with disgust. "Elsbeth, you have been used. This man does not love you. He has been playing at his own game and is responsible for the death of your brother and countless others. I am sorry for your loss, but this is not the way. Don't be a fool."

"You are the fool," she laughed as she lunged for the wall and pushed the secret catch. The panel slid open, and she began to back into it with Raven tucked safely behind her. She reached to hit the catch that would close the door.

To everyone's surprise, she screamed as she was thrust back into the room. A single shot rang out as the panel slid closed with a click. Elsbeth crumpled to the floor.

"No!" Jacob yelled as he ran to her. Even with all the lies, he still loved what his uncle had been to him. Elsbeth smiled at him.

"What can I do? Derby, Englebright, help me," he pleaded as he removed his waistcoat and put pressure on the wound in her side. "Just look at me, Elsbeth. We will fetch the doctor and sort this mess out. Just look at me…No, don't close your eyes. That's right, look at me."

He folded the waistcoat over. It was already soaked completely through, and the wound was hissing as if air was escaping.

"I think the lung is punctured. Help her," he begged the two men. I know how to treat an injured horse, but not this."

Elsbeth raised her hand to his face. "I tried to love you. I did. You were a good boy. I…" She gasped as blood trickled from her mouth and she coughed. "I am just no good at love, it seems. I am sorry for the lies. Raven told me it was the only way. I did…did it for you. For…you.…and…my…baby."

Breath halts after each word. She gently touched his face and smiled.

"My baby," she gasped and smiled again. "I get to see my baby." Elsbeth closed her eyes as she exhaled her last breath, her hand dropping to rest on his arm. Blood pooled around them as Jacob gathered her up into his arms and rocked there on the floor as he cried.

Rosalind goaded her mount to pick up the pace. Though many of their horses were bred for racing, some were more adept at long, breakneck speed journeys than those that could keep that pace for only the length of a track. She had quickly selected the best mounts for them, but it had taken some time to calm them enough to mount after the fire and the tumult that had happened that evening. The horses were more skittish than normal. Rosalind knew she and Nan would have no issues keeping pace with Kristoff, but she was so worried they would all be too late and that something would happen to her Papa.

Her fear was clearly being transferred to her mount, Pepper. The horse was leaping puddles in the road with no provocation from her. She could imagine Kristoff grimacing each time, but he kept the pace going. Rosalind looked back at Nan, who was leaning down low on Cadence. Nan rode as well as any jockey Rosalind had ever seen. Charles had taught them both well and with the patience of a saint when they were younger.

"Whoa," Kristoff called to his mount. He needed a moment to think. He knew that Derby and his new father-in-law were perfectly capable men, but they had no idea what was waiting for them. They had said Raven always worked alone, but given the tales the men had shared with him tonight, he could not reconcile a single man doing all that he was claimed to have done in all regions of England, Belgium, and France simultaneously. The man had to have had a network, and with a network came more than one ringleader.

He had a sudden bad feeling about all of this and just needed to sort out some details before they rushed in, but his abrupt stop had caused confusion. Rosalind's horse reared on its hind legs and danced in a circle in the middle of the road. Kristoff nearly lost his supper right then and there. God, he must have been insane to bring these two, but he knew they would have just followed if he had not.

"Why are we stopping, Kristoff? Father and Derby are in danger…and Jacob, if he is who he says he is," Rosalind said urgently.

"And if Jacob is not who he pretends to be," she said, looking apologetically at Nan, "then they are in greater danger than they know. Papa is only seeing his failure to fulfill the last request of his best friend. He may not see this situation objectively. We must go."

She shouted this, and the horse reared again.

"Whoa, boy," she calmed the horse again. He had nearly unseated her that time. Kristoff's face had turned white. "Are you well? Your face is so pale," she said.

"Could you calm that beast before you are tossed into the road? Something is not right…I can't put my finger on it, but I have learned not to ignore my instincts. The Raven was at the manor, caused some chaos, possibly killed a housemaid, and just left without taking anything that we know of? This seems wrong. If your father and Derby are correct, he was after the letters…and if the maid had been in his employ to get them, she could have done so at any time, but instead just takes a pretend map?" Kristoff thought aloud as his horse pranced in response to the abrupt change in pace.

Nan agreed with Kristoff. Something was off. Nan felt the prickle of being watched. She turned in the saddle, taking in the dark surroundings. Was there something out in the woods watching them in the bright moonlight? Nan faced forward again, heart racing; she felt a growing sense of danger.

With urgency in her voice, she implored, "We must go. I feel there are eyes in these woods, watching."

She spun Cadence again and caught the glint of something metallic in the treeline just behind them, and then she was staring into the eyes of a shadowed figure silhouetted by the moon gleaming through the trees.

"There," she pointed and shouted her warning, causing Cadence to rear again. She could have sworn she heard a deep voice yell, "No!"

Kristoff had heard the yell as well, but could not understand what was happening. He pulled his pistol and charged in the direction she was pointing. He stopped, hopped off his mount, and stepped into the woods. It was too dark to see the ground well, but someone had been afoot; he just could not tell which direction they had gone. He looked back to make sure the ladies were fine. They were no worse for wear but looked frightened. "We need to get to Durham Hall with all haste. I fear they may be riding into a trap."

In full gallop, the trio rushed toward the estate.

"Are we too late?" Rosalind gasped as they closed the gap between them and the front steps.

Jared ran out the front door, stunned to see them as he exited. He remained calm, suspecting only the three in the room knew his true identity.

"A man has been shot. I am going to fetch the doctor," he shouted as he continued toward the stable, palming the gun to keep it from sight as he slipped it into his pocket.

"Oh, dear Lord! Who was shot?" Nan begged. "Is it severe?"

She and Rosalind quickly dismounted and ran toward the entryway of the manor.

"They called him the Raven, M'lady. It was my master," he cried after them, allowing one tear to slip down his cheek for effect.

Kristoff hopped off his mount. "How far is the doctor? Will your master live?"

"I fear it may already be too late, but I must try. It does look quite grim, m'Lord. Lord Englebright, Sir Derby, and the young master Jacob are in the study tending to his injury. I believe they require some assistance," the Raven lied. "Let us both make haste."

As Raven reached for the stable door, he looked back to ensure his quickly deployed bait had been taken… *like a trout with a worm*, he thought and grinned wryly as he saw Kristoff make his way up the steps, the ladies trailing him. With a swift tug of the door, he found his steed, mounted the horse, and goaded him into a full gallop out the back of the stables. The Raven was no more. Jared was no more. He would reinvent himself with ease.

Chapter Fifty-Five

Kristoff bolted through the door but was nearly waylaid as Jacob flew by him, shouting, "Where is he? Where is that villain? I'm going to kill him."

As soon as Jacob had run by, Derby ran out into the hall and yelled, "Go help him. That butler is our villain."

Kristoff realized he had been duped and turned, catching up with Jacob quickly. "We'll need fresh mounts if we are to catch him," he called as he followed Jacob into the stable.

"Take Rebel, third stall on the left. I'll take Lightning. They ride best bareback. Brace yourself. Rebel is one of my fastest," he shouted back as he mounted Lightning in one fluid motion. The horse reared with excitement and took off fast as his name implied. Jacob ducked low onto his back and rode as if hell itself were chasing him.

Kristoff paused at the rear exit and surveyed the ground on all sides to ensure they were heading in the right direction. He hopped upon his steed and followed Jacob.

Jacob had not been exaggerating the stallion's speed. The wind rushed past, whistling around him and muffling the sound of hoofbeats as dirt swirled with each gallop. He stopped briefly to recheck their direction. Two sets of tracks led in the direction Jacob was going, so he took off again, trying to catch up.

Raven was on the open road now, but knew that was the last place he should be. If Jacob recovered from his shock quickly enough, he would run him down in no time, depending on which steed he used, he thought as the cold air rushed past him.

That fool, Kristoff, had made everything run afoul, but he would make amends for that particular error as soon as he had secured his next identity. Clearly, his associate could not be trusted to complete the task he was given, or Kristoff would be dead. He would see them all pay for ruining his comfortable life…and for Elsbeth…sweet, trusting Elsbeth. For her, he at least held as much pity as he was capable of. He had loved her in his own way and did try so hard to give her what she longed for.

She, in turn, had given him what he desired. Her body had just been too broken after her first pregnancy to bear another child. He tried but knew in the end she would be happier dead than to have lost all hope. It was a mercy killing, really, he thought as he reined in his stallion and turned to make his way through the treeline bordering the road and Durham Hall.

"Be in the last place they would expect," he laughed as he circled back toward the manor through the woods. The secret passages would aid him in navigating back to the small wall safe in the lower receiving room. There, he could retrieve the remaining documents that implicated him. It also held a tidy sum of money and the deed to the Haberlin estate in the Netherlands and his brother's estate in Scotland.

The Haberlin estate would be investigated now – best not to go back there for some time. When things quieted, he could go and get the bounty of money he had acquired over the years and stashed there. That estate had lain empty as a grave for decades, and his ingenuity in hiding his booty would leave it all as untouched as a maiden before her wedding day. Perhaps, he would even go visit his brother and revel in the sheer, scandalous spectacle his sudden presence would create for him. He nearly laughed aloud at the thought of the look on his brother's face. Of course, if he went in disguise again, his brother would be none the wiser. That was how he had obtained the deed to his lands to begin with. He did wonder if he even knew they were missing from his locked trunk he thought he had hidden so well…

He frowned a bit as he ducked below tree branches and made his way on through the undergrowth, allowing his mind to wander. He always had a contingency plan, but he had hoped he would not need it.

Perhaps this bit of change had come at a good time. He was far too comfortable living as a servant, directing his spiders from behind the web, as it were. It might be time for him to remind them all of who he was. He was untouchable, uncatchable, vapour on the wind…just out of their reach. The fools did not even realize what was coming for them all. He laughed aloud at that thought before turning grim again. Damn, but he would miss Elsbeth and her passion. Damn them all. If Englebright's Anna were not already dead, he would make Englebright watch him kill her now – slowly and painfully. He scowled.

Slipping back into the house was easy since the passage was near the root cellar, the door of which was neatly hidden behind the spring roses. All of the commotion would be taking place in the study above stairs. So, he knew he would have an easy way of slipping in and out unnoticed. The fools would expect him to be long gone by now. *Oh, how sweet it is to be more intelligent than these learned buffoons,* the Raven mused.

As he closed the secret door behind him, he grabbed an awaiting torch and made his way back to the manor. He walked swiftly through the moldering, musty tunnel and entered a hidden room adjacent to the root cellar. The door to the room was accessible only by this tunnel and through a trapdoor that would allow him to enter the area below the stairs. A quick trip up a wooden ladder would allow him access to the trapdoor.

As he took the first rung of the ladder, he paused to admire volume after volume of his memoirs written in his own hand. A sense of malcontent washed over him, though. He had retrieved the letters from the War Department and thought his collection complete until that horrid, useless Edith informed him that more letters were in the Englebright estates…in the old duchess's rooms.

"Perhaps I was a bit hasty in killing that hag," he thought aloud. She had said they were love letters, but he knew better. Unfortunately, Englebright seemed a suspicious man, and the letters had been removed prior to him being able to retrieve them. That trip was for nothing, he lamented. The fools never knew the delicate web he and his brother had woven over the years. They were such dolts that they would never learn the truth. He would need to come back to retrieve his life's work, eventually. Maybe then, he could revisit Englebright Manor and take the rest. He wondered casually if the government would allow Jacob to actually inherit Durham Hall. Well…that was none of his concern now. The boy was nothing to him.

Rosalind and Nan had just started to follow Kristoff and Jacob out the door, when Derby called them back. "Ladies, you are not to follow. Kristoff knows what he is about, even if Jacob is mad with grief and anger. Stay put!" Derby commanded as he gave Rosalind his gun. "Just in case, take this. I know you can use it just as well as I can. Perhaps you should go to the lower study or parlor. There is no need for you to have the scene in this room imprinted upon your minds. The Raven has flown the coop, so the house should be safe enough."

The ladies looked at each other and nodded acquiescence. Rosalind said, "I feel as though I have just swallowed thorns," her belly was so filled with angst. "If this is what love feels like, then I am not certain that I do want any part of it," she grumbled.

They left the room and slowly went down the stairs and plopped on the landing nestled by a small receiving room. They leaned into each other for support and the strength to do what they had just promised and stay put.

Raven pulled the latch that released the secret wood-paneled opening just under the grand staircase in the foyer. *Just a quick pop in and out, and no one will be the wiser*, he thought as the door squeaked open – he grimaced at the noise, but knew it was unlikely to be heard by those above stairs. He had meant to oil it and had forgotten.

Derby's outraged shouts echoed through the halls of the manor. "All these years and right under our noses…I feel like a new copper on his first beat…bamboozled we were." As the Raven listened to Derby trying to sort out the past happenings, he smiled in satisfaction. Derby sounded like he was in a fine snit.

The slight high-pitched squeak caught Nan's attention as she sat thinking of all that had happened. *Poor Jacob…or Pieter. This has to be devastating.* She thought nothing of the squeak until it came again, followed by a soft click and slow, even footsteps.

She motioned with a finger to her lips to hush Rosalind's disgruntled sigh and mouthed, "Did you hear that?"

Rosalind cocked her head to one side as she heard the steps approach the landing. Quickly looking for somewhere to go, the two rose as silently as mice and made their way to the closest door. It was slightly ajar, so they left it that way and hid directly behind it so if it was opened, they would be concealed by the door.

They entered a small receiving room that was well-appointed with a velvet settee and matching chairs sitting upon a plush rug. The furniture appeared in the moonlight to be of a delicate French blue tone. There was a small, round table on each side of the settee that held an oil lamp and a small blade that used as a letter opener.

There were white curtains that were lined with balled fringe in a hue that matched the settee. The moonlight shone in through them, casting long shadows across the floor in front of the large fireplace that was cold and unlit; the pokers sat in a stand just to the left, its ghostly shadow looming like a particularly thin man.

The only other thing of note in the room was a large painting of a ship beside the fireplace. It appeared to be a pirate ship. Odd choice, Rosalind thought, for someone who was supposed to be a war hero, but perhaps this too was Raven's influence on poor Elsbeth. It might have even been a ship he sailed on. She wished she could grab one of those pokers, but did not want to give herself and Nan away.

She and Nan looked at each other as Rosalind readied her weapon, cocking it with a slow, steady motion so the click was barely audible. Damn it all, if the sneak did not come right into the room they were in. He stole in confidently without so much as a glance behind him.

Just as she was hoping, the door covered her and Nan. All she could see was the picture of the ship and the edge of the settee. She used her body to better cover Nan while pressing her against the inset bookshelf behind the door. She raised the gun so it would be approximately chest level as a tall, lean figure appeared directly in front of the painting. The figure reached up and pushed a small golden gull carved into the frame. Rosalind had to stifle her gasp as the frame swung to the left, revealing a safe behind it.

The figure began to work the tumblers. Rosalind looked at Nan, only to find her shaking her head vigorously, indicating Rosalind should not do anything foolish, but both knew that as soon as he turned, he would see their hiding spot.

Adjusting her aim to accommodate his height, she took a deep breath and called, "Stop right there and throw down any weapons."

Raven froze, slowly turned, and smiled at them coldly, calculating his options. He had only one shot left as he had not had time to reload. He could shoot the girl, but could he escape the way he had come if he did? Thinking quickly, he turned, pulled his gun from his pocket, and raised the weapon.

He was simply shocked at the boldness of these two women who dared to stare him…him…down in contempt. How dare they! The lady and the commoner who acted better than her birth should allow. She was also to blame for this mess. If that hussy had not attracted the attention of Jacob, then he would have married Rosalind, and his Elsbeth would still be alive, and his could continue to weave his web. Now he had to start over. It was such a bother.

"You!" Annoyance dripped from his voice like the blackest ink from a quill.

Making his decision, he took the seamstress in his sights and squeezed the trigger.

Chapter Fifty-Six

Kristoff and Jacob ran up the steps in a panic as soon as they heard Rosalind's demand for someone to drop their weapon. All too quickly, they had discovered that the Raven had doubled back to the house, but they could not fathom why until they barreled through the door, slamming it into both women and knocking them to the floor in a flurry of muslin, just as the bullet struck where Nan had been standing only a breath before.

Kristoff stood beside Jacob with his jaw clenched tightly and his knuckles white and pressed to his side.

"It's over, Raven. You have finally lost," Jacob sneered as he lunged at the man, revenge written in his every movement.

Raven answered by grabbing the fire poker, then swiftly swinging it in an arc to land solidly across Jacob's face. The blow was meant to kill. The infallible Raven miscalculated and connected with his left shoulder instead. A snap of bone echoed through the room in unison with his scream of fury. Jacob was thrown off and fell upon the small round table, sending the oil lamp crashing upon the floor. Oil puddled on the rug, turning it to a darkened hue.

"You damn fool," Raven yelled as his composure snapped. He began swinging the poker at Kristoff, who was advancing upon him cautiously.

As he dodged a particularly vicious blow, the poker lodged into the wooden floor, making a deep gouge. With the split-second pause, Kristoff leapt, seizing the man's lapels while driving him back toward the fireplace.

Nan ran to check on Jacob, but he had already gained his feet and had the shattered remains of the oil lamp in his hand as he ran at the struggling men. Oil leaked down his hand, soaking into his coat and dripping onto the floor.

"Watch for secret doors," Kristoff grunted as he struggled with the man, who was far stronger than his waif-like appearance let on.

Nan, not knowing what to do, retreated to the bookshelf and began hurling books toward the blaggard. Books rained onto the floor, thudding to the carpet as dust billowed around them. As one book met its mark on the back of Kristoff's head, Nan lowered her leatherbound weapon with an exclaimed, "Oh, dear!"

Seeing the shiny letter opener on the floor, she picked it up so that Rosalind and she could guard the open door. It was the only exit. Rosalind kept her gun aimed at the fray, but she could not get a clear shot.

Jacob circled to edge his way behind the man. He was wielding the broken glass like a dagger. Jacob's grasp tightened around his makeshift weapon. Blood mingled with the oil already covering his hand.

Raven refused to go down easily and brought his knee up to connect with Kristoff's groin while swinging his arms in a downward motion to break the hold on his lapels. In anticipation of this known fighting tactic, Kristoff redirected his knee by shifting his hips to deflect the blow from the upward movement of Raven's knee. All the while, he lunged with a swift motion for a well-aimed headbutt. A crack echoed through the room. There was so much force behind the blow, Raven stumbled backward. Kristoff reeled from the impact he had just delivered.

Seizing the opportunity of Raven's dazed look, Jacob stabbed him in the upper quadrant of his shoulder. Unfortunately, Jacob misjudged the slickness of the carpet and slipped onto the hearth when he stepped forward. He collapsed to the ground, then grabbed Raven by the ankles. In combination with the heaps of books littering the floor, the hold Jacob had on his ankles caused Raven to skid across the floor, bringing him to his knees.

Jacob pressed the advantage and jumped on the man's back. Rage surged through him like an uncontrollable wildfire. He drove his fist into his opponent's back and struck him repeatedly. Jacob's blood splattered the room with each blow.

Kristoff intercepted a chaotic assault and yanked Jacob off his target with one strong arm. Jacob fell backward, the fight draining from him like water from a broken vessel.

A shot echoed throughout the room. The men simply stood there in surprise, chests heaving, breath mingling with the dust-laden room.

"It ends here!" Derby shouted as he squeezed between the ladies flanking the open door.

After decades of treason and murder, the Raven had finally been caught.

Jacob's response was a ragged sigh and silence.

Chapter Fifty-Seven

To everyone's surprise, Lady Rosalind had been able to crack the safe – a talent she had apparently learned from Ol' Maude – and removed a series of diaries, some deeds, and a hefty sum of cash. She handed them all over to Derby to aid in his investigation. Jacob had already provided him with the letters he had seen his uncle lock in his desk just days prior.

Derby, his men, and the Raven left for Newcastle to await proper reinforcements from the London home office. Derby was not letting the villain out of his sight. It had been too long a chase to risk losing him again. The rest of the fray returned to Englebright Estates for a long-awaited rest. Everyone was exhausted. Since this whole fiasco started, no one had a proper night's rest.

Jacob lay in his bed, which was offered up by Englebright for as long as he desired. He felt like his life had been turned upside-down, and his entire future was now clouded in the mist of lies and deceit. He definitely wasn't going to stay at Durham Hall to relive his past horrors. He needed time away and some time to regroup his thoughts. As things stood, it was likely that he would be stripped of his inheritance and estates, given the nature with which they had been obtained: murder, lies, espionage.

Englebright was truly a good man. Jacob thought perhaps he could offer his assistance and advice to rebuild the stables. His true love and passion had always been working with horses. That distraction would at least give him somewhat of a reprieve from his inner chaos during all the legal proceedings that would be required. Elsbeth…Uncle Elias, whichever she claimed to be, had been broken; a wretched being shaped by a torturous past. It was unfair what had happened to her, but did she arrange to have her own brother killed, or was that the Raven's doing? So many unanswered questions…so much hurt and loss.

Jacob lay and stared at the ceiling. He loathed that he was at least partially at fault for this whole tragedy. He had not recognized the villain he was living with his entire life. What did it say about him that he was not able to recognize the evil that lurked under his own roof? He should have been able to prevent at least some of this.

As it stood, he was unsure if he would be a pauper after all of this or actually allowed to keep anything from his past, including his beautiful horses, and was not sure he believed he deserved such a reprieve anyway for his part in the entire farce. He was bone weary and saddened almost beyond comprehension. In one night, he had lost all he had known, but had also lost a life of joy and love that should have been his if his father's wishes had been carried out. And Nan…what must she think of him now? He shook his head and chalked that up to another gift he did not deserve anyway.

A tear slipped down his cheek, and he angrily swiped it away as he lay in his soft bed awaiting sleep that would not come.

A soft knock sounded on the door. Jacob had no desire to speak with anyone. Oh, he was tempted to ignore the tapping. Unfortunately, it might be Englebright needing additional information. He felt as though every ounce of knowledge, history, travel…everything had been wrung out of him like so much wet, dirty laundry. Rising from the bed, he shuffled toward the door with a sigh. He jerked on a robe, opened the door, and gasped in surprise.

Without any warning, Nan threw herself at him and wrapped her arms around his waist. He sank into the comfort her arms offered and broke on a sob. No matter how much he felt he did not deserve comfort, he could not make himself release her. She was a light in this bleakness – a soft reminder that there was still good in his world.

Chapter Fifty-Eight

The moonlight shone through the cracked window of the small cottage the following night. A gentle breeze stirred the air within the bedroom, bringing with it a calm sense of balance. It was as if the forest were breathing a verdant sigh of relief.

After everything that had happened, Kristoff and Rosalind would have their wedding night, Kristoff thought. At least, that was the plan. Tucked away in Anna's forest cottage, the couple secluded themselves from the rest of the family. They needed some long-awaited privacy.

Kristoff leaned against the cottage door, his wife wrapped in his arms. He rested his head atop hers, contented as a hound by a warm fire. In truth, they both could probably sleep for a week before the thought of a wedding night could intrude, or so he thought until his sweet wife pressed against him rather insistently.

They had rested briefly in the manor the night before after contending with the task of assisting his father-in-law and Jacob with accounts of the week's activities for Derby to use in the case against one Jareth Bentley Wilmington, III, if that was his true name. The documents they had found indicated it might be accurate, but the man had created a web of deceit so intricate that a spider would have been jealous of the weave. It was likely that only the man himself could sort it out. It would take at least a fortnight for them to go through the documents and detailed memoirs the man kept.

Who knew if there were not more hidden within the bowels of Durham Hall? But those were thoughts for another day. He felt his soft bride wiggle against him like a kitten cozying up to be stroked, drawing his attention back to more pressing matters. He smiled down at her upturned face.

She kissed the pulse at his neck and flicked her tongue across his warm skin. A surge of desire spread from where her mouth touched him like lightning to his loins. He could feel her sweet mouth curve into a smile against him as she did it again.

"Are you sure your father is situated at the manor?" Kristoff inquired with a small smirk as he kissed the top of her head again, trailing his hands down the length of her back and resting them on the swell of her hips.

"He promised not to disturb us for the next fortnight. He assured me that no one is allowed near the cottage, not even the serving staff," she said, leaning back to gaze into his eyes.

"That is why Mrs. Gowan stocked the shelves with plenty of supplies for us to use." She smiled

"And the twins?" Kristoff asked with a cocked brow.

"The twins are *en route* back to school, much to their displeasure, with both Charles and Andrew in escort. We are alone, I assure you. Now, where shall we begin?" she asked as she scanned his body up and down, then gently tugged on his cravat and led him to stand beside the plush bed.

"Ah, my sweet Rose, I believe I left off here," he whispered against her neck with a kiss and began unbuttoning the tiny pearl buttons of her dress. Thankfully, Nan was such a practical seamstress that he was able to undress his wife with ease. He would need to make sure Nan made all his wife's future clothing.

The front of her dress exposed the valley between her two soft breasts. Kristoff sucked in a breath and growled low as he realized that his vixen of a wife had not donned her undergarments.

He slowly began to slip the garment from her shoulders, kissing a trail along her exposed collarbone. He lifted his head slightly as his eyes traveled down the length of her body. She was perfect in all ways feminine. Her curves were accentuated by the flatness of her abdomen. Faint freckles were sprinkled across her porcelain skin, as if angels had kissed each spot with a blessing. She was his angel-kissed gift from God. Why had he not noticed her dappled skin before— each freckle connecting to another like a constellation of sensuality just for him.

He lowered his head again so that he could capture the soft mound of her breast in his mouth and began to suckle the red rosebud of a nipple. It became taut and velvety in response as his mouth moved over to its twin. Rosalind arched her back so that her husband could have better access. A soft moan escaped from her mouth as she let the blissful pleasure wash over her.

He slid his hand down to the triangle of auburn curls, caressing the inside of her thighs, allowing his fingers to delicately trace over the lace-trimmed hosiery fastened with soft, silken ribbons. She reached to untie them for him.

"Leave them," he told her in that sultry voice that caressed her like flames from a fire, quickening her pace and causing moisture to gather in her feminine folds. His request made her feel both brazen and alluring.

"As you wish, husband," she sighed and slid her hands to his firm flesh still hidden by tight trousers. The heat there blazed against her fingertips as she began to kindle the flames by stroking her hands across his breeches in flicker light touches, exploring the length of him. She moaned and leaned her body into his mouth as he kissed one breast then the other.

She was enticing, beautiful…and his. A smile spread across his lips as he stepped back to look at her, grasping both her hands in his to keep her from stroking him to completeness before he could pleasure her and consummate their vows. After so many interruptions, he was determined to give her the wedding night she deserved.

His eyes fell upon the naked vixen standing before him in her erotic attire, bare except for her silken stocking tipped with delicate lace. Her eyelids were half closed in surrender. He could see the quickened pulse at her neck and the heated rise and fall of her chest as she leaned toward him again, drawn in like a moth to a flame. She was his undoing and his fulfillment. He loved this woman, though he would not give her the words yet. One battle at a time, he thought and smiled to himself. But he had no doubts or regrets.

"Can I help you with your things, husband?" she cooed like a sultry vixen, she hoped, pink tinting her cheeks as she experimented with trying to be alluring. It must be working; she smiled coyly at him.

"Yes, please," he said in a husky voice, barely audible. He let her hands roam over his buttons, undoing each with a building anticipation.

With each button, Rosalind stepped a little closer, closing the little gap between them. When she reached the top button, she began untying his cravat as she kissed a trail across his broad chest, flicking her tongue across his pert nipple. His indrawn breath told her how much he enjoyed her boldness.

His breathing was becoming more and more ragged with each button as his pants became increasingly uncomfortable. The anticipation of a proper wedding night had him as anxious as a young buck in its first season. He needed to shed his blasted breeches.

As she kissed and tormented him further, he reached and unfastened the buttons. His breeches fell to the floor, along with his constricting undergarments. They were both as God intended, naked in natural beauty.

With one swift motion, Kristoff scooped up Rosalind in his arms and walked purposefully over to the bed. Pulling back the covers, he placed her gently upon the soft mattress. Passion gleamed in his eyes, mirrored by Rosalind. She breathed heavily and licked her lips, waiting for him to join her.

He crawled into bed beside her, lying on his side, melding his body with his wife's. He could not take his eyes off her well-formed curves. He gently ran a fingertip from the tip of her breast down through the valley of her stomach. Her muscles contracted in response.

"Oh, Kris…show me what to do," Rosalind whimpered.

"Lie back and let me love you." He nuzzled into that sweet little spot where shoulder met neck. He gazed earnestly into her beautiful eyes of deep blue pools. "Our bodies belong to each other, my Rose. You can touch me anywhere you like, kiss me as you like. There is no shame or wrong in what we do together as husband and wife." He kissed her lips gently.

He needed her to understand that he was hers as much as she was his, and though he was not a virgin, he had never taken a woman to his bed in love. The taking this night would be by both of them. She leaned up and kissed him, parted her lips, and touched her tongue to his, swirling in the delicious flavor of mint and sweetness that was always her Kris, as he caressed her body.

He teased his fingers down her belly to the soft triangle of hair hiding her intimate parts and eased his finger between the delicate furrow of her feminine folds and easily slid it in and around the flesh. She was wet in anticipation of the lovemaking. Slowly, he eased his finger inside her, gently stretching her and spreading the silky wetness until she was slick in every crease of her petal-like flesh. She was warm and soft in all the right places, whereas he was hard all over. He loved the contrast where their bodies touched.

Slowly, he eased his finger in again and then withdrew it just as slowly and began rhythmic movements; in and out, swirling around her delicate bud, stroking her into a fever. How she pleased him with soft moans as she raised her hips, wanting more. She held none of her passion back, like ladies were often taught. She was perfect.

His control was quickly vanishing with each slick glide of his fingers into her molten heat. His movements were becoming more and more demanding, mimicking how he wished he were embedded in her soft heat. He would lose his control if he wasn't careful.

On a groan of sheer sexual need, he abruptly withdrew his fingers.

"What's wrong? Is someone coming?" Rosalind said through gritted teeth.

"Let's end this torment," Kristoff growled as he lowered his hips between her thighs and edged his hard length toward her wetness. He knew he had to be gentle, but it was damned hard not to let go completely.

He eased slowly into her sweet opening. She was ready for him as her liquid heat smoothed over his shaft. She tilted her head back against the pillows and instinctively raised her hips, groaning in response to his new invasion. Her eyes had turned the deepest blue, the hue of a storm-tossed sea, foreshadowing the torrents of passion that were about to wash over them.

"My Love, this may hurt you. I am so sorry, but there is no other way," Kristoff whispered when the tip of his manhood reached her maidenhead. She was so tight, so wet. He held back, awaiting her permission.

"Kris …I…I love you. I know you will keep me safe," Rosalind admitted as a single tear ran down her cheek. She wrapped her arms around his neck and pulled him closer so that she could kiss his mouth, his chin, his neck.

"And…I ache for you," she whispered shyly.

The declaration of love was nearly his undoing. It was all he could do not to spill his seed then and there. He knew this was a moment of vulnerability that he could not ignore.

Ever so gently, he kissed her tenderly and whispered, "I love you, my sweet Sprite, my moonlit nymph, my heart. Your love is all I will ever need."

He eased deeper into her moist sheath, gently breaking the barrier that separated them from true fulfillment.

Rosalind gasped in surprise at the sting of pain that attempted to clear through her passionate haze. Kristoff stilled so that her body could adjust to its new invasion. Whispering words of love, he eased outward and reached between their bodies, stroking the nub of her sex back into a flurry of passion as he slowly eased back into the entrance of her body.

Rosalind moaned as his finger stroked her outer nub and his length worked in her innermost folds. The pain was quick and hot, but she was so far gone that the pleasure mingled with the pain. She only cried out and stilled for a moment before she demanded his movement by experimentally rocking her hips against his. The pleasure was a white-hot flare that was concentrated in the sensitive spot he stroked with his fingers, but also inside.

She felt molten heat spread from that little spot all through the core of her body. It ached and throbbed with a need for something that was growing ever hotter. She felt her inner muscles begin to quiver around his shaft; it completely overshadowed that sting of being stretched and filled. She could not help asking him to move within her by raising her hips gently at first. He slowly slid a bit deeper. The taut muscle above his hard sex rubbed against that sensitive spot again as his head dipped and he sucked upon one pert nipple and then the next, waiting for her to direct his movements when she was ready.

"I…oh, please…can you do that again?" Rosalind nearly begged him as she wrapped her arms around his neck and pulled his head to hers and sealed her mouth on his, licking and tasting his lips. She wanted all the sensations at once.

She wrapped her hips around his waist and deepened the kiss as her tongue swept into his mouth and he stroked back into her body ever so slowly. She began to ache in that spot. Kristoff returned the love play in kind by mimicking the sweeping action with his tongue as his hips moved in a slow rhythm in and out of her tight sex, rekindling all the pleasure she had felt before his invasion.

He moved slowly, steadily, delving deeper and deeper into the slick folds. She rocked up, pulling her knees up higher around his hips to take more of his length and allow that sensitive spot to rub against his hard abdomen. She whimpered love words as he worked inside her, then withdrew and ever so slowly delved back in as he licked and bit at her lips. He raised his hand back to her breast and rolled the nipple between finger and thumb. Something about that action caused the ache in her feminine parts to grow more insistent. She rocked harder against him and sucked his tongue into her mouth.

The mating instinct took over both of their bodies. She was wet, soft, and sweet heavens, so tight. Kristoff tried to be gentle, but Rosalind knew no pacing or reservation. She gave over to the passion completely. Each time he subsided, her sex tightened around him as if to pull him back. Each motion forward created a new sensual feeling of exhilaration for both of them. He had not anticipated such intensity with each movement.

Rosalind had no thought of holding back anything from him now. She was his, and he was hers. The sensitive nub ached and thrummed with each stroke of him, weaving with a thread of sensual pleasure. Slowly, the feeling began to blossom from that one spot, bursting into a cacophony of sensation that seared her to her toes. Every nerve hummed as the sensation spread. She cried his name as she came undone. It was as if they were soaring into the heavens to be with the stars, higher and higher until, in a crescendo, his body shuddered with hers as he found his release. She continued to quiver around him, gasping in pleasure as she felt each throb of his length inside her until they were both replete with fulfillment.

He looked down into her passion-glazed eyes and gently kissed her lips. "I love you, Lady Arabella Rosalind Van Reede. You are my life, my breath, my world, my Sprite. Whatever is in my power to give, name it, and it is yours...the stars, the moon...all the pants in the world...yours for the taking," he said playfully and kissed her nose.

He had never experienced anything like this in his life. He felt complete, like he had finally found all that he had been missing. It felt like returning home from a long journey. This was the way it was supposed to be. In each other, they had found what had been missing, and neither of them even knew it. She smiled at him in return.

"And I love you, husband," she said with a sigh.

"The only thing I ever need is you," she said sincerely. Then he noted the most devilish look upon her face as she nipped his nose. "But if we could do that again, I would not complain."

At last, on their wedding night, they understood what their hearts had long been whispering to them; that in each other, they had found home. And with that truth, the fear of love, of loss simply faded into the distance.

They both knew they would live each day fully, hand in hand, adventure by adventure for all the days God gifted them..

Epilogue

The day was gloriously warm with the sun shining brightly as Rosalind and Kristoff set off across the woods. Rosalind looked down at the parchment and began to read aloud:

> *"At the oak that never yields to storm, where two initials carved in an emblem of love lie, find under a root that hides the next hint to your intent."*

"I know of only one tree on the estate that has Mama and Papa's initials carved into a heart…an emblem of love, as the clue says. It is just outside the maze garden." Rosalind beamed with excitement. She clutched the parchment Charles had given her on her wedding day to her breast, as if giving it an embrace.

This was an adventure that both the newlyweds welcomed after the tumultuous hunt of the Raven had ended.

Kristoff and Rosalind walked hand in hand as they approached the large oak near the opening of the woods. There were the initials of her dear mother and her beloved father, delicately carved with love so long ago. With its scrolling letters of an "A" and a "G," the two letters were intertwined with darkened wood from years of weathering.

"See, this is Mama and Papa's carving. Papa engraved it on this oak for us all to see. You can see here that there is a carving for each of us below. It's a carving of a family tree. Papa always laughs at the irony of the family tree on a tree. It's quite silly." Rosalind smiled at the memory of him retelling the story of carving each letter for each family member.

Kristoff gazed fondly at the old tree, then he heard a gasp of delight from his beautiful bride.

"Look, Kris! Your initial has been added next to mine. Charles must have done this…adding you to the tree. This is so beautiful. You are part of the family tree." The words settled between them, heavy and beautiful all at once. Kristoff covered her hand with his, steadying them both. A tear slid down her cheek as she traced the initial with her index finger, the lighter wood contrasting with those that had been carved years before. She looked at him and was thrilled to see his joy at being added.

"The clue mentions a root," he said gently as he broke the spell passing between them, tracing the letters of her initials beside his. "But all these roots are large. This tree is massive." Kristoff marveled at its grandeur as he walked around it, smiling again at his initials beside his wife's. The whole family held the same sense of whimsy, and he adored them all. How fortunate he was to have landed in this strange mix.

They circled the oak until he found it. It was a massive root with a hollow knot. From within, he drew a small glass bottle corked tight. Inside lay another rolled scrap of parchment.

Rosalind smiled as she unrolled it, her eyes bright with recognition even before he read it aloud.

Love is the stream that ever flows,
Where water murmurs over stone,
And wych elms groan,
Upon a verdant bed.

"My mother," she whispered. "She always loved riddles that led us through the woods."

As they followed the sound of water, the forest seemed to open around them. The sunlight dappled the path, and birdsong weaved through the air. It felt achingly familiar, as though the land itself remembered the joy and adventurous times the Englebright family enjoyed together. Rosalind felt the warmth of the day upon her shoulders.

"Near the stream beneath a nearly ancient wych elm, the moss lies thick and green. We played there as children…I even napped there a time or two," she instructed Kristoff, pointing in the direction to go. "'*A verdant bed,*' See? That is what the clue must be leading us to." Heat rose to her cheeks as she thought of the bed they had shared last night.

Kristoff smiled as he saw the blush creep up her lovely face. He pressed his hand to the small of her back and whispered a promise.

"After, my love. You are a true vixen."

They reached their next destination, and Rosalind gently peeled back the moss near a spot that was nearly as thick as a mattress, and two pillow-sized rocks sat proudly as if waiting for a weary head to rest upon them. Beneath lay an approximately dinner-plate-sized, heart-shaped stone. It was out of place amongst the other rugged stones surrounding the base of the tree. There was no doubt that it was their target. With tender hands, she removed the stone, only to find a carefully laid oilcloth. It sealed the damp earth away from the treasure that was protected underneath – a slender wooden case.

Rosalind held her breath as she opened it. Inside was a small, delicately carved family tree that was gilded with golden leaves and gemmed fruit of every birthstone color for each family member. The branches were etched with names she knew by heart. Her parents stood at the center, their names joined just as they had been on the oak. Below them, each sibling, each connection, each life shaped by love, with room to add names as the family grew.

And there, a newly carved name. It was still pale against the darker, more aged wood. Their two names intertwined – Rosalind and Kristoff.

She pressed her hand to her mouth, tears blurring the fine lines of the carving.

"He finished it," she whispered. "Charles finished what Mama started. He must have stayed up all evening to complete it. It's a masterpiece."

Kristoff wrapped his arms around her, holding her as the meaning settled in. This was not an ending, nor a remembrance meant to bind them. It was an invitation for them to continue their story, to grow the family branches, and to carry love forward.

Rosalind traced their names once more, then closed the case with care. "Let's take it home," she said.

Hand in hand, they crossed the stream and followed the path northward, no longer searching for what waited at the end. Their adventure was just beginning.

Ms. Gowan's Famous Nutty Bun Recipe:

A note to the reader: This recipe is adapted from Leanne's grandmother, passed on to her sister, who still makes these fabulous cinnamon roll-like pastries for our family. We hope you will enjoy them as much as we do.

Ingredients

Rolls

- 2 cups self-rising flour
- ½ cup shortening
- ½ cup cold butter (grated)
- ½ cup ice water
- ½ cup sugar
- 1 teaspoon vinegar salt
- 3 tablespoons cinnamon

Caramel Sauce

- ½ cup (1 stick) butter
- 1 cup packed brown sugar (dark or light)
- ¼ cup heavy cream or buttermilk
- 1 cup chopped nuts
- ¼ teaspoon vanilla extract
- pinch of salt

Instructions

For Plain Rolls

- Preheat oven to 350 degrees
- Cut shortening into flour and salt mixture
- Add vinegar/water to form dough
- Chill
- Roll to about ⅛ thickness in a rectangular shape, squaring the dough
- Brush with butter
- Mix ½ cup sugar with 3 tbsp. cinnamon

- Sprinkle onto buttered dough
- Roll dough into a tight log
- Slice into ¼ or ½ inch using a sharp knife or kitchen string
- Place on parchment-lined pan
- For a soft edge, the buns should touch
- For a firm edge, leave ~2 inches between buns
- Bake until done, ~20 minutes

For Nutty Buns with Caramel Sauce

- Melt butter over medium heat
- Add cream orbuttermilk (for a tangy sauce with a bit of zip), vanilla, salt
- Mix until smooth
- Add nuts
- Melt butter and brown sugar over medium heat
- Pour caramel sauce into a 13-inch pan and tilt to cover bottom of pan
- Place cinnamon rolls on top of the caramel sauce
- Bake at 350 degrees ~25-30 minutes, watching closely so not to burn the caramel sauce
- Invert immediately to serving platter

The Wasp and The Widow

Second Book in the Shadows & Silk Series

2027

WARRINGTON
PUBLISHING

Acknowledgments

To our publisher, Mikael Carlson: thank you for taking a chance on us and on this, our first of hopefully many projects together. Your faith in our voices means more than we can ever express, we won't even mention those "few" edits.

To our editor, Michael Waitz: THANK YOU for catching our many (many) screw-ups and helping us shine. Your sharp eye and endless patience are the unsung heroes of this book.

To John, Leanne's husband, and to their two kids, Jack and Gillian: thank you for cheering us on, for the quiet moments you gave us to write, the numerous weekends away, all the brain-picking and research, but mostly for believing in this dream right alongside us.

To Mark, Adra's husband, and her two kids, Nathan and Clayton, along with her beloved fur babies: thank you for enduring the endless grilling for storyline ideas and the deep-dive research conversations you never asked for but listened to anyway. We couldn't have done this without your support.

To our dear friend, Denise: thank you for letting us read countless hours of romance aloud to you, often in *truly* terrible accents. You inspired us, encouraged us, and reminded us that stories are meant to be shared. This book exists because you helped bring the first spark to life.

To Beth Anne: thank you for introducing Adra to the romance genre in the first place. Without that nudge, this journey might never have begun.

And to Cathy: thank you for the tastiest nutty bun recipe that could be passed on to the next generation of readers.

To each of you: this book carries a piece of your love, patience, and influence within every chapter. Thank you for helping us bring this dream to fruition. We cannot express our thanks enough for those who have helped, supported, and guided us on this journey.

About the Authors

Leanne Blakemore and Adra Mayfield met during their freshman year at college, bonding over the love of adventure and storytelling. Leanne became a dedicated research scientist with a passion for unraveling the mysteries of life while adding a fun, whimsical spin on everything she does. Adra, a compassionate speech therapist, has a gift for understanding people's feelings and helps them find their words so they can communicate with the world around them.

Their friendship deepened when they took a train trip across America in their senior years, where countless hours of conversation and a shared love for romance novels blossomed. This journey led them on a new adventure, writing their first romance novel. With Leanne's sharp wit and intellect and Adra's sympathetic nature, it became a passion to create a captivating story with love, intrigue, and a family anyone would love to be acquainted with.

Their debut novel is a result of their collaboration and love for storytelling. This story mirrors their own friendship and celebrates the magic of unexpected connections. When they are not writing, Leanne is a research scientist specializing in finding treatments for the illnesses that plague us, while Adra is helping students and parents find better ways to communicate as a speech language pathologist. Together, they continue to write, laugh, and dream as lifelong friends. They are both happily wed to their soulmates and have two beautiful children each.